✓

‖‖ ‖ ‖ ‖‖‖‖ ‖ ‖‖‖‖ ‖‖‖
D0363638

F 28, 818

Date of Return | Date of Return

25 MAY 2005

DARK WINTER

www.**booksattransworld**.co.uk

Also by Andy McNab

Non-fiction
BRAVO TWO ZERO
IMMEDIATE ACTION

Fiction
REMOTE CONTROL
CRISIS FOUR
FIREWALL
LAST LIGHT
LIBERATION DAY

F 28. 818

DARK WINTER

ANDY McNAB

BANTAM PRESS

LONDON · NEW YORK · TORONTO · SYDNEY · AUCKLAND

TRANSWORLD PUBLISHERS
61–63 Uxbridge Road, London W5 5SA
a division of The Random House Group Ltd

RANDOM HOUSE AUSTRALIA (PTY) LTD
20 Alfred Street, Milsons Point,
New South Wales 2061, Australia

RANDOM HOUSE NEW ZEALAND LTD
18 Poland Road, Glenfield, Auckland 10, New Zealand

RANDOM HOUSE SOUTH AFRICA (PTY) LTD
Endulini, 5a Jubilee Road, Parktown 2193, South Africa

Published 2003 by Bantam Press
a division of Transworld Publishers

Copyright © Andy McNab 2003

The right of Andy McNab to be identified as the author of this work
has been asserted in accordance with sections 77 and 78 of the
Copyright, Designs and Patents Act 1988.

All the characters in this book are fictitious, and any
resemblance to actual persons, living or dead, is purely coincidental.

A catalogue record for this book is available from the British Library.
ISBNs 0593 050258 (cased)
0593 050266 (tpb)

All rights reserved. No part of this publication may be reproduced,
stored in a retrieval system, or transmitted in any form or by
any means, electronic, mechanical, photocopying, recording,
or otherwise, without the prior permission of the publishers.

Typeset in 11/13½pt Palatino by
Falcon Oast Graphic Art Ltd

Printed in Great Britain by
Mackays plc, Chatham, Kent

1 3 5 7 9 10 8 6 4 2

Papers used by Transworld Publishers are natural, recyclable products made from
wood grown in sustainable forests. The manufacturing processes conform to the
environmental regulations of the country of origin.

DARK WINTER

1

Penang, Malaysia
Sunday 20 April, 20:15 hrs

The huge billboard explained in English, Chinese, Malaysian and even Hindi that the penalty for drug-dealing was death, and a picture of a hangman's noose rammed home the message in case a language had been missed. What it didn't say was that Malaysia had the highest concentration of al-Qaeda terrorists outside Afghanistan and Pakistan, these days, which made it a fucking strange place to take a holiday.

I rested my crash helmet in the crook of my right arm. I was too hot and sweaty even to bother saying no to the market traders waving tacky souvenirs in my face. The pavement wasn't wide enough for us to walk side by side, but I knew Suzy was close behind. Her estuary English was unmistakable, especially as she was shouting to make sure I heard her above the din: 'Hey, Nick, did I tell you my Dad came here to do his National Service?'

It had rained only an hour ago, a heavy tropical downpour, and the air was thick and sticky. The road through the market was narrow, packed with cars and rusting diesel buses; scooters and Honda 70s buzzed through the gaps between them like pissed-off mosquitoes. The beach front of Batu Feringhi, where we were staying at the Holiday Inn, was

7

dotted with smart hotels and lined with casuarina trees, but the further we got from the not-so-white beaches, the more corrugated-iron shacks we saw. This was where the ordinary Malaysians lived and worked.

The Bali bombing, war in Iraq, then the SARS outbreak, had all affected the tourist trade, which made those of us who had turned up even more of a target for the guys trying to flog counterfeit Rolexes, pirated CDs, ethnic wooden masks and trinkets that had probably been made in China. Fumes poured out of the small petrol generators supplying power to stalls churning out chicken kebabs on home-made grills. Tacky neon signs did their best to entice us into street-side cafés.

Suzy wasn't deterred by no response: she kept prattling on regardless. 'Yeah, he was only here for a while. He wanted to join the Navy, but they shoved him into the Army Catering Corps and sent him out here.'

I gave a grunt of acknowledgement, not really listening. Our holiday wasn't going badly, apart from her chain-smoking. She didn't do it in the room, but I was sure she'd like to, just to annoy me.

'He only stayed for a couple of months, then did a runner. Couldn't stand frying all those eggs, I s'pose. I guess he's still technically AWOL, still a deserter,' she said. 'Even though he's dead.'

I turned my head and gave her a quick smile. Most of her dark brown shoulder-length hair dropped forwards round her face as she looked down to avoid falling into the storm drain that ran parallel with the pavement. The rest of it was stuck to her neck by small beads of sweat.

We were nine days into a two-week romantic break after a chance meeting in a London bar a couple of months ago. I'd been sitting nursing a beer, and when she came up to give her order I made fun of her accent. She told me she was 'Bovis class' and proud of it – it meant she was one rung up from Barrett, apparently, several above Wimpey, and a whole ladderful ahead of me. We got talking, and I ended up with her number.

She worked in a travel agent's but, apart from that, I didn't know too much about her. Her parents were dead and she was an only child. She shared a flat with two other women in Shepherd's Bush. She didn't like tomatoes or the size of her feet – and that was about it.

Now that the war was over and the looting of Baghdad and Basra had calmed down a bit, SARS was really grabbing the headlines. Fuck knows why – I'd read in *Newsweek* that other forms of pneumonia killed more than forty thousand a year in the USA alone, malaria nearly three million worldwide, and tuberculosis about the same. Not to mention the fifteen hundred who died each year in the UK falling downstairs. But every cloud has a silver lining – that was how we'd come by the holiday so quickly and cheaply.

It was the first time we'd been together longer than a night; our jobs got in the way, but we were working on that.

Well, that was the cover story, anyway.

The flat in Shepherd's Bush really existed, and so did the two women who lived there – it was her CA [cover address]. The travel agent would vouch for Suzy.

The market was petering out and we'd got to where we wanted to be. Our rented Suzuki 250 was parked where we'd left it, between the roadside café and the Palace restaurant, which was just starting to get a few tourists for the evening. Maybe they were lured by the sign promising 'The Magic of Fine Indian and Western Cuisine'. The roadside caff suited us better. Opposite it, on the other side of the road, was the mosque, a solid brick-and-plaster building in the middle of the shanty town. Right now, though, I was more interested in the lone old, white and rusty Toyota Lite Ace people-carrier that was parked on the hard compacted mud alongside.

It seemed all you needed to set up in the catering trade round here were some corrugated-iron sheets, a few concrete slabs to cover the storm drains and a couple of rusty birdcages filled with little green birds that couldn't be arsed to sing. Suzy and I pulled out plastic garden chairs and faced each other across a long, flower-patterned Formica trestle table. As we sat down, someone inside the Palace began to knock out 'Climb Every Mountain' on an electric keyboard.

A barefooted Indian girl appeared and I asked for two orange juices. There was no need to ask Suzy what she wanted; we'd both been drinking gallons of the stuff since we'd arrived.

The smell of kebabs from a street stall fought its way through the diesel fumes and the stench of the drains as the English commentary blared from a TV set fixed on a bracket above our heads. Leeds United were playing someone or other, and a few British lads a couple of tables along were up for it.

Suzy was still in Catering Corps mode. 'Yeah, AWOL. But you know what? The strange thing is, until the day he died he'd sit in his chair and bang on about why they should bring back National Service to sort out the yobs.' She dumped her hemp beach bag on the table and fished out a purple disposable lighter, a fresh pack of duty-free Bensons, and a guidebook to Penang.

I looked around me as she lit up and started to flick through her book. A group of middle-aged Germans with shiny red faces wandered past, all dressed up for a night out. They reeked of scent and aftershave and looked far too hot for their own good. Coming the other way were half a dozen twentysomethings in faded T-shirts and shorts with Australian flags on their backpacks. One had an arm in plaster. Hiring a scooter was a big adventure until the rain got between the rubber and the tarmac, and we'd seen a constant stream of people coming back to the hotel with skin needing to be repaired.

The gold pack and purple disposable went back into the bag and Suzy blew a cloud of smoke in my direction. She sat back in her chair and grinned. 'Oh, stop whining. I have to pay for this stuff. You're getting nicotine for free. Besides, you're going to feel really stupid when you're lying in hospital dying of nothing.' She studied my face for a reaction, still smiling, her hand held high with the cigarette between her two fingers facing me. She soon realized she wasn't going to get one, so went back to thumbing through her guide. As I shifted to look up at the television I felt the small of my back sticking to the chair through my T-shirt.

My gaze wandered to the mosque. Set back about thirty or forty metres from the road, it was a one-level building, with a blue roof, a white muezzin tower with loudspeakers, and a couple of corrugated carports. It was definitely a working-man's mosque.

Just down the street was a Buddhist temple, and Hari Krishna was ready to bang a few cymbals only ten minutes further along. I'd worked in Malaysia before, during my time with the Regiment, and I knew it was one of the few places on earth where Buddha, Allah, Hari and even Jesus could go out for the night and not have a fight. Earlier today I'd seen Australian mothers on the beach in tiny bikinis shoving chips into their children's mouths, alongside women covered from head to toe in black doing the same to theirs.

Our drinks arrived as the organ-player in the Palace began to tell us he'd left his heart in San Francisco. Suzy took another drag; her eyes didn't leave the page. I had a sip of juice as the mosque parking area began to fill with people arriving for evening prayers. A small gang of bikers buzzed in, dismounted and headed straight for the brightly lit reception area. I had a good view of the immediate interior as they took off their shoes and washed their hands and faces before disappearing to talk with God.

'Have you ever considered colonic irrigation?'

I snapped my head back to Suzy.

She took another drag and turned the pages towards me to show a woman lying on her side, covered in towels and drinking cappuccino through a straw. The pupils of her large brown eyes dilated as she looked up into the lights. 'A lot of people

11

come to South East Asia just for the detox spas, you know. Apparently it does wonders, really gives your insides a spring-clean.'

I shook my head slowly. 'I've tried to be a bit careful about what I let people shove up my arse.'

'The average American male dies with five pounds of undigested meat inside him.'

I guessed it was only natural for her to be concerned about the new love in her life. 'I'm not American.'

'Same difference. I've seen what you throw down your neck. You should think about it. You are what you eat, you know.' She put the book on the table and lifted her cigarette to her mouth.

'So that would make me a double burger with fries, would it?' I pointed at her. 'And you a fucking nicotine-stained banana.'

'Can't be that bad – I've seen you looking at me by the pool. Those shades of yours aren't as dark as you think.' She pulled a face and went back to her book.

2

I was with her here in Penang on George's instructions. As he kept on saying, 'If someone hits you and they threaten to hit you some more, you've got to stop them. Period.' But as always, of course, I was also here because I needed the money.

Suzy and I didn't know the whole story, and that was fine by me. Too much information gave me a headache, and Suzy probably felt the same. We were just small cogs in a big machine. I'd learnt the hard way that it's better to be just clever enough to plan and carry out the task you're given, and not to ask the reasons why.

The job was deniable. The Malaysian government had no idea what was happening – not because they couldn't be trusted: Malaysia had a strong, stable government and a good record against terrorism. It was just that the fewer people who knew what we were here for, the better our chances of success.

It was a joint US/UK operation, a first for me. There weren't many Americans on vacation in Malaysia, especially with the current situation, but a Brit couple was quite a normal sight. Being sent back to the UK had been a bit like going back in time because it was the Yes Man who had given us our final brief, the very person I'd gone to the US to escape. I couldn't say I enjoyed it much, but it was great knowing that I was only his property for a short while before I returned to the US and became George's again.

The other first was that I'd never worked with another K. In fact, it was the first time I'd ever knowingly been within a hundred metres of one. It probably never occurred to Suzy that I was anything but a Brit operator like her – my cover documents certainly wouldn't have told her. I was called Nick Snell again, the same cover as when I'd been a K.

On the final day of our preparation he'd sat on the settee in the safe flat in Pimlico, as wired as an army officer about to give a pep talk to his troops before they go to war.

The Yes Man always liked to talk about things he'd read in reports, forgetting that people like me and Suzy had got hold of the stuff in the first place. 'Don't you two believe the hype,' he'd said. 'That's for those out there.' He pointed at the window. 'They need to think we are fighting the ignorant, destitute and disenfranchised – but we're not. Nor are the enemy crazed, cowardly, apathetic or anti-social. If any of these terror groups relied on such maladjusted low life, they simply wouldn't be able to produce effective and reliable killers who are prepared to sacrifice themselves in the process.'

'No, sir.'

Suzy always called him 'sir'.

I avoided calling him anything – just in case the words 'arsehole' or 'bastard' slipped from my lips by mistake.

All around us mobile phones started tuning up: it was like the digital version of the 'Hallelujah Chorus'. Their owners just stood up and walked away, not even looking to see who was calling. They knew it was God.

Suzy knew too. 'Not long to go now.'

Malaysian mobiles could ring you five times a day for prayer, and also had a Kiblat finder to point the faithful in the direction of Mecca if they were stuck in the shopping mall and couldn't make it to a mosque.

Suzy went back to mugging up on arse tubes, and smoked

14

and drank without lifting her eyes from the page while I watched a couple stop and look at the menu board outside the Palace, then listened to the excited waiter rush out and try to lure them under the corrugated sheeting. He had to shout to make himself heard above the organist, who was now going on about a girl from Ipanema.

No need to hustle for business over at the mosque. Scooters and cars kept arriving, and plenty more came on foot. I let my gaze wander to the left, to a shack with a blue plastic tarpaulin over a scaffolding frame as an awning, surrounded by scooters and motorbikes in various stages of cannibalization or repair.

It was the entrance to the left of the workshop that I was most interested in. A neon sign with Chinese lettering was set into the road close by. I didn't have a clue what it was advertising, but it lit up the doorway beautifully.

Five minutes went by before the target appeared. He was wearing a clean white shirt over grey tracksuit bottoms and flip-flops. He turned to his left, and walked along the cracked, greasy pavement past the workshop. I leant closer to Suzy and tapped the table lightly. 'There's our boy.'

Smiling at me, she closed the guidebook and put it into her bag. The Indian girl must have taken this as a sign we were leaving, and immediately came over and asked if we wanted more drinks. Suzy nodded. 'Two more, the same.'

The target was in his late forties, Indian, Pakistani, maybe even Bangladeshi. He climbed gingerly over the metre-high spiky fence that divided the motorbike graveyard from the mosque. His short black gleaming hair was neatly combed back and kept in place by gel or tonic. We both watched as he removed his shoes, headed for the taps, then disappeared inside with the rest.

The drinks arrived and Suzy paid the girl, letting her keep the pound's worth of change. Her face said we'd just made her day, but Suzy wasn't being generous. We didn't want her having to come back to us when we needed to leave in a hurry.

A couple of backpackers, gap-year age, came and sat down at a nearby table and ordered the cheapest thing on the menu as they checked out their red, peeling skin. Their conversation was drowned as the call to prayer wailed out from the loudspeakers in the tower, even bringing the organist to a standstill.

All we had to do now was wait for the target to reappear. We didn't know his name. All we knew was that he was a member of the militant Jemaah Islamiyar [JI] group, and active in Indonesia, Malaysia, Singapore, the Philippines and Thailand – all countries in the region that weren't seeking to establish a Muslim fundamentalist state.

Jemaah Islamiyar means 'Islamic group' in Indonesian. Over many years they had attacked US and western targets all over South East Asia. George and the Yes Man weren't the only ones who suspected that JI was a wholly owned subsidiary of al-Qaeda. Others argued that they weren't too closely linked, and that JI's original goals didn't fully dovetail with the global aspirations of Osama's boys. Whatever, it was only after the Bali nightclub bombing in October 2002 that the US finally designated them a foreign terrorist organization – something Malaysia had been wanting for years.

Indonesia had been the principal obstacle: the overwhelming majority of its 231 million population were Muslim – the largest Muslim population on the planet – and it hadn't been willing to alienate its own people until JI had been caught planning simultaneous truck-bomb attacks against US embassies in Indonesia, Malaysia, the Philippines, Singapore, Taiwan, Vietnam, even Cambodia.

My eyes were still on the mosque, but my ears were with the tableful of Brits knocking back the Tiger beer. They'd just been watching a government commercial during half-time, warning that if you were caught using a pirate satellite card you were liable to a fine of up to the equivalent of five thousand pounds, ten years' imprisonment, and a whipping. 'Shit,' Suzy muttered, 'you don't want to mess with Murdoch, do you? It's almost safer being a drug-dealer.'

The call to prayer stopped and the electric organ sparked up again, this time announcing the appearance of the Phantom of the Opera.

'Taxi's here.' Suzy gave a slight nod in the direction of the workshop area, as a knackered red-and-yellow-topped Proton saloon pulled up. The cracked plastic Teksi sign on its roof disappeared from view now and again as a bus or truck rumbled past. The last four numbers on the plate were 1032, and that was the VDM [visual distinguishing mark] we'd been given. The driver was definitely our man.

I caught a glimpse of him waving no at a group of tourists in brand-new counterfeit Nike T-shirts. They drive on the right in Malaysia, and the vehicle was parked with the driver at the kerbside, so I couldn't see his face clearly. In the glow from the neon sign he seemed to be lighter-skinned than the target, but not as light as the locals. Maybe he was Indonesian. He stayed in the cab, reading a newspaper with his arm out of the window, a cigarette in his mouth. He was the source, the one responsible for informing on the target. Perhaps he even knew what the target was up to. Whatever, he was the one who was going to help us.

We didn't know the source's identity, and I didn't want to. He probably felt the same about us. All he would have been told was that people were going to be waiting out there for him to finish his part of the job so that they could do theirs. Once he was finished, that was it, he was out of the equation.

Now all three of us were waiting for the target to show his face, while everyone around us was either swigging beer, watching TV or comparing sunburnt shoulders. Suzy got out her guidebook again. It would have looked unnatural for both of us to be looking over there and not saying anything.

3

Worshippers began to emerge from the mosque and before long there was a frenzy of cars and scooters revving up in the parking lot. The first vehicles tried to edge out into the traffic, but nobody on the road was giving them an inch. The air was filled with the din of horns and screeching brakes.

Suzy rested her guidebook on the table and I looked up. The target had come out of the door and was soon climbing back over the fence. The source waved, then got out of his cab. In the stronger light I could see he was definitely Indonesian, with high cheekbones, short black hair and a moustache, about the same height as Suzy. His stripy shirt hung out of his jeans, maybe because his massive shoulders were stretching the material so much – he looked as if he'd forgotten to take out the extra-wide coat hanger before putting his shirt on.

The two men came together without greeting, then went through the same door the target had come out of. Suzy packed her book back into her bag as the Brits eyed up a group of girls walking by, and the organist got a ripple of applause. The source was coming out again, carrying some sort of white box with a handle. As he got nearer to the taxi I could see it was a cardboard gift pack of six bottles of wine, with the sides cut away to make the labels visible. He went round to the passenger door, the side nearest us, and opened it, placed the box carefully in the footwell, then walked back round the front of the cab, climbed in and the vehicle started rolling. It was all over and done with in less than a minute.

Suzy's hands were securing the rolled-up top of her bag as the taxi melted into the traffic. 'So much for Muslims and alcohol, eh? Maybe it's Ribena.'

The Brits next door cheered and slapped the table. It wasn't Suzy's joke: Leeds had scored.

As we sat there and waited, I felt in my trouser pocket for the bike key. The target would be leaving for work soon. Even terrorists need to make money and have a cover story.

He was illuminated by the sign as he came out a couple of minutes later. He was a little early tonight. There was normally a fifteen-minute window after prayers before he set off. His white shirt was now tucked into a pair of black trousers, and he was wearing black patent leather shoes. He crossed the fence once more and headed to his Lite Ace, dodging the puddles in an attempt to keep his shoes clean.

I got to my feet. 'Right, might as well get back to the hotel.'

Suzy nodded and stood up. I picked up my helmet, putting it on as I walked to the bike. She hooked the bag over her head and shoulders, then put her helmet on as I kicked up the side-stand and turned the ignition. She waited while I revved up and added our share of black exhaust to the rest as I manoeuvred the bike with my feet to get it facing the road.

The Lite Ace moved towards the mosque gates. There was no indication of which way he was turning, but if he followed his own script of the last week and a bit he should be going with the traffic: to his left, our right. Suzy climbed on, and fiddled with her helmet to buy us time while we waited for the Lite Ace to get on to the road. My head was already hot and sticky inside the crash helmet, which stank of years of tourists' greasy hair. The plastic strap under my chin was slippery against my two days' growth.

She tapped me on the shoulder, just as the Lite Ace merged with the traffic. We turned right, against the flow, in front of the massed headlights, and began to take the target. There were four cars and a swarm of Honda 70s between us. He slowed for a group of tourists crossing the road, then accelerated to catch up with the flow. We followed, stopping and starting, guided by his flickering right brake light. If I lost him, this would be an excellent VDM for me to look out for either in the dark or in general traffic confusion. I knew it was there because I had slipped out with a screwdriver a couple of nights ago. If whipping was the penalty for using a dodgy satellite card, I dreaded to think what it would be for tampering with a vehicle.

The cars and heavy vehicles came to a halt again, but the scooters carried on weaving in and out. Instead of following suit, I stopped and kicked down into first, kept the clutch in and stayed well back.

Suzy adjusted herself behind me, wiggling her arse either side of the seat to unstick her thin trousers from the plastic. Her right hand was round my stomach and the bag was squeezed between us; her revolver, an old six-shot .45, Second World War vintage, almost silver with wear, dug into the small of my back as I inhaled another lungful of exhaust fumes.

Keeping two vehicles behind the van, I played the cautious tourist, making no attempt to copy all the others on two wheels. My legs were sweating inside my cheap night-market trousers, and it was nice to get a bit of breeze through my trainers as we moved.

There was a burst of light inside the Lite Ace before cigarette smoke leaked from the driver's window. Suzy leant forward over my shoulder and breathed in deeply, then I could hear her laughing behind me. I didn't know whether to be pleased she wasn't flapping on the job, or to flap myself because she wasn't. I liked people who got scared.

The coastline of Penang was low-lying, but as soon as you turned inland you began to climb. The target worked as a waiter in a Dutch restaurant up on the high ground in the centre of the island; I knew we'd be coming up to some lights soon, and he should be turning right. But something was wrong. He wasn't moving into the right-hand lane; instead he fought his way past the traffic at the junction waiting to turn inland.

Suzy was on my shoulder. 'What's he doing?' I ignored her and carried on with the take; there was nothing we could do but follow.

The traffic stopped and started before the left indicator flashed up ahead and the Lite Ace headed into a world of rusty corrugated iron. I slowed at the junction and followed, just as he hung another left and disappeared.

We were on a narrow, rough concrete road, flanked by shacks. I took the bike down into the darkness, stopping just short of the turning. There was a glow of static light hanging above a group of tin roofs. Suzy jumped off and I just managed to grab her arm before she ran towards it. 'Not here, OK? Not here.'

Her helmet came off and she faded into the darkness.

I carried on past, turned to face the junction in shadow, and killed the engine. The ghostly glow of TV sets flickered inside most of the shacks, and I could hear kids playing and dogs barking. There was a strong smell of drains.

Vehicle lights soon sparked up along the track out to the junction, and I could hear an engine heading my way. I couldn't see inside the Lite Ace as it turned right, towards the main; I hit the ignition but kept my lights off as it stopped at the junction then tried to fight its way back out and head right.

Suzy reappeared, running as fast as she could. I rode up to meet her as she waited and shoved her helmet back on. Jumping on the back, she sucked in air as she held on to me. 'He was picking up – it's two-up. Of all fucking nights.' I could feel her warm breath against my neck as we watched the vehicle disappear. I turned the lights on and we started to move.

21

'Did you see who it was?'

'No. What now?'

I shrugged. I never really knew what to do until I was doing it when these fuck-ups happened. We got out on to the main and this time I gave it some throttle and joined the rest of the mosquitoes weaving in and out. Her arm tightened round my waist and her legs squeezed tight against mine.

She saw the brake light at the same time as I did, pulling at my stomach with her right hand and pointing over my shoulder with her left. I exaggerated my nod as the glare of neon and traffic lights merged in my badly scratched visor.

The Lite Ace was nearing the crossroads, in the left-hand filter. I passed another car and was now just one vehicle behind, trying to get a better view inside. I pushed up the visor and a rush of cooler air hit the sweat.

Neon bathed the two bodies in the front seats. The passenger was a man, younger than the target, and Malaysian. The good news was that he also wore a white shirt, and was obviously a model employee. When he turned his head to talk to the target I could see he'd already put on his bow-tie.

The vehicle's indicators flashed for the left turn and they left the coast road. The route inland was busy but not as chaotic as the one we'd just quit, and I could feel the contours almost immediately as we started to make height. After less than a kilometre the breeze-block shacks petered out, and with them the clatter of petrol generators and the yelps of their scabby dogs. As we climbed even higher there was nothing at the roadside but vegetation. Lights twinkled occasionally behind the greenery, suggesting habitation, but even those soon disappeared. The road narrowed; two vehicles could just have squeezed past each other.

I let us fall back as we became the only vehicles in sight. I was anticipating a sharp left-hand bend before long, and sure enough his rear lights flared in the darkness, one flickering, as he hit the brakes to negotiate it, then disappeared.

Suzy's head came over my shoulder, her .45 digging deeper into my back. 'We sticking to the plan?'

There was nothing for me to do but nod as she sank back behind me. The job must go on. I felt Suzy's right arm delve into her bag as her legs squeezed round mine to support her. She was putting on her rubber gloves.

The red lights in front of me came and went as the target followed the bends uphill, but I didn't need to be right on top of him for about another kilometre. I knew where he was going.

I glanced in the rear-view mirror. The coastal plain was way below us now. The road ahead had been carved through rain-forest and our headlight glistened on the solid green stuff that reared up on both sides of us, still wet with rain, as I dodged fallen palm leaves and water-filled potholes.

Five hundred metres further on we passed our marker – a big stone Buddha on a log, looking down on to a junction with a mud track that went right into the forest. Maybe it was some sort of accident black spot and Buddha was there to bring good luck.

Suzy tapped my arm with a hand in a red rubber glove, and pointed to make sure I'd seen it. Then I felt her left hand go completely round my waist and her right push into the bag wedged between us. A few seconds later the barrel of the revolver ran up my back.

We were nearly at the ambush point, a narrow, staggered crossroads where the target would have to stop to negotiate a stream that cut across the junction. That was the point we were channelling him to: why force a target into the killing ground when you can pick a route he always uses? He would have to slow almost to a standstill as he forded the water.

We were less than fifty metres from the Lite Ace now. Suzy pushed down under my arse with her left hand, the .45 in her right, ready to jump herself off.

The red lights flared and flickered as the target braked for the junction. He'd have to turn right, cross the stream, then do an immediate left.

I approached the Lite Ace on its right-hand side and could smell cigarettes. As we slowed, level with the rear of the vehicle, the bike wobbled. Suzy had leapfrogged off the back as I carried on.

There was a shout from the cab.

I twisted the throttle to get myself forward to block him, but this boy wasn't for stopping. The Lite Ace crashed into my front wheel and I curled up, taking the fall. My right hip hit the tarmac, then skidded along the road with the bike following until we finally came to a halt in the stream.

I dragged myself to my feet, yanking the helmet back in time to see the vehicle roll backwards down the hill, headlights blazing skyward. Suzy was running after it. I hobbled forwards, trying to get my leg to work. It felt like someone had taken a cheese-grater to my thigh.

The vehicle kept rolling and the lights arced higher into the sky as Suzy dived in through the driver's window. What the fuck was going on?

It hit the trees fifteen metres further downhill, and came to a halt. Suzy's legs disappeared inside the driver's window at the same time as the side door slid open and the interior light came on. A figure leapt out and crashed through the foliage as two shots were fired.

'Which one? Which one?'

Suzy scrambled out. 'He's in the cover!'

'Wait, wait.' I drew level with her and grabbed her arm to stop her jumping into the forest. It was the pickup who was dead, his head twisted and pushed up against the blood-soaked seat.

I ripped off my helmet, gulping down oxygen. 'Sssh, listen.'

It was secondary forest, small bushes and plants growing wherever the sun had penetrated the canopy. This stuff was difficult to move through, especially when it was dark. The target wouldn't be able to see his own hands in front of his face.

24

We heard nothing; we'd have to go in after him.

Four paces in and I couldn't see her any more. I reached out into the inky blackness and gripped her arm, pulling down until she dropped with me on to the wet leaf litter and mud of the rainforest floor. We crawled a few paces, hands and knees sinking into the mud, before stopping and listening. Still nothing.

I'd just started to move again when there was a noise. I stopped. She bumped into me. I held my breath, opened my mouth to block out my own sounds and let the saliva dribble out of me. He was close, a little to my right. It was barely audible above the engine ticking over, but I could just make out whimpering.

I felt behind me very slowly and grabbed her spare hand, passing my helmet to her before feeling my way to her face and pressing my fingers against her lips. She still had her helmet on, which was good: we didn't want to leave either of them here.

I turned my right ear towards the sounds of a frightened man. He probably didn't know what to do, where to go, whether to hide or run blindly into the forest. I hoped he kept choosing to lie still and think the darkness would save him.

I put out my hand in his direction, feeling the invisible ground just below and in front of me, then inched forward. Mud, roots and leaves collected between my fingers before I came into contact with the cool, clammy bark of a tree. I moved very slowly round it. I heard Suzy behind me, swallowing a mouthful of saliva.

He was close now, moving his legs. I heard them scrape across the rotting leaves.

My face was getting attacked by whatever flew around here and ate skin. Not that it mattered at the moment. My whole being was focused on finding the target; even the pain in my leg had gone as I inched a little further.

He was so close I could hear him gulp with fear, then he moved his legs again and leaves rippled across my hand.

There was nothing to do but jump in that direction. My body fell clumsily on him and he screamed. My nose landed on the side of his face. He curled into a ball, begging and pleading as I got up on my knees. I didn't know the language; I wasn't listening.

Suzy was up behind me. 'Where is he? Where is he?'

I got my right knee pushing down on the side of his head. His begging became louder.

'Ssssh, it's OK, it's OK.' My right hand went down and fell on to his sweat-soaked face. I kept hold of his head and held out my spare hand into the darkness. 'Come to me, quick.'

She moved into me and I grabbed her, feeling my way up her arm. My fingers found the revolver and guided it down on to his head. 'You've got it. I'll hold him.'

I felt the muzzle digging into his skin as he sobbed and started to struggle. I wanted to get this over with. 'You ready? I'll let go on three . . . one, two, three.'

I released his head and pushed myself backwards, and in the same instant she squeezed the trigger. There was a bright flash and the sound seemed much louder than I knew it actually was.

'Stay still, stay still. Got to make sure.'

I heard the hammer go back.

'Wait, wait.'

I heard her feeling around for what was left of his head. There was another bright flash and loud bang. The smell of cordite hung between us, trapped by the canopy of leaves, and the pain in my leg returned with a vengeance.

'So, how the fuck do we get out of here?' Suzy sounded almost normal.

We were no more than ten metres or so into the rainforest, but we'd only got where we were by following the sound of the target. Getting out was something else.

'Let's just wait, calm down, see if we can hear the Lite Ace.' I held my breath. Gradually, the ringing of the shots in my ears faded, and I came to hear the gentle ticking of its engine. It was easy enough to home in on. I felt about for my helmet, and we crawled out of the trees, hitting the road only three or four metres from the vehicle.

I could see Suzy's blood-splattered face in the headlights. 'What the fuck were you doing playing Spiderman?' I inspected my leg as she did the same with her hand. 'All you had to do was shoot them.'

'By the time I got level they were already flapping to get out the side door. The wagon was rolling. I didn't know what to do. Then I thought, Fuck it, just dive in.' She was smiling: I could see a big grin in the red glow of the rear light. 'Anyway, it's done, isn't it?'

She was right. 'We need to get the wagon off the road and you need to clean up your face. The trees are too dense here to drive through – take it down to the Buddha junction, dump it out of sight as best you can, and I'll follow you if the bike's still OK. If not, we're walking back.'

She got into the Lite Ace, engaged first gear with blood- and mud-covered gloves, got it back on to the road, and drove down to the junction. I went over to the grounded bike and hauled it upright. The bike's clutch was twisted down so it faced the tarmac, but it was still in better nick than some of the machines we'd seen around town. The main thing was that it worked.

I waited at the top of the Buddha junction for Suzy, and as she came back up the hill and threw her leg over the saddle she leant forward. 'Didn't we do well? I think we deserve to go jet-skiing tomorrow, don't you?'

The right side of my leg was raging so badly from the gravel grazes that I had to grit my teeth.

4

Washington DC
Friday 2 May, 07:04 hrs

It was a miserable day. The weather just couldn't make up its mind – never quite raining but looking like it wanted to at any moment.

I walked along D Street just a couple of blocks south of the Library of Congress, on my way to meet George, moving as fast as I could while trying to sip from a lip-burning Starbucks. I'd got the metro from Crystal City, where I now lived in a large grey concrete apartment block that made me feel like a UN delegate. There was a Bosnian concierge in the daytime and a Croatian one at night. All the cleaning women seemed to be Russian and the superintendent was from Pakistan. They all understood English really well, until something needed repairing or cleaning. Especially the superintendent – every time I hassled him about the problem with my washer-dryer he went deaf.

I tested my Starbucks again. It had cooled down a little so I took a longer sip through the top cover. I'd been thinking that only George would call me into the office for seven in the morning, but apparently he wasn't alone. The whole of DC seemed to be on an early start; the traffic was heavy already and plenty of people were walking purposefully past me in both directions, almost power walking, cell phones stuck to the sides of their heads so everyone knew they were doing really important stuff. Not that they needed the cells; their voices were loud enough to carry the message right across town.

I took another swig and checked my traser watch again as I kept moving. I should be on time. The mission in Penang had been simple enough – to kill the target once he'd handed over a box to the source, after prayer that same evening. But just as important, George had stressed, was that Suzy and I both had to see the source physically in control of the box – which must have been why he'd brought it round to the passenger door.

It was a shame about the target's pickup. He was one of life's unfortunates: wrong place, wrong time. It didn't take a brain surgeon to figure out that whatever was in those bottles, it sure wasn't wine, or even Ribena; I just hoped it had been worth him dying for.

The big problem facing Suzy and me afterwards was that we still had four days left of our package holiday. We couldn't just pack up and take a scheduled flight home: everything had to look normal; we had to brass it out. We did a lot of the tourist sights rather than lying by the pool – I needed to keep my gravel-graze out of view and keep as low a profile as possible. It felt like we spent entire days in trishaws going from temple to temple.

I took the bike back; it cost me $150 for the damage, but I was just dismissed as another incompetent tourist. The killing, even the disappearance of the two waiters, hadn't made it to the *New Straits Times* in the remaining four days, which probably meant that no one had come across the Lite Ace or a fly-infested body by the time we left the country. In fact, the main event in the papers was some politician's wife being accused of *khalwat*, an offence that involved being in close proximity to a member of the opposite sex who wasn't a relation. She had been watching television with three students from the International Islamic University when a team from the Federal Territory religious department raided the

29

apartment following a complaint from neighbours. If found guilty, they could be fined three thousand dollars and jailed for up to two years. As Suzy said, she should count herself lucky she hadn't been sitting with three drug-dealers watching satellite channels with an iffy Sky card.

Suzy's revolver had been dropped off by a courier in the Firm into a dead-letter box in the women's toilet at Starbucks. I took another sip of their coffee; globalization was a reality, these guys were getting everywhere. That one had been in the shopping mall in a good part of Georgetown, the island's capital. The weapon and six rounds were all we'd been given, so Suzy had to make sure she did a good job. No wonder she'd acted like a lunatic, diving in through the Lite Ace's window. She knew she couldn't afford to waste a single shot.

It would have been better for us if the handover of the wine box had been done on the last night, so we could have carried out the task and left Penang the following day. But I was just pleased that it hadn't happened on the first night, which wouldn't have given us enough time to do the recces and would have exposed us on the island for a whole fortnight. We'd spent a lot of time establishing his routine: the route from his house to the restaurant, what time he started work, what time he finished, whether there was anyone else living in his house. We knew where he kept his vehicle, and we knew the best time to go and tamper with the brake light. We knew almost everything about him, except his name – but then again, it wasn't as if I'd wanted to have coffee with him.

By the time I reached the mansion block there was still about half a paper cup of *latte* left. I walked up the six or seven steps of the large Victorian brick building, long ago converted into office space and flanked by modern concrete blocks at either side. Large glass double doors took me into the hallway and down towards a huge black guy in a white shirt and blue uniform at the front desk. I showed him my Virginia driver's licence, as required everywhere since 9/11. I hadn't got round to buying a car yet because I had my bike –

if I could get hold of it – at Carrie's house in Marblehead.

I glanced at the security guy's name badge. 'Hi, Calvin. My name's Stone – I'm going to the third floor, Hot Black Inc.'

'Can you sign the book, sir, please?'

I signed in while he checked the visitors' list and gave me the once-over. DC was still quite a formal town when it came to dress codes and I was in my jeans, Caterpillar boots and brown leather bomber jacket. I placed the pen back on the desk and gave Calvin a smile. 'It's dress-down Friday.'

Calvin didn't bat an eyelid. 'Thank you, Mr Stone. The elevator is just round the corner there to the right, and you have a good day, sir.'

As I walked away I gave him the standard, 'And you.' I had a smile on my face: the name Hot Black Inc still made me laugh. I'd always thought it was only in *The Man from U.N.C.L.E.* that they invented weirdly named companies as fronts.

I'd been on Hot Black's payroll for just under a year now. It was a marketing company that didn't really have anything to market, which was just as well because I didn't know the first thing about that. Life was good. I got paid a salary of $82,000 a year, my apartment was taken care of, and on top of that I got cash in hand after every job. It was a much better deal than working as a K for the Firm on £290 a day, all in. As a Hot Black employee I'd been given a US social-security number, and I even had to file tax returns. It gave me the chance to have a kind of real life. After George's daughter, Carrie, had binned me, I'd even managed to have a new girlfriend for about six weeks. She was the area manager for Victoria's Secret for DC and Virginia, and we lived in the same apartment block. It worked out quite well until her husband decided he wanted to try to make a go of their marriage. I guessed he'd been missing the free samples she brought home.

I even had a pension plan. It was one of the ways George could slip me extra cash without it being noticed in the real world: walking into a bank with $20,000 in cash, these days, would do more than just raise eyebrows. For the first time in my life I was starting to feel a bit secure.

The elevator arrived, pinged open, and I stepped in and pressed the button for the third floor.

5

I still wasn't too sure what military or government department George worked for and therefore who paid my salary, but I wasn't complaining. Things had been really busy for me since I'd thrown in my lot with him: in the last few months I'd been in Bombay and Greece on 'rendering' operations; the targets were three suspected al-Qaeda operators who, I presumed, were now shuffling around Guantanamo Bay sporting shaved heads and orange coveralls.

I finished my coffee as the elevator doors closed behind me, and turned left down the corridor towards Hot Black's offices. It was a world of shiny black marble walls, alabaster statues in alcoves, and bright fluorescent lights set into suspended ceilings. The corridor had just been refurbished and the smell of thick new carpet was in the air. Hot Black Inc was no two-bob company.

I went through the smoked-glass double doors into the deserted reception area. A large veneered antique table served as a front desk, but it was unmanned. To the left of it, two long red velvet sofas faced each other with a low glass coffee-table between them. There wasn't as much as a daily newspaper or a copy of *Marketing Monthly* in sight. The desk was the same, completely clear apart from a phone. Even the drinking fountain was missing its huge upturned plastic bottle; there were just six lonely crystal glasses to one side.

I carried on to the main office doors, tall, black, very shiny and substantial. When I was just a couple of paces away they were pulled open. George spun on his heel without a word of greeting and strode back towards his desk, framed by the window a good ten metres away. The cleats in his heels clunked on the maple floor. 'You're late. I said seven a.m.'

I'd known he'd say that. He'd probably been up since five, gone for a run, said a prayer over his healthy bowl of granola, and left his house at precisely the time he'd planned. Not five or ten past the hour, that wasn't precise enough, and would have meant time wasted. It was probably eleven minutes past or something like that, to get him to the office at exactly six fifty-six.

I closed the doors behind me. 'Yes, I know, I'm sorry. There were a few delays on the metro.'

He didn't reply. The Washington metro was never late. What had made me late was the line at Starbucks, and the not-too-bright people behind the counter.

He rounded the desk. 'What's that one called?'

'A *latte*.'

The windows were triple-glazed so I could see traffic moving beyond the blinds but not hear it. The only sound, apart from our voices, was air droning through the air-conditioning ducts.

'Doesn't anybody just buy a cup of plain Joe any more? You're paying over two bucks a hit just because it's got a fancy name.'

The room was well furnished. One wall was panelled with oak and had what looked like an eighteenth-century portrait of a guy wearing a tricorne hat and a mason's apron, with a bunch of American Indians in the background killing someone.

As George finally turned to face me I realized it really must be dress-down day in Spookville. He wasn't wearing his

34

normal button-down shirt and tie under his cord sports jacket but a white polo shirt. Maybe next week he'd go completely overboard and undo the top button, but I wasn't going to hold my breath.

George sat down on a dark wooden chair, which squeaked with newness as it took his weight. There was nothing on his desk, except a phone and a dark brown briefcase. He motioned for me to take a chair, then wasted no more time. 'So, what happened to the weapon?'

I still had the empty coffee-cup in my hand: there was nowhere to put it. 'Suzy went jet-skiing and dumped it about three hundred metres out to sea. The cases were still in the chamber. I didn't go with her, but she'll have done it OK.'

George raised an eyebrow.

'I couldn't – I didn't want the gravel burn on display.'

'How is it now?'

'Fine. I just can't resist picking at the scabs at night.' I raised a little smile but it had no effect on George. He was looking up at the fluorescent lighting set into the false ceiling. 'I'm going to get some dimmers put in here. These things are a health hazard, not good for the eyes.'

I nodded, because if George said so it must be true.

He got back into the real world. 'You and the woman . . .'

'Suzy.'

'Yes, you both did very well, son.' He pulled the briefcase towards him and played with the combination locks.

I put my cup on the highly polished floorboards. 'I was wondering, George, what was in the bottles?'

He didn't even bother to look up. 'That, son, you don't need to know. Your part is done.'

The case opened and he looked up, forcing a smile. 'Remember what I told you? Our job is to make sure these scum get to see their God earlier than expected. Period.'

I remembered.

'Where are you headed now?'

'Maybe away for a while, who knows?'

'I want to know. Make sure you keep your cell with you. My beeper number is the same until the end of the month when I'll give you my new one.'

A brown Jiffy-bag came out of the briefcase and he pushed it across the table, along with a sheet of typed paper. I leant forward to pick it up as he checked out the ceiling lights once more and glanced at his watch.

It said that I'd received $16,000 in cash from George and required my signature – maybe to stop him keeping it and buying a pony to go with his shirt. 'I thought you said it was going to be twenty thousand?'

'It is – but you just made a twenty per cent contribution to the welfare fund.' He looked around at his plush surroundings and opened his arms. 'There are old operators out there who didn't have a marketing pension to fall back on when they were retired or got themselves all busted up. Life was different then, so I got to thinking that those old guys are entitled to share a little of our good fortune. Those guys find it hard in the real world, Nick. As I don't need to tell you, it's a jungle out there . . .'

I took a breath, ready to say I didn't have a choice.

George got in before me. 'Now you've settled in, this is the way it's going to be. We all do it. Who knows? You might be calling for help yourself some day.'

I didn't bother opening the envelope to check. All my cash would be there: George would have counted it out himself. Everything was correct with George, everything was always on time. I liked him for it.

He checked his watch again, then closed his briefcase and concentrated on the locks as he reset the combination. 'This is where you leave, with your cup.'

I'd got to the door with cup and cash in hand when he gave his parting shot. 'There'll always be a place for you here, Nick. Nothing's going to change that.' I knew he was referring to Carrie, and turned back to see his face break into a smile. 'Until they kill you, of course. Or I find someone better.'

I nodded and opened the doors. I wouldn't have had it any other way. As I turned to close them again, I could see George looking up at the lights once more, probably planning a memo to the building superintendent. I hoped he had more luck with his than I did with mine.

6

Laurel, Maryland
Monday 5 May, 10:16 hrs

I sat in the back of a taxi on the way to Josh's house, after the half-hour train ride from Central Station to Laurel. With all the messing about and waiting, I'd probably have been quicker hiring a car, but it was too late now.

We turned the corner into Josh d'Souza's new estate of prim and proper weatherboarded houses, and I directed the driver to his cul-de-sac. My last visit had been only six weeks ago, but it was just as hard to tell the houses apart, with their neatly trimmed grass fronts, obligatory basketball hoop attached to the garage wall, and Stars and Stripes waving in the breeze. Some front windows even displayed a blown-up photograph of a young son or daughter in military uniform, virtually swamped by Old Glory. Josh's house was 106, about half-way down on the left.

The cab pulled up at the bottom of the concrete drive. Josh's place was set back from the road by about twenty metres, and on a slight rise, with his front lawn sloping up towards the house. A couple of bikes, a basketball and a skateboard lay outside the garage, and his black, double-cabbed Dodge gas-guzzler stood in the drive.

I caught sight of Josh looking out of the kitchen window, as if he'd been twitching the curtains waiting for me. By the time the taxi had pulled away, he was standing at the white-painted wooden front door, agitation etched all over his scarred face.

That was nothing new. Despite the I-forgive-you stuff, I still wasn't too sure that he liked me. 'Endured' would probably have been a better word. I hardly ever got the warm smile he would have greeted me with before the shooting that fucked up his face. He accepted me because I had a relationship with Kelly, and that was about it. We were like divorced parents, really. I was the errant father who popped in now and again with a totally unsuitable gift, and he was the mother who had all the day-to-day problems, who had to get up in the morning and find her clean socks and be there when things went wrong, which was most of the time recently.

He turned, closed the door behind him, and double-locked it. 'Why don't you ever turn your cell on?'

'Hate the things. I just check messages. Calls normally mean drama.'

We shook briefly and he waved the bunch of keys he had in his hand. 'I've a drama for you. We gotta go.'

'What's happened?'

He headed us towards the Dodge. 'The school called. She got pulled up by the math teacher for being late for first period, so she told him to go eff himself.'

The indicators flashed as he hit the key fob.

'Do *what*?' I climbed into the cab beside him.

'I know, I know. That's on top of walking out on her gymnastics teacher last week. The school's had enough. They're talking suspension. I said you were visiting today and we'd get down there as soon as you arrived. We got ourselves some firefighting to do.'

The massive engine kicked into life and we reversed down the drive.

'You know, Josh, I sometimes think that in a past life I must have really offended someone really really deeply . . .'

'You mean, as well as in this?'

The school was just twenty or so blocks away. I couldn't remember if Kelly walked there or got the bus. Probably neither. Kids could drive at sixteen in Maryland, and she hung around with a slightly older crowd.

Josh waved his hand despairingly. 'I can't control her. She slips out at night. I've found cigarettes in her dresser. She's so moody and irritable that I don't know what to say to her. I'm worried about her future, Nick. I spoke to the school counsellor last time, but she hasn't any answers because she can't get anything out of her either. Nobody can.'

'Don't beat yourself up, mate. Nobody could be doing more than you are.'

Josh was half black, half Puerto Rican. His looks had changed quite a bit since the first time I met him. Standing next to Kelly's family's grave site in the sun, his hairless head and glasses had glinted as brightly as his teeth. But what you noticed first these days was the rough pink scar along his left cheek that looked like a split sausage in a frying-pan, edged with spots of dried blood where he couldn't get used to shaving around the lumpy tissue. However much Christian-forgiveness shit he splashed around, and however much I tried to cut away, tell myself the damage was done, I still felt as guilty every time I saw it as he did about Kelly.

He was wearing a blue sweatshirt tucked into his black-leather belt with the same grey cargo fatigue trousers his Secret Service training team always wore, and a pair of Nike trainers. In the past, they'd always been accompanied by a very worn, light brown pancake holster on his belt, tucked against his right kidney, and a double mag carrier on the left, alongside a black beeper.

Five years earlier he'd been on the vice-presidential protection team, part of the Secret Service, until Geri had left him and their three kids for her yoga teacher. He'd had to sell the house in Virginia because he couldn't afford to keep up the mortgage, and had taken a job up here at Laurel, training baby agents. We hadn't come into each other's lives at that stage, but

I knew the first few years had been a nightmare for him and the kids. That was when the born-again Christian stuff had happened.

The Service was finished for him now. Like he told me, it had been an easy choice to make: quit, or his kids never seeing their father. Now he was a baby vicar or reverend, something like that; the God thing had given him a new career. He had another year to go before he was officially able to shout and breakdance in church with the best of them. I'd told him he ought to think bigger than that and go the TV route. I'd be his sidekick. He could talk up God for the first part of the show and after the break I would explain how the two of us, God's little helpers, could do with a shedload of dollars. That hadn't gone down too well.

'You got the devil, Nick.'

'That's right, I'm an agent of Satan – but my duties are now mostly ceremonial.'

That hadn't gone down too well either.

The bell rang for the end of a period and a tidal wave of students and noise surged into the corridor.

'I wish I could help her.' Her maths teacher was very frustrated about the whole Kelly situation. He slowed kids down so the three of us didn't get swept away. 'I try to get her to talk, but I guess I just don't choose the best days. Sometimes it's so hard to communicate with her.' He ran his hand over the top of his balding head and checked his fingers as if expecting to find more fallen hair. He was only in his late thirties, but already seemed broken on the wheel of life. 'You've both seen it, she's withdrawn one day, then high as a kite the next. She takes some keeping up with. The school counsellor would like to help if you're willing to – look, here we are. I had to send her straight to the principal's office. We have to maintain standards in the classroom for these kids. Here we are, in here.'

He opened a door and ushered us into the principal's waiting room. 'Now, Kelly, look who – oh . . .' The chair I guessed

41

Kelly should have been sitting on had a half empty paper cup of water next to it, but that was about it. The room was empty.

'She took off an hour ago.' The principal's secretary was big and black, radiating efficiency but still unable to hide the distressed look on her face. 'The principal has been trying to call you, Mr d'Souza. We were about to call the police.' She shook her head. 'All she said to me when she first came in was she was going to Disneyland.'

'Save us.' Josh sighed as he turned to me, his right hand cutting the air. He got out his cell and started to dial. It went up to his ear and stayed there for just a second. 'Her cell's off. OK, we go home. If she's not there we'll have to call in the police.'

'No need, mate.' I started for the Dodge. 'I know exactly where she's gone.'

7

We headed west, and it wasn't long before we were following signs for Baltimore and Washington. Josh had called his house three times already but no one was answering. Soon we were taking the ramp left on to the I-95 towards Washington. 'Disneyland, huh? Is that what she calls her old house?'

'Sort of.'

He shrugged. 'Did I tell you she doesn't come to church with us any more? She says religion is a con. I don't even think she believes it, she's just saying it to pain us.'

'You know her take on that, mate – if there's a God, then how come her family's dead?'

He shot me a telling glance. 'I'm not getting into that – and I keep telling you, go read the book.'

I looked at the dash. The Puerto Rican in him revealed itself in the recent picture of Kelly and his three mounted there in a small but ornate gold frame. Dakota was now sixteen and had the mother of all braces in her mouth. Kimberly was fourteen and the biggest concern in her life was her hair, and the boy, Tyce, was thirteen and thought he was Tony Hawks. Their skins were all lighter than Josh's because their mother was white, but they looked just like their dad. You couldn't move in their house for framed photographs. There was Josh when he used to have hair, as a young fresh soldier, looking very much like the ones in his neighbours' windows; Josh becoming a member of Special Forces; Josh and the kids; Josh, Geri and the kids, plus all the horrible school portraits with gappy-toothed grins and scabs on their knees.

It must have been clear he wasn't going to get an answer out of me and, like a good Christian, he turned the other cheek. 'So tell me, man, what you been doing?'

'I'm fine. I've been working in the UK the last few weeks. It's been quite strange standing in the foreigners' line at Immigration. But, hey, it pays the bills.' Which reminded me why I'd come to see him in the first place. I reached into my bomber for the still-sealed envelope and pushed it under his thigh. 'Get yourself a decent car, will you? And a wig.'

'Thanks. But I think I can put it to better use.'

I was sure he could. Kelly wasn't the only one who needed the cash.

He drove a while in silence, then leant forward for his cell from the dash mounting and passed it over. 'Get to "Names", will you, Nick? Look under B for Billman. They're neighbours in Hunting Bear. Keep an eye on the house and stuff.'

I hit a few keys and listened to the ringing tone. After a while an answering-machine kicked in.

He shrugged. 'We'll try later. ' He turned his head and gave me a wry smile. 'They're probably at another of their community meetings, still complaining about the way we're messing with their real-estate prices. Maybe we should give in, you know, let them have it cheap. No one's ever going to buy a house with that kind of history. Let them knock it down and make a play area or whatever it is they want.' It had taken a while, but Josh was slowly coming round to my way of thinking. 'It might help Kelly in a funny sort of way. Some kind of closure, know what I'm saying?'

He flicked the indicator to come off the I-95 at the next exit, towards the Outerloop, the I-495 around DC. Electric road

44

signs constantly flashed out their instruction to report any suspicious terrorist activity. 'What are we supposed to do with any unsuspicious activity we see, mate? Just keep it to ourselves?'

He'd obviously spent the last few miles collecting his thoughts. 'Look, Nick, this is my take on things. It's nothing new, I'm just more sure. First of all, we're not going to give up on her, whatever. Her acting out, she's trying to cope. She's coping with her family being dead, coping with the fact she feels abandoned. She's coping with living with us. She's got a lot weighing on that heart of hers, man.'

I pulled down the visor to shade me from the glare. 'I didn't abandon her, she knows that. She knows we thought it was the best thing for her to come live with you.' I knew I was sounding defensive.

'You gotta take a look at it from where she stands. No matter how much love our home is giving her, it's gotta be tough.' He leant forward over the wheel to stretch his back. 'She alienates people, you know she does. It's her way of coping, Nick. She withdraws from us before we have a chance to do it to her. She's insulating herself. We've got to make sure she learns how to cope another way. A good way.'

'You've been watching too much Dr Phil, mate.'

He ignored me again. 'We all have ways of handling stuff, OK? Me, I've got a devout belief in the Lord, I know that He loves me. You would, too, if only you'd let Him in. Let anybody in, come to think of it.' He pointed a finger while trying not to cut up a truck. 'You, you're Mr Distractive – when things get a little too hot for you, you try to head off somewhere different, get busy, get funny, anything to get away. That Dr Phil gag, you're still doing it – what you call it, cutting away? Yeah, you're still cutting away, huh?' He turned towards me and I took over looking out of the windscreen. 'You know why you never look me in the eye, you never look at my face? It's because you feel guilty, so you just do your little thing, you cut away.'

45

I wasn't cutting away, I was completely blanking out. 'Load of bollocks.'

His head shook slowly from side to side. A road sign announced we were entering Virginia. 'The way it looks to me, she's doing exactly what you do, cutting away, keeping a lid on things. She just can't bear to let her feelings out – she's scared of what might happen. She's scared it might be like leaving the gate open in the zoo, so the lions and the elephants escape, know what I'm saying?'

I shrugged a 'maybe'.

'Man, I know you were doing your best for her, I know there were outrageous circumstances, but what goes through her head at night? What does she dream about? It may be too late for you, but we gotta help her take the lid off. But, like, real slow.' We came off the highway, taking the ramp right and following signs for Tyson's Corner. 'It's going to take a long time, know what I'm saying? But we'll get there with her in the end.'

'You reckon?' Sometimes I admired his unshakeable Christian certainty, but just as often it tipped me over the edge. 'You had a word with God then, have you?'

It was a cheap shot, and we both knew it. His face looked very sad all of a sudden. I must have been a constant disappointment to him. 'No, Nick, I've told God we are going to sort this one out for Him. Or, rather, that you're going to sort it out. I'm taking the kids to Baptist college for my module tomorrow. Kelly was only coming under sufferance anyway. We'll be back Saturday p.m. Spend some time with her, man.'

The moment we left the freeway we could have been in leafy suburban Surrey. Large detached houses lined the road, and just about every one seemed to have a seven-seater people-carrier in the drive and, of course, a basketball hoop. I remembered only too well the route we were taking to the estate – or community, as it liked to be known – where Kev and Marsha had lived with Kelly and her younger sister, Aida.

We turned on to Hunting Bear Path and carried on for about

a quarter of a mile until we reached a small, one-level parade of shops arranged in an open square with parking spaces, mainly little delis and boutiques specializing in candles and soap. That was where I'd stopped that day to buy sweets for Aida and Kelly that I knew Marsha wouldn't let them have, and a couple of other equally unwelcome gifts.

Far up on the right-hand side among the large detached houses I could just about make out the rear of Kev and Marsha's 'de luxe colonial'. The Century 21 for-sale sign had been up for five years now, and had become faded and weatherbeaten. As co-executor with Josh of their will, I knew not to get too hopeful when anyone came to view it. They never stuck around long once they discovered its history.

8

'Mrs Billman's back.' Josh nodded at the blue Explorer in a driveway fifty metres ahead. The houses round here were quite a distance apart. He stopped, blocking in the other wagon, and arched his back to reach into his cargoes. 'I'll go check with them, you go look around the house. Here.' He threw a bunch of keys at me on a Homer Simpson ring. 'I won't come looking, OK? I'll stay in the truck to give you kids some time. Know what I'm saying?'

We both climbed out of the Dodge, and as he went up the Billmans' drive I stood looking up the road at the light-brown brick and white weatherboarded house. I hadn't seen it for a year or two, but not much had changed: it just looked older and a bit more tired. At least the 'community' cut the lawns and trimmed the hedges so it didn't make their world look untidy.

I began to walk up the driveway. I was kidding myself – everything had changed. In the old days, I'd have been ambushed by now. The kids would have jumped out at me, with Marsha and Kev close behind.

I'd known the Browns a long time by that spring of 1997. I was there when Kev first met Marsha, I was best man at their wedding, and was even godfather to Aida, their second child. I took the job seriously, even though I didn't really know what I was supposed to do.

I knew I'd never have any kids of my own; I'd always be too busy running around doing shit jobs for people like George. Kev and Marsha knew that too, and really tried to make me feel part of their set-up. As a kid on a run-down estate in south London I'd grown up with this fantasy of the perfect family, and as far as I was concerned Kev was living the dream.

I went straight to the up-and-over garage door, but it was locked, and none of Homer's keys fitted. I skirted round the left side of the house and headed for the backyard. No sign of her. Just the big, wood-framed swing, a little the worse for wear, but still there after all this time.

I slotted a Yale in the front door and gave it a turn. Six years ago, as I remembered only too well, I'd found it ajar.

Kev's job with the DEA [Drug Enforcement Administration] had been mostly deskbound in Washington for the previous few months. He'd made enemies in the drug-dealing community when he was an undercover operator, and after five attempts on his life, Marsha had decided enough was enough.

He loved his new, safer life. 'More time with the kids,' he'd say.

'Yeah, so you can carry on being one!' was my standard reply.

Luckily Marsha was the mature and sensible partner; when it came to the family, they complemented each other well. Their house was a healthy, loving environment, but by the end of three or four days I'd have to move on. I'd joke about it and complain about the house smelling of scented candles, but they knew the real reason: I just couldn't handle people showing this much affection.

The stale, musty, unlived-in smell hit me the moment Homer did his stuff and I stepped inside. The corridor opened up into a large rectangular hallway with doors leading off to the

49

downstairs rooms. Kitchen to my right. Lounge to the left. All the doors were closed. I stood just the other side of the threshold, spinning the key-ring slowly on my finger, wanting badly to smell those candles again.

All the carpets and furniture had been taken away a long time ago. It was the first thing the realtor had got us to do when we put it up for sale. Prospective buyers didn't go a bundle on bloodstained shag pile and three-piece suites. Kelly hadn't minded anything going, but insisted we hung on to the swing. Next, we'd got every trace of blood steamed away. The smell was still there, though, I was convinced of it: the haunting metallic tang was starting to hit my nostrils and catch in the back of my throat. Shoving Homer in a pocket of my bomber, I ventured deeper into the house.

As I passed the solid wood lounge door, my heartbeat quickened. I couldn't help myself; I had to stop and face that fucking door. I even started reaching for the handle, but then my hand dropped away. I knew I couldn't do it. And this wasn't the only door here that made me feel like that.

I'd come back more than once to oversee removal men and cleaners, but I'd never made it further than the kitchen. In the end I'd had to leave that side of things to Josh. I'd never told him why, never told him about the doors I just couldn't bring myself to open. Smartarse that he was, he probably knew anyway.

I just stood there, staring at the handle, my forehead against the closed door. My hands went into my bomber pockets. My fingers closed around Homer's head and the keys, clenching them until they gave me pain.

Sunlight had cascaded through the lounge door that day in April 1997, but I hadn't bothered looking in. I'd been too intent on making a beeline for the soft rock music in the kitchen. Something must have snagged in my peripheral vision, though, because after a couple of steps I froze in my tracks. My brain must have taken in the information, but for a split second refused to process it.

I gripped Homer hard, while a wave of nausea washed through me. My internal video had begun to play back what I'd seen, in full technicolour. Hard to believe it had been six years ago, even harder to believe it could still be stored so close to the surface.

Shit, I thought I'd got this under control.

Too late. It was running.

Kev was lying on his side on the floor, his head battered to fuck by a baseball bat. It was the one he'd shown off to me, a nice light 'aluminum' job. He'd raised his eyebrows and laughed as he told me the local rednecks called them Alabama lie-detectors.

Then I was checking his body, just in case he was breathing. No chance. His brains were hanging out, his face pulped. Blood all over the settee and chairs. Some even splattered on the patio windows.

What about Marsha and the kids? Was the killer still in the house?

I'd needed one of his pistols, the very fucking things that had been supposed to be there to protect them. He'd once shown me all the places they were concealed, always above child level, always loaded and made ready, a magazine on the weapon and a round in the chamber. I'd soon got my hands round a Heckler and Koch USP 9mm, a semi-automatic pistol. This one even had a laser sight under the barrel; where the beam hit, so did the round.

My eyes welled as the song from the radio came back to me, some Arrowsmith thing, one of Marsha's favourites. I stayed leaning into the door, waiting for my heartrate to slow, then pivoted my head to the right, towards the closed kitchen door. That had been the room I'd checked first for Marsha and the kids. It had been the nearest, the one with music.

I pushed away from the door, my Cats echoing as I walked across the bare hall, Arrowsmith providing the soundtrack to the video in my head.

51

Pistol out in front of me, ready to fire as soon as I saw a target, I had given the door a push, and moved back from the frame. The radio had become louder, and the washing-machine was on – turning, stopping, turning.

I'd moved forward and pushed the door fully open. Nothing. Just a small dot of brilliant red light where the laser splashed on the opposite wall.

Today, no radio, no washing-machine, no nothing. But even then it had been like stepping aboard the *Mary Celeste*. There'd been food on the side, in the midst of preparation. Kev had said Marsha was going to cook something special. There were vegetables and opened packs of meat. The table was half laid.

I had moved slowly to the other end of the room and locked the door to the garage. I hadn't wanted to clear the bottom of the house only to have the boys come in behind me.

I suddenly realized I was still throttling Homer, and released my grip. As blood rushed back into my hand, I leant against the sink and stared at the garage door. That was the one I should be going through, but I couldn't help myself, I needed to go upstairs.

I went out into the hallway again and put my foot on the uncarpeted bottom step. The bare wood creaked unnaturally loudly.

The girls' old room was waiting for me at the top of the stairs. Six years ago, it had been the world's biggest shrine to *Pocahontas* – T-shirts and posters, bed-linen and even a doll who sang something about colours when you pressed her back. The door was closed, but that door wasn't the problem.

The next room down on the left had been Kev and Marsha's. The door was slightly ajar.

My heart sparked up again, my mouth went dry.

Why the fuck have you come up here? You promised yourself you never would again.

I couldn't help it. I edged nearer, as if the door was a dangerous animal, and smelt that faint, metallic tang again, as strongly as if it was really there – and then the stench of shit.

Fuck this. I headed back towards the stairs, but stopped and turned back, lying to myself that I had a reason to stay.

Get a grip! You're here to find Kelly.

The video was running. I wasn't able to stop it. Sinking down on to the bare floorboards of the landing, I just stared at the part-open door, my head replaying every last fucking detail.

It had only been when I'd inched round the frame that I'd got my first glimpse of Marsha.

She'd been kneeling by the bed, arms spreadeagled on it, the bedspread covered with blood.

I'd gone in, forcing myself to ignore her. The room was clear. The en-suite was next, and what I'd seen there had made me lose it, totally fucking lose it.

Bang, I'd smacked back against the wall and slumped on to the floor. Blood everywhere. I'd got it all over my shirt and hands; I'd sat in a pool of it; it had soaked the seat of my trousers.

Stop this – fucking stop it! Cut and run . . .

Too late. Much too late. Aida had been lying on the floor between the bath and the toilet, her five-year-old head nearly severed from her shoulders. Just three inches of flesh left intact, the vertebrae scarcely attached.

Then I'd *really* seen Marsha. Her dress had been hanging normally but her tights had been torn, her knickers pulled down, and she had shit herself, probably at the point of death.

All I had seen in that moment was somebody I really cared for, even loved, on her knees, her blood splattered all over the bed. And she'd had the same done to her as Aida had.

Not even Homer could divert me now. I was taking deep breaths and wiping my eyes, just as I had done then. Feeling the same shock and disbelief, the same devastating feeling of failure.

What if you'd got here earlier? Could you have stopped this fucking nightmare?

I wiped my face.

I had to cut away, or I'd go crazy. It had taken me years to learn how to keep the zoo gates closed, and I'd done myself no favours by giving them the chance to open.

I gripped the banisters and pulled myself up, and then went downstairs to see her.

9

Kev had shown me the 'hidey-hole', as he called it, the same day he showed me where all the weapons were concealed, just in case shit happened. It was built from the boxes the kitchen appliances had come in, under an open staircase in the garage that led up to a little makeshift loft where he used to stack his ladders and stuff. The kids knew they had to run straight there if Kev or Marsha ever shouted the word 'Disneyland!' They were to keep very quiet, and they weren't to come out until Daddy or Mommy came and got them.

Back down in the kitchen, I took a deep breath and got myself together, then went through into the garage.

In the old days they could easily have fitted three extra vehicles beside the company car Kev always used to keep there, a navy Caprice Classic bristling with aerials. 'Fucking thing,' he would always complain. 'All the mod cons of the nineties, in a motor that looks like a nineteen-sixties fridge.'

The kids' bikes had used to hang from frames on the breeze-block wall. They'd been disposed of with all the other clutter that families accumulate. All that was left was a collection of unused removal boxes that we'd stacked under the staircase. Kelly had made herself a new Disneyland.

I moved towards them, calling out gently. 'Kelly? It's Nick. Are you there?'

When Kev had made his cardboard cave he'd provisioned it with a few dolls, bottles of water and chocolate bars. Last time I'd approached it on my hands and knees, the pistol down my waistband. I hadn't wanted Kelly to see a weapon, hadn't wanted her to know there was a major drama going on.

I'd tried to coax her out as I moved Kev's boxes aside, inching towards the back wall.

And that was where I'd finally found her, eyes wide with terror, sitting curled up, rocking backwards and forwards, holding her hands over her ears, her eyes red, wet and swollen. It was only much later that I discovered she'd seen and heard the lot.

This time I only had to move one of the packing cases. She was sitting against the wall.

'Hello.'

She was wearing a green T-shirt with some kind of sports logo, red and white trainers, and a pair of low-cut jeans that exposed her hip bones. It wasn't terror in her eyes this time, they were just kind of sad and tired, and a bit puzzled, as if she was trying to work out why mine looked red as well.

'Found you at last.' I grinned. 'You play a mean game of hide-and-seek.'

She didn't return my smile. Her blotchy, tear-stained face stared at me as I crawled towards her.

It didn't matter what state she was in, she was as pretty as ever. She'd inherited the best of both her parents: her mother's mouth and her father's eyes. 'Biggest smile this side of Julia Roberts,' Kev used to say. His mother came from southern Spain and he looked like a local: jet-black hair, but with the world's bluest eyes. Marsha reckoned he was a dead ringer for Mel Gibson.

'Come on, let's get you out of here. I need some fresh air.'

She stared at me for what felt like for ever, as if she'd been travelling to some far-off place and just come back, and was trying to work out how everything had changed. Finally, she gave me the briefest and bleakest of smiles. 'Sorry.'

I shifted a box to make it easier for her to get out. 'About what?'

She glazed over again, as if she still wasn't quite connecting. 'Today.' She shrugged. 'Everything.'

'It's OK, don't worry. Hey, you still like playing on swings?'

10

I closed down my cell as we walked into the back garden and put my arm round her. I'd told Josh she was fine, we just needed a bit of time. He said he'd go down to the stores and grab a coffee. Call him whenever.

Last time I'd found her in the hidey-hole I'd taken her hand and guided her gently out. Then I'd picked her up in my arms and held her tight as I carried her into the kitchen. She was trembling so much I couldn't tell if her head was nodding or shaking. When we drove away from the house a bit later, she was almost rigid with shock.

Dr Hughes had told me some things early on in her treatment, which felt like it had happened a lifetime ago. 'Kelly has been forced to learn early lessons about loss and death, Mr Stone. How does a seven-year-old, as she was then, understand murder? A child who witnesses violence has been shown that the world is a dangerous and unpredictable place. She has told me that she doesn't think she'll ever again feel safe going outside. It's nobody's fault, but her experience has made her think that the adults in her life are unable to protect her. She believes she must take the responsibility herself – a prospect that causes her great anxiety.'

We walked over to the swing and she wiggled about to get comfortable on the rubber tyre seat as I lay on the grass beside her.

'Push me, Nick?'

I got up and stood behind her. She sat there passively at first, not helping me with the momentum, then it seemed to come back to her.

'What have you done to your finger?' She had a plaster on the knuckle of her right index finger, and the skin below it looked red and sore.

'I did something a bit silly in science. It'll be fine.'

I pushed her in silence for a while. I liked it. It made me think of the great times I'd had in this backyard too.

'First thing Dad used to do when he came home from work,' she said. 'He'd go and give Mom a kiss, then come out and play with us. It was good. Not all dads do that.'

'Not all dads love their kids as much as he did.'

She liked that. 'Mom used to bring us out cookies and Kool-Aid. Sometimes we'd all stay out here right until supper-time.' She grinned. 'We used to love it when you came visit. Mom would tell us to say thank you if you gave us candy, but to give it to her. She was the candy police.' As she came back towards me her face went serious again and I slowed her to a stop, my head on her right shoulder as I listened. 'I used to feel safer when you were here with Dad. Don't you remember? Mom used to call you guys "my two strong men". I was always worried when it was just him on his own because I knew people were after him.'

'That was because he did his job so well.'

'Did you work together?'

'We were soldiers together in the army. When he married your mum he came here.'

She looked down at her trainers, then sharply up again, her blue eyes piercing mine. 'Why did Mom and Aida have to die, Nick?'

We'd never talked about it. I somehow assumed she just

59

knew, maybe that her grandparents or Dr Hughes or Josh had told her. I felt like I hadn't explained the facts of life to her, and just hoped she'd pick them up on her own. Then again, maybe she did know and just wanted to hear me try to make sense of it one more time.

'Your dad was one of the good guys. But his boss got mixed up with drug people and your dad found out. His boss killed him – and then he killed everybody who might be a witness.'

'Mom and Aida?'

'Yes.'

'How come he didn't kill me, Nick? How come I'm the one who got to stay alive?'

'I don't have those answers, Kelly. Maybe if the people had come into the house five minutes earlier or later, they'd have got you too.'

'It would have saved everybody a lot of hassle.'

I lifted my head and walked round to face her. 'Hey, don't say things like that. Don't even think things like that.' Hunching down in front of her, I held both her hands.

'Sometimes I feel so shit, Nick. Just kind of disconnected. Do you know what I mean?'

'I spend most of my life feeling like that.' I hesitated, drawing her close to me. 'You know, I saw somebody die when I was eight.'

She sat up straight. 'You did?'

I described the disused old factory building near our estate. The windows and doors had been boarded up and covered with barbed-wire, but that wasn't going to keep us out. 'There was an old sheet of corrugated iron nailed over the frame of a small door down an alleyway, but it was loose. We got in, up on to the roof. I remember puffing out hard and watching my breath form into a cloud.' It had felt much colder thirty feet up than it had at ground level. 'I walked to the edge of the roof and looked down at the pools of light underneath the lamp-posts. The street was deserted, there was no one around to see us. It was so peaceful. I'd never known the streets round my way be so quiet. And then there was a sound, a really horrible sound.'

'What was it?' She was pressing into my side.

'Breaking glass. I turned and saw my three mates standing near one of the skylights. There should have been four.'

A split second later, there'd been a muffled thud from deep inside the building. 'I knew even before I looked through the hole that John would be dead. We all did. We ran back to the roof hatch and down the stairs. He was lying very still, and we just scarpered.'

'Did the police come?'

'There were police swarming all around the flats the next day, but we made sure we all told the same story. We thought we were murderers. I'd never felt so scared.'

Kelly looked up at me. 'Do you ever get scared now?'

'All the time.' I chanced a smile. 'And before you ask, I have absolutely no plans to die until I'm very old.'

'But no guarantees, right?'

'Whoa, that's one for Josh and his Bible college.'

She winced. 'Not funny, Nick. I know you don't care what happens to you, but I do. It really matters, you know? I mean, what if people come after you like they came after Dad? What happens to me then?'

I squatted down in front of her, our faces now level. 'There'd be Josh. They all love you.'

'I know that. But it's you I need, Nick. Like I said, Mom used to call you and Dad her two strong men. Now there's only one of you left.' She let go of the ropes and touched my cheeks with surprisingly cold hands. 'Will you be my strong man, Nick? Will you?' There were tears in her eyes.

She took her hands out of mine and looked down at her trainers again before I could answer, which was just as well because I didn't have a clue what to say. 'There aren't many places I've felt safe since ... well, since I was on my own. I listed them to myself once. There's the house in Norfolk. Remember, we put up that tent in the bedroom? You nailed it

61

to the floor instead of pegs and I thought that was so cool. I loved that. Then there's here – sometimes. And . . .' She looked away. 'That place you took me to . . .'

I gave her shoulder a squeeze. 'Dr Hughes?'

She nodded. 'She understood.'

In the silence that followed, I realized it was time for me to start being her strong man. Josh was right. 'Would you like to talk things over with her again?'

Her face lit up as if I'd thrown a switch. 'Could I? I mean, how?'

'The twin miracles of flight and Mastercard. We could be there tomorrow if we wanted.'

'I'm supposed to be going to Josh's Bible college on Friday and—'

I waved my hand. 'Not a problem. Let's go to England instead. I'm sure he'll understand. We can go and see your grandparents, spend some time with Dr Hughes, spend some time together, just you and me.'

Practically falling off the tyre, she threw her arms round my neck and planted a huge kiss on my cheek. Her face was radiant. 'I feel better already.' Then she frowned. 'How did you get here? Did Josh bring you?'

'Yeah. He's gone down to the stores for a coffee.'

'He doesn't know about Disneyland, does he?'

'Our secret.' I gave her a grin. 'How do you get in anyway?'

'I borrowed the key way back and got one cut, stupid.' She couldn't stop smiling about it. 'OK, let's go.'

We walked around the backyard a bit as Kelly looked at the swing and then we locked up. A bird swooped across the grass and up into the sky, and I called Josh on my cell as we headed out of the driveway.

11

Bromley, UK
Thursday 8 May, 09:10 hrs

Kelly's grandparents stood outside their 1980s bungalow, beneath a small wooden sign saying 'The Sycamores'. Carmen was still fussing. 'Have you got your key? We're going to Safeway's later.'

I dangled it at her as Kelly put on her seat-belt, the expression on her face as dull as the day outside. I started the engine and they waved us off as if we were leaving for ever, not just for the day. Carmen always got anxious when it came to departures. Apparently she hadn't been the same since her sister, her only other flesh and blood, went on holiday to Australia soon after Carmen's wedding and ending up marrying a guy in Sydney who had the money to buy his own house. Something like that, anyway – I'd glaze over when she got to the bit about Jimmy never really earning enough to buy a whole house in Bromley.

Carmen and Jimmy hadn't changed at all since I'd last seen them quite a few years ago, and neither had anything in their lives. But I guess they must have been like that pretty much since they first got married and Jimmy started to work his bollocks off to keep Carmen up with the Australian Joneses. He still had the same nearly spotless fifteen-year-old Rover, and

63

Carmen still kept the place as immaculate as a show-house. She still blamed me for her son's murder, even though I hadn't been there. We'd both been in the same line of work, and that was good enough for her. They were both still pissed off that Kev and Marsha had made Josh and me joint guardians of their kids in their will.

Kelly just sat there, not saying a word, staring out of the window at the busy streets. Josh was right about the mood-swings; right now she was so down I wasn't sure she'd ever swing back, but then I remembered how far she'd come since I first found her. I wondered if it was something I'd said, or something she'd heard me saying to her grandparents. I'd always tried hard not to let her know what I really thought about them. This morning it was especially tough, because I'd overheard Jimmy agreeing with Carmen that Kelly's problem was entirely my fault. Nothing to do with that nice man Josh: he'd taken her on out of the kindness of his heart, introduced her personally to God and given her lots of love and care. No, mark her words, none of this would have happened if I hadn't insisted on looking after her myself in the beginning, and left her with that good Christian family instead. Well, tough shit. It had happened and, fuck it, they'd be dead soon, so they'd better get all their complaining in while they could. I caught a glimpse of myself grinning like an idiot in the rear-view mirror. Somehow Carmen and Jimmy really brought out the best in me.

We were just south of the Thames and passing a big McDonald's. I felt a need to fill the silence. All I'd been getting for the last ten minutes was 'yes', 'no', 'maybe', 'whatever'. I pointed at the McDonald's window posters, doing my best to keep the grin in place. 'Hey, look, the McRib's back. Shall we get some afterwards?'

'Yeah, whatever.'

I stole a glance at her. What the fuck was going on inside that young head of hers? Probably much the same as went on in mine. I'd just learnt to hide it better.

The Moorings was a large townhouse in a leafy square overlooking central gardens that were fenced and gated so that only the residents could enjoy the trimly cut grass. Everything about the area and the building said that this was an institution that specialized in the disorders of the rich, which was unfortunate because I wasn't.

I found a parking space for the cheapo-hire-deal Corsa, turned off the engine and looked at Kelly as I undid my seatbelt. 'Looks as lovely as ever, doesn't it?'

No response.

'I always wonder why they call it the Moorings. I mean, we're half a mile from the Thames – where are the boats?'

Still silent, Kelly unbuckled her belt as if the weight of the world was on her shoulders. I got out and fed a few pound coins into the meter, and we walked together up the three stone steps, between the nicely painted wrought-iron railings and through the glass doors. The reception area was as plush as the head office of a private bank, had Victorian oil paintings on the walls and smelt of furniture polish. An immaculately dressed woman came out from behind the desk and ushered us towards the waiting room with an offer of drinks. Kelly was still in 'whatever' mode so I asked for a Coke, and white, no-sugar coffee. We knew the way, and settled down side by side on a big red leather chesterfield. A spread of property magazines for the South of France and the Caribbean lay on the low glass table in front of us. Nice work if you can get it, this therapy business.

Kelly rested her hands on her jeaned thighs, but the rest of her seemed to crumple. Her index finger was still red and the skin was flaking under the plaster. I nodded down at it. 'Does that thing hurt? I thought it would have cleared up by now.'

'It's just gone a bit weird. It's fine, OK?'

The receptionist came in with the drinks and Kelly seemed to brighten. Then Dr Hughes walked into the room, with a big, warm smile. 'Hello, Kelly, it's been quite a while since we last met.' She ignored me, which was reasonable: she wasn't here for me. 'What a wonderful-looking young lady you're turning out to be.'

Kelly's cheeks turned pink as we both stood up, but at least there was a hint of a smile at the sight of Dr Hughes, and that made me feel a whole lot better.

Hughes looked as striking as ever behind her half-moon glasses. She must have been about sixty now, and still had a big grey hairdo that made her look more like an American news-reader than a psychiatrist. She was dressed in the kind of black trouser suit that you can only buy on a platinum Amex card. Chatting away with Kelly she got a few little nods in return, but then there was a huge grin, and suddenly whatever I was paying was worth it.

'Shall we go upstairs for a while, Kelly?' She opened the door and ushered her through.

Kelly turned to me. 'You're waiting here, right?'

'I'll be here.'

I sat down again as the fire door closed with a whisper.

12

Exactly fifty-five minutes later the door opened again and Hughes appeared. She looked back down the corridor and said, 'Yes, he's here.'

Kelly came into the room, her face looking much the same as it was on the way here. That was fine: I trusted Hughes. This wasn't about getting an instant fix. She still gave her full attention to Kelly. 'So, same time on Saturday?'

Kelly nodded as her coat went over her shoulders and we walked back out to the car. I knew from last time round that it wasn't the thing to ask how it went. Hughes had said that if she wanted me to know, she'd tell me of her own accord. She'd also told me she wouldn't discuss anything Kelly had said to her, unless it was putting the kid in danger. I just had to shut up and wait.

The sidelights flashed as I hit the key fob and we climbed in. 'The old girl hasn't changed much, has she?'

She fastened her seat-belt. 'No.'

There was no more conversation as we crawled back towards south London. I checked traser. It was ten past six. There was no way we'd be in Bromley by seven. I got out my tri-band cell phone and she looked at me suspiciously.

'I'm going to give them a call. We're not going to make it.'

No surprise who picked up the phone at the other end: Jimmy wasn't allowed anywhere near it. 'Carmen, it's Nick. The traffic is a nightmare and I don't think we're going to be back by seven.'

Kelly pointed at the mobile, shaking her head.

'Oh dear, what a pity. We went to Safeway's specially. I've spent ages preparing it. Jimmy won't be able to wait. We always have dinner at seven.'

'I'm really sorry. We'll get something on the way.' I managed to stop myself saying I'd be looking for an extra-large slice of humble pie.

'Are you going to be late every time?'

I took a deep breath. 'Depends on the traffic. Listen, we should be back by nine at the latest.'

'Can I speak to her? How is she? How was it?'

'She's fine. She's asleep in the back. I'll tell you later. I'll get her something to eat, don't worry. We're just going into a tunnel. I'd better go. 'Bye.'

I hit the red button and grinned at Kelly. 'That's going to cost you big-time.' At last I saw the faintest flicker of a smile in the light from the oncoming cars.

'Sorry I didn't want to talk to her,' she said. 'But she'd just be telling me to keep my coat on and make sure you feed me properly.'

'I think you're being a bit unfair. She might have wanted to discuss something like the humanitarian crisis in Iraq.'

Kelly's smile broadened and I felt my own spirits lift. 'Talking of food, how about that McRib?'

It wasn't long before we were in line at the crowded McDonald's on the Wandsworth roundabout. It was full of people like us who'd just thrown in their hands at the end of the day instead of going home and cooking. After taking for ever to get to the counter, we couldn't be arsed waiting even longer for a new batch of McRibs so both opted for the quarter-pounder meal and large fries. Kelly also wanted a milkshake.

She went off to grab a table where she'd spotted some people just leaving, and I followed with the tray.

We shovelled fries into our mouths as hyperactive kids piled past us into the play area. Kelly had always been a streak of piss, and had got even skinnier the last few times I'd seen her. I didn't know where she put it all.

She dipped her burger in extra ketchup and it was soon heading for her mouth, but she suddenly stopped, staring at the bun. 'Dr Hughes says being honest with yourself is the key to recovery.'

'Does she? I guess that's right. It's probably the key to everything.'

Eyes still downcast, she shifted slightly on the plastic bench. 'Nick, you want to know some stuff I told her today?'

I nodded, but braced myself. Even if it was part of her therapy, I didn't want to hear her saying she hated me.

'Did you ever mess with drugs when you were young?'

I shook my head. 'Only alcohol. I never fancied the other stuff. Why? You been hitting the wacky-baccy?'

She gave me one of her really exasperated smiles. 'Pot? Get out of here!' Her face clouded again. 'No. Something else. You heard of Vicodin?'

'Painkiller? Matthew Perry?'

'I'm impressed. OK, look. No judgements, OK? No sermons?'

I shook my head, if only to release the steam building up in it.

'And not a word to Granny and Grandpa. Josh, well, I'll tell him myself, if the time seems right.'

'Whatever you want.'

She took a slurp of milkshake with her eyes angled up at the TV, as if gathering her thoughts, then she looked back at me with her piercing blue eyes. 'OK, here's the thing. At my high school, it's easier to get Vicodin than children's Tylenol. Whoever's got them shares them around.'

'Where do you get them? Are there dealers at school?'

69

Adults taking this shit was one thing, dealers getting to kids was another. Those people deserved the heavy end of a sledge-hammer. I could feel the skin on my face start to prickle, but I was determined not to let her see it.

'No, my friend Vronnie, remember? Last fall, her boyfriend had his wisdom teeth out. He was prescribed a lot more Vikes than it turned out he needed, so he gave her the leftovers for her migraines. That's how it starts.'

She looked around the room. 'Vicodin numbs you to the pain and soon that numb feeling is something you want again. We all know it's addictive, because we see it on TV. Melanie Griffith and Matthew Perry had to go into rehab for it. We know Eminem's got problems. But Vikes do the job, that's the problem. My friends and I are always stressed about grades and getting into college. We stay up all night doing homework or cramming. Vikes give you a high, release the stress. And before you say anything, Nick, I'm not in with the wrong crowd.' She gave a hollow laugh. 'It's the medication of choice for kids whose moms take Valium to relax.'

She put on a weird face. 'This is Vronnie's mom, OK? "Doctor?"' Her voice rose an octave and her hand flew up to her forehead. '"Doctor, I just have to have something for my nerves. My Amex has gone into hyperspace and my ex-husband doesn't understand me . . ."' Her voice went deeper. '"Sure, Mrs Housewife, I've got just the thing. Here's a hundred good pills."' She gave a sigh. 'See? It's that easy. Then Vronnie steals the pills from her mom.'

'Hang on, Kelly, you're going to have to rewind a bit. When did you start taking them?'

She shrugged. 'About six months ago. Vronnie and me were talking about stuff, like her parents are divorced and her dad drinks way too much, and it's been horrible for her. I told her about Mom and Dad and Aida, and then about you and Josh, and she was like, "Whoa!" At least she still lives in the same house and her dad's still alive. Just.'

I took a deep breath. 'What did you say about me?'

Another shrug. 'You know, looking after me, sending me to Josh because you were busy. Palming me off because of work. That kinda thing.'

'You know me and Josh thought it was the best thing for you . . .'

She cocked her head. 'Stability, right? That really worked. Why was it so long before you came and saw me?'

'We have weekends and stuff. It was just that Josh and I felt you needed to settle down, and me just appearing out of the blue every so often would go and mess that up.'

Her eyes narrowed. 'Vronnie's parents fight all the time, but at least her dad hasn't totally abandoned her. He turns up every weekend and takes her out. He's never missed a weekend – and he's a drunk.'

She concentrated on dipping a fry into the little ketchup pot. I started to speak to the top of her head as the rest of the quarter-pounder was shoved into the front of it. 'You know my work keeps me away a lot. I was doing the best I could.'

She took her lips away from the burger but didn't look up. 'But, hey, that's history now, isn't it? I'm here, you're here, and we're going to go and get things sorted out, right?'

'That's right.'

She looked up and wiped the grease from her mouth with the napkin. 'So your next question is going to be, why did I try them in the first place?'

I had to agree.

'OK, well, Vronnie and I were discussing drugs that time, I asked her for the list of what she'd done and she gave me the usual – alcohol, pot, ecstasy, all that stuff. And then she said she took Vicodin to stay chilled. One of her friends told her that she could crush it up and snort it. I asked her what it was like, and she said, "Hey, why don't we try it? Let's go to the restroom."

'Vronnie had a film-canister thing and a little flip-out mirror, and she started to do two lines. She crushes the pills at home and keeps them in the film canister.' Kelly flipped the

71

top of her straw. 'She even had one of these in her bag. Anyway, she took a line and handed the straw to me.'

It was clear from the way Kelly was babbling that she liked talking about this. It worried me, but I still wasn't going to show it. 'What did it feel like?'

'There was, like, this real stinging in my nose and throat and it really hurt, but only for a few seconds. Then it kicked in and my head felt like it was floating. It felt like a balloon, floating right away from all the bad stuff around me. I was happy and it felt amazing, even in my fingers and toes. Then all the colours got brighter and sounds were, like, deeper. And that's how we went off to class, chilled.' She giggled. 'Hillbilly heroin, that's what they call it. It's not like I'm addicted or anything, but that's what Dr Hughes and I were talking about today.'

She stood up, felt around in her coat pocket and headed for the toilets, as if to give me time to consider my answer.

She was away for ten minutes, and by the time she came out I was waiting by the door. We got back into the car and headed for Bromley, with the strong smell of toothpaste and mouthwash in the air.

13

London
Friday 9 May, 08:30 hrs

Kelly was still in bed when I tiptoed in and dumped my sleeping bag next to the rest of my stuff. I was sleeping on the settee but had to be up before eight. Dr Hughes's receptionist had called last night to arrange for us to talk this morning. She'd promised to give me some sort of indication of where we went from here, and what conclusions she'd come to after their first meeting.

Carmen and Jimmy were munching their muesli and toast in the kitchen, so I excused myself and went and sat outside in the front garden with a brew. My cell rang exactly on time. 'Good morning, Mr Stone.' Her tone was very no-nonsense: she obviously had a lot more calls to make after this one. 'I have two questions for you. The burn on Kelly's right index finger. Can you tell me how she got that?'

'She said it happened at school, something in the science class.'

'Is she eating normally?'

'Like a horse.' I hesitated. 'Listen, she's told me about the Vicodin.'

'She has? That's good. Were you alarmed?'

'Should I be? I put on my happy face when she was talking

73

about it, but it did worry me. I guess it conjured up images of drug-dealers outside the school gates, but I really don't know anything about the stuff.'

'Vicodin is an opiate, with the same active ingredient as heroin and codeine, and can lead to a serious dependency. We can go into it in detail when I see you. In fact, if she's already talking to you about it, perhaps you could come in together?

'Mr Stone, I fear she may also be bulimic. The acid burn on her finger could very well be from her own gastric juices. I suspect she pushes it down her throat to make herself vomit, and it's rubbing against her teeth. It's a common problem with girls of her age, but not a complication we'd welcome in Kelly's case.'

I suddenly felt pretty fucking stupid. 'She's always brushing her teeth and using mouthwash strips like they were going out of fashion.'

'I see. Has she started her periods yet?'

'Last year.' Josh had found some tampons in her schoolbag and Kelly had felt very grown-up about the whole thing.

'Do you know if she's still having them?'

'No, I'm not very . . .' I wondered where this was going.

'Please don't worry, I may be asking you more of these sorts of questions as we go along. It's just that when bulimia becomes extreme, women stop menstruating.'

'You say it's quite common?' I was starting to feel like a complete idiot. This girl didn't need me and the God Squad on her team, she needed her mum.

'As many as one in five girls of her age. It starts as a way to control weight and then it develops a life of its own. Again, it's an addiction. Bingeing and purging are the addictive behaviour. Yes, of her own admission she has the drug dependency, but she hasn't admitted to the bulimia. I just wanted you to know that because we might have a long and rather rocky road ahead.'

As I was listening to this, I got the signal for an incoming call. I ignored it and raised my voice as it kept bleeping. 'It must be a good thing that she's opening up to me, don't you think?'

'Yes, of course. But we can't discount the possibility she's doing it because she's angry with you. She might want to shock and punish you. '

'Then why would she hide it? Wouldn't she go to town and hit me with bulimia as well?'

'Possibly. I just wanted to warn you, though, that it could be a long time before there is light at the end of this particular tunnel. She'll need all the support you can possibly give her.'

'Where do we go from here?'

'There are a number of concerns. There's the dependency, and in some ways that's the most urgent. It's more immediately life-threatening.'

'Life-threatening?' My heart sank. What the fuck was going on here?

'That's the worst-case scenario, but it cannot be discounted. Opioid painkillers are dangerous because they are so seductive. They work by throwing up roadblocks all along the pain pathway from the nerve endings in the skin through the spinal cord to the brain, where they open the floodgates for the chemical dopamine, which triggers sensations of well-being.'

'Chilled?'

'Exactly. The dopamine effectively rewires the brain, so it becomes accustomed to those benign feelings. When an addicted person stops taking the drug, the body craves the dopamine again.

'If Kelly takes Vicodin over a long period of time, she will become mentally and physically dependent on it, and may find the drug no longer works at the prescribed dosage. At that point a dependent user will increase dosage until the effect is felt once more. At the moment Kelly's mostly just being bad-tempered and withdrawn, with noticeable mood swings. If the dependency is allowed to grow, she can expect blurred vision, hallucinations and severe confusion. Even if she does not decide to experiment with other drugs to achieve the required effect, this can lead to overdose, liver failure, convulsions, coma and, in some cases, death.'

I gripped the phone hard. 'These dealers, selling that shit to kids, they hang them in Malaysia. I'm starting to understand why.'

'I'm not sure how much that would help us in Kelly's current situation. Addiction and bulimia might only be part of a bigger picture, and that's why I think it would be helpful if you and I were to meet again. I've been talking with my American colleagues who deal specifically with Vicodin, since my experience over here is more with prescription and over-the-counter painkillers. They say there's a number of ways in which her therapy could continue once she has returned home. First of all we need to establish that she is bulimic, and that will affect where I think we should send her. But nothing is going to happen unless she wants it to happen. That is where you come in.'

'Yes, of course. I'll see you tomorrow. In the meantime, should I say something?'

'No. We can talk further once I've confirmed the diagnosis. The greatest gift you can give her now is simply support.'

'Be her mum?'

'Exactly. I will see you both tomorrow.'

I hit the button on my mobile to see who'd been calling, hating tri-band cells more and more by the second. It was a blocked number, and just as I was pondering the possibilities it rang again. I stuck the phone to my ear, to be told I had one message, and then treated to the unmistakable public-school-headmaster tones of the Yes Man. 'Tuesday, 08:57. Call me back as soon as you get this message, same number you used last month.'

Fuck, no!

I turned off the phone. He could only know I was in-country from George – and by tracking the phone signal he would know exactly where I was to the nearest ten metres. It meant trouble, and I had plenty of that already. I hit the keys.

He answered on the second ring. 'What?' The Yes Man had never been what you'd call a people person.

'It's Nick.'

'Listen in, there's a fast ball. Be here at one p.m. It shouldn't take you long from Bromley.'

'You listen.' I hated the way he talked as if he still owned me. 'I don't work for you any more. I don't even live here.'

He sighed, just like my school teachers had used to. 'The child's grandparents can take care of the to-ing and fro-ing to Chelsea.' The bastard wasn't even listening. 'You've been seconded again. If you want to waste your time, contact your American employers. They will confirm. I don't care if you do or you don't, just get here on time. Expect to be away for a number of weeks.'

The line went dead and for several moments I just stared at the phone in my hand. No way. No way could I be away for weeks.

I walked down the drive and began to wander along the pavement, gathering my thoughts. Not that that took very long. Within seconds I was tapping in the numbers for George's beeper. Fuck the time difference, he was paid 24/7.

I listened to the prompts and was pressing home my number when I heard a vehicle draw up just behind me. A Jock voice shouted, 'All right, boy?'

I turned and saw two smiling, hard-lived-in faces that I'd hoped never to see again. Fuck knows what they were called. They were Trainers and Sundance to me, the Yes Man's regulators, the ones who would have killed Kelly if I hadn't done the job for him in Panama.

My cell rang and I saw Trainers pull up the handbrake, keeping them a few metres back.

'It's me. You paged.'

I stood and stared at the Volvo as Sundance got on to his cell as well, probably to the Yes Man.

77

'I've just got the call. Why me? You know why I'm here.'

'Yes. But I'm not a social worker, son.' He didn't sound as if I'd just woken him up.

'I can't do it.'

'I'll call Osama, have him put things on hold, shall I? No, son, duty calls.'

'There must be somebody else.'

'I want my man on it, and today that's you because you're there.'

'But I've got a duty here, I need to be with her . . .' I was suddenly aware how pathetic I must be sounding.

'What do you imagine I do all day? I'm paid to think, that's what I do. I've thought – and no, there isn't anyone. It's an unsparing world, son. You're paid to do, so do.'

'I understand that but—'

'You don't understand, and there are no buts. Get to work or she mightn't ever get to appreciate that fancy therapy.'

I got a sudden dull pain in the centre of my chest as Sundance carried on gobbing into his cell. I'd had George down as a better man than that. 'Fuck you! That stunt's been pulled before with these two fuckers he's sent for me. Why bring a child into this shit again? Fucking arseholes.'

George remained calm as Sundance closed down his cell and smiled at Trainers. 'You misunderstand, son. We're not the threat here.' There was a few seconds' pause. I kept my mouth shut. 'Don't call me any more. Report to London until I say otherwise, you hear me?'

I closed down and walked over to the Volvo. The headful of dirty blond hair that had reminded me of a young Robert Redford the first time I saw it had gone. Sundance poked his head out of the passenger window, looking like he was just growing out of a Number One.

'I said, all right, boy?' He had the kind of thick Glasgow accent that you could only get from forty-odd years of chewing gravel. 'In a bit of a huff there, ain't ya? That girl of yours must be getting a bit older now. You know, getting a bit of a handful.' He held his hands up as if weighing a pair of breasts, and gave me the kind of leer that made me want to smash his face in.

Trainers liked that and joined in the laughter as he pulled out a packet of Drum and some Rizlas. He was about the same age and had the dark brown version of Sundance's haircut. They'd obviously kept up hitting the weights since their days in the H Blocks as prisoners of the UK's anti-terrorism laws, but still looked bulked-up rather than well honed. With their broken noses and big barrel chests they wouldn't have looked out of place in ill-fitting dinner jackets and Doc Martens outside a nightclub.

I could see Trainers's forearms rippling below his short-sleeved shirt as he started to roll up. Last time I saw him his Red Hand of Ulster tattoo had just been lasered off, and all traces had now disappeared.

I knew this wasn't the time to do anything but breathe deeply. Trainers handed the first roll-up to Sundance, and his one hundred per cent Belfast boomed through the passenger window: 'The boss said to make sure you come to the meeting. Don't want you wimping out on us now, do we, big man?'

I leant down to get a better view of him as he got to grips with the second roll-up, and had a chance to admire his trademark shop-soiled Nikes. Sundance flicked unsuccessfully at a disposable with hands the size of shovels. 'What if I decide not to?'

'Ah, now, that would be nice.' Neither could help but smile as Sundance shook the lighter to try to get it working. 'We could all go back to the garage, couldn't we? Things could get interesting again.'

The garage was in south London. That was where they'd beaten the shit out of me while we waited for the Yes Man to come and explain the facts of life: that I would be going to Panama or else.

I straightened up and turned to walk away. 'I'll be there.'

79

'Ah, now, that's a shame.'

As I went back to the house, I saw that Sundance wasn't leaving anything to chance. He pulled the Volvo into the kerb and parked, and they set about filling the car with smoke.

14

Carmen was in the living room, watching transfixed as Lorraine Kelly guided her GMTV audience through the minefield of organic moisturizers.

'I've just had a call from work.'

She couldn't be arsed to look up.

'I've got to go to a meeting at one o'clock – I'll have to leave in a minute to make sure I get there on time. There's some sort of emergency going on.'

What else could I do? Lock the front door and just hope Sundance and Trainers got bored and went away? No, I'd see if the Yes Man could find someone else. Shit, I was even prepared to beg if I had to.

Carmen was tracing the cracks in her face with her fingertips, her eyes still glued to Lorraine. If she knew what was coming, she wasn't going to make it easy for me. I spoke up a little. 'You know how these things sometimes drag on, and I might not get back tonight. Just in case that happens, I'll need somebody to take Kelly to Chelsea in the morning.'

For a moment I wondered if she'd heard anything I'd said. 'Oh dear, I don't know,' she said finally. 'I'd have to ask Jimmy. I don't think he'd be happy about the traffic. What with the congestion charge and everything ... And then there's the parking. How long would we have to wait?'

'Just under an hour. Look, I'll pay the petrol and the—'

'We *can* afford petrol, you know.'

'But you just said ... What's the problem, Carmen?'

'Well, I mean, what will we tell the neighbours? No one knows she's seeing a psychiatrist.'

'You're not going to have to put a fucking sign up. And for the millionth time, it's no big deal. Kelly isn't mentally ill, she just needs help with some stuff, that's all.'

'Well, and can you blame her, poor thing, the life she's had? Pushed around from pillar to post, having to listen to your foul language all the time ...'

I couldn't take any more. This woman was so negative I could actually feel her draining the energy out of me. She'd spent her entire life either sniping at other people or feeling sorry for herself, and she wasn't about to change. The only thing that would do that was a two-pound ball hammer to the back of her head.

'Thanks for the support, Carmen.' I turned and got out, tempted to add something sarcastic like, 'I don't know why I've paid a shrink all these thousands of pounds when I've got you on hand' – but I didn't think of it until I was in the corridor.

I was looking forward to the next bit even less. I was just about to confirm everything I knew Kelly felt about me.

I needn't have worried. It had already been done. As I went down the flowered carpet to her room, Kelly was standing out-side her door. I couldn't read the exact expression on her face – anger, disbelief, disappointment, abandonment, maybe a mixture of them all. But I knew it meant I was in the shit. 'I don't believe you, Nick.' She was so close to tears she almost choked on the words.

'I don't have a choice, Kelly. It's just a meeting. All being well, I'll—'

'There's always a choice, Nick. That's what you keep

saying, isn't it? Why don't you just say no to them, eh?'

'It's not that easy.' I went to stroke her head but she jumped back as if I'd touched her with a Taser.

'Don't.' She moved backwards into her room. 'Fucking hypocrite!'

I heard a gasp of shock from Carmen. Either Lorraine had suggested going non-organic on the moisturizer front or she'd been eavesdropping. Either way, I'd be to blame.

Kelly slammed the door but it didn't have a lock. I knocked gently. 'Let me explain. No, don't let me explain – just let me come in and say I'm sorry.'

I heard a sniffle and I opened up. She was lying face down on her bed, a pillow over her head. When I came in she flung it away and sat up to face me. 'I've told you so much, Nick. Too much for you to take, was it?'

'I know I should be able to tell these people to shove it but I can't. I just can't.'

She buried her head in her hands. 'When will you be back?'

'Not long. Tonight, maybe tomorrow.'

'OK, off you go.'

I went to touch her but she flinched again. I turned for the door, picking up my Caterpillars and bomber jacket. No one was allowed to wear shoes in Carmen's house. 'Hey, listen, make sure Granny doesn't go into my bag for any dirty washing. I'll do it when I get back, OK?'

'Whatever.'

15

It had taken me at least an hour to reach Chelsea Bridge, still seething at George and the Yes Man, and still being followed by the Volvo. The traffic thundered about me as I edged my way back into the flow towards Pimlico and the apartment where Suzy and I had stayed while preparing for the Penang job. The Firm had safe-houses dotted all around the country, but Pimlico seemed to have more than its fair share. They tended to be in mansion blocks that had been divided into self-contained flats, the sort business people used as *pieds-à-terre* while they were working in London during the week, or as shag pads before going home to their families in the Cotswolds at the weekend. They were good for security because they were impersonal and anonymous.

The flat I was going to was furnished, had a TV and a video, but no phone. The Firm serviced it and paid the bills, but it belonged to an alias company.

After cruising around for about fifteen minutes, I finally parked in Warwick Square. I fed the meter with as many coins as I had, hoping that would be enough. With any luck I'd be on my way back to Bromley within an hour or two.

I walked across the square to number sixty-six with

Sundance and Trainers helpfully at my shoulder, and hit the intercom of flat three, which was on the top floor. The voice that answered belonged to Yvette, the Yes Man's PA-cum-fixer-cum-who-knew-what. She always spoke softly, as if life was one big conspiracy. I had to put my ear right up to the speaker to hear her 'Hello?'.

'It's me, Nick.'

There was a buzz as the front door unlocked and I was pushed into the narrow hallway. It was the kind of push that left me in no doubt that the boys were looking forward to a return match.

When the house had been converted it had obviously been at the expense of the common areas. The staircase was almost directly ahead and I started climbing. The last time this place had seen a lick of paint must have been in the 1980s, when magnolia was all the rage, and the carpet wasn't a lot younger. Fuck knows what colour it was meant to be.

The staircase turned on itself and followed the woodchip wallpaper up a few landings to the top floor. Yvette was waiting for me in the doorway. Suzy and I had christened her the Golf Club. She had shortish and thin brown practical hair, and was slim, maybe too slim. A night out with Kelly for a few chip suppers wouldn't have done either of them any harm – even the arse in her skin-tight jeans was baggy. She was in her mid forties and, from the neck up, wouldn't have looked out of place at a WI meeting. Her only jewellery was a wedding ring, though, and she was dressed for Everest. I'd seen her in several different Gore-Tex mountain jackets, and the rest of her looked as if it was sponsored by Helly Hansen. I glanced down at her feet. Sure enough, the mountain boots were in place; side-on she looked like Tiger Woods could have used her to drive off from the first tee.

She'd been extremely professional on the Penang job. Even before dropping off the revolver in the Georgetown Starbucks, she'd done all the admin, collated our passports and cover documents, got hold of any information we needed, and

85

relayed instructions from the Yes Man, all without raising her voice above a whisper. Thanks to her, we never had to see him after the initial briefing, which suited me just fine. I decided I really must find a way to kill this man and then take care of Sundance and Trainers before I got old and grey. It would be a job no one would have to pay me for.

She opened the door wider and whispered me inside. 'Hello, Nick. We never got to say goodbye.'

'It would have been a bit of a waste of breath, wouldn't it?' I whispered back. If I'd talked normally to her, it would have sounded as if I was using a loud-hailer. I hoped I'd never find myself on top of a mountain depending on her to shout for help.

I got a little smile out of her, and returned the compliment as I walked into the flat. I could hear the Yes Man immediately. Excellent: I was already rehearsing my speech in my head. The small rectangular hallway had bare walls, another riot of magnolia. Directly in front of me was the door to the bedroom, and to the right the bathroom and a rather tattered white MFI kitchen. I went left, following the cheap grey office carpet, and into the living room, which overlooked the startling green of the square.

The Yes Man had his head down, and was taking up the whole of the red velour settee as he flicked through a pile of files and spoke into a cell. Suzy was sitting on one of the chairs, dressed in jeans, black leather jacket, and a jumper nearly the same colour as the carpet. At her feet was a large blue nylon sports bag.

The two remaining chairs stood against the wall. One was taken by a red Gore-Tex jacket I hadn't seen the Golf Club wearing before, with a thousand pockets and zips. I took the other. Lying between them were two brown briefcases, each attached by about nine inches of chain to a worn steel handcuff.

Nobody said a word. The Yes Man didn't greet me because he was an arsehole, and because he didn't, Suzy couldn't. I didn't hold it against her. She got a bit overexcited at times, but if I had to work with someone, she was at the top of my list – and not just because the rest of the list were dead.

I sat on the edge of the chair and waited for the Golf Club to prepare a brew. Meanwhile the Yes Man kept nodding as he turned the pages and began to get flustered with whoever was at the other end of the phone. 'OK . . . yes . . . No! Tell him he will meet them this evening – even if he hasn't confirmed how many the meet is just as important. Remind him what he is, and that he has no choice.'

He slammed the phone down on the table and speed-read the remaining pages. I'd never seen him like this before; he was really starting to flap. Suzy and I just sat and exchanged glances while he continued reading and nodding. Fuck it, she looked as if she was looking forward to this. I knew Suzy was dying for a B & H, but I bet she wouldn't be lighting one in front of him. The Yes Man didn't drink or smoke, and was a born-again Christian – Scientologist, something like that – so he was pretty frightening at the best of times. I wondered if I should introduce him to Josh; perhaps they could bore each other to death.

There was clinking and clanking in the kitchen, and the sound of the electric kettle getting filled.

I leant forward and rested my forearms on my thighs as I watched the Yes Man making notes on the pages that flicked through his hands. His ginger hair was going even more grey around the edges – or it would have done if he'd left it alone, but he'd been at the Grecian 2000 again and I was catching more than a hint of copper.

As always, his blue, diamond-patterned tie was knotted really tight up to the collar. Maybe that was the reason for his permanently blushing complexion. Maybe he did it to try and hide his neck, which always seemed to have a boil on the go. He was in his mid-forties now, and the mind boggled as to what he must have looked like as a kid. The pockmarks all over his face suggested a miserable adolescence. Maybe that was what had turned him into an arsehole.

Judging by the sound of mugs being moved around in the kitchen it wouldn't be long before the brew turned up, but here in the living room we were still waiting for the headmaster to take assembly. He turned a few more pages and dialled on his cell. I tried catching his eye, but he was just too distracted to notice as he read on and changed his mind about the call.

The clomping of Yvette's boots on the thin carpet telegraphed her arrival with a tray. She put it down on the small table in front of the settee, and poured the Yes Man's coffee first. He had what Suzy called Nato standard: white with two sugars. Suzy got black without; me, white without. The Golf Club never forgot a detail.

She sat down in her seat and bent to pick up one of the briefcases. The cuff rattled about on its chain as she manoeuvred the case on to her lap and flicked open the locks. The Yes Man passed a couple of his pages to her, and glanced briefly in my direction before returning to the ones remaining on the table. 'So glad you could make it on time.'

I looked at Suzy. 'I think I'm early, actually, even without the prompt at my door. Sir?' I hated calling him that, but I had to attract his attention somehow. 'Can I talk to you alone?'

'What?'

'There's something I need to discuss with you.'

One glance at Suzy and she got the hint and made herself scarce, closing the door behind her. Yvette stayed where she was. A private word with the Yes Man automatically included her.

'Well?'

He hadn't even looked up. I knew I was on a loser straight away.

'Sir, I have a personal problem that I need to deal with urgently. I just need a little time to sort things out.'

'You don't get it, do you? You have no personal problem, because you have nothing that is personal. That headcase of a child stays with her grandparents, or goes home. It's as simple as that. What happens to her really doesn't matter, because you're going to stay here and do what you're paid for.'

'Sir, I understand but—'

'No buts. Shut up and get on with your job. Do you understand?'

I nodded. For now, what else could I do? Storm out of the flat and straight into two regulators who'd like nothing more than to park me all over their garage? It was too early for that. There had to be another way.

16

He straightened himself on the settee as Yvette went to let Suzy
back in. His eyes stayed on his files as the two women passed
him, and Yvette handed Suzy and me a Jiffy-bag each from her
briefcase. I checked my passport. It was in the name of Nick
Snell again. Everything was in order: the date of birth was
correct, but some of the stamps had been changed. For starters,
the Malaysian holiday visa had disappeared. I checked the
worn-looking Bank of Scotland credit cards, making sure they
were still valid.

Yvette was helping herself to a sip of brew.

'Is it the same CA?'

She nodded.

I looked at Suzy, who was doing the same as me, but much
more enthusiastically. Her eyes shone, but she was trying to
control her excitement in front of the boss.

The Yes Man had put his file to one side when the phone
rang again. The Golf Club picked it up and left for the kitchen,
although she didn't need to: it was impossible to hear what she
was saying from more than six inches away.

The Yes Man leant forward to pick up his brew, and fixed his
gaze on Suzy. That was fine by me. I wanted to be anywhere

but here, and it helped if I didn't have to look at him. 'The wine bottles that were collected in Penang contained pneumonic plague . . .' He let the words hang, as if waiting for a reaction. He wasn't going to get one from me: I wouldn't have been here if it had been Fat Bastard Chardonnay.

'That was the last batch produced for JI. We have no idea how much they've stockpiled in the last eleven months, but we know they've been planning bio attacks for some time now, mainly Far Eastern targets. Meanwhile, ASU [Active Service Unit] members have been disappearing from Malaysia. It seems they have ambitions to move further afield, which can only mean one thing. They consider themselves third wave.'

By the look on his face, he probably hoped we'd have to ask him what it meant, but it wasn't rocket science. Third-wave terrorism just meant these people were switched on and highly technical. They weren't knuckle-draggers: their greatest weapon was their brains. They knew it wasn't that hard to access information and, scarier still, they knew where to look. They had already learnt how to develop biological agents – and it was probably only a matter of time before they figured out how to split the atom in the kitchen.

Suzy twisted on her chair. 'Is that why the barriers are up around the Houses of Parliament?'

He shook his head. 'The sort of attack they have in mind can defeat any barrier.' He put down his mug and stared at it for several seconds before jerking his head up and re-establishing eye-contact, this time with us both. 'The problem we face, as of six hours ago, is that there are already up to six bottles in this country, possibly more. It appears they were brought in as duty-free wine by one of the four-member ASUs. Every available bit of CCTV footage from all ports of entry is being looked at to try and identify who they are – and then, of course, find them.'

The Yes Man's cell rang yet again in the kitchen, and Yvette answered as she came back into the room, then cut the call. His eyes followed her as she headed for him. 'We have a source on the ground but so far very little information. The fact is—' The Golf Club whispered into his ear.

'You sure?' He was a worried man.

The Golf Club gave a yes as she went to her chair.

'Right, source int says that there are twelve bottles, but we still do not know where they are or when they will be used.' He paused, checking us both to make sure we'd taken in the full weight of his words. Yvette, calm as ever, picked up her coffee and sat back in the chair with the barest rustle of Gore-Tex.

'How would you do it, Susan?'

She took a breath. 'Is it contagious?'

The Yes Man stared gloomily into her eyes. 'Extremely.'

'Then I'd concentrate on densely populated areas with transient people traffic, so that those infected move on swiftly and infect others, like their families. Their kids pass it round at school, their wives or husbands pass it on to friends and colleagues. The chain is endless.'

Suzy was more or less on the edge of her seat as the Yes Man took a sip and placed his mug carefully on the table, keeping his focus on her. I might as well not have been there. 'Remember the anthrax attacks in the US?'

She hung on his every word.

'People afraid to go to work, afraid to open mail? The US suffered huge economic damage from a microscopic amount of agent. And how many deaths? Five?'

Suzy kept nodding. If she wasn't careful, her head was going to fall off.

'It was the psychological effect that was most damaging. But this would be far worse.'

I thought I'd chip in with my twopence-worth now, before their love fest developed into a full-scale shag. 'So, those experts who argued that JI's goals didn't fully engage with the global aspirations of al-Qaeda weren't absolutely on the money?'

The Yes Man turned and fixed his eyes on mine, probably surprised I was using words with four syllables. 'Exactly. And

92

because everybody is focusing on the Arabs, South East Asians are slipping through the net. See an Arab today and the public think they see a terrorist. See a South East Asian or Indian and they just think he runs a takeaway.'

'So what does this stuff look like?' Suzy asked. 'How is it disseminated in an attack, and what protection do we need? More important, where do we start looking?'

He kept his look of derision on me a second longer, then turned back to her. 'Not even the government has been completely informed about this situation. The cabinet would overreact, and Number Ten leaks like a sieve – we'd have anarchy on the streets within hours. Which is why you are here. It simply mustn't come to that.'

The cell started to warble again, and the Golf Club disappeared back into the kitchen. The Yes Man carried on. 'The words "plague" and "pneumonic" will not appear on any report or briefing paper. You will refer to the agent as Dark Winter. I say again, at no time will the words "pneumonic" or "plague" be mentioned. It is Dark Winter. Have you *both* got that?' He pointed at Suzy and she nodded, then at me, and I nodded too. I wasn't intending to hang around any longer than I had to, but in the meantime I needed to go through the motions. The Yes Man sat back and put his hands on his knees. 'Your task is very simple: to take control of Dark Winter.' As it was the mission statement, he repeated it to make sure everything was clear.

'However –' I might have guessed this was coming: there was always a 'however'. He jabbed the air with his index finger. '– if you are confronted by a person or persons preventing you taking control of Dark Winter, you will react as the situation dictates to ensure the safety of the public and yourselves.'

It was the standard gobbledygook. Expedited killings couldn't happen legally unless either the home or foreign secretary, I could never remember which, gave the OK, and if this went wrong, the Yes Man would need to cover his arse by saying that he'd never ordered the killing of the ASU on the UK mainland.

'The first thing you'll do is contact our source. Yvette will give you the meet details later.' He exchanged glances with the Golf Club. 'Once our friend sorts himself out.'

Suzy sat back and crossed her legs. 'So no one else is involved?'

'No one.'

'Bit like using a nut to crack a sledgehammer, isn't it?'

The Golf Club got up as the Yes Man gathered together his papers. Her jacket rustled as she leant forward and pushed her arms into the sleeves. 'This operation is somewhat more complicated than most. The service has a difficult balance to achieve,' she said.

It was the first time I'd heard her raise her voice.

'We have got to get out there and find Dark Winter, but also keep the details of its existence and planned use from the public – which unfortunately includes the government and other agencies, plus some in the service itself. It's the only way we can protect the public and at the same time achieve our goal. However, we have only a small window of opportunity to eradicate this problem before circumstances may make it prudent to inform the relevant agencies in the very near future.'

It sounded like something out of *Yes, Minister* and I really didn't understand a word she was saying. But I got the message: if errors were made, others would be blamed. Dark Winter had been the name given to an American exercise conducted in June 2001 with the aim of educating US policy-makers about the possibility of a bio-terrorist attack. In the simulation, terrorist networks attacked American cities, including Atlanta, Oklahoma City and Philadelphia, with smallpox. Within a fourteen-day period the virus had spread to all fifty states and several other countries, making the simulation a terrorist success. Thousands of Americans 'died', and countless others were 'infected'. A friend of mine had been

94

involved, and that was the only reason I'd heard about it. The whole world should have sat up and taken notice, but it was three months before 9/11, so nobody batted an eyelid.

I could see what was happening here. The Firm was covering its arse in case information about the attack leaked out, or we were compromised. If the service was accused of acting unilaterally or suppressing information from the Prime Minister, the Yes Man could turn round and say: 'Of course we informed government – doesn't everyone read the intelligence reports, doesn't everyone know what Dark Winter is?' The relationship between government and the Firm hadn't been brilliant after the latest Gulf War. I bet the Yes Man was loving keeping this from them. Suzy was even more excited. I realized now for sure that she just lived for this shit.

The Yes Man shoved the last of his files into his briefcase. Yvette followed suit and continued her bit as she ratcheted the cuff round her wrist up tight. 'At fifteen hundred there will be a brief to address your concerns about the contents of the bottles. His name is Simon and he will come here. He is not aware of any aspect of the operation and will think he is giving a general tutorial to the FCO.' She looked up with a smile, making eye-contact with us both as the Yes Man cuffed himself to his briefcase. 'I'll be back at eighteen hundred, hopefully with details of the source meet and communications, and two Packet Oscars.'

The Yes Man got to his feet. It had never been his custom to ask if anyone had any questions: as far as he was concerned, once he'd finished speaking his audience knew everything they needed to know.

They both made for the door. Suzy was just ahead of them with the mugs before she veered off towards the kitchen.

The Yes Man leant down for a moment as he came level with me, so close I could feel his breath condense in my ear. 'Make whatever arrangements you need to for that child before the three o'clock briefing. After that, you're mine.'

As the front door closed, Suzy reappeared, all smiles. 'Well,

95

this is freaky here-we-go-again shit, isn't it? Though I'm not sure the boss is as pleased to see you as I am . . .' She reached into her back pocket and pulled out a blister pack of gum, then jumped backwards into the Yes Man's sofa, her feet up on the arm. 'OK, what do you make of all this, then?'

'I'm keeping an open mind.'

'Thanks. No need to go overboard.'

She studied me while shoving two chunks of gum into her mouth. 'Well, at least you won't die of passive smoking. I've given up.'

'Thank fuck for that.' I headed for the front door. As I turned the handle, I called back to her: 'Listen, we've got an hour before the Simon thing. I'm going to get some washing and shaving kit. See you in a bit.'

'OK . . .' She didn't sound convinced.

17

When I got back to the car and hit the cell keys the meter was just about to run out. I'd come out expecting to get a fond farewell from Sundance and Trainers, but they weren't anywhere to be seen. With their job done for the day they'd probably slunk back into their holes.

How the fuck was I going to get out of this? I didn't know yet. What I did know was that I'd better get my act together and prepare for the job, just in case I really did land up belonging to the Yes Man. It was an unsparing world. George was right – but, then, he usually was.

I got a crackly 'Hello?' Carmen must have been stuck down a well for him to have permission to answer. 'Jimmy, it's me, Nick. Listen, I—'

'Here, best I pass you over to Carmen.' The sound of the TV in their front room filled the earpiece and world order was restored.

'Hello?' It was her martyred voice.

'Sorry, Carmen, I don't know if I'll get back tonight.'

'Oh, really? What does that mean?'

'You'll need to take her to Chelsea. It's important she doesn't miss any of the sessions. Look, I'm trying to get back and take her myself. I want to see her.' I could hear the sharp intake of breath as she prepared to give me a speech, but got in before she had the chance. 'Listen, Carmen, let's cut the bullshit, I haven't enough time. It's only a few more years before she's old enough to look after herself, and then we'll never have to talk to each other again. The only reason I put up with your constant moaning is Kelly. So just talk normally, will you? Are you going to take her or not?'

She huffed and puffed. 'But we don't know how to get to this psychiatrist. Jimmy won't be able to manage the Underground.' She just couldn't stop herself.

I tried to keep my voice level. 'Carmen, don't take the Underground. I'll tell you what, book a taxi tonight – a pile of those minicab cards comes through your door every day. I'll pay. There, it's all done.'

'But what time does she have to be there? We can't just go on a wink and a nod. Taxis need a time to come and collect, you know. We just—'

'I'll give you all that stuff in a minute. Is Kelly there? Can I speak to her?'

Her tone changed again. She was rather pleased with herself. 'She's very angry with you at the moment, I can tell you. We can't get a word out of her. Whatever you said to her certainly made her very upset. But never mind, we'll get by.'

'Carmen, why can't you just cut the crap? Are you going to take her tomorrow or not?'

'I'll take her.' She had to force it out.

'That's good. Thank you very much. Oh, and I nearly forgot. I'm expecting a package in the post. It'll be arriving tomorrow or Monday. Can you just hold it for me until I can pick it up?'

'Well, I suppose so.' She made it sound as if the package was going to be the size of a small car.

'Thanks. Now, can I speak to Kelly?'

There was mumbling in the background as she got up and took the telephone out of the living room. I wished Kelly had a mobile, but hers wasn't tri-band so she'd left it in the States.

The TV chatter died and there was scuffling before I could hear breathing. 'Kelly?'

'I know, you can't make it. You're working. Whatever.'

'It's not like that. I'm stuck. I'm trying to get back tonight but if not they'll take you to Dr Hughes's tomorrow and I'll try to meet you there. I'm sorry, I'm trying to get out of it, I really am.'

She'd heard it all before. 'Sure, whatever. Do you want to talk to Granny now?'

'No. I just want to talk to you.'

'What's to talk about? Maybe I'll see you tomorrow, then, eh?'

The phone went dead. I understood why, but it still pissed me off. I redialled and Carmen answered. I gave her the contact details and timings for Hughes, then hung up.

I drove out of the parking space and headed for a multi-storey, eyes skinned for the Volvo.

One carrier-bag full of washing kit and a black nylon bum-bag from Superdrug later, I went into a corner shop-cum-post office and bought a pen and an A4 Jiffy-bag. In went my Nick Stone passport, wallet with Citibank credit cards, and all my other Nick Stone bits and pieces including the key to Carmen's front door. I hated it when the Firm took away my real documents: it was like losing my personality, my life; I felt exposed, undefended. This way, at least I knew where they were, and if all went well and I got binned I'd be picking them up soon any-way. I couldn't help a little smile as I addressed the bag to myself. Carmen had decided to call the bungalow the Sycamores, and got Jimmy to put up the sign – but you still had to write No. 68 or your mail never got there.

18

With ten minutes to spare, I buzzed up to the flat. Suzy let me in and I almost choked on Benson & Hedges. The windows were all double-glazed and had more locks than the Bank of England. I followed her into the bedroom and into a cloud of nicotine that even the French would have been proud of.

'I know, Nick, I know. Sorry. But I was gagging. The gum's shite.'

'Well, get some patches or something, will you?'

'I promise it's the last one, ever.'

It was obvious that the Golf Club had already been and gone – so much for coming back at six. There was an open suitcase on the bed in Suzy's room. It looked as if she was in the process of unpacking. She held up a Nokia moan-phone. 'We've got one each, one spare, three batteries and a fill gun. The rest looks like the Packet Oscars.'

I dropped my carrier-bag on the bed and noticed the wardrobe door was open. The couple of shelves on the right were full of underwear and socks, a hairdryer and a washbag. In the suitcase were two MP5 SDs, the normal Heckler and Koch MP5 machine-gun but with a very bulky barrel, together with five or six boxes of ammunition and three magazines for each weapon. For us to respond with as the situation dictated to ensure the safety of the public and ourselves.

The SDs were suppressed and not 'silenced'. There's no way of totally silencing a weapon's muzzle report. A suppressor just diminishes it with a series of rubber baffles and fine meshing inside the barrel, which dissipate the gases that propel the round. By the time the round leaves the muzzle there is just a dull thud and no flash, and the faint click of the working parts moving backwards before the return spring pushes them forward again to pick up another round and ram it into the chamber.

Both weapons were fitted with holographic sights, a small window mounted where the rear sight would normally be. When you turned it on, it was like looking at a heads-up display on a windscreen.

There were different packets for different jobs. Packet Oscar was a covert killing pack. As well as the SD, it contained the basic kit needed to make entry covertly into a building in order to kill, all rolled up in a black PVC MOE [Method of Entry] wallet.

These particular Packet Oscars had come with a few extras. I picked up one of the moan-phones as Suzy busied herself with the other two, connecting up the jack that led into the fill gun, a slim green alloy box about the size of a pound bar of chocolate.

Suzy depressed the black button and kept it down until the red light flickered, indicating that the encryption code was downloaded. The phone could now be put into secure mode at any time, and anyone listening in would just get mush. Just as importantly, it would cut out the phone's footprint; digital phones are notoriously easy to track, but once these were fill-gunned and on secure mode we became invisible. Two, ten, even a hundred phones could be filled with the same encryption code, and everyone could dial up and talk to each other in clear speech knowing they were secure.

The money to update kit had miraculously appeared after

9/11. The phones were light years ahead of the old system of one-time pads to encrypt a message into a series of numbers, then key the numbers over the phone. It took far too long, and there was always the possibility of fucking up under pressure.

Some fill guns had a number of codes so they could be constantly changed throughout an operation, at specified times and dates. Normally there was a numbered dial on the gun, one to ten, so you might get the instruction, 'On Thursday it will be number six.' But on this fill gun there was just one fill. We would still try to fill the phones once every twenty-four hours anyway, to ensure the fill didn't drop – that the encryption didn't get corrupted. Each phone had a sticker on the back with the PIN security code to access it, just like any other Nokia, and all three were the same – an unimaginative 4321.

Suzy leant down next to me as I turned the phones on and plugged them into the charger to make sure the batteries were full. Beneath the aroma of hastily smoked B and H she smelt of freshly washed clothes and apple shampoo. 'Get everything you needed, then?' She sounded bouncy enough, but studiously avoided any eye-contact.

'Yeah. Spent most of the time trying to find somewhere to park the car.' I paused. 'You all right?'

'Of course I'm all right,' she snapped. 'Why wouldn't I be?'

I'd annoyed her. I hadn't meant to.

She started to fill the last phone, and the red light flickered before she looked up. 'How well do you know the boss? I thought when we got briefed before Penang that you two might have a little history . . .'

'Hardly know him – we've just got that fatal-attraction thing going on between us.'

She wasn't having any of it. 'Yeah, right.'

'You called your CA yet?'

'Nope. We got to sort our story first. Penang's history now, isn't it?' She stood up, her face beaming, almost taunting, just inches from mine. 'Switch on, will you?' The B & H was just still on her breath. 'Anyone would think you didn't want to be here.'

We spent a few minutes working something out, then I went into the front room and hit my own cell keys while Suzy headed for the bedroom to do the same. I was greeted by a happy, middle-aged female voice.

'Rosemary, how are you? It's Nick.'

'Really well, thank you. Good holiday?'

'Fantastic.'

'You forgot to send us a postcard, naughty boy.'

They were good people, James and Rosemary. Their job was both to confirm my cover story and be part of it. When I was a K, I used to visit them whenever I could, especially before an op, so that my cover got stronger as time passed. They knew nothing about the ops, and didn't want to: we would just talk about what was going on at the social club, and how to keep greenfly off the roses.

All my documentation, all my credit cards, anything that needed an address, was registered to theirs. I subscribed to three or four weekly and monthly magazines to maintain a steady flow of mail and regular charges on my card. I was even on the electoral register. I hadn't seen them for over a year, since moving and working for George, so I'd had a lot of catching up to do before the Penang job. It had been quite a surprise for all of us.

'Sorry about the card, but you know what Spain's like – and the weather was fantastic.'

'You're making me green with envy, dear. We'd love to go to Spain ourselves this year.' She'd got the message: Malaysia was history. 'So, what can I do for you, Nick?'

'The holiday went so well I'm thinking of going to London with my new girlfriend for a while, maybe for a couple of weeks. Romance is definitely in the air – you still think her name is Suzy or Zoë, something like that. But I really called to say thank you very much again for the lift you gave me to the station this morning.'

'Oh, yes. The eight sixteen wasn't it? The express to Waterloo?'

'That's the one.'

'A couple of weeks, that sounds lovely. I hope you have a good time. She sounds like a really nice girl. Are we going to see her one day?'

'All in good time, Rosemary – no need to buy a new hat just yet. Anything I should know about?'

'Not much at all, really. We've got a new TV in the lounge, it came last Tuesday. You were out, so you weren't here to see the delivery. It's a Sony widescreen, black, twenty-four-inch. You and James like it, but I don't because it makes the cabinet it's on look too small. You know, the brown veneer one?'

'I know it well. But never mind – just think, Delia will be even bigger and better than usual. Anyway, say hello to James for me, won't you?'

'Of course. He isn't here at the moment, he's gone to Waitrose. After doing nothing but complain and chair that damned committee to stop the thing being built, you can't keep him out of there!'

We both laughed, said goodbye, and I headed towards the kitchen to make us a brew.

The intercom buzzed and I hit the button. A slightly anxious voice crackled, 'Hello, I'm Simon, I believe I'm expected. A lady called Yvette told me to be here at three.'

I hit the entry button as Suzy came out of the bedroom and shut the door behind her, then started to check round the flat in case we'd left the odd SD sitting on the tea-tray.

I flicked the kettle on in the kitchen, then opened the front door. Looking down the stairwell, I could see the top of a neatly cut and combed blond head making its way towards me from a couple of flights below. As he got closer, I saw he was in his early thirties, tall and thin, and very well groomed. That made sense: you probably would give yourself a good scrub after spending the day surrounded by flesh-eating bugs and all that sort of shit.

When he reached the landing I stepped back to let him in. He had to be at least six four: I was looking into his neck. He was clutching a battered canvas shoulder-bag he must have had since his student days. He could have been captain of the basketball team, but was probably too polite.

'Hello, mate.'

He hesitated in the hallway, his hand half out, not too sure what to do. We shook and smiled at each other. He was very clean-shaven, and his cheeks had the kind of bright red patches you usually only see at the circus. Maybe it had been an effort climbing the stairs, or maybe he was just flapping. He struck me immediately as one of those people who had pocketfuls of niceness. I hoped we weren't going to spoil things for him.

I pointed to my right, and he followed me through to the front room. I offered him the settee. 'I've just put the kettle on – want a brew?'

Suzy came in and held out her hand with a welcoming 'Hello.' He was half-way down into the settee but still as tall as she was when her hand disappeared into his. 'Nothing for me, thanks. I won't be staying long, there's a car waiting for me. I have another brief at four thirty.'

Suzy was all smiles as her eyes locked briefly on mine. It wouldn't be a brief he was going to at half four but isolation, until this job was over. 'You don't want any of his tea? Wise move – I bet most of the stuff in your laboratory tastes better.'

Terrible joke, but he laughed all the same, still not sure whether to stand up again or sit right down. Suzy waved him into the seat. 'Simon, isn't it?'

'Yes, Simon, Simon Ma—'

She held up her hand. 'Simon'll do just fine. Well, Simon, what have you got for us today?'

19

'May I?' His bag hovered above the table while he waited for permission.

'Of course.' Suzy was doing a good job of making him feel comfortable, but with his arse sunk down in the settee and his knees up by his chin he certainly didn't look it.

The bag went down and he took off his coat to reveal a maroon cardigan over his brown checked shirt. He still looked nervous; maybe it didn't look like an FCO brief and he was worried we'd have to shoot him afterwards.

Once he'd unbuckled his bag, he pulled out a clutch of ten-by-eight colour photographs and put them on the table. He cleared his throat.

'Simon, quick question before you start?' I always wanted to know who was giving me a brief. Not having enough knowledge to pass on is sometimes more dangerous than not knowing anything at all. 'Can you tell us where you're from?'

Suzy's chewing filled in the second or two of silence while he wondered if that would be OK.

'Of course. I'm a doctor, formerly working in Namibia, before becoming a consultant at the School of Hygiene and Tropical Medicine here in London. After the US anthrax attacks

I became a technical adviser on biological agents slash weapons for the Foreign Office – briefings for embassy staff, that sort of thing.'

Suzy interrupted, with a smile, 'What have you been told about why you're here today, Simon?'

'Just that I'm to fill you in on pneumonic plague and its potential as a weapon. No more than that.'

She nodded her thanks and I signalled that I had no further questions. He picked up the dozen or so ten-by-eights and passed them to me. 'This is the type of case I've tried to treat over the years.'

I looked down and found myself inspecting a series of close-ups of a bloated old man's body – head, arms, torso, legs – covered in swellings and weeping pus. His gangrenous fingers and toes looked like they'd been pushed into a food processor. I tried not to look at the one of his face, at the terror in his eyes. This guy was being eaten alive. The foil rustled on Suzy's blister pack and I knew she was trying to avoid it too.

Simon's eyes flickered between the two of us with a nervous smile, trying to establish if this was the level of information we wanted. As Suzy put the last of the scary pictures back on to the table, he took it as his cue to carry on. 'There are two main variants. Bubonic plague, you'll have heard of – it was responsible for the Black Death in the fourteenth century, killing over thirty million in Europe alone. Bubonic plague was what the nursery rhyme was all about – "Ring a ring o' roses, a pocketful of posies".'

Suzy finished it for him. '"Atishoo, atishoo, we all fall down!" '

I didn't join in. It was another nursery rhyme I'd never learned. My stepdad didn't like things like that going on in the house. My mum had to be at work at the launderette, not wasting time teaching her kids that sort of nonsense. Knowing shit like that never got anyone a job.

He cleared his throat again. 'Yes, thirty million in Europe alone, the biggest chunk of population ever killed by any epidemic. But bubonic plague is the less deadly variant of the two.' His eyes flicked between the two of us again. 'The variant I am talking about today is pneumonic plague, which infects the lungs and is so highly contagious that it's an A-class weapon. The only other two with that designation are smallpox and anthrax – that's how bad this disease is. If treatment is delayed more than twenty-four hours after infection, the mortality rate is virtually one hundred per cent.'

Suzy was leaning towards him now. 'So its supply or whatever is tightly controlled?'

He smiled fleetingly. 'It cannot be controlled. Pneumonic plague is caused naturally by the bacterium *Yersinia pestis*, found in rodents and their fleas on every continent except Australia and Antarctica. It occurs in humans when they're bitten by plague-infected fleas – but thankfully there are just thirty cases a year, on average, worldwide.' He tapped the ten-by-eights still on the table, and looked sad. 'Old Archibald had the misfortune to be one of them.'

I didn't really give a shit about poor old Archibald. I wanted to keep Simon on track. 'It can be used as a weapon?'

He sighed and shook his head. 'It doesn't bear thinking about. Just fifty kilograms sprayed over a city the size of London would infect as many as a hundred and fifty thousand people, nearly a third of whom would be expected to die. And those are just the primary victims. That figure would be multiplied many times if infected people carried it to other cities or countries. Pneumonic plague spreads like wildfire, transported by respiratory droplets – a simple cough or sneeze will infect anyone within range. The trouble is, there are no effective environmental warning systems to detect plague bacilli, so you wouldn't know you'd been infected until symptoms appeared.'

I realized I still had my jacket on and semi-stood to take it off. 'How long does that take then – you know, the symptoms?'

'The time from exposure until development of first

symptoms is normally between one and six days, but most often two to four.'

'So, what are we looking for?'

'Well, the first indication of an attack would most likely be a sudden outbreak of illness, presenting as severe pneumonia and sepsis. If there are only small numbers of cases, the possibility of them being plague may at first be overlooked, given the clinical similarity to other bacterial or viral pneumonias – and the fact that so few Western physicians have ever seen a case of pneumonic plague. It may be up to ten days before public-health authorities recognize what's happened, and by then, anyone infected will be dead.' He pulled up the sleeves of his cardigan. 'Using this form of plague as a biological weapon would be simply catastrophic.'

'If you were a terrorist, how would you use it?'

'*Yersinia pestis* can be grown in large quantities and, with just a little skill, could be quite easily disseminated. The agent would have to be milled into a very fine powder so it could be dispersed in aerosol form. A crop-sprayer could be used over a town or city, or individuals could disperse it using compressed oxygen bottles, maybe large hospital bottles in a vehicle, to pump the agent out as they drove round the streets. Then again, it could be hand-held – a smaller compressed oxygen bottle concealed in a rucksack, or even a conventional aerosol can. It really doesn't matter how – once it's delivered an infectious and invisible cloud would remain suspended in the atmosphere for up to an hour, waiting to be inhaled.'

Suzy pursed her lips. 'This powder, Simon, could it be transported in a bottle? And how big an area would, say, twelve full wine bottles contaminate?' She placed her wet gum on the edge of the table before standing up and going over to her handbag.

Simon's eyes followed her. 'A bottle, yes, if it was well sealed.'

Suzy sat down with her cigarettes and lighter in her hand. He looked at me as she took out a Benson & Hedges, and the expression on his face told me the penny had dropped.

'That's why I'm here isn't it – some *pestis* has been discovered? Twelve seventy-five-centilitre bottles – nine litres. Where? What control measures are in place? Has the public health—'

Suzy interrupted him with the offer of a cigarette and, to my surprise, he took one.

'No, Simon, we don't know what control measures are in place. We're trying to find the stuff.' She glanced at me and I nodded as her disposable clicked into life. Considering where he was going after this, it didn't matter if he knew or not. She dragged in a lungful of smoke and handed him the lighter.

He studied it for several seconds before lifting it to the cigarette in his mouth. 'First in three years.'

'Glad you cracked too, Simon.' Suzy was all smiles. 'I only gave up a few minutes ago.' She wiggled the cigarette between her fingers at him. 'This is all your fault.'

The smoke from two cigarettes soon filled the air. 'What more do you have to tell us, Simon? What about infection? How close do we have to be?'

Emptying his lungs, he leant forwards again and gave his ash an experienced tap into the coffee-table ashtray. I was sure his eyes were watering but he still took another quick drag. 'Direct exposure to the *pestis* obviously means you're infected. After that, anyone within six feet of an infected person will be exposed – two metres, two yards, whatever you want to call it – and they, too, are likely to get infected. It would be simply a fucking biblical event.'

Simon flicked non-existent ash as he stared into the ashtray, his mind clearly elsewhere. It seemed an eternity before he looked up at Suzy. 'Is it really going to hap—'

'Tell you what, Simon, just do your job. OK?' If he thought she was the soft touch of us two he was wrong.

'Yes, of course, sorry.' The next drag was a lot longer and smoke spilled out of every hole in his face as he continued. 'The first sign of illness is fever, headache, cough, general weakness. Victims will feel under the weather, but think it's just another round of colds and flu. Most people, like Archibald, will just get on with life. He was a gardener. And all the time they're doing that, they're part of the contamination chain.'

His spare hand waved in front of him, pointing at his body. 'Then, within a few days, they'll get a bloody or watery cough due to the lung infection – the pneumonia. There will be shortness of breath, chest pains, along with intestinal symptoms – nausea, vomiting, abdominal pain, diarrhoea, that sort of thing.'

Suzy blew a lungful of smoke towards the ceiling. 'This isn't going to have a happy ending, is it?'

Shaking his head, he slid backwards into the settee. 'As the pneumonia worsens over two to four days, it can cause septic shock. Not that you'd be too concerned because you'd be as good as dead anyway.' He squinted and looked up as he took another long drag. His hand had started to shake. 'By the time the disease is recognized in the population, after anything from ten days to two weeks, it will be too late for tens, maybe hundreds of thousands of us.' Simon sank back, his eyes on the ceiling, as if contemplating the enormity of it all. Shit, he wasn't the only one.

Suzy and I exchanged another glance. Her smile had disappeared as Simon's cigarette moved up and down in his mouth. 'The one good thing is that there is no spore form in the *Yersinia pestis* lifecycle, so it's susceptible to the environment – and particularly sensitive to the action of sunlight. That's why plague aerosol is infectious for no more than an hour.' He sat up and tried me this time. He sounded as if he was having difficulty breathing. 'With that amount of *pestis*, we're talking hundreds of thousands of innocent people. Why isn't any action being taken out there? People have a right to know of the risk, surely.'

'What about protection, Simon?'

He shrugged in submission. 'Close-contact transmission can

111

be prevented by wearing a surgical mask of a US rating of N95 or UK standard FFP3, then there's surgical gloves, eye protection, that sort of thing.' He didn't sound at all convincing. 'Look.' He stubbed out his cigarette in the ashtray. Suzy was only moments behind with hers. 'To be honest, it's all bollocks. If I was playing about with this stuff in its powder form, I'd only feel safe in an astronaut's suit.'

Suzy offered him another cigarette, which he gladly took, and the smoke was soon billowing out of them again.

I thought it, Suzy spoke it. 'Is there anything out there that we can take? A vaccine or a drug or anything like that to protect us?'

He shook his head. 'A vaccine, no. Manufacture was discontinued in 'ninety-nine. But the use of doxycycline, I think, has some effect as protection and post-exposure.'

I was straight in there. 'That's good enough for me – we need a shedful. Can you get it to Yvette today?'

He nodded. 'Sure, I can arrange all that.' He looked at Suzy. 'Are you pregnant, or do you think you may be?'

She held up her new cancer stick. 'What do you think?'

'It's just that some antibiotics have an adverse effect on foetal growth.'

Suzy stood up and had regained her smile. 'Lovely. Everything we always wanted to know about pneumonic plague, and probably a whole lot we didn't. Thanks, Simon.'

He gave a little smile that soon faded. 'I don't know exactly what's happening and I don't want to know, but the thing is . . . I've got a family, and I'm thinking . . . I'm thinking I've always wanted to take them to visit my sister-in-law in Namibia. Do you think now would be a good time?' His hand was still shaking as he stubbed out the cigarette.

Suzy and I looked at each other.

'Please, I just need to know.'

Fuck it, why not? 'Let's put it this way.' I stood up to join Suzy. 'If I was one of your kids and you said, "We're going on holiday to Auntie Edna's tomorrow," which would mean

112

leaving school and going somewhere nice and hot, I would be really, really happy and feel really, really safe.' I looked at Suzy. 'Wouldn't you?'

'Absolutely. A kids' dream. But you won't be going with them, Simon.'

I couldn't tell whether the look on his face was shock or resignation. 'Everything's OK.' I did that stupid lowering-of-the-hands thing, trying to calm him down. 'But you won't be going to another meeting after this. Sorry, mate. Are there two guys waiting for you downstairs?'

'Oh, God, no. I have a family and—'

'Calm down, mate, it's nothing like that. They'll be driving you somewhere safe until we've done our job – or fucked up – that's all. In any case, if we do fuck up you'll be thinking how lucky you are to be in isolation. That's just the way it is.'

There was no way the Yes Man was going to take the chance of a leak. Simon was about to spend some time in a house in the country, with his family thinking he'd been whisked away to carry out some important bug stuff in the jungle.

Suzy picked up his bag for him as he slowly got his coat back on and I moved towards him. 'Simon, you got a mobile?'

'Er, yes . . .'

I patted him on the back in best-mate fashion. 'I'll tell you the best thing to do. Call your wife on the way down, tell her you've got to go and do some African disease stuff. Tell her to take the kids to your sister-in-law's for two weeks and you'll meet them there – the company's paying, free trip, chance of a lifetime, shit like that.'

He buttoned up his coat. 'Thank you so much.'

I shrugged. 'No problem. Just don't forget our drug deal – and be careful, mate. Be careful what you tell your wife. Don't fuck up with what you know or next time you see the boys downstairs they'll not be as nice. You understand, don't you?'

He gathered up his bag from Suzy and thanked us again as he headed for the door. Suzy walked with him. As he opened the door she put a hand on his shoulder. 'Forget what he just said.'

He looked up sharply. I was confused, too.

She said, 'If I was your wife and you said the holiday was for a couple of weeks, I'd be happy. But if you said we were going for a couple of months, I'd be over the moon.'

'Thank you, I hear what you're saying.'

She rubbed his shoulder. 'Speak to her, sort it out.'

Simon gave her a smile that was full of sadness. 'Oh, that won't be possible, I'm afraid. She died six years ago. Gillian would have loved to go home, but she never got the chance. Archibald was our gardener, you see. They used to walk the garden together every day.'

20

Suzy stayed by the door. Her expression told me we were both thinking the same thing.

'Facemask, my arse.' I gave a thumbs-down. 'N95 or UK standard F something or other? I want full NBC [Nuclear, Biological and Chemical warfare protection] kit.'

'I'll phone the Golf Club.' She disappeared into the bedroom.

'And tell her we want the older stuff, not the newer camouflage version,' I called after her.

She got on with it as I just sat there, trying to feel pleased with myself for doing a nice thing for Mr Niceness instead of worrying myself sick about Kelly. George had been right: if these people weren't stopped, then all the therapy in the world wasn't going to help her. There was no way round it. She had to go back to Laurel.

Suzy came into the room with two of the Nokias. 'The Golf Club is coming later tonight. If we're at the source meet she'll just drop the NBC kit off.'

'The older suits?'

She nodded, trying to untangle the car chargers from the hands-free sets, then passing one to me. We both set about programming out the start-up tune.

Suzy did her best to look as though she was concentrating on her cell, but I could see a little smile creeping across her face. 'So, Austin Powers, International Man of Mystery, you're not Mother Teresa, but you're not a K either, are you?'

I was too busy hunting for the sound-options menu to look up. 'Come on, you know the score. You're going to have to work a lot harder than that . . .'

'Fair one.' She shrugged and went back to the administrative side of Nokia ownership for all of five seconds. 'You're obviously ex-military and a Brit.'

I just got on with what I was doing and listened.

'I was in the Navy – 'eighty-four to 'ninety-three. I ran away to sea – well, sort of. The last six years of it were in the Det.'

I did look up then.

She grinned. 'I knew that would ring a bell.'

'What is this? I'll show you mine if you show me yours?'

She was right, though. Northern Ireland in the seventies was a nightmare for the Firm and the Security Service, and the quality of information they were gathering was piss poor, so the Army started its own covert intelligence-gathering unit. Recruited from all three services, operators worked in a series of area detachments or Dets.

She was in full flow now. 'I did two tours in East Det, then became an MOE instructor down in Ashford.'

'Is that how you became a K?'

'Yep, I was approached when I left.'

'Why leave the Navy? Meet the man of your dreams or something?'

'Come on, now, no personal shit, remember?'

'So, all that stuff about your dad going AWOL – was that all bollocks?'

'No, but he's dead and it fitted with the cover story. So, come on, how do you know about the Det?'

Fuck it. I wasn't going to spend the next few days in

total silence. 'I was a team leader in North Det in the late eighties.'

'North Det?' She laughed and waved her hands about as if she were holding a set of reins. 'One of the cowboys? A bit of a law unto yourselves, weren't you, you lot?'

'Let's get these moan-phones up and running, shall we? What's your number? 07802 . . .'

She called out the last six digits and I hit the newly silenced keys. I'd got that much right. I finished dialling, then hit the hash key twice. 'Hello, hello . . .' In the background I could hear a low bleeping tone every three seconds, and so would she. It was the signal that we were on secure, the fill hadn't dropped.

'Good, that works.' I hung up, then saved her number to speed-dial.

Her expression suddenly became more intense. 'Nick, does it worry you – you know, working with me?'

I frowned.

'Course not. Why should working with a woman be a worry? I wish you'd be a bit more scared now and then, but we did OK in Penang, didn't we?'

'I'm not talking about that, dickhead.' Her face was still serious for a moment, then split into the world's biggest grin. 'I'm talking about me being so five-star good.' She laughed, but I wasn't sure just how much she was joking.

I always worried about people who thought they couldn't get hurt. She was starting to sound a bit like Josh, but without God's Kevlar jacket.

'Being so wonderful, I suppose you're permanent cadre?'

Permanent cadre were Ks, and some of them were deniable operators. They were on a salaried retainer, not freelance like I'd been, but they still had to do the shit jobs that no one else wanted.

'I will be after this. So don't fuck up, all right?

'Only if you promise to empty the ashtray.'

She picked it up and disappeared into the kitchen. I heard

117

the tap running. She shouted through, 'Do you want that brew now, or what?'

'Good idea.' I put the Nokia in my bumbag with my own cell. I needed to break the news to Kelly soon, and get hold of Josh. I tried to forget the look on Archibald's face.

The kettle was bubbling away as the moan-phone rang. Reluctantly, I pulled it out. The Yes Man was on the other end and the moaning started at once. 'Hello? Answer me.'

'Hello.' The gentle bleeps did their stuff in the background.

'Starbucks, Cowcross Street, Farringdon. Do you know it?

'I know the station.'

'The source meet is at twenty hundred.' He carried on with the meet details as Suzy appeared and stood expectantly at my elbow, like a schoolgirl waiting for her exam results.

Once he had finished, and I had finished with Suzy, we both headed for the bedroom and got the two 9mm Brownings out of the suitcase, a little extra treat Yvette had popped into Packet Oscar. The Browning had been in production for something like a million years, but I still liked it and saw no need to go trendy and plastic or whatever the latest fashion was in pistols. These two were starting to look their age. They'd been jazzed up a little: the wooden sides of the pistol grip had been replaced with rubber. There was no extension welded on to the safety catch above the grip, where it could be flicked on and off with the firer's right thumb, which was a pity, since I had fairly small hands, but I had no complaints. It was a simple weapon: you knew that if you squeezed the trigger, it was going to go bang. What more did you need?

We carried out NSPs [normal safety precautions]. With my right thumb and the side of my forefinger I pulled back on the serrations at the rear of the top slide and checked inside the ejection opening to make sure there wasn't a round stuck in the chamber, then released and let the top slide return under its own steam. Then, placing an empty magazine in the weapon so I'd be able to squeeze off the action – it wouldn't fire without a mag on – I rested the top pad of my right forefinger on the trigger and felt for the first pressure.

Most triggers have two pressures. The first is normally quite loose, allowing a little play between its resting position and the point at which it will actually fire the weapon. This one's trigger had maybe three or four millimetres' play before it became solid again. I squeezed gently on the second pressure and the hammer came forwards with a click.

Knowing the position of second pressure is critically important. I always took up first pressure if the target was close and I'd have maybe a second to react once I'd seen them. There might only be a few millimetres in it, but that could make all the difference and, despite everything, I was still in no hurry to end up dead.

We put on surgical gloves and started to load the half-dozen thirteen-round magazines. When we fired the SDs or Brownings, empty cases would be flying all over the place. No matter who found them, friend or foe, neither of us wanted to leave any evidence of our presence. This was a deniable job. Even the ammunition was German, judging by the markings on its base.

Holding the short magazine so that the base of the stubby 9mm rounds would be facing away from me once loaded, I grabbed a handful and pushed them down one by one into the top recess, then eased them back to make sure they were correctly seated.

Suzy did the same, stopping now and then to take a sip of brew. 'So, tell me, what is it with you and the boss? Really.'

I started to load my second mag.

'I mean, it's obvious you two aren't exactly on each other's Christmas-card list.'

119

The fishing rod was well and truly out but, fuck it, what did it matter?

'I used to be a K until just over a year ago, but then got offered a better job somewhere else. Maybe he just can't live without me.'

'Somewhere else?'

'In the US.'

'Oh.' She smiled as she held up a magazine to the light. I had no idea why. 'Why are you back here now?'

I picked up my third mag and began the process all over again, but all I could think of was the look on Kelly's face when I found her among the boxes. 'It seemed like a good idea at the time.'

I pushed the third magazine into the pistol grip and slid it home until it clicked into place. I never slammed them in the Mel Gibson way: it just damages the mag, and that's going to give you stoppages.

With the grip of the weapon jammed firmly in the web of my right hand, I pulled back sharply on the top slide with my left, releasing it so that the slide sprang back into position on its own. As it did so, the working parts picked up a round and fed it into the chamber. Then, turning the weapon to the left and exposing the ejection opening, I pulled back just a little on the top slide again to make sure that a round was bedded.

Because I found it difficult to use the safety catch, I always half cocked these things if there wasn't an extension. I put the little finger of my left hand in front of the hammer, and gently squeezed the trigger. The hammer swung forward and bit into my knuckle, then I pulled it back until it stopped half-way. It wasn't going anywhere now, even if I squeezed the trigger. If I had to draw down, I'd pull the hammer all the way back, so that it clicked into its full-cocked position, then I'd fire.

There were two thick black nylon pancake holsters in the suitcase, but I wasn't interested. My pistol went down the front of my jeans. It was too late in the game for me to change now: actions need to be instinctive – my hand had to go straight to the weapon.

Suzy, however, was going by the rule book, cocking her weapon, checking chamber and struggling like I would to apply the safety catch and picking up a pancake holster to feed into her belt. As she unbuckled it I tightened mine, so the Browning was nice and secure.

'You're not worried about the family jewels, then?'

'No. But I'd hate to get gun oil on my nice new boxers.'

Her pancake went over her right kidney. She checked her safety catch once more and holstered her weapon.

I pulled off my gloves and flicked one at Suzy before we put them back into the suitcase, zipped it up and shoved it under the bed. As hiding places went, it was about as inventive as the phone codes.

I went and got my bumbag from the front room, threading the straps through the belt loops of my jeans so they wouldn't get in the way if I had to draw down the Browning. Then we carried out SOPs [standard operating procedures] on leaving the flat – checking windows, unplugging electrics – before we switched back into boyfriend and girlfriend mode by the open door in the hallway.

I punched the code into the alarm as if we were a happy couple leaving for our weekly trip to Tesco. It didn't make any noise – the last thing the Firm wanted was for the police to turn up and sort through a safe-house – and was linked directly to the QRF [quick reaction force]. The door was reinforced with a steel liner to prevent access, and every room had a panic button in case you got bored and wanted to piss off the QRF as they settled down to tea and biccies. An armed four-man team would respond immediately, whether we were taking the piss, the place was being burgled or there was a drama during one of the many 'interviews' that were held in flats like these.

The door closed behind us and I double-locked it. We

walked out of the square and turned right to get to the main. After about five minutes we managed to flag down a black cab and Suzy adopted the tone she reserved especially for cab drivers from Penang to London. 'Farringdon, darling.'

'Whereabouts do you want, love?'

'By the tube station will be fine.'

We hit the Embankment and were soon passing the new ring of concrete designed to stop suicide bombers driving into the Houses of Parliament. We listened to a radio talk-show piece about the heightened state of alert. Some dickhead from the mayor's office said that the security measures should reassure tourists, not deter them. The cabbie cracked up. 'I've heard of spin, but is this boy taking the piss or what?'

I looked at traser. It was six forty-five, and the meet was at eight, which gave us enough time to do a recce and sort ourselves out once we got there.

We turned off the Embankment at Blackfriars and headed up towards Farringdon, stopping at a set of lights. I noticed a Ford Mondeo parked up on the left, with a motorbike so close to the driver's door that the rider's helmet was nearly through his window. The car was two-up, man and woman. She was leaning over from the passenger seat to join in the conversation as another bike drew up. I glanced at Suzy, and she'd seen it too. There was a big surveillance team on a serial [surveillance task], and either they were staking something out or they'd lost the target and were trying to decide what to do next. They were probably E4, the government's surveillance group, which keeps tabs on everybody from terrorists to dodgy politicians.

The lights changed and the bikes peeled away in different directions as we passed, then the Mondeo pulled a U-turn that brought the traffic to a standstill. The cabbie saw the commotion in his rear-view mirror. 'Some people'll do any-thing to avoid the congestion charge.' He laughed at his own joke as Suzy nodded thoughtfully and settled back in her seat.

Within ten minutes we were confronted by a checkpoint,

part of the ring of steel around the City. Armed police stood beside two cars with flashing lights. The taxi driver leant his head back. 'Don't worry, we're turning off here. But it's all go, innit? Wonder what's happening?'

Suzy shook her head. 'Not a clue, darling. Like this all the time, is it?'

'Sometimes it is, sometimes it ain't. Bit of a bleedin' lottery these days. I blame that Bin Liner nutter myself, know what I mean?'

The driver chuckled as he made a turn into Cowcross Street, and I could see Farringdon tube station up ahead. Clerkenwell was the place to be, these days. Every old storage building had been turned into loft-living for City types, just a short walk from their offices in the Square Mile, and every other shopfront was a bar.

We paid off the cab outside the tube station. Starbucks was around here somewhere.

'The source will be wearing a blue suit over a white shirt, and carrying a copy of the *Evening Standard* in his right hand,' the Yes Man had told us. 'He'll also have a black overcoat on his left arm.'

Suzy was sponsoring the meet. She'd be sitting inside Starbucks having a coffee; on the table in front of her would be a folded copy of the *Independent*. The source was to approach her and ask if she knew the way to the Golden Lane estate. Suzy would reply that she didn't, but she had an A–Z. Once she had made contact, she would get on the cell and tell me to come in.

Farringdon station was an old Victorian building with a little stall outside selling newspapers, porn mags, *Private Eye*, that sort of stuff. I waited while Suzy got herself an *Independent*. Cowcross went slightly uphill and was quite narrow, built for horses and carts. It was still busy, mostly with bond traders not wanting to go home. Among the fashionable façades there was a scattering of corner shops, Indian takeaways, sandwich joints and hairdressers, like bad

123

teeth in an otherwise perfect set, all waiting for the landlords to put their rents up so high they'd no longer be able to stand their ground.

I spotted the Starbucks sign further up Cowcross on the left. The source was due to approach from the direction of the station and on the same side of the street. He would cross at the junction with Turnmill Street, about fifteen metres further uphill. There was a pub on the opposite corner called the Castle, which looked as if it had been there since Jack the Ripper was doing his thing, and would be still when all the chrome-and-smoked-glass pleasure palaces had fallen down. Our coffee shop was thirty metres beyond it.

Suzy put her arm through mine. 'Do you see it?'

I nodded. There didn't seem to be much up Turnmill Street apart from a long, high wall that followed the railway line.

We crossed. The pub was packed with briefcases, raincoats and laughing people. If we needed them, there were seats all the way along the window, with good exposure to the road.

The Starbucks looked brand new, and pretty much the same as the one in Georgetown, with its mix of leather and hardwood seats, sofas and low tables. It was about a quarter full. A set of stairs led down to what I assumed would be more seating and the toilets. Beyond the glass doors at the far end were a few sets of shiny alloy chairs and tables in what appeared to be a courtyard. More than one entrance and exit. Perfect. Either this was one of the Firm's regular venues or the source knew his stuff.

We headed down an alleyway beyond it that opened into a large, recobbled square. There were a couple of balls-achingly trendy bars, with lots of stainless-steel shit outside, and to our left the Starbucks seating area.

Suzy looked up like she'd decided what she wanted for dinner and I was on the menu. 'If this turns into a bad thing before you get here, I'll be coming out this way. After that, who knows?'

I put my arms round her. 'We'd better make sure the doors are open, then, hadn't we?'

As we stood there, two couples came out almost immediately. Suzy was happy. 'That's it, then. Once I'm out of the area, I'll call.'

21

We wandered back down to Farringdon station and got ourselves a brew from a soup and sandwich bar. As we leant
against the wall outside and took the odd sip we did a casual
scan of the general area. Suzy bit gently into the rim of the
polystyrene cup, her teeth leaving a pattern much like the scar
an Alsatian had once left on my arm. She kept her eyes on the
road while turning the cup a little for a fresh site to chew.
'Can't see a thing to worry us. You? Seen anyone standing
about with peepholes in their *Evening Standard*?'

She was right: no one was concentrating too hard on looking
normal. Most people had their heads down, thinking of getting
home.

'Nope, but I hate source meets all the same. In fact, I hate
sources, period. No matter what side you're on, they're betray-
ing someone, and that gives me a prickly feeling between my
shoulder-blades.'

She took another sip, her eyes never straying from the street.
'We can't do without them, though, can we? And it's not as if we
have to invite them back for dinner, is it?' She glanced at her
watch, and I checked mine. 'Twenty to go. You'd better make a
move, otherwise you're not going to get that drink, are you?'

She turned and smiled at me while she put in her hands-free earpiece. I hit the moan-phone's speed dial, pressed the hash key twice and put it to my ear. She answered before the end of the first ring. 'We have comms.'

I listened and heard the reassuring bleeping in the background. 'See you later, then. And don't go making any improper suggestions to strange men.' I gave her a quick peck on the cheek and walked away.

I threw the rest of my coffee into a bin, crossed the road and ambled towards the Castle, inserting my earpiece when I got to the door. Suzy overtook me on the opposite pavement, on her way to Starbucks.

Cigarette smoke curled towards the ceiling inside the pub, which was full of happy, raucous people unwinding after a week's work. The men's ties were undone and the women's lipstick mostly on their glasses. I queued at the bar to order my Coke, then wormed my way through the crowd towards the windows overlooking the Turnmill junction. The music was loud, and the sounds of laughter and chat drowned the background noise in my earpiece, but I had a fantastic view down the road to the station, then all the way to Farringdon Road.

I heard the screech and squelch of espresso machines. 'Hello, have you got me?' I pressed my earpiece in deeper. 'Can you hear me?'

'Oh, hi, yes, I'm in Starbucks.' She spoke gently, as if talking to her boyfriend. 'I'll wait here for you if you want.'

'Yeah, I have the trigger.'

I sipped my Coke and watched the world go by, eyes peeled for a man in a blue suit and white shirt, with a black raincoat over his left arm. A guy came down from the direction of Starbucks, on the opposite side of the road. He was early thirties, skin very dark brown, Indian, maybe Sri Lankan. His side-parted short-back-and-sides had a thick streak of grey at the temple. He was wearing a brown suede bomber jacket over a black pullover and jeans – not the kit I was looking for but he attracted my attention all the same. He was checking out the

127

street, turning to look back the way he'd come before crossing as he checked down Turnmill. Once over the road he headed towards the station, and disappeared inside.

It wasn't long before I got a possible coming out. He looked to be South East Asian, and had a blue suit and a black raincoat, but he was wearing it. He stepped over to the stand and bought himself a paper.

I lifted the mike on the hands-free to my mouth. 'Hey, guess what – I have a possible, and he may have brought a mate.'

I watched as he turned back into the station entrance. 'He's disappeared.'

'OK, fine.' I pictured Suzy sitting in Starbucks with a nice big frothy cappuccino, holding up her own mike and smiling away like an idiot as we exchanged sweet-nothings. She left a few seconds' pause. 'Yes, I understand that. That's good. I'll talk to you soon, then.'

He reappeared. 'Here we go, he's got his coat over his left arm, and the paper folded in his right. Might just be three of us for coffee. No sign of his friend.'

He looked familiar. I let him pass the pub window. 'It's the *Standard*.' I looked at his face and felt my pulse start to race. 'It's the fucking taxi driver from our holiday.' I tried to keep sounding casual. 'He's on his way . . . he's past me . . . towards you now. The taxi driver . . .'

'Oh, lovely. It'll be just like old times.'

I eyeballed the street, looking at everyone and everything who might be following our guy, and sure enough Grey Streak reappeared at the station entrance, and he wasn't alone. 'I reckon there are two others with him. Brown suede on blue, and navy on blue. Both Indian. Be careful.'

'He's here now. See you in a minute. 'Bye.'

They crossed Turnmill and passed my window, eyes peeled, concentrating too hard to talk. They both had very dark, smooth skin, and looked as though they shared a barber: their hair was cut square, and their neck shaves hadn't grown back yet. I waited a bit longer, then left the pub and crossed the road to get a better view of the coffee shop.

I couldn't see them, but heard an educated South East Asian voice in my earpiece. 'Excuse me, do you know the way to the Golden Lane estate?'

Suzy came over loud and clear. 'No, sorry, but I've got an A–Z if you want to have a look.'

I cut in. 'You OK? Can't see the other two.'

'Yep.'

'OK, that's me now moving in.'

I walked up the road, listening to her establish his cover. My heart was pounding, but she sounded cool as a cucumber. 'The reason you're here is that you've just asked me the way to Golden Lane estate. I'm now going to get the A–Z out of my bag and put it on the table, and we've got talking because my boyfriend and I went on holiday to Malaysia over Easter. Do you understand?'

I could hear him agreeing.

Since Suzy was sponsoring the RV [rendezvous], she was responsible for the cover story. 'OK, my boyfriend is going to join us any minute. We all know Penang and we're going to meet up and have a little chat over a nice cup of coffee.'

Again, I heard him agree.

'If anything happens, my boyfriend and I are going to go out the back door. You go out the front, the way you came in. Do you understand?'

As I entered the coffee shop I spotted the two of them sitting in the far left-hand corner. Suzy had the commanding position, with her back against the wall so she could see both exits. I waved to her, and he looked round. Her A–Z was sitting on the table.

I went over and kissed her. 'Hang on, let me turn this thing off.'

She turned hers off too. 'This gentleman is trying to find his way to Golden Lane estate. Can you believe it? He was in Penang the same time we were.'

129

Everyone else around us was doing their own little thing, and no one took the slightest notice. I gave him a nod and a smile. 'We had the best holiday ever. I'd love to go back.'

We all sat down. Cover and escape routes were established: we could carry on with the meet.

There was silence as he sat and waited for us to start, which was strange because it should have been the other way round. I smiled at him – maybe he was nervous. 'What have you got for us, then?'

He was in his late forties, slim, about the same height as Suzy. He wore a simple stainless-steel watch but no rings or other jewellery. He had lost the moustache and had a few dark brown freckles over his cheeks, and a lot of lines everywhere else. They complemented his bloodshot eyes, which made him look as if he'd been up all week, or was just fucked in general. What was most noticeable, though, were his hands – maybe even bigger than Sundance's, with nails that were perfectly manicured yet knuckles so rough they were almost white. He must have been a Jap slapper, into martial arts and all that kit, doing press-ups on them and punching through lumps of wood. I was certainly glad not to be a lump of wood. 'What do you people expect from me?'

Suzy and I exchanged a glance.

'You people have to realize that finding this ASU will be extremely difficult.'

Suzy leant closer. 'So, what's the point of meeting if you haven't got anything?'

'But I told your people I have nothing yet, it was they who wanted this meeting. We are fighting people who want to be martyrs. These are serious people and their successes depend on concealment. They do not make mistakes. All you people keep saying is where are—'

I raised my hands. 'Hey, listen, whatever you're pissed off about doesn't mean a thing at our level, all right?'

He stared at me for a few seconds, as if weighing me up. 'It

130

may take a little while. These are not your boy terrorists in Northern Ireland . . .'

Suzy's eyes flashed. 'People have died fighting those "boy" terrorists.'

I put my hand on her arm. 'OK, what now?'

The source looked grave. 'They are here, they are in the UK. What are my contact details, who am I dealing with?'

I pointed at Suzy. 'Her. Give him your number.'

Suzy looked at me but didn't object: we had to show unity, even if he was dicking us about. She told him and he closed his eyes as he loaded it into the software inside his head.

When he opened them again, they seemed even more blood-shot. 'I will call if and when I have something.' He stood up to leave.

'Are you sure you'll be able to locate the ASU?' I said. 'Have you got any help?'

'I do not need any. I am perfectly fine on my own.'

He got up and left through the back doors.

22

'Stay put, Suzy. Watch.'

Outside, the street-lights had come on. Less than thirty seconds later Grey Streak passed the front window, heading back towards the station.

'That's the first one I saw.' The source also walked past as she sat back in her chair and picked up her brew. He didn't bother looking in. Finally, as she took a sip, Navy followed suit. I powered up my cell. 'He's lying. Let's take 'em. You start.'

She did the same with hers, then her bag went over her left shoulder as she stood up, making sure that her leather jacket covered the Browning on her right hip as we kissed goodbye. I hit redial as she stepped out of the front door and disappeared. 'Hello? Do you have me?'

'Yep, good. That's Navy on the right . . . approaching the station . . . into the station now. All three unsighted.'

I was on my feet and out on Cowcross. Suzy was maybe twenty metres ahead of me on the right-hand pavement, just short of the pub.

'I'll go complete the station.' I could hear the PA system and the noise of the ticket hall before she spoke. 'All three still unsighted, still checking.'

There was a lot of rustling as she checked the area. 'Wait, wait, wait. Yes . . . I have all three down on the platform, can't make out what direction. They're still split up, but on the same platform. I'll get the tickets.'

I joined her a minute later. She greeted me with a smile and 'Nice to see you', as we walked arm in arm towards the turnstiles. CCTV cameras were everywhere.

'Look down the stairs.'

A flight of wide wrought-iron steps led down to the platforms. I could make out the top third of the source's head above the billboards, and further along the platform a tell-tale streak of grey. Navy was nearer to us, sitting on a bench between a middle-aged black woman with two Tesco bags and a white man with a leather bag at his feet.

Suzy moved into me and laid her head on my chest, nodding as I whispered lovingly into her ear. 'We'll just have to wait for—' A train roared in immediately below us. People shuffled to the platform edge. Navy and the two on the bench got up to join the shuffle. 'Fuck the other two, they don't know us. We take the source. You take the far carriage and I'll do this one.'

She handed me my all-zone ticket and pushed hers into the turnstile. The gate flapped open as the train doors did the same below us. I followed her through, and down the stairs. She walked briskly on to the opposite platform, using the billboards as cover. My eyes didn't leave the back of the source's head. I needed to be as close as possible, which meant taking the carriage immediately to his right. I moved behind her, head down, losing myself among the waiting passengers until she'd overtaken him. Then I ducked back as the source boarded the train.

Shit. Navy was heading for the same carriage as me. No time to change direction: I was committed. The woman took a seat with her back to the platform, and so did Navy. I sat opposite her, trying not to get my feet tangled in her bags.

The carriage was only about half full. A couple of kids stayed standing because they wanted to look cool, but everyone else sat. I looked to my right, through the connecting door, but couldn't see the source. Half standing, I leant across to pick up a discarded *Guardian* supplement a few seats to the left of the woman. As the PA told us all to mind the gap, I caught a glimpse of him on my side of the next carriage, seated about half-way along. I couldn't tell if he was aware or not. Navy certainly wasn't. He stared blankly ahead, his hands resting on his legs. That was it now, no more looking. I couldn't afford eye to eye: I didn't want to be someone he remembered later.

The doors closed and the train rumbled off, still above ground, although the grimy brickwork ran very close on either side. I checked the route card above the woman's head and discovered we were on the Circle line. I felt myself rock from side to side as the train speeded up, then slowed. I played with the phone as if I was dialling, and brought the mike closer to my mouth. I smiled as if I'd just got through. 'Hi, how are you?'

I could hardly hear her above the rattle of the tracks, so I lifted the phone right to my ear and pulled out the hands-free.

'I'm fine. Are you seeing him today?'

My lips were touching the phone. 'Yes, I'm seeing two. I'm going to lose you soon.'

She gave a girlish giggle. 'Me, too. That sounds really great.' I guessed there was somebody sitting right next to her. Maybe it was Grey. She went quiet and I checked the phone signal. It disappeared as the train was swallowed by a tunnel. I glanced around at my fellow passengers. They were all in their own worlds, reading books and newspapers, or avoiding eye-contact with the people opposite. Some, like Navy, just sat there letting their heads wobble from side to side. To my left, the man with the leather bag at his feet picked fluff obsessively from his corduroy trousers.

The woman bent down and rustled about in one of her bags, produced a copy of *Hello!* and started to flick through the pages. I played with the idea of Corduroy Man walking along crowded platforms in the rush-hour with his bag, letting its deadly cargo of Dark Winter leak from a small hole in the bottom of it. No one would give him a second thought as he moved about the Underground. He could walk as far as he liked until he needed to refill and start all over again.

Like thousands of others, the woman wouldn't have seen, heard or smelt DW as it floated about her to be breathed in. She would go home tonight, and in a couple of days think she had a bit of flu and almost certainly infect her husband and kids. The husband would give the good news to everyone he passed on the way to work, then once there, he'd keep on going. The kids would go to school or college and do exactly the same. You didn't need to be Kelly's maths teacher to work out how quickly it added up to what Simon had called a biblical event.

The train's PA system crackled and a female voice from Suzy's neck of the estuary told us the next station was King's Cross. The platform lights rushed in from the opposite side of the carriage, and long blurs gradually became Greek holiday posters. The train stopped with a gentle squeal of brakes and the doors lumbered open.

Navy got up. I looked through the interconnecting door. The source was on his feet too, overcoat on. I waited where I was, not knowing which end of the platform was the exit. Would he turn left or right? If I went too early and got it wrong, I might walk straight into him. If I waited too long, the doors would close.

Most of the people disembarking from my carriage turned to the right, and Navy followed them. If the source did too, Suzy would pick him up for sure.

I waited a while before falling in with the rear of the herd. I couldn't see any of them, even Suzy, as the crowd followed the way-out signs. We were still all heading in the same direction, but I kept an eye out for other exits: King's Cross was a major tube interchange, and there were two rail stations at street level.

I still had no signal on my phone as I pushed my way

through a group of dithering foreign teenagers and joined the stream of business people hurrying for their trains.

I spotted Navy about half-way up the escalator – static, not aware. He glanced at the odd poster now and again, as everybody did. One signal bar flickered on the mobile's display. 'Hello, Suzy?' Nothing.

By the time I'd got maybe half-way up he'd reached the top and disappeared. I started taking the stairs two at a time, barging past people when I had to, muttering apologies.

The escalator spilled us into an area from where maybe five or six tunnels led off in different directions. Navy could have gone down any of them, but he didn't matter. The source did. I took the first option left, with only a one-in-five chance of being right, and made about a hundred metres.

'Hello, Nick, hello?'

'Suzy, you're weak, you're weak.'

'He's out of the tube. He's in the main-line station, I have all three.'

'Nearly there.' I turned and moved against the flow, back to the top of the escalators and followed the sign for King's Cross main-line station. More pushing, more apologies.

Suzy kept up her commentary: 'All three heading out of the station towards the main, they're taking the main exit, they're still separate. You getting this?'

'Yeah – nearly there. Excuse me, sorry, sorry.' I pounded up the final flight of stairs and into the enormous high-roofed concourse. A large digital display showed the times of departing trains, most of them delayed. Pissed-off commuters stood around drinking hot stuff from paper cups and muttering into cell phones.

Suzy was nowhere to be seen, but I heard traffic in my earpiece and then her voice. I had to block my other ear with a finger to hear what she was saying, because the station tannoy had started up as well. All I caught was something about the main.

'What's he doing on the main?'

'They're all held at the main. Outside the station, they're still apart and static. You get that?'

'Got it. Can you hear me?'

'Yes, yes.' She shut up and the traffic took over in the earpiece. Then, 'Stand by, stand by, they're moving. Still apart. They're at the main, still station side of the main, heading left.'

'Coming out now.'

23

The whole place was a building site, metal fences and machinery everywhere, and boards apologizing for any inconvenience during the construction of the high-speed Channel Tunnel rail link, 'Britain's Rail Gateway to Europe'. Immediately beyond it was the main, a brightly lit fucked-up mess of roadworks and traffic, clogged in both directions.

'They're crossing the first junction left, the road running alongside the station.'

I walked towards it, with Suzy still gobbing off in my ear. 'That's Grey and Navy now at McD's the other side of the junction left ... wait, wait ... target's intending right at the crossing, over the main, towards the island. The other two are going straight, he's crossing the main.'

I couldn't see her but that didn't matter: I could see the target through the crowds, lit up by the golden arches. He stood waiting obediently with a few others for the green man, then realized the traffic was so clogged he could cross anyway. He was aiming for the paved area in front of a three-storey derelict building, shaped like the bow of a ship and splitting the main into two separate roads.

'Stand by, stand by, he's towards the island now.'

I could see him, no more than sixty metres away, and could just hear Suzy over the traffic. 'I still have, still have. Held on the island. Intending the second road, still held.'

I headed across the junction left, past McDonald's, to the crossing that led to the island. I didn't have to watch him, she'd tell me what he was up to. I was looking ahead: Grey and Navy were taking the next option left further along the road, then disappearing.

'Stand by, stand by, lights green, now crossing. He's heading right . . . now on the pavement, he's gone right. Still unaware.'

I looked back towards the source just in time to see him disappear inside an over-lit Costcutter, a 24/7. We both sparked up simultaneously. 'Stop, stop, stop!'

I crossed on to the island and walked along the pavement to the left of the wedge-shaped building to get out of line of sight of Costcutter. Suzy still had eyes on. 'I've got the trigger, and can give direction once he goes foxtrot.'

'Roger that, mate. I'm on the dead side of the derelict building. The other two took the first option left past McDonald's. Wait . . .' I moved a little further along the road to get the street sign. 'That's Caledonian Road, Caledonian. I'll wait for your stand by.'

'Caledonian, OK.'

This had always been a sleazy, run-down area, a jumble of kebab, chip and burger joints, and corner shops selling porn. It was the home of down-and-outs, drug-dealers and their addicts, many of them prostitutes. The derelict building was boarded up, awaiting redevelopment, the chipboard sheets at street level covered with an already grimy artist's impression of a brave new world.

I could just make out Suzy again, above the impatient revving of engines. 'Stand by, stand by. That's him foxtrot, he's foxtrot. He's gone left, blue carrier-bag, your right with a blue carrier.'

I went back to the ship's bow. 'I have, I have.'

I was about twenty-five metres behind him. 'That's him approaching the first junction left.'

We were now walking along the main once more, opposite the station, when he disappeared. 'He's gone left, unsighted to me.'

'Roger that. I'm behind you, I'll try and parallel.'

'Roger that.' Suzy was going to try to find a road that ran parallel to the one the source had gone down.

I got to the junction and waited by the small police station on the corner. It looked like a converted corner shop with mirrored glass. 'Suzy, it's Birkenhead Street.'

'Roger that, Birkenhead. I'm behind you on Gray's Inn – it dog-legs after a hundred. I'm now parallel to Birkenhead.'

'Roger that.'

I crossed the road as if to go straight past the junction towards the flashing lights of the amusement arcade opposite the police station, and glanced left as arcade machine-gun fire and screams of death filtered through the doors. 'He's about half-way up Birkenhead. The street's about two hundred. At the top there's a T-junction. Must link left with Gray's Inn.'

'Roger that, I have a junction right. St Chad's Street – St Chad's. I'm going static, see if I can see him coming up to the T.'

I waited on the corner, wanting him to make a bit of distance before I followed. In any case, as soon as he reached that junction Suzy should know which way he was going. 'OK. Roger that. I still have, on the left on Birkenhead.'

Birkenhead was a street of Edwardian houses that had been converted into seedy private hotels. They all seemed to have identical net curtains and condensation on the windows, the sort of place you'd bring one of the station hookers if you didn't fancy an alleyway.

'Stop, stop, stop! What the fuck is he up to? Just short of the T junction.' He just stood there. 'Wait, wait . . . lighting up.'

'Roger that. I'm static by the snooker hall on Gray's Inn Road and have a view all the way down St Chad's.'

'Roger that. Still static, he's smoking.'

He stood with the carrier-bag in his left hand and his cigarette in the right. Why had he stopped so suddenly? Did he know he was being followed? If so, why didn't he look round to check? Was he waiting for someone?

'He's still static, smoking. He's head up, plane spotting or something. I haven't got a clue what he's up to.' He wasn't looking at the stars, that was for sure. The sky was the colour of mud.

Suzy came straight back. 'It's the CCTV. I can see a camera at the first junction, right on St Chad's. The camera is starting to move, the camera is—'

'Stand by, stand by. He's foxtrot.'

I stayed where I was. 'He's at the junction left. He's going left, towards you, he's going left.'

Suzy cut in just as he disappeared from my view. 'I have, I have. That's him now towards . . . No, that's stop, stop, stop! That's keys out. He's at a door, he's going complete. I'll walk past.'

'Roger that. I'll wait short of the junction and meet you there.'

I looked back at the railway station behind me, no more than fifty metres across the main, and could now see the reason why all three had held at the exit. At the first junction past WH Smith and Boots another CCTV camera was set high on a steel pole. It swivelled, then settled more or less directly facing the entrance to McD's.

I crossed back over Birkenhead to the side of the street he'd taken. The source had gone left. He'd been watching the camera, waiting for the right moment to make his move, like an escaping PoW timing the progress of a sentry.

I could hear Suzy's breathing in my earpiece as she moved along St Chad's. I stopped about five metres short of the junction, next to a steel-barred gate, about seven feet high and padlocked, that guarded the gap between two buildings. Through it I could see the rear of a three-storey block of flats, which formed the corner of Birkenhead and St Chad's, and also the back of the row of Edwardian houses that the source had gone into. Light spilled from the clear plastic sheeting of a small DIY conservatory on to a haphazard pattern of downpipes.

A light went on behind a droopy net in one of the top-floor windows, then the main curtains were pulled swiftly shut.

The camera began to turn with a gentle electric whine. I got my cell out and put it to my ear instead of using the hands-free, so anyone watching would see I had a reason for being there. 'The camera's on the move again.'

'I've got it.' There was a pause. 'The house is thirty-three. It's thirty-three. It's the one nearest the block of flats.'

'OK, thirty-three, got that. Just carry on round the corner and you'll see me.'

The camera focused on Birkenhead, which meant I must have been exposed below the street-lamp. I smiled broadly as Suzy came into view and held out her arms. We kissed, cuddled, and turned off our phones. The camera stayed where it was as I leant against the gate to give her a good look at the rear of the target house.

'Third floor.' I felt her head move on my shoulder as she looked up. 'See the crack of light between the curtains?'

'Yes.'

'It came on within a minute of him going into the house. It's got to be him, and he must be alone. Let's get clear of the camera. We'll turn right on to St Chad's.'

I held her hand as we walked across the road, under the camera. It didn't swivel to follow us. We couldn't see any more cameras ahead of us, just signs stuck on lamp-posts announcing that Neighbourhood Watch really worked.

She poked me in the arm. 'Hey, why did you say he could have my number? What's the matter with yours?'

'I'll tell you once we're back at the flat.'

Suzy took out her pack of nicotine gum and nodded towards

142

the red neon sign on a Chinese Methodist church as she lit up. 'Like being back on holiday.'

'Run out of B & H then?'

She turned and blew pretend smoke at me.

'I just wish the Yes Man had told us who the source was.' She put the pack away as she started chewing.

'He must know how much we love surprises.'

'You know what? I have a bad feeling about this so-called source. Boy terrorists, my arse – who does he think he is?'

'I thought you didn't care.'

She studied my face. She wasn't sure if I was taking the piss.

'"They serve a purpose," ' I mimicked. 'I don't care why they do it, as long as they do.'

She spat her half-chewed gum into the gutter, looking disgusted by it. 'Tastes shit. Listen, I reckon we need to be careful with him and those other two.'

I told her about Grey and Navy's haircuts and smooth faces. 'They could just have gone for a job lot at the barber's – or they've cut off not only their hair but also their beards to blend in. That may or may not be good for us.'

'Let's look on the bright side, yeah?'

As we passed the church, a figure stepped out from the shadows. He was a white guy in his early twenties, wearing a black leather jacket and ripped jeans. Even in this light I could see his eyes were bloodshot and wild. 'Oi, you want any whites or browns?' It sounded like a threat rather than this week's offer.

We didn't break step. 'We're all right, thanks, mate.' I shook my head. 'We don't want anything.'

He started following. 'Come with me, come down here.' His voice sounded like a tape-recorder with the batteries running low. 'Come on, come on.' He waved his hands towards the rear of the church. 'I got whites, I got browns, tenner a go.'

Suzy was sharper this time. 'Which bit of "no" don't you understand?'

He stopped and swayed. 'You taking the piss, slag? I'll rip

143

your fucking guts out.'

We kept walking but both kept him in sight, just in case this was going to get out of control. He slipped his right hand into his pocket. 'I'll cut you both. Fucking slag.'

Suzy laughed quietly as we carried straight on. She was right, we didn't want to attract any attention; it was better just to keep walking.

He wasn't going to follow us on to the main – it was clear he preferred the darkness. He just shouted instead, 'Fuck you, slag,' then laughed to himself. 'If you don't want 'em, I'll sell 'em to your fucking kids – your little girls would suck my cock for a baggy.'

Spinning on my heel, I headed straight back towards him, my face burning. I knew I shouldn't, but fuck it.

Suzy was close behind. 'Leave it, Nick, let's go. We're not here for that.' She came up level and grabbed my arm, trying to look into my eyes. 'Not now, mate, not now. We've got to go.'

The little bastard staggered back towards the side of the church, cackling like a hyena. 'Come on, then, fucking wankers . . .'

'For fuck's sake, Nick, what was that all about? I'm trying very hard at the moment to imagine you with a brain. If it's still in there, switch the fucking thing on.'

She dragged me down to the main and we headed west until we managed to flag down a cab.

24

The small red LED on the alarm panel blinked as I tapped in the eight digits so that we wouldn't disturb the QRF as they sat down to *The Bill*. Suzy was already past me and on her way to the fridge with our two bags of microwave food. We were becoming a proper little domestic couple.

I could see things had moved on efficiently while we were out. Yvette had dropped off the NBC kit: it was stacked on Suzy's bed, still in its vacuum-packed plastic bags. Sitting on the coffee-table in the living room was a brown cardboard box, about ten by eight, its lid open, filled to the brim with blister packs of shiny dark green capsules. I picked one up and turned it over. 'We've got the doxycycline.'

'Oh, great.' Suzy's voice drifted from the kitchen. 'Party time.'

Two cards of pills went into my back pocket; the bumbag and Browning went on top of the TV.

There were also two sets of keys and a handwritten note. 'The cars are in residents' parking. You fancy the Mondeo or the Peugeot?'

'Oh, come on, what do you think?'

Both of the cars would have been prepared for ops. Any

VDMs – such as a dealer's sticker in the rear window or scratches on the bodywork – would have been removed. The interior bulbs would have been taken out too so that we could work at night without being seen getting into and out of the vehicles. There would also be two rocker switches under the dash to cut out the brake and reversing lights.

The next item on the note was Yvette asking if I wanted someone to take my hire-car back. These people did know everything: there was no such thing as a personal life.

I fell on to the settee and hit the Sky remote control, scrolling the twenty-four-hour news channels to catch up on all the gloom and doom.

Suzy came in, munching her gum, not liking the taste at all. 'I'll get used to it, don't worry. We might as well load up the SD mags now, don't you think?'

I plugged my cell into the charger and followed her into the bedroom. She pulled the suitcase from under the bed, lifted out two clear plastic bags full of loose rounds and threw me a pair of surgical gloves.

I picked up one of the SDs and carried out NSPs by pulling back on the cocking piece at the top of the barrel and checking there were no rounds in the chamber, then letting the working parts go forward under their own steam and gently squeezing the trigger until I found the second pressure. It had a lot less play than the Browning, which would be a pain in the arse when we had bulky rubber NBC gloves on, plus the thin white cotton inners to soak up the sweat.

The pistol grip had a three-round-burst and single-shot selector on the safety catch. Push it down with your right thumb until the first click and it would only fire one round each time you squeezed the trigger. Push it down again as far as it would go and you'd fire a three-round burst.

If you ran out of ammunition with the original MP5, the working parts would still move forwards and lock into position as if it had collected a round from the magazine and rammed it into the chamber. Then you'd be left with a dead-man's click as you squeezed the trigger on an empty chamber. To change magazines you had to cock the weapon, reload, then slam down on the cocking handle to let the working parts move forward to pick up a round before you could resume firing. A pain in the arse, especially if you had people firing at you.

These MP5 SDs worked the same way as M16 assault rifles and all semi-automatic pistols: after the last round was fired, the working parts remained to the rear. All you had to do was replace the magazine and hit the release lever. It made life just a little bit simpler, and I was all for that.

What I liked most, however, was the HDS [holographic diffraction sight]. The heads-up sight was just like a tiny TV screen. I pressed the right-hand button just below the screen and Suzy looked over to see what I was up to. 'Ever used one of these before?'

She nodded. 'Last year. Nothing exciting, just took out some street-lights and a dog the night before going into an office block. Good kit, isn't it?'

'That's the understatement of the century.'

I brought the weapon into the aim: the bedside lamp was about to get the good news. The heads-up inside the screen was a dull white light, in the middle of which was a circle with a dot in its centre. The light couldn't be seen from the barrel end of the weapon. Hitting rapidly moving or multiple targets in a closed environment couldn't be easier. It was a bit like taking a picture with a digital camera – you could keep both eyes open, but lock the sight on to a target as quickly as you saw it, even through the eyepieces of a respirator.

A lot of people didn't like these things, but I did. If you're firing in CQB [close quarter battle] conditions, both eyes have to be open: you've got to be able to see all the threats around you, all the time.

I turned off the HDS and started to load the thirty-round magazines. I couldn't tell by the markings, but I hoped they were subsonic rounds. The SDs would work with high-velocity rounds, but the power of the gases that propelled them could blow out the baffles and produce a normal muzzle report. I supposed we'd be finding out soon enough.

We sat together on the bed. 'A bit like old times, this,' Suzy said. 'Like being back in the Det.'

I stopped what I was doing and watched her for a moment. For me, this was never more than a job: at best, it delivered a regular flow of cash, at worst, it stopped me from having to pay attention to a lot of shit that I'd spent my whole life running away from. Keeping that lid on, as the all-knowing Josh would say. For her, it was something different. I was curious. 'How come you're so sure you're going to get permanent cadre?'

She didn't look at me, and kept on feeding in the rounds. There seemed to be a bit of pride at stake here as to who could do it quicker. She shrugged. 'Because I'm good and I'm committed, and because I've been told I'm going to get it.'

'By the Yes Man?'

'Yeah. By the end of the year, he said, but who knows after this job? What's your story? You get approached while you were in the Det?'

'No, after I'd left the Regiment.'

She seemed surprised.

'I know, I know. Sad but true. I left in 'ninety-three, then worked for the guy who ran the desk before the Yes Man.'

'Colonel Lynn? I worked for him too. You ever get permanent cadre?'

My hand went into the bag and grabbed another half-dozen shiny brass rounds. 'What do you think?'

'That the reason you moved?'

'No, I did just the one job for the Yes Man a couple of years ago, and we didn't really get on. Like I said, I was made a better offer in the States.'

'So why are you here?'

'Because somewhere along the line I ran out of choices. But enough of my shit. Why are you?'

'Well . . .' She stopped loading her magazine and looked up. 'I want to do other things, another life, but deep down I know it just wouldn't work. You know what I mean, don't you?'

'What're you going to be when you grow up?'

Now she smiled. 'Yeah, that's right. Dunno. You?'

'Haven't really thought about it. They keep telling me I'll be kept on until I'm killed or they get somebody better.'

We both fell silent and the gentle click of rounds and the sound of her chewing took over.

'Suzy, I need a favour.'

She just carried on.

'I've got to do some stuff between about ten and twelve thirty. That's why I gave the source your number, because you'll be on it all the time.'

'The boss said sort the child business out by three o'clock, Nick – I was only in the kitchen, wasn't I? I wasn't listening – you know the difference, don't you? The child, is it yours?'

'Look, I got the call in the middle of my holiday, and I've got to sort just a little more of my shit out – and hers.'

She stopped loading again. 'Are you married? Can't her mother do it?'

'No, she can't. And the Yes Man doesn't need to know. Two and a half hours tomorrow morning, and it's done. I'll only be twenty minutes away.'

She looked at me with what I guessed was something close to pity, and went back to loading. 'Don't fuck this up, Nick. I'm doing it for her, whoever she is.'

'Thanks.'

It wasn't long before we were both finished and she announced she was going to take a shower. I checked traser: it was just after eleven p.m., which would make it sixish in Maryland. I got my own cell from my bumbag in the front room and took it into the kitchen. Cradling it beneath my ear, I filled the kettle.

The plumbing's reaction time was lightning fast. 'Bastard!'

It made me smile, anyway.

The phone kept on ringing, then a smily version of Josh

came on the answer-machine. 'Hey there, you know what to do: just let God bless you.'

I put the phone down. Of course, he was away until Saturday on the happy-clappy thing with his kids. Kelly wouldn't be able to fly back until Sunday because Josh had to be there to pick her up. Shit.

The kettle boiled, and a few seconds later Suzy came out of the bathroom wrapped in a big fluffy green towel, followed by a cloud of steam. She pulled her hair back as she walked the few steps down the corridor to the bedroom, giving me the V sign all the way.

'Fancy a brew?'

'Yeah, arsehole.'

She only part closed the bedroom door behind her, and I didn't try too hard to look away as she dried herself and walked to and from the wardrobe; she still had her bikini line from Penang.

'Don't think I can't see what you're up to, you sad little man. Get on with the brews.'

I turned back to the kettle. 'You been spending some time at the electric beach?'

Her laughter bounced out into the hallway. 'In your dreams, mate. In your dreams.'

By the time she came to join me in the front room, I was munching a very cold sausage roll, watching the pastry crumble on to my jeans and gather in a pile on the carpet. Her hair was combed back and she was in the same jeans and trainers, but now with a blue sweatshirt and fleece. She bent down near me to take one of the mugs. The smell of her shower gel reminded me that I really did need to keep the gun oil off my boxers. I had no other clothes.

She sat down and I threw her a card of doxycycline. I'd taken two capsules out of my own. 'How many should we be taking?' I swallowed them both with small sips of tea.

She wasn't too sure. 'I'll take mine with some food. They give me a stomach ache on their own.'

'Want some?' I offered her half of the sausage roll, but she waved her blister pack at me with a look of utter disgust.

'Why did you rev up like that with the drug head? It looked pretty personal . . .'

'I just hate those fuckers.' I tried to conjure up a smile. 'I hate it that they're making more money than me.'

'Hey, Nick, I'm not the enemy. I won't tell anyone – I'm covering for you tomorrow, remember.'

I pushed a bit of pastry that was hanging on my lips into my mouth and pressed out another two capsules. 'Yeah, OK. The child's got problems, and I thought I was going to be able to sort everything out here, but then I got the call and—'

'It's OK, Nick, that's all I want to know. Personal stuff, remember.' She got up and disappeared into the hallway. Just before she closed the bedroom door she said, 'Good luck tomorrow, Nick. Just make sure you keep the fucking phone on.'

Later that night I lay on the settee under a couple of blankets, but I couldn't sleep. I couldn't shake off thoughts of the nightmare that tomorrow morning was going to bring. She was going to be devastated to be sent home just when she was getting somewhere with Hughes – and just when she and I were establishing some kind of connection again. But, fuck it, at least she'd be alive. If this ASU really got going, the consequences didn't bear thinking about – for all of us.

25

Saturday 10 May, 08:55 hrs

I'd got as far as the door when she called from the kitchen, 'Remember what I said – keep the phone on, yeah?' I had it half open when she appeared in the hall with a bowl of bran, her jaws working overtime. 'Hope it all goes well – you know . . .'

I went down the stairs, checking my inside jacket pocket. My hand connected with the carrier-bag last night's dinner had come in; it now contained ten packs of doxycycline.

I was going to leave the Mondeo where it was. The UK is the largest user of CCTV in the world. There's so much coverage in London linked to numberplate-recognition technology that the Yes Man would know immediately where I was going and might even be waiting for me when I arrived. The addition of eight hundred congestion-charge cameras was the final nail in the coffin. Ken Livingstone kept saying that they'd wipe all information at the end of each day, and maybe they would – but not necessarily before they'd passed it on to the Firm, Special Branch and anyone else who wanted to know about our lives. Even on foot around here the fucking things could capture the average person on film at least once every five minutes. Many of the cameras were 'smart CCTV', combining video surveillance with facial-recognition technology, searching one million faceprints per second.

My own cell was turned off, but the moan-phone stayed on as promised. Because it was on secure, I knew it couldn't be tracked – but I knew that wouldn't stop them trying.

I took a taxi to Chelsea and spent the entire journey grappling with how best to break the news to Kelly. At the turn-off for the Moorings I realized I was most of an hour early, so got the driver to take me the few hundred yards back up the road to Sloane Square. I went into WH Smith and bought a Jiffy-bag, a Bic and a book of stamps. Sealing the antibiotics inside, I wandered down Kings Road to the post office. Addressed to myself care of Jimmy and Carmen, and with enough stamps on to get it to the South Pole, the Jiffy finally made its way through the appropriate hole in the wall.

There were still another forty-five minutes to kill, so I walked into Next and bought a pile of underwear, socks, sweatshirts and jeans. It must have been the quickest three hundred pounds they'd taken in a long time. My disposable life hadn't changed much. I still didn't own many things; I just used kit and then binned it, whether it was razor blades, toothbrushes or clothes. The apartment in Crystal City was bare, apart from three sets of sheets, towels and jeans: one clean, one on, and one in the wash. Well, that was the theory: it all depended on whether I'd get the machine repaired. The rest – a second pair of boots and some trainers, a couple of shirts, a few bits of crockery and a job lot of house stuff from a cable TV channel – I didn't really need. It wasn't as if I was entertaining every night. That was how I'd landed up buying it in the first place.

I got to the Moorings on time but the others hadn't arrived. The receptionist hadn't received any calls to say they were going to be late so I called the bungalow from her phone, but all I got was the BT messaging service. Carmen was always fucking up answering-machines by pressing the wrong buttons. Letting BT take care of it made much more sense.

153

Dr Hughes came into the waiting room with a smile on her face that made me think she'd been expecting Kelly rather than me.

'Her grandparents are bringing her.' I smiled back. 'Maybe they're caught in the traffic.'

She nodded. 'No matter, we'll just sit and wait awhile, shall we? What would you say to a cup of tea? Catherine, could you organize that for us?'

No wonder Kelly felt safe with her. She might have stern hair, but there was something about her, some kind of soothing aura, that made it impossible not to relax in her company.

'Dr Hughes, I need to have a word with you. I'm afraid things have changed.'

'By all means, Mr Stone. Do sit down.'

We sat at either side of the coffee-table, her half-moons nearly falling off the end of her nose as she gave me her full attention.

'Kelly will be going back to the US tomorrow, so unfortunately this is going to be the last time she can come.'

Her expression didn't change, but I heard the concern in her voice. 'Are you sure that's wise? She still has a—'

I cut in with a shake of the head. 'I'll be quite happy to pay for what time we have booked and anything else I owe you. I really do appreciate all you've done for us, in the past and, of course, now, and I'd be very grateful if you would still recommend someone to help sort things out for her in the States.'

She seemed to know it was pointless taking the conversation further. 'Very well, Mr Stone, I understand. Your work again, I presume?' The tone was sympathetic, not accusing.

I nodded. We'd been through a lot together, Dr Hughes and me. Three years and tens of thousands of pounds ago, I'd turned up at her clinic with Kelly in pieces. She was like a big bucket with holes – everything was going in, but then it just dripped out again. At boarding-school, before she went to live with Josh, she started to complain about 'pains', but could

154

never be more specific or explain exactly where they were. It slowly got worse, Kelly gradually withdrawing from her friends, her teachers, her grandparents, me. She wouldn't talk or play any more; she just watched TV, sat in a sulk, or sobbed. My usual response had been to go and get ice cream. I knew that wasn't the answer, but I didn't know what was.

One particular night, in Norfolk, she'd been particularly distant and detached, and nothing I did seemed to engage her. I felt like a schoolkid jumping around a fight in the playground, not really knowing what to do: join in, stop it or just run away. That was when I nailed the tent down in her room and we played camping. She woke much later with terrible nightmares. Her screaming lasted until dawn. I tried to calm her, but she just lashed out at me as if she was having a fit. The next morning, I made a few phone calls, and found out there was a six-month waiting list for an NHS appointment, and even then I'd be lucky if it helped. I made more calls and took her to see Dr Hughes the same afternoon.

I'd had some understanding of Kelly's condition, but only some. I knew men who'd suffered with post-traumatic stress disorder, but they were big boys who'd been to war. Hughes told me it was natural for a child to go through a grieving process after a loss – but sometimes, after a sudden traumatic event, the feelings could surface weeks, months or even years later. This delayed reaction was PTSD, and the symptoms were similar to those associated with depression and anxiety: emotional numbness, feelings of helplessness, hopelessness and despair, and reliving the traumatic experience in nightmares – exactly what had happened to me at Hunting Bear Path.

Hughes's diagnosis rang so true, but then, as I was to discover, just about everything she ever said rang true. Kelly hadn't fully recovered from the events of 1997, and I didn't know whether she ever would. Seeing your whole family head-jobbed took some recovering from. But she was a fighter, just like her dad had been, and had made dramatic strides.

Under Hughes's care, she'd moved from being a curled-up bundle of nothing to being able to function in the big bad world. It was just a fucker that that world was full of sex, exams, boys and drugs, all conspiring to send her back down the black hole it had taken her so long to escape from.

26

There was a gentle knock on the door before it opened and the receptionist popped her head round. 'Kelly's here.' We stood up as Dr Hughes put her special smily face back on.

'Dr Hughes, I haven't told her yet, and I want to myself later today.'

Kelly came in, apologizing. 'The taxi driver didn't know the way. He had to get his book out.'

Carmen and Jimmy were still in the reception area, and I could hear Jimmy getting a hard time. Carmen was somehow managing to make the driver's incompetence his fault. I sneaked a look at the new plaster on Kelly's right hand.

'Shall we go up, then, Kelly?' Hughes had an arm out to usher her away. 'There's still quite a bit of time left.'

Kelly looked pleased, then gave me a raised eyebrow. 'Are you going to be here?'

I nodded. 'See you in a bit.'

I got a slight smile from her as they left the room. I didn't know whether she was pleased to see me or just glad to escape from those two for the best part of an hour.

Jimmy looked relieved as I walked into Reception. He always made the mistake of assuming there was safety in numbers. I opened the door for them. 'Shall we go for a cup of tea round the corner? It's pointless waiting here, isn't it?'

Jimmy was up for it but we had to wait for Carmen to agree. Eventually we walked along to the main and found a table in a pretend French café staffed entirely by Croatians.

'Have any letters come for me yet?'

She shook her head while studying the menu. 'No, but we left before the post. It's such a long way, you know. That stupid man didn't know where he was. Don't they have to sit a test? Look at these prices – one fifty for a cup of tea.'

Jimmy nodded his thanks to the waitress as she wrote down our order and took it to the counter. We all went back to studying our menus, already stumped for conversation.

The girl rescued us a few minutes later by returning and plonking down two teas and a coffee for me. I pushed two antibiotic tablets through the foil of the card, which didn't escape Carmen's eye. 'I've got a cold coming on,' I said. 'Just trying to knock it on the head.'

'As long as you don't knock it in my direction. I've only just got over one. Well, it was more flu, wasn't it, Jimmy?'

Jimmy sparked up. 'I think it's just black-cab drivers, dear. Our one was a minicab.'

'Well, they should have to do the test too.' She turned and gave me a theatrical aside. 'He's going deaf, but he won't admit it. I told him to see the doctor, but, oh, no . . .'

I swallowed the first pill with a sip of frothy coffee. I bet he was deaf. I would have been in his position. 'There might be another letter coming to you,' I said. 'It's not important, I can always come and pick it up after I've finished this work.' I scooped a bit more of the froth from the top of the brew to help the pill down. There was no point putting this off any longer. It was time to cut to the chase. 'Carmen and Jimmy, I've got some disappointing news. Kelly's got to go back to the States tomorrow.'

'But—'

'I know, I know, but I'm going to be working for longer than

I thought. Dr Hughes is already finding somebody in the States for Kelly, so that's a good thing.'

'Surely it's not a good idea to chop and change—'

'What I need,' I cut across whatever she was going to say, 'is for you to change her flight. Can you do that for her?'

'Oh, but we haven't got that sort of money.' No problem was too small to escape Carmen's radar.

'If you just change it, I'll pay any extras with my card, I'll phone them with my details. It's just I haven't got time to do the organizing, and she has her ticket. I have to start work at twelve.'

'How do we do that?'

'Have you got a pen?'

She fished in her bag and I wrote, 'London Heathrow to Baltimore American Airlines; Sunday 13th', on a paper napkin.

'That's all they'll need to know,' I said. 'Give them her ticket and they'll do the rest. Just call American, the numbers are on the ticket. If they can't do it, just book any airline to Baltimore for tomorrow. Any travel agent will do it for you. Tell them that once they've got a seat reserved I'll phone in and get everything squared away.'

I was removing obstacles before Carmen could zero in on them, but she was still looking like she'd swallowed a wasp. 'When are you going to tell her? It'll upset her even more, you know, the poor mite.'

'I know. In a minute.'

Almost unconsciously I checked the signal on the phone, and Carmen looked even more anxious. 'Do you have to go?'

I was tempted to say yes and just bin her, but the Croatian coffee was good. And for all Carmen's faults, Kelly loved her, which was why I'd posted the antibiotics for them in case there was a drama once Kelly had got away safely.

We all lifted our cups and drank in uncomfortable silence. Jimmy fidgeted with his spoon and Carmen looked at the traffic outside one moment and back at me the next, as if she was trying to say something but couldn't find the words, which wasn't a problem she normally had.

A minute or two later I was finished and went to dig out my wallet.

'Oh, no, we'll see to this – won't we, Jimmy?'

I smiled. 'Thanks. Well, I suppose we'd better—'

'Nick?' Carmen's hand was on my arm. 'There's something I'd like to ask you. Before you go. In case, you know . . .' She was still struggling.

Oh, fuck. Please don't let them be asking for money.

'I – well, we, Jimmy and I – there's something we'd like to ask you. It's about Kevin.' She spent some time trying to clear her throat. 'He never told us what he did, but we could guess. It was the same sort of job you do, wasn't it?'

This was difficult. If Kev had chosen not to tell them, why should I? What the fuck. 'Yes, sort of.'

'It was for the government, wasn't it?'

'Yes.'

Carmen smiled, and Jimmy looked as if he was going to burst with pride. 'We thought as much.' Then her smile faded. 'Nick, that's why we worry so much. Look, we've had our differences, but we know that deep down you care for Kelly and want the best for her. We do know that, and we understand that you don't have the sort of job you can say no to when they call you. It can't be easy for you, trying to juggle all these things at once.'

I opened my mouth but Carmen hadn't finished. 'There's something else, Nick. It's embarrassing for us to say this because we're her grandparents, but you see, well, the truth is we're not really up to looking after her – not for more than a day or two at a time, anyway. We love her dearly, of course, but it's just too much of a strain. We can't bear to see her so unwell, needing a psychiatrist and so on. If anything happened to you and Josh, well, we just don't think we could cope with her ourselves, and then what? And Kelly – what about her if something happens to you? I'm sure Josh would do his best, but how would Kelly survive, having to go through it all a second time? I know you think we're just silly old fools, but we do worry. We worry about it all the time.'

It was my turn to look away. 'I guess it's not easy for any of us, eh? But things will get better. Kelly will start her treatment in the States, I'll be with her again in two or three weeks. As soon as we can, we'll come back over. It'll be like none of this ever happened.'

She looked at me expectantly. I wasn't sure what to do, so I just stood up. They both smiled uncomfortably before Jimmy stammered, 'We— we're g-getting a black cab back, so he should know the way.'

I thought I'd leave them to it. 'Tell you what, you two stay here and I'll go and pick up Kelly, OK? It'll give me a moment to talk to her. I'll leave my bags.' I got a smile from both of them as I turned and walked away, but with the exception of Kelly, I didn't think I'd ever seen people look so lonely.

27

There was going to be no easy way to tell her. In the past I'd just have lied, but somehow I couldn't do it any more.

I checked the signal again as I walked into the waiting room and sat down with a magazine. It wasn't long before Kelly emerged with Dr Hughes. She said her short goodbyes to the doctor, thinking that she was going to see her on Tuesday. 'Where's Granny and Gramps?'

'They're having a cup of tea round the corner. Fancy one?'

We came out into the April sun and I psyched myself up – but Kelly got there first. 'Nick, can I tell you something?'

'Of course. Unless it's something horrible about me.'

A smile flickered across her face, then a more serious look. 'I want to tell you what Dr Hughes and I have been talking about. She's so brilliant, Nick. I can tell her everything and it's like she really understands. It's like chilling out with Vronnie, only her advice makes sense.'

I took her hand and squeezed it. She probably thought it was because I was pleased with her or something. She looked up into my eyes. 'The thing is, Nick, I've been, well, not all the time, but I've been making myself sick.'

I resisted the urge to look away. I didn't want her to think I was disgusted with her, or that I already knew. If I was disgusted with anyone, it was myself. 'Really? Why have you done that?'

'Well, you know about my gymnastics, right? We get together and count each other's ribs, and if they're hard to count that means we're too big. Vronnie's in gymnastics too, and one day she pinched my side and got hold of some fat, and it just totally freaked me out. I made myself sick after dinner that night and it was horrible, but I did it again and it wasn't too bad, and now it's not that hard to do at all.'

I didn't know how to respond. I just couldn't believe the timing.

I felt like Carmen, struggling to find the right words. 'Are you going to tell Granny and Gramps?'

She looked at the ground and shook her head. 'I don't think so, do you?'

'Probably not. What about Josh?'

'What do you think?'

'I know you probably don't want to, but he loves you and he's really trying to help.'

'Yeah, I suppose.'

And then I took a deep breath. 'Kelly, I've got a drama . . .' I felt her hand stiffen in mine. She knew what was coming. 'I've got to go away. Yes, it's work. I've thought about it, and I reckon it's best that you go back early. Josh and everyone are back later today, so if you went tomorrow—'

She pulled her hand away. 'But I'm due at Dr Hughes's on Tuesday, right?'

'I've told Dr Hughes, she knows you're leaving tomorrow. I asked her not to say anything because I wanted to tell you myself. Look, you're better off getting back to the States and starting with whoever she's organizing to help you.'

'But I want to come back on Tuesday.' Her voice quavered. She stared at me, tears welling and just starting to fall down her face. 'I want to see her, I need to see her, she's the only one who—'

163

'It's better this way. You'll just be starting with the person she recommends a little early.'

'How am I supposed to get better when you keep doing this to me?' She moved her head sadly from side to side. 'You say you want to be with me, but you don't. You don't understand . . .'

'Be fair – how can I get to understand if you don't tell me what's happening?'

Her tears had stopped and her body stopped moving. 'But I have now, haven't I? You're still leaving.'

Shit, she had me on that one. 'Look, going home now means you can start seeing another therapist all the sooner. We were only ever going to be here for a short while, and Dr Hughes has done well, hasn't she? I mean, look what you've been able to talk about. Now we have a good base to work from back home. Isn't that for the best?'

Bastard! The cell rang and Kelly put on her most sarcastic voice. 'Hello, work calling. Hello, work calling.'

I hit the key, then rehashed it. Suzy was out on the street. 'He's called and we've a meet in an hour and forty-five.'

I put on a happy voice. 'OK. I'll call you back in a few minutes.'

Her voice was full of tension. 'Do you understand? I'm leaving now for Starbucks. You need to be there – don't let me down.'

'Yes, I've got that. I'll talk to you in a minute.' I cut the phone and looked down at Kelly. 'I know, I know. I've got to go in a minute. I'm sorry, but I can't help it. I'll call you later.'

We stood on the pavement outside the café. 'Granny and Gramps are inside.' I opened the door and we went in. Kelly took the conversation out of my hands. 'Nick has to go to work now, don't you, Nick?'

I looked down at her. 'We'll talk later about . . . you know, what we just talked about. OK?'

She nodded weakly as she accepted my hug. 'OK.'

As soon as I was outside with my bags I got back on to the

164

phone. 'Suzy, pick me up, will you? I'll meet you in Sloane Square, the bus stop outside WH Smith.'

'Better be there.'

The phone went dead and I walked up to the square, still trying to convince myself that I was doing the right thing. But, then, I'd spent most of my life doing that, and wasn't sure I'd ever won the argument.

28

Suzy was late. It shouldn't have taken her so long. I was waiting against the Smith's window with my shopping bags piled up at my feet, concentrating on the vehicles coming from my right on the one-way circuit round the square. While I looked out for Suzy, I took a mental note of every female driver of about her age, as well as the model of their car, its colour and registration number – anything to stop me thinking about Kelly.

I checked traser again and pulled out the moan-phone. 'Where the fuck are you?'

'Nearly there. Gimme two.'

I got out my own cell and dialled Josh, just in case they'd got back early. If so, I'd be waking the house – they were five hours behind. But all I got was his answerphone.

I spotted the Peugeot 206 first, a shiny silver thing straight from the showroom, then Suzy's hair flying round as her head swung from side to side, looking for me. She saw me and swerved, her right hand on the wheel as her left changed down, and a cabbie hit his horn as he moved to avoid her. I stepped out on to the pavement and waved to her, then went back and gathered up my shopping.

I did a smily 'Hello, how are you?' as I opened the door and climbed in, dumping the bags in the back as she responded with her pleased-to-see-you routine.

'Fucking traffic.' She chewed hard on her gum. 'We gotta get a move on.'

We nudged out into the flow, following the clockwise route round Sloane Square, and immediately had to stop at the lights. 'Phone the boss, will you, Nick? Tell him what's happening. I waited in case he wanted to talk to you.'

'Can't you do it?'

'What – and break the law?' She lifted both hands from the wheel. 'Go on, you like him, really.'

I pulled out the moan-phone from the bumbag and dialled.

He answered with a gruff 'What?' The Yes Man had only wrong sides on his bed, and the moan-phone lived up to its name.

'It's Nick.'

'Well?'

'We've got a meet in just under an hour. We're on our—'

'Call me back when you've finished with him.' The phone went dead.

'There, you see?' She shrugged her left shoulder and lifted a hand. 'That didn't hurt, did it?'

I didn't answer, instead concentrated on putting the moan-phone back in the bumbag.

'Just because I'm right. Anyway, what did he say?'

'We've got to call back with a sit rep afterwards.'

She checked her watch. 'I brought all the kit with me – there's two ops bags in the back. I reckoned it's better with us than back at the flat. Another blast from the past, eh?'

She was talking about the stuff that sat in the back of our cars when we went out on ops with the Det: a set of Gore-Tex, including boots, warm-weather kit, wellington boots, Mars bars rewrapped in clingfilm to cut down on noise, and a weapon. A lot of us chose the G3, a 7.62 assault rifle with a fixed butt so you could take good, sturdy, long-range shots, rather than collapsible stocks that tend to move about. It would have been my weapon of choice for this job, too, but the SDs in the boot would do just fine.

We left the square and headed east. Suzy nodded as we drove by Victoria station. 'Look, they're busy again.' Parked at the roadside ahead of us were two unmarked police cars. The occupants looked nonchalant enough, but the sunlight glinted on the blue lights hidden behind their plastic radiator grilles.

I hit the radio and got a phone-in about post-conflict Iraq. Suzy powered down her window. 'Were you in Gulf War One?' She spat out the gum. 'You know, with the Regiment?'

'Yeah, looking for scud and stuff. It was the last time I wore NBC kit. Even then I wasn't too sure what to do with it.'

The window got powered up and she laughed. 'Come on, you know how to use this shit, don't you? You want me to—'

'I know – sort of. Not that it mattered much then. I reckoned that if I was in the middle of getting zapped with anthrax or whatever, trying to pull one of those things on was definitely shutting the stable door after the horse had bolted.'

'But they work.'

'Sure, but the fucking things also start to fall apart after a day. The only benefit I ever got from mine was that it kept me warm at night. But this time,' I levelled my hand above my head, 'I'm going to be up to here in charcoal and rubber.'

Twenty minutes later we found a parking space in Smithfield. I pumped in enough coins to take the whole two hours on the meter while Suzy put my shopping bags with the rest of the kit and locked up. The congestion charge wasn't a worry for us because the cover company paid a yearly fee, but getting towed away would ruin our day. Those guys just slap on a ticket and the tow truck is there in quick time. We both double-checked inside the Peugeot before moving off.

'Same as before?'

She nodded, extracting some more gum from her bag, and I dialled her phone to check comms. She pushed the hands-free into her ear and I waved her goodbye with a smile as we passed Starbucks and she went inside. There were fifteen minutes to go until the RV.

The pub wasn't as packed as last time. I got myself a Coke, and could hear the Starbucks espresso machine gurgling and gasping in my ear as I headed for a seat back from the window. Over the sound of soft violin music Suzy ordered two cappuccinos. A minute or so later she sparked up. 'Hello, I'm facing the main door, half-way up on the left.'

'That's me in position too.'

With three or four minutes to go a familiar face came out of the station and turned left, towards me. 'Hello, stand by, Navy is here, same jacket on jeans. Approaching Turnmill.'

'OK, that's great, I'll see you soon, then.'

Navy crossed the junction and looked into the pub as he passed. At that moment, things got even more interesting. 'Here we go, Suzy. Our man is out of the station, towards me, same raincoat, now on. Grey is behind him, still suede on jeans, crossing over the road. Both heading your way.'

'Yep, got it, just seen Navy pass. See you soon.'

The source walked past the pub, doing a good job of blending in with the world around him.

'They've just passed me.'

'OK, I've got that.' Suzy spoke as if she was chatting to her mum about the prices in Sainsbury's. I could still hear the violin music, and also catch some loud Italian gobbing off over the counter as people ordered coffee. Then an edge of concern crept into her voice. 'Why don't you come and have your coffee now?' Maybe she'd seen something.

'You OK?'

'Don't trust him, that's all.'

29

I could hear Suzy talking to the source as I left the pub. 'Oh, hello – I didn't expect to see you here.' I could just imagine them exchanging surprised smiles. I heard the scrape of chairs, and by then I was passing the front window. I glanced to my left. They were both seated at the table Suzy had described. She was in a leather chair and he was perched on a stool, facing her with his back towards me.

I carried on past, turning left just a few metres later, and down the alleyway. As I came out into the square I made sure I kept looking dead ahead. Out of the corner of my eye, off to my half-right, I caught Navy, sitting on one of the steel benches. He was eating a sandwich, alongside a group enjoying their lunchtime break.

I went in through the glass door and Suzy flashed me a smile. The two women next door to her looked up nosily to see who'd come in, then settled back to their gossip. I pulled up a seat next to Suzy and faced the source.

Suzy took charge. 'We're here for the same reason as last time, OK? Any problems, we're going to go out the back way, and I want you—'

She was pointing at the source, but before she could

complete her sentence I cut in: 'No, we'll go out the front door, he goes out the back.'

She knew better than to ask why just now; she could do that later. 'OK, that's what we'll do.' Then, with a smile, as if she was asking him to pass her the sugar, she said, 'So, what do you have for us?' She leant forward and took a sip of coffee, and I did the same.

The source also leant forward, and started playing with his sachet of sugar. 'The ASU – I know where they are.'

I said, 'Do they have what we want?'

'Of course.'

We waited for him to carry on, but there was nothing. He just played with the sachet on the tabletop with his massive hands. I wondered what he really did for a living.

Suzy had soon had enough. 'Well, where are they?'

He looked up sharply. 'Why did you follow me last night? You could have just asked me.'

'Why have you got two men outside if you're on your own? Who's following who?'

He quite liked that, sitting back a little and taking a sip of his coffee while he thought it over. 'The terrorism you're dealing with now, the kind I know, it's not about tactical attacks to get a government to the bargaining table. It's about killing as many people as possible. You're now fighting men and women who pray five times a day to die a noble death.' He paused for effect. '"As you kill us, we kill you."'

I raised my hands. 'Hey, listen, whatever.'

'You people know nothing. You're all about now, all about nine/eleven. You have no understanding of history. You talk about *jihad*ists as if they inhabit a world where time is compressed, and all the murders and wrongs that their people have suffered for hundreds of years can be righted with just a few years of martyrdom. This is just the beginning of the third wave . . .'

'Where are they?' Suzy was getting as pissed off as me, but was starting to show it. He liked that. He closed his

171

eyes. 'They're in a city called King's Lynn.'

Suzy looked surprised. 'What? East Anglia?'

He hunched his shoulders with irritation, went back to the sugar. 'How do I know where it is? All I know is that's where they are.'

'Is that all you've got?' I said. 'It's a big place.'

His eyes swivelled. They were so bloodshot I thought they might fall out of their sockets. 'The house is in Sir Lewis Street. Number eighty-eight.'

'How many are there?'

'I don't know anything else. Nothing.'

I continued to hover over my cup. 'Are they armed?'

'Enough! I've told you everything I know.'

Suzy had one other question. 'How did you find out about King's Lynn?'

Without answering, he stood up, made his polite goodbyes for the sake of appearances, and left via the back door.

I nodded at him. 'That's where Navy was as I came in.'

A pen came out of her bag and she wrote down the King's Lynn details before we left through the front door and walked towards the car. I tapped her bag. 'Better give a sit rep.'

'Don't you want to?'

'Nah. My horoscope advised me to minimize communication with arsewipes.'

She powered up and made the call as we walked through Smithfield. 'We've just had the meet.' There was a pause. 'King's Lynn.' Another pause. 'Yes, that's right. Eighty-eight Sir Lewis Street.' She shook her head. 'I don't know, maybe four or five hours?' She nodded. 'Yes, sir.'

I held up three fingers and mouthed three.

'Sir, we should be there in three hours.' It was a while before she could get another word in edgeways. 'OK, sir, yes, we will.'

I beckoned the phone over.

'Sir, Nick wants to talk.' She handed it to me.

'What is it?'

172

'What do we know about the source? Is this int reliable – is he reliable? It sounds bullshit to me. Only yesterday he was telling us how hard it is for him. Why should we rush up there on what could turn out to be—'

'Because no matter how unreliable the information or even he may or may not be, there is no other option. So, until the decision is made to inform others about this, you will rush wherever I want you to. Do you understand?'

'Yes.'

The line went dead.

'You know King's Lynn, then? You don't sound like a Norfolk boy.'

I ignored her and told her what the Yes Man had said as we got to the car. She rubbed her hands with what looked almost like excitement. 'Which way, then?'

'Just get us to the M11.'

We stopped at a garage once we were on the North Circular and bought sandwiches and a bottle of Coke for me, and four apples and a yoghurt for her. Eventually we got on to the motorway towards Cambridge. I'd been brooding about the reasons the ASU might have chosen Norfolk, and it suddenly dawned on me. 'If Fuck-face back there is right, King's Lynn could make sense.'

She took her eyes off the road for a second and turned to look at me through her light blue sunglasses.

'The train goes direct from there to Liverpool Street and King's Cross. Good stand-off location, considering the state of alert around the City.'

'So they'd rig everything up in King's Lynn, take the train to King's Cross, and start sprinkling – maybe even splash some about on the way?' Suzy indicated to overtake a truck. 'But wouldn't a few Malaysians, Chinese or whatever stick out up there?'

What did I know? 'There are some docks up there, and one or two takeaways. Fuck-face better be right.'

We left the motorway and began to drive through the

flat, boring fields of Cambridgeshire. I got the blister pack out of my jeans and threw two more capsules down my neck mixed with by now very warm Coke, then waved it at Suzy.

She shook her head. 'Had some before picking you up. Listen, maybe Fuck-face knows the ASU, maybe he's taken the train up – that's why he's staying in St Chad's? Whatever – if he's right, we get this done quick, you get to sort your shit out, and I get to be in the cadre, know what I mean?'

She nodded away as I pushed the antibiotics into my back pocket, then obviously decided it was time to get off the subject of Fuck-face. 'So what's her name, then? How old is she?'

Ignoring the question, I got myself comfortable, but she wasn't giving up. 'Come on, I know you want to tell me. Besides, we may not see each other after tomorrow if Fuck-face is right, eh?' She turned back to the road and gave me some space.

'Kelly . . . Her name is Kelly, and she's fourteen.'

'She's not your daughter?'

'No, I sort of look after her.'

'She could have worse, I suppose.'

A sign whizzed past – 'King's Lynn 42' – and what seemed like twenty miles later another said, '38'. The road was elevated in places and there were dykes either side, waterways draining the fenland, and miles and miles of jet-black earth growing spuds or carrots or whatever.

'So, foster-dad, step-parent, whatever you are, what's it like having to look after someone else?'

'It's all right.'

'That your great insight to parenthood, is it – all right?'

I pushed the seat back so I could stretch my legs. 'Here's what I reckon.' I turned to face her. 'First off we buy a town map, find out where this place is, then get into the town and have a look, yeah? What time does it get dark?'

Before she could answer, the moan-phone rang. I passed it across. 'Here. I'm an arsewipe-free zone, remember?'

174

She hit the keys and put it to her ear. 'Hello? Yes, sir, I'm on secure.' She looked at me and rolled her eyes. He wouldn't have been able to talk to her if she wasn't. There was a pause. 'Oh, no, he's driving, sir.' She nodded in response to whatever was being said, then looked at me, her face very serious. 'Yes, sir, I will.'

Pressing the off-key with her thumb, she passed the phone back to me. 'The address has been flagged up for two years with Immigration and local plod.'

'Is he doing anything about it – you know, unflagging it?'

She shook her head. 'Nope – deniable, remember, Norfolk boy.'

'Fucking idiot.'

She nodded slowly. 'Are you ever going to tell me what you've got against him?'

We were just coming into the outskirts of King's Lynn and Suzy pulled into a BP station. You always start an op with a full tank, and in any case we needed the town maps.

As I walked back across the forecourt looking at the folded-out map I could already feel the breeze off the North Sea. King's Lynn was at the bottom right-hand corner of the Wash. The Great Ouse ran through it, which was presumably how the boats made it into the docks.

We crossed a ring-road lined with DIY, furniture and electrical superstores with a few burger franchises thrown in, and as we followed signs for the town centre things began to change for the worse. It was a sad mix of 1970s concrete and hundred-year-old red-brick housing. The whole place looked as if it needed a massive dig-out and a coat of paint. Quite a few of the shops were boarded up. We passed a huge open-air car parking lot alongside a drab grey concrete shopping precinct, then a few crumbling, peeling Georgian houses.

Suzy was looking as pissed off as I was, screwing up her face and shaking her head, chewing even faster on her nicotine gum as we passed a group of three teenage mums with prams and badly dyed blonde hair.

We kept on the main artery coming out of town towards the bypass. I checked the map. We weren't far away from Sir Lewis Street now. Huge fuel-storage tanks and industrial pipework started to come up on our left, half painted, half rusting. 'We need Loke Road – on our right.'

We both saw it. We were just short of the dock entrance as we turned right off the main, alongside a vast area of wasteground. 'Sir Lewis coming up, over a stream and first left.'

Suzy looked even more depressed as we made our way behind the back yards of Sir Lewis, row upon row of two-up, two-down red-brick terraced houses straight out of *Coronation Street*.

We continued past the target road and Suzy was still complaining: 'It's so fucking soulless.'

As I looked down the narrow alleyways that punctuated the terraces I could see washing in almost every yard, and bin liners spewing out their crap on to the street. Somebody in the sixties had made a fortune convincing the residents to shell out on stone cladding and pebbledash. There were plenty of tired for-sale signs stuck to the fronts of houses, along with the obligatory Sky dish, and none of the cars parked on either side of the narrow road seemed to have a registration plate higher than J.

We passed a local store, a handpainted sign for a hairdresser's, and a pub. Then, within a minute or so, we were surrounded by 1950s council houses and low-level flats. We turned right, towards the railway station.

'Let's park up there and come back to do a walk past.' If you park in a residential area, people expect you to go into a house nearby.

The road signs ran out but we eventually found the station, an old Victorian brick and glass building, with a brand new Morrisons superstore next to it and a Matalan clothes shop.

176

Suzy turned into the Morrisons car park and we sat studying the map to get our bearings.

30

'It's an old map.' I ringed Morrisons. 'But that's where we are now, in that open ground. The target is maybe ten minutes' walk north.'

Sir Lewis Street was part of a six-block grid of terraced houses lying along three roads, each about 250 metres long and parallel to each other, cut across the middle by Walker Street. It backed on to the stream, and was a little longer than the other two. The wasteground stretched all the way from the stream to the main.

Suzy pulled a face. 'How can anyone survive here? I fucking hate these places.'

I shrugged. 'People don't always have a choice, do they?'

We worked out a strategy for the walk-past, not knowing exactly where the target house would be. According to the map, the top of the road was a dead end.

Suzy ripped the corner off and furled it into a pointer. 'If we walk down Loke, back to the shops we just drove past, and take a right down one of the alleyways, we should be able to work our way down to the dead end of Sir Lewis. If we can get on to it, we can then walk the whole length of the street back towards Loke.'

'Done. OK, the story is we're here for a few days' holiday. We were just taking a walk, we got lost and we're looking for the station.'

Suzy locked up, double-checking all the doors and making sure the kit in the boot was out of sight.

The parking lot was swarming with cars and trolleys. Suzy and I walked side by side, heading for a gap that led into the housing estate. Suzy slipped her arm through mine and chatted happily about the make and colour of each car we passed. Anything to look natural from a distance as we wormed our way through.

People had made efforts to stamp their individuality on their council houses, and that seemed to piss her off even more. Some had stone lions mounted on their gateposts, gnomes sitting on the front doorstep or fishing beside little ponds; others had bird-boxes with windmills. The smartest had carports. Suzy particularly admired some loose half-bricks in the wall next to a telephone pole. 'That'll be the DLB [dead letter box], yeah?'

I nodded as we hit Loke and turned left, going back the way we'd driven, past all the *Corrie* two-up-and-two-downs. A stone panel set into one of the walls said '1892', which must have been the last time anyone had had the decorators in. Through net curtains I could see patterned brown carpets and brass dogs sitting on tiled fireplaces.

Suzy hadn't cheered up much. 'I really hate this.'

'What's the matter? Don't you like Norfolk?'

'I ran off to sea to get out of a shit-hole like this. Look at it, it's like fucking West Belfast on a bad day. Give me Bluewater and my new conservatory any time.'

I looked around, knowing exactly what she meant – apart from the Bluewater bit.

We carried on down Loke, passing the first two roads that paralleled Sir Lewis. A twentysomething Chinese guy came out of a corner shop with a newspaper under his arm and his finger in the ringpull of a Coke. He knocked back a mouthful, jumped into an old red Lada and drove away from the target road.

Suzy looked up and smiled at me lovingly. 'D958?'

I nodded, not that we needed to remember the plate. There couldn't be that many old red Ladas left on the planet.

I took a deep breath. 'My shit-hole was a council estate. They all smell the same, don't they?'

She shuddered. 'Coal fires and boiled cabbage. Hate it, hate it, hate it.' As if I didn't know by now.

Sir Lewis was the next junction right. 'Down that alley?'

We crossed the road arm in arm, turning down the narrow passage a little short of the target road. We could just fit side by side, the backs of the Sir Lewis Street houses on our left. The yards were tiny and washing hung from lines at second-floor level to catch a bit of wind. Old grey vests and very faded blue jeans seemed to be the fashion statement of the week.

Cats or urban foxes had got stuck into the bin-bags, scattering frozen food packets and the contents of hundreds of ashtrays. There was a smell of damp clothes mixed with something like stale tea coming from one of the kitchen windows, and somewhere upstairs a toilet had just been flushed. Some of the yards had doors backing on to the alley, others had been kicked in or rotted away. The houses themselves were just little brick squares.

Walker Street cut across us about forty metres ahead. I could hear TVs in some of the houses, and here and there a dog barked behind a crumbling wall.

We started across Walker, and tried to make out the door numbers on Sir Lewis to our left, but couldn't see any from this distance.

A little half-moon footbridge spanned the stream and led into the vast, bulldozed area of mud, rubbish and heavy plant tracks that ran for about a hundred metres up to the main drag. Beyond that was the fenceline of the docks, where cranes and fuel-storage tanks daubed with the Q8 logo cut the skyline. Hundreds of new joist-sized planks jutted over the fence; someone like Jewsons must have had a bit of a warehouse there. The whole area of the docks was dominated by a huge white rectangular concrete structure. It had no windows, so was presumably some kind of storage facility.

A group of kids came out of Sir Lewis and bumbled up Walker towards us. They all had crewcuts and holes in their trainers, flicked their cigarettes continuously with their thumbs and couldn't stop gobbing on to the pavement. We headed down the continuation of the alleyway, splitting up to get past two abandoned Morrisons' trolleys.

The walk-past would entail far more than just finding the target door. We'd have to take in as much information as possible, because we wouldn't be doing it again. Once we'd walked past the target, the area would be a no-go for us until we went back in to attack the place. We wouldn't even turn and look back: lessons learnt the hard way about third-party awareness ensured that wouldn't happen. Quite apart from curtain-twitchers, we had to assume the ASU had people on stag, looking from windows, or out and about on the street.

Something dawned on me. 'How do you do a walk-past together? I've never done a two-up.'

She seemed quite pleased there was something I didn't know. 'Easy. Don't try to divide up the information. Just do it as if you were on your own. Then we argue later about what we saw.'

We were reaching the end of the alleyway and there was a way out on to Sir Lewis. To our left was *Corrie*-land, to our right, council bungalows and houses that went on for maybe a hundred and fifty before coming to a dead end. We stayed on the opposite side of the road to keep a better perspective on the target, and therefore more time with eyes on, more time to get the information into our heads. We looked at everything, even if it felt as if it wasn't registering: the unconscious is a total

181

sponge and we could extract stored information from each other.

The first number on the opposite side of the road was 136. That was good: it meant we were at the heavy half of the road. A car drove away ahead of us, scaring a couple of manky old cats.

She pulled gently on my jacket arm. 'Don't forget to count.'

I nodded, and groaned to myself. I hated the counting bit, but it had to be done. Eighty-eight was coming up. It was pebbledashed and had a solid white door. To the right of it was a single bare aluminium double-glazed window, a sealed unit with a smaller skylight at the top, which opened outwards. There was an identical unit on the floor above.

Three cars were parked more or less outside: a red Volvo, P reg; a green Toyota, C reg; and a black Fiesta whose plate I couldn't see, but it had a VDM of two red go-faster stripes down the offside.

No immediate signs of life. The curtains were drawn behind nets. There was no smoke from the chimney, no milk outside, no post or newspaper sticking out of the mail-box, and both skylights were closed.

As we got closer I took Suzy's hand and we crossed at an angle, not looking at the target, just meandering. The nearside of the Fiesta had stripes too. A couple of small house fronts later, we were passing the door. There was no noise, no light, nothing. The windows were grimy, the net curtains knackered. The window lock was a simple handle. The door paint was peeling, and the lock was just a dull brass Chubb lever with an ancient B&Q-type imitation brass handle above it – though who was to say there weren't a couple of dead bolts thrown on the other side?

We passed the door and I started to count. One, two, three . . . each house we passed, I pressed one of my digits into the palm of my hand . . . eight, nine, ten, and then I started again . . . eleven, twelve . . .

We got to the junction with Walker, turned right, and were walking over the little footbridge almost immediately. The stream two metres below us was muddy and rainbowed with oil. We turned right again the other side, on to a worn mud path. I put my arm round her and smiled. 'I've got seventeen. You?'

'Yep.'

'Looks empty.'

'Yep – shut up.' She was counting again and I joined her. One, two, three . . .

The stream was about two metres wide, its steep bank the other side almost right up against the backyards of the houses, with just a narrow well-trodden path between them. By the looks of it, it was pretty popular with people coming out to toss their garbage into the river. Old cigarette packets and butts, drinks cans and bits of paper were scattered everywhere. The place was a shit-hole.

It looked as if the wasteground between us and the main drag was being cleared for redevelopment. A chipboard fence, painted white, had been erected to keep people out, but it was already covered in graffiti and mostly pushed over.

Nine, ten, eleven . . . The front of a house might bear no resemblance to the back; the front might be well looked after and painted green, the back neglected and painted red. Terraces can be a special nightmare. Some of these had the same aluminium units as at the front, others still had their old sash windows.

Twelve, thirteen, fourteen . . . We got level with a brown wooden door, set into a crumbling red-brick wall; there was no washing hanging up the other side because there wasn't a line. Old net curtains covered filthy windows.

Suzy jerked her head. 'The one without the washing, with the brown window frames and back door. That's my seventeen.'

'Me too.' We carried on. There were no lights, no steamed-up

183

or open windows, no fresh bin-liners strewn down the bank of the stream.

The door was fastened with a latch, but like the front door there could have been some bolts the other side. The wall was climbable; there'd be no problems with that. I studied the wasteground, trying to get a marker from the docks. At night everything was going to look totally different. 'It's in line with the Q8 oil tanks.'

We continued down the path, the walk-past now finished whether we liked it or not. An OAP was cycling towards us on a very new, shiny mountain bike. We just carried on chatting about nothing until he, and the target, was well behind us and the terraced houses had been replaced by bungalows, then houses.

My head was full of a hundred different things as she put her hand into mine and we walked in silence, following the path. The first consideration is always the enemy, in this case the ASU. Chances were, they were going to be in the house; for now, concealment was their best weapon.

What were their aims and intentions? We knew their objective, but we knew nothing about their training, their leadership, their morale. These people weren't fighters: third wave had brains the size of Gibraltar. But all the same, what sort of people were we going up against? We didn't even know if they were armed. All the source had said was that they were fundamentalists, more eager to go to Paradise than we were to leave King's Lynn. But what did that mean? Would they fight? I hoped not.

Next priority was ground. Going in on white would be a nightmare because, apart from the sealed window units, there were only the skylights and the front and back doors. Even if one of the skylights was left open, we couldn't get through, so that left the doors – and that could mean waiting for darkness so that the Yale could be attacked on the front. But there was a high risk of compromise with so many curtains to be twitched.

Suzy was coming to the same conclusion. 'It's got to be on black, hasn't it?'

Target zones are colour coded to make them easier to identify. The front elevation is always called white, the right-hand side red, the left green, and the back is black. This being a terraced house, all we had to work with was black and white.

'Yeah, unless the Golf Club gets us a Packet Echo and we blow our way through from one of the neighbours' walls.'

She played with her gum between her teeth and couldn't help a fleeting smile at the thought. 'All we have to do is get into the yard. After that we get plenty of cover to get the NBC kit on and attack the lock.'

I nodded. It was a simple plan because we had very little information.

She grinned, taking big exaggerated chews now. 'Shit, sometimes I'm so good it scares me.'

'First we need to get out of town somewhere and prepare the NBC kit so we're not opening all the bags and stuff on target. Then we can walk back on to target with the ready bags, get over the wall and Bob's your uncle – kit on, make entry and get on with it.'

'The only refinement I've got to that is I want to buy some rubber gloves. I don't want the NBC ones. It's really hard to manipulate the trigger, especially with the inners on as well.'

I nodded. 'Good thinking. And once we're inside you can have a crack at the washing-up.'

We got back to the car park with just over two hours to go before last light. 'Fancy a brew?'

She nodded enthusiastically, and we went into Morrisons' café and got a couple of teas, sandwiches and biscuits. I kept checking my traser.

'Relax, Nick.'

The Best of Janet Jackson banged out of the loudspeakers at us, interrupted now and again by a member of staff explaining all the wonderful deals they had in-store.

185

Suzy looked at her watch too. 'I'm going to go and get those gloves. You want some?'

'Madness not to. Get us a can of foam and some razors too, will you?'

She rubbed my face. 'No worries. Who knows? If you took a bit more care of yourself, you might get lucky.'

She left me to the biscuits she hadn't touched, and I pulled out my phone. I got Josh's answering-machine again; it was still only about midday on Friday for them. I cut the call and redialled.

'Hello?'

'Carmen. Is Kelly there?'

'I'll get her.' I heard the noise of the TV as she walked from the kitchen, and then, 'It's Nick.'

I heard a weepy 'Hello?'

'Hi, Kelly, listen – I just wanted to phone you up because we didn't have a lot of time to talk. I'm so sorry I can't come and say goodbye, but I'm up north now. Carlisle.'

'Where's that?'

'Almost in Scotland. Listen, I'm sorry—'

'Is Josh back?'

'Not yet. Some time tonight, his time.'

I looked up and Suzy was in one of the checkout queues with her basket of stuff. 'Listen, I've got to go. I'll call you again, maybe not tonight because I'm going to be travelling. I'll try in the morning, OK? Have they fixed your flight?'

'I'm not sure.'

'Look, I'd better have a quick word with Granny – is she there?'

I heard her call out, then the phone being shuffled over to Carmen.

'Did you manage the flight?'

'No, it cost a hundred pounds to change the ticket and they wouldn't wait for you to call. They wanted the money now and you know how much it costs to use a credit card, when we paid—'

'Look, just pay it, please – I'll send the money off, whatever it costs.'

I powered the phone down and got it back into my bumbag just as Suzy finished paying.

31

It was good to be in the non-smoking area with her for once. We ordered up a plate of sandwiches, a couple of bananas and a yoghurt, then drank tea and spun the shit like every other couple seemed to be doing. The café stopped serving at six p.m., but we'd nursed our food and drink for an hour beyond that. Now the cleaning woman was doing her best to mop round us and it was time to go.

We took the main drag out of the town, via the docks and towards the bypass, Suzy still at the wheel. I took off the interior light cover and felt around in the door pocket. 'Where are the bulbs?'

'In the glove thingy.'

I screwed them back in, then plugged my phone into the charger dangling from the lighter socket. I got the shaving kit out of the carrier-bag, flipped open the visor mirror and worked a handful of foam into my stubble.

To our right, beyond the wasteland, lights glinted in the back rooms of the houses in Sir Lewis, but not in the one that, from this distance, we thought was the target. The odd figure walked or cycled along the river path, and a couple of chimneys were spewing smoke. Suzy was already getting herself worked up about going back in there. 'They'd better not be boiling cabbages.'

I was making quite a bad job of shaving as Suzy drove past estate after estate of flats and houses set back from the road, then a fire station with its strike posters still stuck to the doors. Finally we hit the new steel-and-glass trading estates, where shiny new Audis and Citroëns were on display in the show-rooms, just waiting to be delivered to the detached houses nearby; the ones in their own grounds with stone lions stand-ing guard over the gateways. I wiped my blood-nicked face clean with tissue paper from my Next bags, and was left reek-ing of menthol.

We eventually hit a major roundabout on the bypass. The second left looked the darker option, and Suzy took it as I ripped open the packaging on our smart new Morrisons washing-up gloves. She turned right into a B road and finally pulled up in a dried-mud layby next to a field.

Instead of reflecting quietly on what we could be getting involved with in the next few hours, Suzy seemed to be getting increasingly revved up about it. She picked up her gloves and gave me a flick. 'You into rubber?' She laughed. Her door opened and the interior light came on as she held out her hand for the boot bulb. 'I'll get the kit.'

I heard the back open and her rummaging about inside. It wasn't long before six packs of NBC kit were tossed on to the back seat. Large white cards beneath the Cellophane simply said, 'Trousers', or 'Smocks'. We would prepare one bit of kit at a time, leaving everything else packed in the back. If someone was out walking their dog or another vehicle stopped along-side, it would be easier to hide.

I peeled back the outer covering, then ripped at the thick, air-tight plastic packaging with my teeth. There was a rush of air as the pressures equalized. The NBC suit inside was made of a dark grey-green cotton shell, laminated to layers of tiny carbon spheres. Fingers crossed, it would absorb any biological or chemical agents before they made contact with the clothing worn underneath and, more importantly, my skin.

To cut noise, Suzy let the back down gently so that it locked only on the first click, before getting back into the driving seat and gripping one of the trouser packs. We each had three packs in all: the trousers, a hooded smock, and rubber boots. The trouser legs felt as if they'd been overstarched in a Chinese laundry; I had to push my arms through to unstick them. Suzy pulled apart her smock the same way. She was still on a high. 'This is great,' she whispered. 'It feels like we're on our way to a fetish party.'

Once we'd dealt with the smocks and trousers, we rolled them up and unwrapped the black overboots. They were one-size-fits-all and had to be laced up like Roman sandals. We threaded the strips of rubber through the loops round the sides of the soles, and that was the NBC kit ready to go.

The windows were misting up. We wrapped our suits round the boots, then got out to pack them back into the ready bags. I pulled apart the Velcro at the top of a green nylon bag and removed my standard British Army S6 respirator. It was a black-rubber job with two eyepieces, and a canister already attached. No spares had been provided but that wasn't necessarily a problem; a single canister should last for days. It just would have been good to know whether this was a new one.

I checked that the rubber bladder that formed a seal round the side of the respirator was properly adjusted so no bad stuff could get inside. Forward of where my chin was soon going to be there was a small valve: I twisted anticlockwise to let the air pressure in the bladder equalize with the ambient air pressure to form a tight seal. That was why I'd had to have a shave; stubble got in the way. Short hair is an advantage for the same reason: you don't want bits of your fringe getting in the way of the seal either.

I left it open for a minute and watched Suzy wiping her eye-pieces with the cuff of her fleece. Then, tightening up the valve and brushing back my hair, I put the respirator to my face and adjusted the elastic straps round the back of my head. My nose filled with the smell of new rubber.

The canister was mounted on the left-hand side – so you could get a weapon into your right shoulder. Unscrewing it, I covered the gap with my hand and sucked in hard to make the respirator squash against my face. The seal was good.

Next was the SD. We had three thirty-round magazines each, more than enough. If we needed anywhere near a hundred and eighty rounds on this job we'd be severely in the shit and probably land up dead. We had nowhere to carry the spare mags; for some unknown reason, Packet Oscar didn't come with mag carriers, or even a chest harness for the weapon. This meant we wouldn't be able to run round and fight with both hands free; we'd have to put them down and maybe even leave them on target, which was where the Morrisons gloves came in.

I put them on and pressed the on button of the HDS with a rubbery finger. The heads-up sight started to glow. In theory the batteries in these things lasted for days, but I'd had bad experiences with them in the past and switched it off again immediately.

We each pushed a full 10mm mag into the SD's housing. I listened for the click before giving the mag a shake and pulling on it a bit to make sure it was fully home.

Suzy held her right hand over the cocking piece. 'Ready? After three. One, two, three.'

We made ready together, both pulling back our cocking pieces, which ran along the side of the chunky barrel, then letting them slide forward so the working parts picked up a round.

I checked chamber by pulling back slightly on the cocking piece once more, then applied safe. Suzy was ahead of me again: she'd already undone her NBC kit and was ripping apart the Velcro that secured the top flaps of the map pockets on her trousers. An SD magazine went into each; it meant they wouldn't rattle. I copied her, thinking about my Browning. 'I'm not bothering with the short. Even if I need it, I haven't got anywhere to put it.'

There was no reply as she placed her pick-and-rake wallet in the chest pocket of the smock, closed the Velcro fastening and checked it was secure. We couldn't afford for anything to fall out: we didn't want to make any more noise than we had to, and we didn't want to leave anything behind. If we weren't able to pick up our empty cases, then so be it, but that was it.

'Is that your way of insisting the shorts stay in the car?'

I twisted the bottom off my mini Maglite and reversed the bottom battery so that I had power again – something else I didn't want to run out on me when on target. 'Yeah, along with our docs – why risk leaving anything in there?'

'Done. But this car park of yours had better be safe.'

My MOE wallet stayed in the boot.

She was silent for a moment. 'Nick, what happens if they do contaminate us – you know, start throwing DW about?'

'We'll just have to assume we're in the shit, and hope the suits work while we wait an hour or so for the stuff to lose its fizz.'

'Just sit tight and wait?'

'What else can we do?' I reached into the back of my jeans. 'Apart from giving it a bit of help.' I pressed out four capsules and offered her the card as I felt them make their way down my gullet.

A set of headlights approached from the direction of King's Lynn, disappearing for a few seconds as the road dipped. We got back inside the Peugeot and I took my respirator with me, cleaning the eyepieces with my sweatshirt as the lights got nearer. For a few seconds we were bathed in a misty glow as the passing headlights cut through our steamed-up windows. I glanced at Suzy. She no longer looked so hyped-up as she polished her eyepieces all over again, with short, distracted strokes. I checked that the pressure valve was screwed up tight for the last time, wondering if maybe she had a capsule stuck in her throat or something.

We collected up all the plastic wrapping and shaving kit and threw them into the boot. Everything we needed on target was now stowed in the ready bags, so I could take off my gloves and shove them into my pockets. Nothing that came out of the car on to the target area would carry our fingerprints: we'd be going in sterile and, with luck, coming out the same.

'How come you know this place?' She closed the boot. 'Family holidays?'

We walked back either side of the car. 'Very funny,' I said. I couldn't see her face in the darkness. 'We didn't do holidays.' The truth was, we didn't do family either. 'I used to live a few miles down the coast. Just for a while.'

'With Kelly?'

The doors opened and the interior light came on as we both got back in. Suzy was waiting for an answer, but she wasn't going to get one. 'OK, what about this, then? How much of a coincidence is it that the source is shacked up in King's Cross?'

'All I want to do is get this job over and done with so I can get back to the States.'

'Sort out Kelly?'

'All kinds of shit.'

32

Both doors closed and the light went out. She turned the ignition, and I rearranged the Browning because the half-cocked hammer was starting to make my stomach sting. The red sore had never gone away after years of carrying one of these things, but it was now starting to weep.

Another couple of cars sped past. The driver of the last punched his horn four or five times and we were treated to a chorus of ribald yells from his passengers.

Suzy was back to her normal hyped-up self. 'They think we're shagging.' She cupped her hands and pretended to shout back at them as they disappeared into the distance. 'Hey, I'm not that desperate.'

I checked my traser as she wiped a hole in the condensation on the windscreen. 'You mean that shave was all for nothing?'

As Suzy drove back past the docks the arc lights on the other side of the fenceline were shining like a floodlit stadium. Over to our left, across the darkness of the wasteland, the *Corrie* houses were doing their best to compete. The street-lamps on Walker Street started by the bridge and stretched away from us, but cast no light on the narrow path along the canal. There was a secure triangle of shadow alongside the back walls and fences for us to work in.

Suzy reminded me there was one more thing we had to do before we parked up and headed for the target. 'You've got to call him, Nick. I'd do it but, hey, I'm driving.'

'Let's just call him when we're done and then we keep control.' The more the Yes Man knew, the more he might want changed – and the more influence he'd have over what we were doing. It wasn't the way I liked to work.

'We can't do that, we've got to call him now. I will if you don't want to, it's no biggie. He needs a sit rep.'

He needed a kick in the bollocks, but that would have to wait. Reluctantly I opened up the moan-phone and dialled. I hated him knowing what I was up to; it made me feel exposed. The phone rang just once.

'You should have called earlier.'

'Well, we've done the recces. We should be on target in about an hour. How long after that depends on making entry. We've seen no sign of life.'

'The second you get out, I want to know if you've got Dark Winter and how much of it. You will take control of it at all costs.'

'Yep.'

'Yep what?'

I took a deep breath. 'Yep, sir. Is there anything more about the target being flagged?'

'No. It's a local issue. The town has a huge South East Asia II [illegal immigrant] problem. Chinese gangs use the derelict housing as a holding tank before spraying them around the country. Nothing to do with us.'

'Yes, sir.'

The phone went dead from his end. Suzy was all smiles. 'That went well, I take it?'

The railway station was coming up and Morrisons shone a big yellow welcome at us as we headed for the car park. I bent down into the footwell and unthreaded my bumbag belt from my jeans, shoving it under the seat along with all my Nick Snell cover docs, the Browning and its spare mags.

I got Suzy to stop by the pay-and-display machine. 'My treat. You park.' Nine pounds twenty's worth of coins later, I had a ticket that would see us through till midnight the next day.

The Morrisons and Matalan signs on the other side of the tracks glowed against the sky as Suzy dumped her documents under her seat and I stuck the ticket inside the windscreen. I threw my remaining coins into the glovebox, and joined her as she retrieved her ready bag. The boot went down, and we checked everything was locked and out of sight before she hit the key fob.

We walked past the little tea-cum-newsagent's shop and into the station. To anyone watching, especially the CCTV that covered the almost empty car park, we were travellers about to catch a train. I just hoped they didn't follow us all the way through the station because we walked straight out the other side, past six or seven waiting minicabs, and into the Morrisons' lot. From there we retraced our earlier route.

Nothing had changed, except that it was dark. Lights were on in most of the houses. Some curtains were closed, but through others I could see people watching TV with plates on their laps. Suzy pulled out two of the bricks set into the wall at the DLB, and threw in the car keys, then replaced them. If the shit hit the fan and we had to do a runner, at least one of us would be able to get to the car.

When we got to Loke Road I checked left, down towards the shops. The burger bar was doing a roaring trade, judging by the steam billowing out of the extractor vent. The corner shop next to it was shut, its windows protected by heavy grilles.

We crossed the road at the point we had earlier, just short of the shops. Two Chinese teenagers, a girl and a boy, aged maybe fifteen or sixteen, came out of the alleyway, giggling to each other as they clumsily tried to hold hands and walk at the same time. There was a dark Ford Focus, two-up, parked a bit further along. The driver was as bald as a snooker ball. He turned his head to look at the youngsters as they crossed the road, and studied them a bit too long before he turned back and said something to his mate.

We entered the alleyway to the sound of a lot more TVs on the go. Most downstairs lights were on, and there was the occasional blurred movement behind thin curtains and frosted glass. Suzy changed hands with her bag so she could get closer. 'You see the Focus?'

'They were checking out those kids. Could be drug-dealers, could be police. Or just a couple of perves. Fuck it, let's just get on with it.'

We hit Walker Street and turned left, towards the junction with Sir Lewis and the footbridge. 'You check the target and I'll check left.' As we walked over the crossroads I looked up the other half of Sir Lewis Street. Four kids shot past on bikes with ice-lolly sticks threaded through the spokes, and the headlights of two cars swept towards us. The one further back turned in and parked about half-way down. I knew it was the Focus. They could just have stopped at the chip shop on their way home, but if it was anything to do with us, we'd find out soon enough.

Suzy looked up at me and gave a loving smile. 'No life on target.'

I smiled back as we approached the bridge. 'The Focus just parked short of the junction.'

She knew we were now committed. 'Fuck it, so what?'

We got to the bridge and turned right instead of crossing. There was no other way to do this job except brass it out. No point just hovering around and looking indecisive: we had to look like we belonged, like we had a purpose.

We carried on along the path, in the shadow of the yard walls and fences. Suzy kept a little behind me because the path was too narrow for both of us and the bags. We counted the houses. Three lights, four lights ... I could see the Q8 tanks in the docks to my half-left, and the street-lamps of the busy main casting a weak shadow over this side of the lumpy wasteground.

We reached the target and still there wasn't any light from the top windows. Traffic droned along the main behind me and I heard a bath running upstairs in the house next door to the left.

We moved up against the garden wall and stood in its shadow. It was about seven feet high, with access via a wooden door. The general clatter of domestic life filled the night air as we pulled on our gloves. A couple of screams came from the direction of Walker Street, then the rattle of bikes, getting louder. Almost immediately, the kids flew over the bridge, turning right. Suzy and I cuddled into each other as if we were kissing in the shadows. The lights of the main turned them into silhouettes. They were too busy trying not to fall into the river while cutting each other up to pay attention to strangers.

Suzy was taking the performance a little further than I expected: she put her arms around my neck, pulled me down and kissed me hard on the lips. It only lasted a few seconds, not enough time for me to think about what was happening, only that I got a faint hint of strawberry yoghurt and it tasted good.

'I thought you weren't that desperate . . .'

She still held my head, and pulled it back down, but this time to talk into my ear. 'Don't flatter yourself, Norfolk boy. It's just if you screw things up that could be the last chance I ever get to kiss a man.'

We waited for the kids to go away, laughing and screaming at each other as they pedalled into the darkness. Suzy and I disentangled ourselves as Bathroom Billy shouted at Maureen to bring him up a towel.

I moved against the wooden door and peered through the gap around the latch. The backyard was still in darkness, but I could make out an entrance to the right and a window to the left. There was no sign of life inside the target. This could mean the house was deserted, or that the ASU were down at the burger bar. It could also mean that they'd blacked out all the windows, or were on hard routine, no lights or smoking, not even cooking, just sitting there waiting to give us the good news.

I eased the door towards me before squeezing down on the rusty thumbpiece to release the latch, then pushed it the other way. It yielded no more than a quarter of an inch. Either it was bolted somewhere, or it was stuck. I didn't want to push any harder and risk noise, so, keeping the lever depressed, I nudged the bottom of the door with my foot. No resistance. I did the same with my free hand at the top of the door, and that was solid. I stepped back, grabbed the top of the wall, and cocked my right leg. Suzy cupped her hands under my foot and I heaved myself up until I could lean my stomach across the coping. I looked and listened. Everything seemed all right, so I swivelled round and eased myself gingerly down the other side. My feet connected with a pile of wood. Feeling round it, I toed myself on to the concrete yard as Maureen shouted at Bathroom Billy to get a bleedin' move on 'cos his tea was ready.

There was a bin with no lid, and no rubbish either. Nothing in the yard gave the impression that people lived there. I felt along the edge of the door until my gloved fingers came into contact with a small bolt. I wiggled it gently, and finally opened the door just enough for Suzy to slip through with the bags. She stood against the wall while I closed and bolted it once more.

Water cascaded down next door's wastepipe: Billy must have liked her cooking. Suzy stayed put as I moved slowly to the back of the target. There was enough ambient light from the houses on either side to see what I was up to, but in any event my night vision was kicking in.

The window to the left of the back door was a simple latch job that opened outwards. The frame was old softwood, and its paint was peeling. The problem was it had a Chubb window lock screwed down tight. We would have to smash glass to make entry via the window. The door, to the right, was a DIY-store hardwood special, with just a lever lock and handle. It obviously led into the kitchen; I could see a pair of chrome taps through the glass.

I got the mini Maglite out of my pocket and, holding two fingers over the lens to minimize the light, I shone it through the window. The kitchen looked like it hadn't been touched since Formica ruled the earth.

I moved two paces to the right and got down on my knees so my head was level with the keyhole. It was an ordinary lever lock. I put my ear to it and opened my mouth to listen. I couldn't hear anything inside. The ambient noise still came from the main drag, punctuated by the odd quick burst of TV from the neighbours. I checked inside the lock with the Maglite. It was a four-lever, but there was no key still in it on the inside. That would have made life a lot simpler: all I'd have had to do was turn it with one of the rakes from the pick wallet. I pulled down slowly on the handle in case it was already unlocked. It wasn't. I pushed the bottom corner of the door below the lock and it gave a little. Standing up, I checked the top corner as well, and that did too.

I glanced around the yard for flowerpots, bins or other obvious places to plant a key. There was no point in going to all the trouble of picking the lock if someone had been kind enough to leave us the spare. I reached down and lifted a brick or two, but found nothing.

I could hear a slow, deliberate rustling behind me. Suzy was starting to get into her NBC kit. She had her trousers on and was messing around, trying to get the boots over her trainers. I checked the window again, just in case, but the door seemed the sensible first point of entry.

A car drew up on the other side of the house, and we stepped back into the shadows, waiting for lights to go on. Billy was getting screamed at by Maureen for using all the hot water. Now she couldn't have a soak before they went out, and

200

what was it with him, anyway, having a bath just to go down the pub?

A front door slammed across the street but I waited a couple more minutes before I took off my bomber jacket and pulled my ready bag apart. To cut down on noise, Suzy had unzipped it for me before coming into the yard.

33

A kettle was being filled in Bathroom Billy's kitchen as, very slowly and deliberately, I pulled on my kit. I'd asked for the older versions of the NBC suits because, although they might be harder to put on than the modern ones, there was a whole lot less Velcro to undo first. There was still a noise, but at least it was reasonably controlled.

I turned and realized something was wrong with Suzy. She bent over, her body suddenly convulsing, and pulled out her SD just before she emptied the contents of her stomach into her ready bag.

By the time I leant across to her it was over. I put a hand on her shoulder. 'It's OK,' I said. 'I do that all the time.'

She finished wiping her mouth and snorted back a couple of lumps that had caught in the back of her nose. She leant close enough to make my eyes water. 'Don't fucking patronize me. That yoghurt must have been off.'

I nodded and started pushing my Caterpillars into my trousers, then pulled them up high round my stomach. So Suzy was human, after all. It wasn't a bad thing to be scared. I'd served with guys who'd shit themselves with fear but still got on with the job.

Stitched to the back of the trousers were two long cotton tapes that acted as braces. I put them over my shoulders and crossed them over my chest, guiding the ends through the loops at the front of the waistband and tying them up.

Suzy had already got her smock on and was nearly ready by the time I put my hands into the bottom of mine and started wrestling it over my head. The rough fabric scratched my face.

Canned laughter spilled from a TV next door. I imagined Billy now had a brew to watch it with, while Maureen got busy with the deodorant. When my head finally emerged, Suzy was a foot or two in front of me, her face a picture of concentration, her eyes fixed intently on the back door as she psyched herself for the task ahead.

I lowered my arse on to the cracked concrete as Maureen got a shout to hurry up or they were going to be late. Her reply from the bedroom was loud and clear: 'Shut the fuck up and turn that bleedin' TV down, will yer?'

I picked up the first of the boots, which looked to me like a kid's Christmas stocking but made of rubber, and pulled it over my left boot, lacing up the tapes from the bottom. Once the second was on I pulled the trousers over them and tightened the Velcro at the ankle.

Billy was at the end of his tether. 'For fuck's sake, that's enough. We're going down the pub, not the bleedin' Monte Carlo casino!'

Suzy picked up her SD and leant over it with her Maglite to check chamber for the last time, then pressed on the sight. I tapped her arm and she leant over and shone her light so I could do the same. As we exchanged a glance in the semi-darkness the kids reappeared along the bank, heading back towards the bridge with their lights still off and their ice-lolly sticks still rattling away.

We only had to make sure our rubber gloves overlapped the cuffs of the smocks, then fix our respirators. I grasped mine in my left hand, and pulled back on the elastic harness with the right to get it over my face. The smell of new rubber filled my

203

nostrils again as I made sure that no hair was in the way of the seal. I checked the canister was tightly twisted on before pulling down my hood and tightening the toggle. Breathing immediately became a tug-of-war; I fought to suck in air through the cylinder, and fought to push it back out. These things certainly weren't designed for lovers of open spaces, and would be a nightmare for anyone with even a touch of claustrophobia.

The noise of the respirator was going to be a major problem tactically: our own sounds would be louder in our ears than those around us. But there was nothing we could do about it. Besides, if DW was the other side of this door, being deafened by my own breathing would hardly be a major concern.

Suzy lifted her head so that I could check her hood was in place, then she checked mine. We were ready to go.

The fire station on the main drag had just had a call. Sirens wailed and blue lights flashed across the wasteground as they sped past the docks, and I could suddenly see Suzy's eyes behind her lenses. They were fixed, unblinking, her attention totally focused.

I sounded like Darth Vader with asthma as I stooped and picked up the SD, checking the safety catch by pushing it all the way to three-round bursts before returning it to safe. I didn't want grit off the ground or anything to catch between the safety and the pistol grip, preventing me taking it off. It didn't happen often, but once was more than enough. Detail matters.

Suzy approached the door very slowly, taking big, careful steps so the unwieldy boots didn't trip her up. The chest pockets of these NBC suits were held down by a Velcro square at each end. She tucked her hand under the flap in the middle to save having to undo it, and pulled out her MOE wallet. There was something about the way she moved that made me feel the domestic four-lever lock wasn't going to put up much of a fight.

She unrolled the wallet and took out a lifter pick and turning wrench. Normally a lock is opened by the bit of the key, the part with the combination cut into it that lifts the four levers into alignment. She was going to have to shift each of the four levers with the lifter pick, then move the bolt back into the lock with the turning wrench.

I watched as she began to probe with the steel pick, her left hand letting a small amount of light from her mini Maglite filter into the keyway. There is a Zen approach to the art of lock-picking. The idea is to use all your senses to create a picture of what is happening inside the mechanism as it responds to your attack. It can only happen if you concentrate completely on the job and don't have to worry about what is happening around you. That was my job. I stood by the bin, eyes and ears peeled. The bypass continued to hum on the other side of the wasteground.

Minutes went by. Voices moved along the bank of the stream. A car door was slammed, then Billy's front door got the same treatment. Suzy was right, it was like West Belfast. I was beginning to get concerned, but then she laid out her wallet on the concrete, replaced her tools, and tucked it into the end of her vomit-filled ready bag.

Leaving her to sort herself out, I moved to the door and sank on to my knees, slowly putting down the SD. I felt her standing behind me now, bringing her SD slowly into the firing position above my head, butt into the shoulder, leaning into the weapon.

Sweat started to run down my face as I grasped the handle with my right hand and applied pressure to the door with my left. It held firm. I gave another push, and this time it gave way silently, enough for me to get my head through and, more importantly, Suzy's SD.

At the end of the kitchen there was an Artexed archway, beyond which I could see dull street-light leak into the hallway from the front room and spill across the bottom few steps of the staircase.

Still on my knees, with Suzy hovering above me, weapon

up, I listened as carefully as the hood and respirator allowed. I heard nothing.

I opened the door a fraction more, enough for Suzy to slip past me, weapon still in the shoulder. She moved carefully across the floor, exaggerating every step so she didn't trip over anything as she focused her attention on the hall. I picked up my weapon to back her, standing up slowly and easing the butt into my shoulder, safety to single shot. I rested my index finger gently on the trigger, feeling the first pressure. Both eyes open, I crossed the threshold, getting behind and slightly to the right of her before going static.

We would clear the house covertly, room by room, and have a rolling startline – if we found the ASU and it went noisy, we wouldn't worry about adding to it with a little of our own.

She moved through the arch, her boots squeaking on the lino, then turned and pointed the muzzle of her SD upwards as she leant back against the wall and covered up the staircase.

I was through the arch, weapon up, concentrating on the doorway into the front room, the sight display in front of me. My throat was starting to dry. I passed Suzy and had four or five paces to go when I heard a noise ahead of me.

34

The lock turned, the door opened.

Street-light flooded in.

A silhouette stood on the threshold, a bag in one hand and keys in the other, then took a few steps inside before noticing me.

It spun to run back through the open door. There was no time to think, just do. Bending down and dropping my SD, I ran towards the shape and jumped on its back. My canister hit the back of its skull and I felt a nose through my gloves as our combined momentum carried us both down on to the pavement and into the street.

The head turned. It was a woman. She kicked out, trying to escape. Suzy grabbed one of her legs, trying to drag both of us back into the house. I jumped up and grabbed the other leg as she kicked and bucked, not letting go of the carrier.

The moment we were inside I got my hands round her mouth and collapsed on top of her. She wasn't coming quietly: she tried to bite me, and drummed her feet against the wall.

Suzy ran back for her SD.

'No! The door, the door!'

She grabbed her weapon, moved over me and kicked the

door closed. We were plunged into semi-darkness as she leant into us. 'Keep her still, keep her still!'

'No! She—'

Thud thud thud.

The three-round burst tore off the side of her head, and blood splattered over my respirator lenses. I kicked myself away from the lifeless body. 'Upstairs!'

Trying to wipe the blood off my lenses, I ran for my SD and started up the stairs. Suzy stayed where she was and covered me. It had definitely gone noisy.

It was a lot darker when I reached the landing. All I could hear was my laboured breathing. The bathroom door was open: it was clear. Two others were closed. Suzy started up behind me as I went through the first one left. The bedroom was clear, no bodies – but there had been. Two cheap nylon sleeping-bags were unrolled on the floor, food wrappers were strewn among gravy-stained plastic trays filled with dog ends. Jeans and shirts lay in a pile. A blanket had been tacked across the window.

Suzy came out of the other room and made her way back downstairs. I glanced in – it was in the same shit state, with another two sleeping-bags – then turned to go and give her a bollocking. It had been outrageously stupid to drop her: she might just have been an illegal, or another source of information if she'd been part of the ASU.

A male voice drifted up towards me, confused, frightened. I heard Suzy respond, calmly but firmly: 'Stand still, stand still.'

I stumbled and nearly fell down the stairs. Suzy was kneeling in the pool of blood, weapon up, aiming down the hallway. 'Close the door, now!'

Everything went darker but I could still make out two of them, both white. One was Baldilocks from the Focus.

They stared open-mouthed at the weapons. This was not a good day out. Suzy was straight in there: she grabbed Baldilocks, pulled him over the dead body and into the front room, kicking the backs of his knees to get him down on to the carpet.

I gestured to the other one with my SD. 'Follow him. On your knees, now.'

I hit the light switch as Suzy passed me on her way back into the hallway, and could hear the rasp of her respirator as she fought to suck air and speak. 'I'll check what we're here for.'

The drawn curtains were cheap and unlined, but they protected us from the real world.

Both men stayed on their knees, heads down at the carpet, their faces contorted in fear rather than pain. My own was cold and clammy, like a dead fish, rivulets of sweat collecting in the chinpiece of my respirator. I heard her throw the front-door bolt and go upstairs.

They were dressed in jeans. Baldilocks had a brown leather bomber jacket like mine; his mate, a tattered old black thing with lapels. Their eyes had shifted, though not towards me: they were too busy looking through the doorway at the blood-soaked corpse. She was very dark-skinned, more Indonesian than Malay, in jeans, trainers and a cheap green nylon jacket. What was left of her face looked university age.

Sweat ran down the long-haired guy's cheeks and dripped off his chin on to the threadbare flowery carpet. The floor-boards creaked above us. We heard the scrape of a chair, then the sound of metal hitting the floor and a glass smashing.

'Get your coats off. One at a time.' I kicked Baldilocks and the woman's blood flicked from my boot on to his leg. 'You first, Baldy.'

He started to take off his bomber jacket, still on his knees, his eyes never leaving the carpet. When he was half-way, I could see that he was clear – he wasn't carrying.

Suzy came down and went straight into the kitchen.

'OK, Baldy, that's enough. You with the hair, get yours off too, then pull up your T-shirt and show me your guts.' He did as he was told, unveiling the start of a beer belly. He, too, was unarmed.

'Now on the floor, both of you. Spread your hands and legs.'

A couple walked past the front of the house, talking and giggling, just feet away.

Suzy came to the door and shook her head, then turned to the dead girl. The carrier-bag rustled as she placed it to one side, then started going through her pockets. I went back to the two live ones. Baldilocks watched as Suzy turned the girl over in her own pool of blood so she could rip through the rear jeans pockets. He looked as though he was about to pass out.

I gave him a kick. 'Who are you?'

'Immigration. We're—'

'Why are you here?'

'Just a routine check, that's all. We saw something going on outside, that's why we came in. We're not armed, we're just doing our job.' He was flapping big-time.

Both of them had wedding rings – and, no doubt, a nice big mortgage to go with them. I jerked my head at the brown-haired one. 'You got kids?'

'Two.'

I nudged Baldilocks. 'What about you?'

He nodded.

'How many?'

'Just the one – she's two months now.'

'Well, just do as I say if you want to see them again. Got it?'

They both nodded enthusiastically. I knew they wouldn't do anything to fuck up their chances of seeing their families again because that was who they were thinking about this very second. 'You, Baldy, show me your ID. Stay on your front, just use one hand.'

He reached back into his jeans pocket and held out a worn black leather wallet towards me. 'Open it up and put it on the carpet in front of you.' He did, and I saw that Russell George was indeed an employee of Her Majesty's Home Office.

'Now you.' The long-haired one turned awkwardly to get a hand inside his jacket and Mr Warren Stacey produced his warrant card or whatever they were called.

Suzy had finished emptying the woman's pockets and was

shoving her stuff into her own, along with the three empty brass cases she'd picked up in the hall.

'One more time?'

She didn't even bother to turn and acknowledge: I just heard her feet hitting the staircase again.

Warren was lying flat on his stomach with the right side of his face flat against the carpet, his eyes fixed on my rubber overboots. He raised his head a few inches and the eyes that made contact with mine were very scared. Who wouldn't have been? But tough shit: if you don't like the job, don't take the money.

'No worries, mate. We're on the same side, you just don't know it. But if you fuck up here, we're going to turn into your worst nightmare. Get it?'

He nodded and his eyes went back to my boots.

'What about you, Russell?'

He was facing the other way. 'We don't want any trouble.' The back of his smooth head rippled as it moved. 'I know what you're wearing. I reckon you're in the job. We just want to come out of this alive, OK? You'll get no drama from us.'

Suzy came downstairs and headed for the kitchen.

'That's good to hear. Just accept you're in the shit, OK? It happens to everybody some time. Just do what I say and you'll get out of here safely. We're going to tie you up now, and then we're going to leave. Someone will be here later to release you – it could be an hour, it could be tomorrow. OK, so far?'

Both heads agreed.

'Good. Do everything they say, and you'll keep your jobs. But fuck it up, and you might not get to see your kids grow up. The people that we all work for can be nasty bastards sometimes.'

I knelt down, placed the SD beside me, untied my rubber-boot laces, and used them to tie their hands behind their backs and then together. 'Just hold on, OK? Don't fuck up.'

211

I put their IDs into my chest pocket. Warren's shoulders were bobbing up and down as he fought back the tears, not understanding how lucky he was.

I checked the time by his sporty diving watch. It was just before ten.

35

I turned off the light and closed the door on them, then headed for the kitchen, my boots adding to the trail of blood prints and bone splinters already left by Suzy.

She shone her Maglite over the woman's belongings on the kitchen table. I moved up close. 'Why the fuck did you drop her? What if she wasn't even—'

The carrier-bag rustled as she held it up and I could see hard cylindrical shapes pressing against the plastic. 'Would you have given her the chance?'

I took the bag from her and put it on the table, pulling out three large spray cans of what I hoped was still red car paint. I put it next to the rest of the kit on the table, eighty pounds in notes and some change, a return ticket from King's Cross, and a receipt for a cheese baguette. There was also a mobile phone and a lone lever key for the front door.

I picked the phone up and switched it on with a rubber-gloved thumb just as Billy and Maureen's lights came back on next door. Maureen hadn't had a good night out. 'You bleedin' spoil everything, you do!' The TV went on as her shrill voice disappeared upstairs. 'Karaoke's my only night out and you've fucking ruined it!' And whoever Cheryl was she was a big fat slag anyway and he was welcome to her.

The Motorola's back light came on, then the display, asking for a PIN code. I tried 1234. Nothing. 4321. Nothing. That gave me just one last shot. I tried a random sequence, but the thing closed down. Shit.

I reached across and shoved the side of Suzy's head to my mouthpiece. 'We've got to go. Get the ready bags in here. We'll keep out the way of next door.'

She moved my head then, so my ear was next to her mouthpiece. 'What if this place is contaminated? Even when we're out we should wait an hour.'

I shoved the woman's belongings into the carrier. 'Another hour isn't going to change anything . . .'

The row next door escalated as we played musical heads.

'No, now – we can't wait and I'm not wasting time explaining. Change outside if it makes you feel better. We're taking the pills, aren't we?'

I picked up the carrier and headed outside. Doors were being slammed over at Billy's and the TV was turned up. I pulled down on the toggle and pushed my hood back before ripping off the respirator. The cool air brushed against my wet face. I got the rest of the kit off as quickly and quietly as I could and into the ready bag. Suzy followed after closing the back door. She took her hood down and pulled off her respirator as well. 'Fuck it.'

We finished packing and checked the yard to see if we'd left anything. We exited by the back gate and headed for the bridge, turning left up Walker Street, ready bags over our shoulders.

A queue had formed outside the chip shop on Loke. The pub was rocking to a bad karaoke singer murdering 'Like A Virgin'.

Suzy had been striding along beside me, waiting for an explanation. When we were well out of any possible earshot she got what she wanted. 'We could be in the shit here. What if those cans are DW? What if the rest of those fuckers have already been spraying this shit about today? Or what if they've

214

split up, and are waiting to press the button? Look, let's get the cell to the Yes Man – he finds the numbers, he finds the location, and we get these fuckers.'

Virtually running now, we got to the brick in the wall, retrieved the keys and carried on back to the Peugeot.

I got the Yes Man on the moan-phone.

'You get it?'

'Maybe, but only some. Listen in.' I told him about the Immigration guys, and that the ASU could have been living there. 'If the cans contain DW, what's to say the attack couldn't already have happened? It's Saturday night, pubs are packed, there's been football matches, the list goes on. But, look, we have her cell. I can't open it and we'll have to be quick in case she has report times and they've actions-on if she misses any. The good thing is, it's closed down – chances are she wasn't expecting any incoming.'

'Get moving.' I could hear a lot of people talking in the background and phones ringing and getting answered around the Yes Man. 'I want that mobile, and the canisters.'

Suzy was silently mouthing to me, 'Immigration.'

I said, 'Are the plates blocked?' I wanted to know if we could speed without being chased by the police, if the registration number was on their computers as one to be left alone.

'Of course. Just get your foot down.'

'What about the Immigration people?'

'Fuck Immigration. A clean-up team will take care of them.'

There was more background chaos in my earpiece and a bleep from the fill before he closed down.

'London. We've got blocked plates.'

The engine revved and we started to fly out of King's Lynn.

I was shaking my head. 'That's the first time I've heard him swear. You?'

'Never. He must be flapping big-time.'

She went straight across a raised roundabout on the edge of town, showing off the fast-driving skills she'd probably learned in the Det. I checked traser. It was nearly eleven – just before six at Josh's.

The ops phone rang. It made me jump, but Suzy's eyes never left the road.

'Change of plan. Go to Fakenham racecourse – repeat, Fakenham racecourse. Call me when you get there. Have you got that?'

'Fakenham racecourse.'

'There'll be a heli arriving within thirty minutes. Hand the phone to the technician. I want you back in London and ready to move once we find out where these scum are. The situation has moved on now that the agent could already be aerosolized. If they are not found tonight we will have to go to government, and that must not happen. Do you understand?'

'Yes.'

The phone went dead and I turned round to drag the map-book off the back seat. 'We have a heli pickup at Fakenham racecourse.'

'And where exactly is Fakenham, Norfolk boy?'

I turned my Maglite on and flicked over a few pages. 'Not the way we're going.'

She braked and threw the car into the side of the road.

'We need to get back towards King's Lynn. Fakenham is about forty Ks east of us, further into Norfolk. The racecourse is south of the town. Better get your foot down.'

She turned the wheel and spun the car round.

'Why does he always makes me feel as if we're the guilty party here?'

She changed straight from fifth to third before overtaking a line of three cars. 'We're not, I am. You were right about getting out of there early.'

'No drama. Anyway, he told me that a clean-up team will be on target tonight to sort out the Immigration boys. They'll be having breakfast with Simon for the next few days. I hope they thank us for the overtime.'

She laughed, a bit too much, but so did I.

She was back to normal now. 'Throw up, that's what you call a U-turn in North Det, isn't it?'

I navigated for her as we screamed along narrow B roads and through villages with no street-lights. The gearbox would be in shit state by the time we got there, but who cared? It was a big firm.

We hit a town called Swaffham and headed northish towards Fakenham. It was a much better road now, but I couldn't stop myself doing some phantom braking as Suzy threw the car into the bends. 'Stop doing that,' she snapped. 'Or drive yourself.'

I smiled, got out my cell and tapped in Josh's number. Suzy didn't say anything as I sat there with something to my ear that obviously wasn't a moan-phone.

Josh answered. I bent down into the footwell to try to find a quieter spot. 'It's me, it's Nick.'

It seemed he couldn't hear me too well over the noise of the high-revving engine. 'What? That you, Nick?'

'Yes, listen – she's coming back tomorrow.'

'Say again?'

'Tomorrow, she's coming back tomorrow.'

'Where are you, man? In a wind tunnel or something?'

'Call Carmen, will you? Find out her flight and pick her up. You'll need to pick her up. She is back tomorrow. You get that?'

Josh had, and was in orbit. 'What are you at, man? You're doing it again – you're butting out. What is it with you?'

'Just call Carmen – she's arranged everything.' I didn't add that I only hoped she had.

Suzy braked sharply and I looked up to see her flashing a VW to get out of the way. Its horn blasted as we overtook near a bend and Josh screamed at me down the cell.

'Fuck you, man, you're doing it again!' The Yes Man wasn't the only one tonight who'd changed his Christian ways. I must have the gift.

'Call her, call her.' I hit the end button. However pissed off he was with me, he'd be on the phone to Carmen right now. We'd just have to patch things up later.

36

Suzy's face was caught in the glow of the dashboard, still concentrating on the tunnel of light created by the headlamp beams and the high trees either side of the road. The rev counter was into the red. Without so much as a sideways flicker of the eyes, she smiled knowingly. 'Kelly going home?'

'Fucking right she is.' I gripped my seat as she took a bump and all four wheels left the road. 'Aren't you worried about anyone?'

'Nope. No one.'

A sign flashed by at 115 m.p.h. 'Fakenham 4'.

Another corner was coming up. She dipped the lights to double-check if any traffic was coming the other way, then switched back to full beam. She braked hard on the straight, block-changed from fifth to second, and accelerated hard through the apex on the wrong side of the road. An oncoming car two hundred metres away flashed us angrily.

I gave it a few more minutes and dialled Carmen.

'It's me, Nick. Did you change the flights?'

'Who?'

'Nick.'

'It's very late, you know.'

'Have you organized the flight for tomorrow?'

'It's so late and what with Josh just calling as well . . . he woke us up.'

'Have you sorted out the flights?'

'Yes, she's flying in the afternoon. We have to be there at one, so we'll leave at eleven – that's if we wake up in time. Now, if we pay as soon as the statement comes in you won't have to—'

'Is she awake?'

'Of course not – I imagine she's only just got back to sleep after talking to Josh. I can't wake her again.'

'Carmen, please? This is really important.'

'Nothing's as important to a girl her age as a good night's sleep. I'm not going to wake her.'

'OK.' I resisted the urge to yell my frustration at her. Maybe she was right. 'I'll call again in the morning. Look, I'm going into a tunnel, got to go.' I cut the phone's power.

We were hitting the outskirts of Fakenham and almost immediately the racecourse was signposted to the right. We took the turn, then another less than half a mile later. The roads were getting narrower each time. Suzy made few concessions. 'Now what?'

'Drive in and park up, I suppose.' I picked up the moan-phone and called the Yes Man. 'We're here.'

'You still have the mobile and the canisters?'

'Yes.' What the fuck did he think? That I'd popped them into a car-boot sale?

'The pickup should be there soon. Bring him in on Quebec.'

'OK, on Quebec. It'll be a Maglite.'

'I don't care what it is. Just bring him in and get on board.' The phone went dead.

The road became a narrow stretch of tarmac with white-painted posts either side, which soon became a long blur as Suzy forgot to relax her right foot. I was looking out for possible landing sites in case we couldn't get on to the race-course itself. We passed tennis courts to the right, some buildings to the left, and arrived in a large gravelled parking area. Cars were clustered round the entrance to what looked like a sports club, with signposts pointing off to squash courts and all sorts. Light shone from the front windows and I could see a group of not-so-sporty figures inside, propping up the bar.

The racecourse was in front of us, fenced off by white-plastic rails. To our half-right was the shadow of the grandstand. Suzy parked and we took our cover docs from under the seats and stuffed our ready bags with all the empty military NBC wrappers. We didn't want the local police finding a car full of interest. They'd be happy with just a few new pairs of socks and my Next boxers.

Suzy brought the key with her as we started towards the grandstand. That way she knew it wouldn't be found in a wheel arch by accident. There had been no instructions from the Yes Man about the car, but it would need to be collected quickly; it was an untidy loose end.

The glow of the town was off to our left, a floodlit church tower dominating the high ground. I began to hear a faint rattle in the distance, which became the more definable clatter of rotor-blades somewhere in the darkness above us. He was coming in without lights.

I fumbled around and pulled out the mini Maglite, turning the top to switch it on as I hummed the Bridal March. 'Here comes the bride, daa-daa-de-daa.' Suzy looked at me as if I was having a fit. 'It's the only way I can remember Quebec. Get it? "Here comes the bride, daa-daa-de-daa."' I kept mumbling it to myself as I pointed the Maglite into the air, twisting and untwisting the end in time with the beats to transmit the Morse letter Q. Aboard the helicopter they would be seeing the pinprick of white light from below in a field of darkness – and if they didn't, I'd just keep on doing it until they did.

Here comes the bride, daa-daa-de-daa.

The noise in the sky became a throbbing roar, and within

221

seconds I could make out the nose of the heli just fifty feet above and in front of us, coming in low. I pointed the Maglite down to the grass and kept it on as a reference point for the pilot, and to make sure it didn't shine into his eyes. From the aircraft's silhouette, I knew it was a Jet Ranger.

It hovered for a few seconds, the downwash from its rotors battering against us as it wavered left to right before plopping down on its skids about twenty feet away. I turned off the Maglite and there was a sudden solitary flash from the navigation light under the Jet Ranger's belly to give us a fix in case we hadn't seen it. As if.

Suzy ran past me to the aircraft's nose, then round to the opening door. I followed, my bag on my shoulder, automatically bending at the waist. I never knew why people did that because the rotors are always well above head height.

The downdraught buffeted my face and clothes as I followed her round, and the smell of aviation exhaust drenched the air.

My bag was soon being bundled into the back, and I had Suzy's arse in my face as I tried to get in and she tried to organize her own bag behind the seats. We eventually made it and I pulled the door closed, cocooning us in a world of warmth and comparatively little noise. I could smell coffee, but not strongly enough to wipe out Suzy's vomit.

The Jet Ranger lifted from the ground. The pilot, seated directly in front of me, was wearing NVG [night-viewing goggles], like a pair of small binoculars held in place by a head harness, about half an inch in front of his eyes. They were bathed in the green glow from the rear of the goggles as he checked the take-off.

Suzy turned and started shoving the bags further behind us, to create more space, then the roar of the engine drowned everything else. It was pointless talking, which suited me fine.

The guy sitting next to the pilot pushed himself round in his seat until he more or less faced us. He had a headset on, with a boom mike by his mouth. In the low light of the instruments I could see he was a small, smily, friendly overweight thirtysomething with dark, curly hair. He stuck his thumb up by his ear and his forefinger down by his mouth, and shouted at me almost apologetically: 'The phone, please? The phone?' He was wearing a padded check shirt, open over a *Lord of the Rings* T-shirt that strained across his stomach. I pushed my hand into my jeans pocket and produced the girl's Motorola. Frodo took it with a nod of thanks.

The lights of Fakenham shrank below and behind us as the pilot got busy talking to whoever pilots talk to when flying these things covertly round the UK. Well, not that covertly because they were operated by commercial companies with pilots who liked to moonlight for the Firm. Why go to the expense of buying and running your own when you can hire them by the hour? Apart from anything else, it was a better cover.

Frodo the tech took the SIM card out of the phone and inserted it into a machine on his lap about the size of a reporter's notebook. Within a few seconds words and numbers were scrolling down the display panel in front of him, and he was jabbering into his mouthpiece. I couldn't hear what he was saying, but guessed he was on a radio net that connected him to the Yes Man, or whoever was checking these out. It would be only a matter of minutes before they knew everyone she'd ever talked to or been called by.

I gazed vacantly out of the window, my mind very much in Bromley. My operational concerns were finished for the moment: I had no control over what was happening to me, I was in the hands of the pilot.

What would I do with her if the attack had already taken place? Would it be safer to keep her in England, or risk her moving through a possibly contaminated airport?

I suddenly thought of something I did have control of. I leant forward and tapped the tech on the shoulder. He turned and I mimicked pulling one of his earphones out of the way. He did and leant closer. 'Come on, I can smell it. Where's the brew?'

He spoke into his mouthpiece and the pilot felt around by

223

his feet and produced a large stainless-steel flask. I took off the cup, unscrewed the top, and poured out half a cupful. I offered it to the two in front, but they shook their heads. Maybe they'd just finished one. Suzy took it and had a few sips before offering it back to me. It was black and very sweet, but it hit the spot.

I dug into my jeans and pulled out one very squashed card of pills. I swallowed four with a swig and passed them to Suzy with the cup. I turned away and looked out of my window again at the bright ribbon of the M11 in the distance, and beyond that the lights of Cambridge.

Frodo talked some more into his mike, nodding as he turned to me and took off the headset, gesturing to me to put it on. As the white, cloth-covered cans went over my ears, all I could hear was the gentle thud of the rotors in the background.

Then – 'Are you there?' It was the Yes Man. 'Hello?'

Frodo held my hand and guided me to the rocker switch on the headset lead so I could flick to send. I nodded my thanks. I already knew how to do it, but there was no point offending him. 'Yes, I'm here.'

'Listen in. You're going into Northolt. Roger so far?'

We were on secure comms, so we could talk in clear speech, yet as soon as he got on a radio he thought he was back running the signals department.

'Roger that.' Play the game.

'Yvette will be there with transport. Roger so far?'

'Roger that.'

'OK, well done with the phone. It has been used once, nearly two hours ago. That mobile number is still static in the area of King's Cross station, operating in the triangle formed by Pentonville Road, Gray's Inn Road and King's Cross Bridge. Roger so—'

'We know it, we know the building. Something's wrong here. The source lives only about three hundred away.'

'Roger that, I'll—'

'Get the source to call us once we're on the ground.

We might be able to use him. There's something going on here.'

'Agreed, out.'

I passed the headphones back to the tech and turned to Suzy, putting my mouth right into her ear to pass on what the Yes Man had said.

Her face lit up. 'She was probably checking in to say she made it OK.' Suzy was actually getting off on all this stuff.

37

Sunday 11 May, 00:04 hrs

The glow of London bathed the horizon, and before long the huge towers of Canary Wharf cut into the skyline, their navigation lights strobing through the low cloud.

The clean-up team probably accounted for one or more of the sets of headlamps below us, heading out of the city on their way to King's Lynn. Their job would be to sterilize the place before first light, on the pretext of investigating gas leaks or whatever. They wouldn't have a clue what had happened, and they'd never ask – the body would be taken away, then they'd throw the Immigration boys into a wagon and eventually introduce them to Simon. The chopper pilot and Frodo the tech would join them later. No way would any of them be let loose until this was over.

The pilot had some chat into his headset and we kicked right. It wouldn't be long now before we were landing at RAF Northolt in West London. For a moment I wondered if we'd be taken to the command control centre for a briefing, as I had been during the Kosovo and Bosnia campaigns. It was like something out of a James Bond film, big screens all over the place and everybody being very busy and efficient as they hit keyboards and drank coffee out of polystyrene cups. But I somehow thought that wasn't going to be for us today. Our shirts just weren't crisp enough.

Soon we were over the A40, the busy dual carriageway cutting into London from the west, and minutes later were starting our approach into the darkened military airfield that bordered it. Rain began to spatter against the Perspex and the pilot gave the wipers a quick burst.

We were coming down near two saloon cars and a van, all parked with their headlamps on. In the orange strobe of our navigation lights I could see the shapes of the people inside them, dodging the downdraught from the rotors and the rain. One of the cars was one-up, the other two were both two-up.

Our skids settled on the hard standing and the rotors lost momentum as the whine of the turbo engines gradually subsided. The pilot turned, gave me the OK to pull the door handle, and I clambered out. The heat from the exhaust, the rotor wash and the stink of aviation fuel meant I hardly felt the rain. Suzy pushed out our two ready bags, then followed.

As we ran towards the vehicles a figure emerged from what looked like a Mondeo, and I realized it was Yvette, pulling up the hood on her Gore-Tex. She stayed by the driver's door as the rotors came to a halt.

Two men in jeans and sweatshirts jumped out of an unmarked white Transit and ran towards the aircraft. As they got closer I could see it was Sundance and Trainers, ignoring me as they went past. Yvette beckoned to us. As we crossed the pan, she was busy opening a large aluminium box down by the nearside wheel. We could only just hear her voice. 'Please, the canisters in here.'

I squatted down with my ready bag. The two crew were led towards the back of the van. The pilot was flapping big-time and looked to me for support. 'What's going on here?'

I shrugged as one of the guys in jeans replied for me: 'Don't worry, everything's fine. Just hop in the back, mate.' The way

227

Sundance and Trainers were gripping them, they didn't have much choice.

'And could I please have the Peugeot keys so we can clean up in Norfolk?'

Suzy put her ready bag down and fished in her jeans while I went into mine. I pulled out the carrier-bag, smeared with dry blood, that contained everything we had taken from the woman apart from the phone, and put it into what looked like a cool-box, except this thing was fastened with four latches to keep it airtight.

By the look on Yvette's face, she was starting to get a noseful of the contents of Suzy's bag as she handed over the key.

'It's in the racecourse car park.' Suzy's voice was uncharacteristically quiet, maybe trying to mimic the Golf Club. 'By the sports centre.'

Yvette nodded a thank-you. 'You need to call him for an update. There are antibiotics in the glove compartment and a complete new set of NBC protection in the boot for you both.'

The back doors of the Transit slammed shut and it pulled away. I closed the lid on the container and saw a smile appear under the Gore-Tex hood. 'Well done, both of you. Over to your right you can just see a flashing blue light where the van is going. Head for that and you'll be let out of the airfield. Good luck.'

She picked up the box and carried it to the back of the other car, a dark Vauxhall Vectra. The engine turned over as soon as the box was strapped in place with a seatbelt. The driver spun the vehicle and drove off towards the flashing blue light as soon as Yvette was in the passenger seat.

While Suzy took the ready bags to the back of the Mondeo and started to scrape out her vomit, I pulled out the moan-phone, turned it on and dialled the Yes Man. The phone rang twice this time but, as normal, the Yes Man had no time for ceremony.

'Where are you?'

'Northolt. We have the car.'

'Well, get mobile. The source says he knows nothing about King's Cross. He will call but doesn't want to get involved. He feels he could be compromised.'

'Tough.'

'Exactly. Do what needs to be done, and I want minute-by-minute sit reps from you on the ground. Roger that?'

'Roger that.'

He'd be lucky. I cut him off and called to Suzy, 'No time to clean up. Get your phone on. Fuck-face is going to call.'

Suzy got the boot open and started preparing the new NBC kit for the ready bags. I helped take it out of its packaging, and punched through the arms and legs.

Damp from the rain, we jumped into the car and she got her foot down towards the flashing light, wipers on double-time. It turned out to belong to an MoD police Land Rover, parked by one of the crash safety gates in the chainlink fence that marked the airfield's perimeter. The yellow fluorescent-jacketed MoD plod waved us through and closed the gate behind us. Not having a clue where to go from here, we just headed for the lights we thought were the A40, then chucked a left, heading east towards the city, every speed camera we passed flashing us a hello.

We didn't speak much: there was nothing much to say. I didn't know what was preying on her mind sufficiently to keep her quiet, but I had more than enough on mine.

I took the antibiotics out of the glove compartment and swallowed four, not having a clue if I was overdosing with these things. They certainly gave me a stomach ache, but didn't they turn your teeth yellow or something? The plastic-coated capsules scraped down my throat as I pushed out another four for Suzy and handed them over on an open palm.

'I'll take 'em once we get there.' She passed a couple of cars on the inside lane and their spray splashed against our windscreen. 'I can't dry swallow, fucking horrible.'

I felt my guts start to rumble. Either they were telling me it was a long time since tea at Morrisons, or the antibiotics were already hard at work killing off all my flora. I didn't care how much good stuff they took with them as long as they blitzed every atom of whatever-it-was-called-*pestis* they came across.

38

It was fifteen past midnight by the dash clock as we hit the elevated section of the A40, past the BBC buildings and White City redevelopment site. Fuck it. I pulled my phone from my bumbag.

Suzy was still focused on the oncoming lights, but knew exactly what was happening. 'You really want to talk to her, don't you? Make your last call? You know, just in case?'

I turned the phone on and the welcome screen glowed at me. 'Sort of.' I hadn't thought about it quite like that. I never did: it wasn't as if I'd be leaving much behind, and right now she probably felt I'd be doing her a favour.

I hit the numbers and got the ringing tone at the Sycamores. It seemed to go on for ever before Carmen answered.

'Hello? Hello?' She sounded confused.

Jabbing a finger in my left ear, I leant down once more into the footwell. 'It's me, Nick. Listen, I need to talk to her.'

Carmen wasn't listening. 'It's past midnight. I told you, I'm not—'

'Carmen, please – please wake her up. I really want to talk to her before she leaves. I might not get another chance. You understand, don't you?'

There was a heavy sigh, and I listened to the rustling as she walked out of her bedroom, on to the landing. 'I'm turning the phone off after this. We need to sleep, you know, we have a busy day ahead of us.'

I heard some mumbling that I couldn't make out because of the noise of the car, but to my surprise Kelly answered quickly and sounded quite awake. 'Where are you? I can't hear you.'

'I'm in a car. You're up late.'

'Well, yeah, just doing stuff. You know.'

'I've got to drive up north, so I won't be able to come and see you off. But Josh will pick you up, yeah?' I carried on before she had a chance to respond. 'I'm so sorry, but there's nothing I can do. I'll try to get there but, you know . . .'

She was scarily calm. 'It's OK, Nick.'

'I want to see you. I want to say sorry you've had such a crap time here, us not being able to spend much time together, not being able to see Dr Hughes any more, but—'

'Hey, really, it's OK. Josh called and it's cool. He's going to call Dr Hughes on Monday and sort things out with a therapist back home. Everything's cool. You know, I think coming here really did help me.'

'He's talked to you already?'

'Sure, and we've got it all sorted out.'

'Really? That's fantastic. Look, as soon as I've finished this job I'll fly over.'

'Will you call me when I get back to Josh's?'

'Try and stop me.'

''Bye, then.'

'OK, 'bye.'

'Nick?'

'What?'

'I love you.'

The antibiotics attacked my stomach again. 'Me too. Gotta go.' I hit the off key.

*

232

The traffic had built up now we were entering the city proper. Suzy's eyes were still on the road as we jumped a red. I was curious. 'You've really got no one to call?'

'No one.'

Her ops phone rang and it went immediately to her ear. 'Yes?' There was no reaction in her face as she listened, her eyes still fixed on the road ahead. 'We don't give a shit – stay there and watch, we'll meet at Boots.'

He must have closed down. 'Fucking slope.' She put away the cell. 'He's complaining this isn't what he's here for. Says he could be compromised. Who gives a shit?'

'Has he seen anything?'

She shook her head.

We passed the British Library on the main, Euston Road, just short of King's Cross. The roadworks stretched towards us from the station, clogging the late-night traffic. Huge concrete dividers and red and white fluorescent tape channelled vehicles and pedestrians through what felt like a series of sheep pens. I pointed up at a blue parking sign and she turned left, taking us down the side of the library to some roadside pay-and-display parking bays. At this time of night there was no charge.

We double-checked the doors and the inside of the Mondeo, then went back on to the main and turned left towards the station. It was less than a hundred metres away. The fast-food joints were doing a steady trade. Wobbly twentysomethings, with wet jackets and hair, tried to walk in straight lines as they attacked their doner kebabs after a night on the Bacardi Breezers. A couple of hookers in a shop doorway tried to catch their eye, and grimy figures were curled up in blankets and greasy sleeping-bags in every vacant doorway.

Suzy tilted her head and I looked over. The girls had cornered a Breezer boy as he tried to eat from a polystyrene tray. 'It's nothing like as bad as it used to be,' she said. 'But it's not as if anything's been sorted – they've just been moved on elsewhere.'

233

We were almost at Boots, but there was no sign of the source. We had a clear view of the target, maybe sixty metres ahead. The triangle of buildings looked even more like the bow of a cruise liner bearing down on us through the falling rain. It had probably been quite a grand sight when it went up in Victoria's reign or whenever, but now the ground floor consisted of boarded-up shopfronts, and the three above of smoke- and dirt-blackened sash windows. The bow cut into the small pedestrian area the source had crossed when we followed him out of the station.

The shop on the right had sold kebabs, burgers and chips in a bygone age. Its cheap, luminous handpainted signs told us Jim used to be the boy cutting the finest chunks of meat off the spinning joint, but it certainly wouldn't have been in this century. It'd been a long time since anyone had raised the metal shutters.

The shop on the left had been called MTC. Its front was covered with sheets of chipboard; the green sign above said it had been a booking office. It must have gone to the wall about the same time as Joe's: the number to call for the best ticket deals in town didn't even have an old national prefix.

We joined the three backpackers who were leaning against Boots' window to shelter from the rain, scratching their heads as they studied an A–Z and got hassled by drunks and drug-dealers. Immediately left, between us and the McD's over the road, the CCTV camera was pointing towards the ship's bow, and no doubt had a clear view of the roads each side of it. I looked down at Suzy and she shrugged her shoulders. 'He isn't here. So what? His phone comes up without a number. Fuck him, let's get on with it.'

'Give it a minute, he could be out there somewhere, making sure we're clear.'

Topping the bow of the brick ship was a tall belvedere tower, looking a bit like a lead-covered Moulin Rouge without the sails. In its heyday it had probably been the pride and joy of King's Cross, but now it looked just like the rest of the

234

building, covered in grime and pigeon shit, completely dilapidated. The sooner they dug it out and got on with the gateway to Europe the better.

I could see straight up Birkenhead Street. The CCTV was about 250 metres away, swivelling into a new position. Neon flooding from the fast-food joints glistened on the wet pavement the other side of the road, casting a pool of light across the dodgy-looking characters hanging around outside the amusement arcade. The only place that didn't seem to have a light on was the police station at the corner of Birkenhead. It didn't necessarily mean it was closed: who knew what was going on behind the mirrored glass?

I got out my moan-phone as Suzy played the girlfriend and cuddled into me. Two policemen in yellow fluorescent jackets came past and decided it was time to wake up a bundle in Boots' doorway and move it on.

The Yes Man was as charming as ever, and I could still hear a load of other voices in the background. 'What?'

'We're here. The car's static along the eastern side of the British Library and we're at the station looking at the target. The source isn't here. You want us to lift him after this, find out what he knows?'

'Negative. There's no need, he's not going anywhere. What can you see?'

'No signs of life yet. We'll give him another five minutes. Wait . . .' A group of teenagers with too much illegal substance in them shouted their way past us and the two policemen eyed them knowingly as I got back to the Yes Man. 'If he doesn't show, we'll bin him. Wait . . . is the signal still there?'

'Of course,' he snapped. 'Otherwise I would have told you. Don't forget, I want sit reps.'

The phone went dead and I powered it down. The Yes Man had to rely on us calling him: he would never make the call in case he compromised us, but it was always best to turn the thing off just in case.

Minutes were being wasted. 'Fuck it, let's go.'

As the police started following the teenagers, Suzy nodded and put her arm in mine. We walked out of cover and into the rain towards Pentonville. We weren't going to cross just yet, but stay this side for the start of our 360 of the target. We'd do two recces: the first to get a general overview, the second for a close examination of locks and other detail.

We crossed the junction to the left of the station, and waded through the McFlurry cups littering the pavement outside the closed McDonald's. Apart from MTC, the hundred-metre stretch of building was covered at street level all the way down to King's Cross Bridge with the purple-painted chipboard I'd stood by when we first followed the source and his two mates from Starbucks.

Suzy smiled away at me, as you would that time of night, after a few hours together in a pub and a romantic walk home in the constant but now gentle rain. I looked up to the sky. 'We won't be able to get in from this side. You seen the street-lighting?'

She nodded. It was the same height as the tops of the windows on the second floor. They were in shit state, but these huge windows would let in enough light to cast shadows everywhere. For anybody on those first two floors, the street-lighting would provide illumination, but they'd have to keep below the sills, even during the day – especially as I could see straight through the first-floor windows to Gray's Inn Road. They'd certainly be on hard routine, no smoking, no lights, no cooking.

Any movement would be easily spotted from the buildings on Gray's Inn. The second- and third-floor windows on this side were a little smaller than the ones below, and I could only see enough of the two upper floors to tell it wasn't an open space.

There was still no sign of life, no lights, no condensation, not even a window covered with net curtains or sheets of news-paper. Further down Pentonville there was a collection of two-storey buildings that were still being used; they made up

236

the rear of the triangle, the stern of the ship. They probably dated from the sixties, and included a mock KFC and a radio shop. No doubt the owners had their fingers crossed that the developers would buy them out as well.

We crossed Pentonville and walked down to the base of the triangle, King's Cross Bridge. Maybe there had been a bridge at one time, probably over a canal, but now it was about seventy metres of road linking Pentonville with Gray's Inn.

We turned right, beneath yet another CCTV, and crossed Gray's Inn as a police car and van, both full of uniforms, wailed behind us.

39

The CCTV camera in front of King's Cross station was now pointing towards the British Library. Suzy grinned as she got to grips with another wad of nicotine gum. 'Maybe they'll take them down again when this place is all nice and shiny.'

'About as much chance as Ken Livingstone getting a second term.'

The traffic splashed its way up Gray's Inn as we checked the Boots shopfront again for the source. The target building made definite sense to me as an FOB [forward operations base]. The construction site probably wasn't working at weekends, so there'd be no one overlooking from that side, even if they could see through the plastic sheeting. The shops this side of Gray's Inn had office-for-rent signs sticking out from the floors above them, but it wouldn't be too much of a problem to keep out of sight of anyone working in one of them over the weekend – especially if the ASU members confined themselves to a high room on the Pentonville side of the building.

I checked the bell pushes on the doors sandwiched between the shopfronts our side of the road. I wanted to try to see if any of the flats were residential, including the ones above

Costcutter. Hardly any had a name on them, and those that did were scribbled on scraps of paper.

Even with CCTV everywhere, there were other factors that made it a good choice of FOB. In a hotel room there'd always be the risk of someone next door overhearing them prepare. With a rented room or flat, there are booking procedures, agreements, deposits, all that rigmarole to go through and potentially compromise. And they hadn't had to force their way into someone's home, take them hostage or kill them so that they could use the location; all they'd had to do was get in there and lie low.

I tried to imagine them inside, maybe in new sleeping-bags, eating more shit in trays. Did they pray before going on a job? Were they shitting themselves, or just totally focused? Were there any more women up there? Was their plan to kill themselves after the attack, or just move round the city for a few more days, contaminating fresh victims until they were incapable of going any further?

A couple of twentysomethings were making the best of their cans of Stella in the shelter of a shop doorway, with a young girl who looked like she was sleeping rough too. She was in ripped jeans, T-shirt and an old green nylon bomber jacket, and couldn't have been more than a year older than Kelly. Her gaunt face was full of zits and her hair as wet and greasy as the pavement. She leant against an *Evening Standard* newsbox that headlined more SARS hysteria, as they swayed and she giggled. One of the guys said they should both get a blow-job after the favour they were about to do her. She took a swig from one of their cans. 'Maybe.' Her eyes were as big as saucers, the pupils huge and black.

'You feeling OK?' Suzy jabbed my arm.

The pain had returned to my stomach. 'You know, those sandwiches could have been a bit dodgy.'

As we neared the top of the road by the ship's bow, traffic was backed up at the lights, windscreen wipers thrashing. The shopfronts this side of the building didn't have nice purple chipboard to disguise them. They mostly just had rusty shutters. I still couldn't see any light coming from inside and, as far as I'd been able to see, all the doors that led upstairs were well and truly padlocked.

We approached the police station on the corner of Birkenhead. Suzy was still upbeat as we passed its CCTV. 'You see, it's not all bad news. At least that one only looks at the station.'

We crossed towards the arcade. The source's no-show was pissing me off. 'Let's do a circuit before we go back round for the locks recce. I want to go past the source's house anyway to see if he's in. I just don't trust that fucker.'

We looked up Birkenhead to check what the CCTV at the T-junction of St Chad's was up to. It had turned away from the direction of the source's flat, and now pointed to the right of the junction.

Suddenly Suzy stopped and turned, as if to kiss me. 'It's him, coming down on the left.'

I glanced up. The source was making his way towards the station. I turned back with her. 'We'll get him at the junction.'

Turning left at the arcade, we stopped and she gobbed out her gum before we cuddled. Seconds later he appeared, raincoat collar up, arms folded. He hesitated when he saw us, then quickly crossed the road. As the flashing lights played across his face I could see he was as pissed off as I was. But that didn't matter. Suzy got in first as he took his final three or four steps to get under the cover of the arcade. 'You're fucking late – we wanted eyes on over there from—'

'Do not be stupid, I cannot afford to do these things. The whole world is watching.' His eyes darted about him as if he expected to see a face at every window. 'I had to leave for a while, there was too much activity in the streets. I was just coming to meet with you.'

Suzy gave him her lovely-to-see-you smile. 'You see anything?'

'No, nothing. What do you people expect of me? I

240

discovered King's Lynn for you, what else do you want?'

It sounded like bullshit to me. 'This ASU is right on your fucking doorstep and you know nothing about it?'

His bloodshot eyes screwed tight. 'There are many things that aren't known. I don't care what you think, I care little for you or your country, but you two had better understand one thing. If there are any JI in there, they have nothing to fear, they're happy to become martyrs. They will attack with whatever is in those bottles. I know these people – I've been fighting for fifteen years.'

Suzy leant towards him. 'You don't like us much, do you, so what are you doing here?'

He pursed his lips and took several deep breaths as his eyes dropped away from us. 'Because you people tell me I have no choice.'

Neither of us answered. I remembered the Yes Man on his cell in the flat saying he had no choice. They had him by the bollocks somehow. I knew the feeling.

He sighed, looked up, then gave a smile. 'I will die fighting.' And with that he walked away.

Suzy and I watched as he disappeared up Birkenhead, then followed. We got to the driveway behind his flat as a crack of light pushed its way through the closed curtains on the top floor.

The zit-faced girl and the two twentysomethings emerged from a dark area further down St Chad's, staggering, not concerned about the rain – or us – as they squabbled over the contents of a small plastic bag. The girl giggled as they passed, recognizing us, and ran her tongue over her scabby lips.

We crossed into the shadows in case the CCTV decided to turn in our direction. The place where the three had emerged seemed to be an entry-point into a Jaguar garage, and as we passed a soft but urgent voice called out to me, 'Oi, mate, you want some?'

I peered into the darkness as a lighter clicked and he lit up. He was a white guy, cocky-looking, about the same age as the two drunks who had just left him. He was in ripped jeans and a rain-soaked leather jacket. He'd been so off his head the last time he saw us we weren't registering at all.

'Want some what?' I knew I'd asked the question, but the voice didn't sound like mine.

The dealer didn't notice. He took the cigarette out of his mouth and gestured with his hand. 'Whatever – whites, brown, take your pick.' He spoke with a lisp. 'Come in here – get off the road, just in here. It'll be all right.'

I let go of Suzy and turned to face him. She seemed to know what I was about to do before I did. 'No, not now, *not now* . . .'

40

She stayed on the pavement as I walked into the shadows. The dealer pulled himself off the wall and shuffled from one foot to the other. 'What you want, then, mate? I got whatever. I got whites, I got brown, you name it.'

I was about three feet away from him, my eyes fixed on his head. He glanced over at Suzy, a bit worried now. 'Here, tell her to—'

That was all he got out. My left hand grabbed the back of his scrawny neck and I punched him hard under his chin with the heel of my right. His head snapped back and he dropped like a bag of shit on to the concrete. I knew now why he'd been lisping: whatever it was that he'd been hiding under his tongue flew out on to the pavement.

'Fuck you – cunt.' There was no lisp now.

He started moving, so I did what I had to. I kicked him in the face. I couldn't tell exactly where it connected in the dark below me, but it didn't really matter. I kicked him again as Suzy grabbed at my arm, whispering loudly. 'What the fuck are you doing? Come on . . .'

The guy was face down so I gave him one in the side, hoping to get a kidney, and a couple more in the gut. I yanked myself free from her and bent down.

'This isn't the time!'

I started dragging him across the wet tarmac towards the kerb. Suzy tried to pull me the other way. 'What are you—'

I got him face down, his shoulder on the edge of the kerb, his elbow above the gutter. He tried to curl into a ball but I grabbed his arm and pulled it out again.

Suzy got down on one knee. 'For fuck's sake! Give him to me.' She grabbed his wrist and pulled the arm out straight. He moved his legs, trying to protect himself. His voice was blurred – his mouth must have been full of blood. 'You cunts, cunts.' He tried to curl up again, trying to protect himself. Suzy still had him in a wristlock, elbow pointing outwards, his fore-arm on the kerb. 'For fuck's sake, get on with it.'

I jumped a foot or so in the air, brought my right foot higher, and kicked back down with all my strength and weight. There was a loud crunch as my right foot made contact and my left landed on the tarmac. He screamed like a pig. I turned and kicked into his face once more to shut him up. Suzy was already moving out on to St Chad's, looking up at the CCTV. 'Come on, come on, come on!' She turned right, towards Gray's Inn, and I followed, catching her up within a few paces.

'What the fuck is going on, Nick?' She looked ahead, check-ing, as I kicked my boots through a couple of puddles to get the blood off. 'Have you decided to devote a little quality time to totally fucking this job up?'

I didn't bother answering: I didn't care what she thought. But she still had a little more to add. 'I don't know what your problem is, but I'll bet it's fucking hard to pronounce.'

She quickened her step. Fuck it, I was sure it was all pretty straightforward, once people understood my point of view, but now wasn't the time to explain it to her. 'Listen, it's done, I fucked up, sorry.' I grabbed her arm to slow her down, then reached for the moan-phone.

The traffic was still busy, so I had to plug my empty ear with my finger again after dialling the Yes Man.

'What?'

'We've done the 360 and we've seen nothing, no signs of life. Are the signals still up?'

'Yes. I want you in there just as soon—'

I cut him short. Once the op started *he* had to listen because I was the man on the ground. 'We've seen the source. He's got nothing. We're going to go and get a closer look at the target building right now.'

We were heading back up towards the ship's bow. 'I'll call back soon.' I closed down. It felt good to have the final word now and again.

Suzy was on my arm again and checking over her shoulder in case of any follow-up. She was like a dog with a bone. 'Have you got a connection loose or something? You shouldn't have done that, it could jeopardize the whole job.'

'No, it couldn't. I did us a favour. If he goes to the police they'll be concentrating on the block back there, so that makes it even better for us when we try to make entry here. That's if he even goes to the police.'

'Fucking hell, that's the thickest thing I've ever heard.'

I held her as we dodged the puddles and double-timed it over King's Cross Bridge. 'OK, MOE girl, next phase – the locks.'

She nodded and changed sides so that she had her left arm through my right. MOE girl wanted to be nearer the locks. As we started to walk along the target, a group of black kids in baggy jeans with hoodies up over ball caps fell in behind us, eating chips and swigging from Coke cans.

A can was shaken and sprayed over one of the crew behind us and they all had a good laugh, apart from the victim who was pissed off that his new trainers were not only wet from rain but had now got the good news with Coca-Cola. Suzy and I slowed down to give them time to pass and get some distance; this was good for us, it gave us a natural reason for stalling, and time to have a look about before we carried on slowly behind the boys.

245

Four derelict shopfronts and adjacent doors made up the ground floor of the target building.

The first looked as if it had once been an Indian restaurant. Did the grime about the door or the locks have handmarks? Had they been pulled open lately? These places looked as if they'd been closed down for ages, so any recent disturbance should be easy to detect.

It was boarded up with chipboard and a dirty, rusting padlock that hadn't been touched for years.

Next along was Mole Jazz, which had either been a club or a record shop – it was hard to tell from what was left of the sign. The padlock on the door was in the same state, grimy and virtually rusted solid, with a bit of old chewing gum stuck in its keyhole by a bored passer-by.

Dress Wright, next up, was covered with heavily locked shutters, which someone had pissed over months ago and taken off the first couple of layers of grime. It was highly unlikely to be an entry- or escape-point: shutters make too much noise and take too long to open and close.

The Eastern Eye had definitely once been an Indian restaurant, and was the last premises before Jim's burger bar. There was a door to the right of the boarded-up shopfront: its padlock wasn't new, but had definitely seen some action. Suzy saw it too and we stopped, held each other and smiled, me with my back to the entrance to afford her a better look. Her wet hair brushed against my face as she confirmed what I'd seen. 'The dirt's been disturbed – the lock's been opened, and very recently. Can't see any tell-tales, but it could have been the girl, locking her mates in before heading back to King's Lynn.' Suzy started to run a hand over the top of the door frame.

'But she didn't have another key with her.'

'What do you think I'm doing this for, dickhead?' She brought her hand back down and her eyes switched into excited mode. 'Got it, she must have been coming back. Bet these fuckers have an escape route if she's locked them in.'

Our faces were just inches apart, and I could feel her breath on my face. 'Better still check, MOE girl. You still might have to work your magic.'

I smiled as I put my arms round her once more as she tested the key. She wouldn't have turned it in case she couldn't close it again, or the key broke. All seemed well. A police car screamed past us on Gray's Inn Road. Sirens were as common as cuddling couples round here; no one took any notice of it or us.

She pulled away from me a little, smiled, and planted a kiss on my lips. 'Third-party awareness.'

'I wish that gum was mint flavour, you stink like your ready bag.'

'Bet you still liked it, though.'

We moved back to the bow of the ship and carried on round to the other side to start a closer walk-past of the Pentonville side. The MTC was number 297. Suzy linked arms and pulled herself into me. 'Two nine seven – you see it? No locks. Escape route?'

'Could be – maybe bolted inside, or just locked then boarded up.'

'I guess we'll find out soon enough.'

We carried on down Pentonville and crossed over King's Cross Bridge before turning left and left again, so we could get back to the car yet keep a healthy distance from the target area. Eventually we found ourselves under some railway bridges that led from the station: it was quiet, very few vehicles, hardly any foot traffic. I got on the phone to the Yes Man and detailed what we'd seen.

'How long before you get in and clear the building?'

'That's difficult to say. Could be an hour, maybe two. We need to go through things first.'

'Be quick. Remember, take control of Dark Winter at all costs.' I heard him take a breath as if to launch into a speech.

There wasn't enough time for that shit. 'I'll call you when I'm ready.' My second chance to close down on him, and why should I care if I pissed him off? I might be dead soon.

247

'What do you think, then, MOE girl? With that camera down on us, we'll just have to brass it out and make it look as natural as we can. I can't see any other way out. Assuming you turn a key, of course.'

She ignored the dig. 'What about the NBC kit? We can't go in there already rigged up.'

'If we're not compromised on entry, we can get into it as soon as we're inside, then clear the building until it goes noisy.'

She nodded, and started to look excited again, I didn't know why: we were probably going to be walking into an absolute nightmare.

41

Suzy ran her fingers through her soaking hair as we skirted the pools of light around the construction area. I slowed down a little: we weren't that far from the car but I didn't want us to be sitting in it longer than we had to. We might get some unwelcome attention from the police in these times of high terrorist alert or, round here, the Vice Squad. The last thing we needed was someone in a uniform inviting us to step out of the vehicle and give him a guided tour of the boot.

'OK, MOE girl, how about this for a plan? We take the ready bags, we get to the door. We cuddle just like before, and you turn that key, yeah? What sort is it?'

I knew she'd have her MOE kit on her body just in case.

'Ward. Shouldn't be too bad.'

'So, you open the lock, I'll move inside and cover you while you bring in the ready bags and close the door. Once you get in, we jam it.'

Suzy glanced across at the world's biggest construction site. 'There's got to be something we could use lying around here.' We needed to stop the entry door from being opened again and block the possible escape route if it went noisy. We had to contain the ASU like pigs in a poke if we were to have a chance of dealing with them.

'Then we get the NBC kit on. I'm not going to put my hood up – it was making too much noise. I'll get my respirator on but keep the hood down until the last possible moment.' This was hardly brain surgery, but we both had to have a clear idea of what was going to happen. 'Once we're ready, we'll clear the place from the bottom up. Unless we hear them, we'll have to go through room by room.'

'What if we've got the wrong door and no one's in that part of the building? We can't walk outside in the NBC kit.'

'We'll have to go across the roof.'

'Dark Winter at all costs, eh?'

I saw that fervent look in her eyes again. 'Something like that.'

She nodded, still scanning the building site. 'Easy money.'

I hoped she was right.

The arches supporting the railway lines in and out of St Pancras and King's Cross were in the process of being stripped bare. But it wasn't the Victorian brickwork I was interested in so much as the scaffolding. There had to be a few stray fixings lying around and, if not, a fresh stock somewhere near. Portakabins stood at every entry-point in the chainlink fence around the sites. I couldn't see any security guards – they'd be tucked inside watching late-night porn on Channel Five.

'Here we go.' Suzy had seen something. She guided me on to the opposite pavement, put her arms round my neck and whispered into my ear. I was getting to like this. 'Time for another of your legendary cuddles, Romeo. You'll find there's some stuff by our feet, just the other side of the fence.'

We embraced and I looked around. I couldn't see any CCTV cameras. 'Right, let's go for it.'

'Last of the great romantics, aren't you?'

I bent down and stretched my fingers through the links. A few seconds later we were heading back to the car, arm in arm, my pocket bulging with five or six steel fixings. Some were triangular, some rectangular, but any of them would do the job.

'The boss needs to know what's happening, Nick. Time for another call.'

She was right, of course. One of the archways had alcove-like chambers, probably a bit of a feature when Gladstone was a boy but only used nowadays by people who needed a piss or a place to smoke some crack. I stepped into one of the shadows to get out of the rain for a few minutes.

'Just one more check.' I pulled out the 9mm and, keeping it by my stomach, put the heel of my right hand on the muzzle and pushed back the top slide just enough to see the glint of brass. She did the same.

I got out the moan-phone, and the first secure bleep didn't even get a chance to sound off before he was up and running. 'What's happening? Where are you?'

I could hear voices behind him. Two sounded American, another I couldn't make out. Maybe Malaysian? Who cared? I had enough worries.

The voices faded, as if the Yes Man was putting some distance between them.

'We're going back to pick up the ready bags and move to target. Should be making entry in less than thirty.'

'Where's the entry-point?'

'Are the signals still in the building?'

'Of course. Where's the entry-point?'

I told him, and for once he sounded nervous. 'Are you sure this is going to work?'

'No.' I was never sure of anything much.

'What are you going to do if you can't make entry?' He sounded almost frantic. He must be under a lot of pressure, and it pleased me to think that a nice big boil might be throbbing on his neck. 'I cannot afford compromise – I don't want to hear about you on the morning news, do you under-stand? Take control of Dark Winter at all costs.'

The American voices came back within earshot, and I realized the other voice wasn't Malaysian: it was German.

251

'If you don't hear from us by first light, you'll know there's a problem. I'll call you afterwards.' I cut him off. I didn't want to stand there all night while he told me how to do the job. He had never been out on the ground: his entire professional life had been spent in front of monitors, sorting out communications and that sort of shit. Being lectured on his third-hand ideas would have pissed me off no end, and I didn't want to be pissed off – I just wanted to be worried, and a bit scared. A little healthy fear was what brought everything into focus and shrank my brain to a size where I could think of nothing but the job and getting away with my body intact. What was it that Josh kept bumping his gums about? 'Courage is just fear that's said its prayer.'

We stepped back into the street-lighting and rain.

'What did he say?'

I studied her face, wishing it would look even a little bit scared. She seemed more distant, but that was all, probably going through her own mental preparation. 'Just the normal shit, reminding me to wear my vest, and no telly or caffeine after nine o'clock.' I mimicked his Home Counties voice. ' "Take control of Dark Winter at all costs." '

Her eyes narrowed. 'He's got a job to do as well, you know.'

We reached the car and Suzy got straight into the driver's seat. 'I'll do first stag.'

I moved to the back of the car as she clicked open the boot and started to unload her documents, just as we'd done in King's Lynn. I began checking my kit, not worried about what was happening around me. Suzy would let me know if there was a problem: the engine would turn on and I'd just slam the boot, walk to my seat and we'd drive. If I got a shout from her, maybe because people were coming towards us, it would be in slow time.

The SD was loaded and made ready, but I still checked chamber and that the mag was on firmly. Then I checked that the top rounds of the spare mags were seated properly and put them into my NBC trousers. I didn't want to be changing mags and have a stoppage if the working parts came forward but got held because the round wasn't correctly positioned – not good if you've got an ASU just feet away wanting to rip your throat out.

I tapped the Mondeo's roof when I was ready and walked along the driver's side. Suzy climbed out and I was pleased to see her face had no expression at all. She was clearly tuning in.

A taxi trundled along the road behind us, splashing through the puddles. I got into the driver's side, checked the keys were in the ignition, and moved the seat back a little. Suzy was mincing about at the rear as I emptied my pockets of everything but the scaffold fixings, including the moan-phone and my own. It all went into my bumbag and was shoved under the passenger seat for what I hoped was the last time. All being well, I'd be back to pick it up in the next couple of hours.

She was ready too. I got the keys, climbed out and joined her as she slung her ready bag over her right shoulder. I chucked mine over my left to make it easier for us to walk together, then hit the key fob. 'I'm gagging for a brew.'

'Good idea. Jack Daniels and Coke will do me.'

She walked round the car and checked each door. Satisfied, she put her arm through mine and we started to walk back towards the main, placing the key under one of the chucks of concrete that diverted the traffic. There'd be no more talking from now. She would be doing exactly the same as I was, trying to visualize every step of the way, trying to create a film in her head of what she wanted to happen, starting with the padlock, as if her eyes were the camera lens and her ears the recording kit.

I visualized going through the door with the 9mm, lifting my feet as I tried to avoid making noise, starting to get my NBC kit on, avoiding any rushed movements. I imagined going upstairs, my feet moving slowly, deliberately, placing themselves on the sides of the stairs to stop them creaking. Finally, I made entry into a room with Suzy backing me as we took on the ASU. I replayed the footage three or four times on the camera inside my head, from entering the target to leaving with Suzy and Dark Winter, and the ASU dead.

Suzy pushed out some gum and her jaws got to work. Now was the time to play the fuck-ups, not later. What if the door had been obstructed? What if they hit us as we were getting the kit on? What if one escaped on to the street with the DW, or threw it out of the window? I hit play, then replay, trying to come up with answers.

It wouldn't go exactly to script – it never did. On the ground, every situation would be different from what we'd imagined. But the films in our heads were a start point; it meant we had a plan. If it all went to rat shit, at least we'd react immediately instead of standing there feeling sorry for ourselves.

42

I checked traser: it was just after two, but the ASU were unlikely to be asleep. They'd be jumping at every hiss of air brakes out on the road or every scratch of a rat on the plaster. If some of them were curled up in their new sleeping-bags, they'd surely have somebody on stag. Which was worse? And did it matter? The fact was, the fuckers were in there and soon we would be too.

We turned left towards King's Cross. All the late-night food places were now closed, but the pavements were strewn with their wrappers and a crateload of old Stella cans. There were fewer drunks hanging around than before, and a couple more whores, but otherwise the cast of characters looked more or less the same. The camera was pointing across the road towards the police station. Maybe its mirrored glass needed more protection at this time of night than members of the public.

As we got to the crossing that took us to the bow of the ship, Suzy pulled her selection of Ward-lock keys out of her jeans pocket. We didn't look out of place round here: this was cheap-hotel land, and backpackers and budget tourists were seen twenty-four hours a day. We crossed the road arm in arm, on to the tip of Jim's kebab shop.

I looked at her and smiled. 'You ready?'

She smiled back. 'You bet.' Her eyes passed mine and moved on to the station CCTV. 'It's still pointing over the road.'

We turned left on to Gray's Inn. When we got to the target, I put down my bag and got into position with my back against the door, holding my arms out for her. She smiled and her bag joined mine as she leant into my embrace. 'Left a bit.' I moved as ordered, and felt the lock press against my left shoulder as I ran my hands through her damp hair and gazed at her adoringly, while she got her arm up for the key then tried to see over my shoulder and get into a good position to open the padlock. 'That'll do, stay there – that's it, just there.'

There was no one else about, not that it mattered. Whatever happened, we'd just have to get on with it, as we did getting over the wall in King's Lynn. Fannying around just gives people more time to take notice.

A steady bass beat came up the road, two cars pulsating with the power of their own speakers. They revved their engines, jumping the lights up by the ship's bow less than twenty metres away as Suzy brought down the key from the door frame. I soon heard the shackle being lifted out of the hasp, and felt her breath against my neck. 'Easy.'

Suzy moved her head a little towards me as I checked the windows above the shops opposite. 'The door's giving.' Her head went back slightly to check out the station CCTV. I smiled and nodded.

I lifted my right hand off her back and moved it between us. If anybody came along now they'd think I was having a feel. Her stomach eased away from me so I could reach under my sweatshirt.

'Wait, wait.' Two figures were approaching from the direction of the ship's stern, on our side of the street.

My hand was still between us, now gripping the pistol. It was just a couple of teenagers, out on the town. Both of them saw where my hand was and obviously thought it was my

256

lucky night. As they passed they gave me a big grin and a 'Wa-hey, get in there!' as Suzy gave me another kiss hard on the lips. She tasted a little more of gum than vomit now. I pulled her a little tighter with my left arm. Maybe this would be the last time I ever got to kiss a woman.

They disappeared towards the station and I had one last check round as I took over holding the door in position with my left hand. 'You ready?'

She gobbed out her gum, then nodded, and I gripped harder on the Browning. I took a deep breath. 'OK, stand by . . . stand by . . . go.'

She backed away slightly to give me some room and I pulled out the weapon, bringing the hammer back with my thumb.

There was a gap of about a foot between the door and the frame. Keeping the weapon low on my chest, I side-stepped and slipped through into the narrow hallway, still controlling the door. It was pitch black inside. The instant I was over the threshold and standing on hard concrete, I thrust out the weapon, bending from the waist to make myself a smaller target, fingerpad resting on the trigger's first pressure.

A shaft of street-light pointed the way to a flight of lino-covered stairs not more than eight metres ahead. I took a step away from the door to let Suzy through, my Browning still straight out in front of me, both hands controlling it now to give the weapon a firm platform.

I pointed the Browning up the stairs as I lifted my foot to make sure I didn't kick any shit on the floor, eyes flashing everywhere. The staircase was five or six paces ahead. A vehicle passed behind me along Gray's Inn, a flash of white light flooding the hall.

There was a closed door to my left. I stopped short of it just as Suzy shut the entry-point behind her, plunging us both into darkness. I stayed still, my mouth open, and cocked an ear at the staircase. A pair of high heels clicked along the pavement. Someone tooted a horn at her. Then there was a gentle rustling

257

as Suzy eased the SDs from their bags. Moments later she was with me.

The pistol went back slowly into my jeans and I flicked up the safety catch with my right thumb. My ears fixed on the closed door, my eyes on the staircase, I held out my right hand and her body moved into it. We fumbled for a moment before my hand gripped the cold metal of the SD. I felt my way to the pistol grip; my thumb found the safety catch and pushed it up.

A very faint glow emanated from the back of the sight as my left hand went down for the Maglite in the front pocket of my jeans. Twisting it on with my mouth, I covered most of the lens with the fingers of my left hand so there was just a pinprick of light.

The door was panelled wood, two lever locks on the left covered with flaking paint, one half-way down with an old brass handle, the other at about chin height. It opened inwards.

I shone the torch just above the handle for Suzy to see as I crossed to the hinge side, doing my best to avoid the lumps of fallen plaster and other crap that littered the floor, making sure the beam didn't shine directly into the keyway and through to the other side.

Suzy knew what I wanted. Her fleece-covered hand closed slowly but firmly around the handle. The rest of her body stayed against the wall, in case someone with a weapon was standing on the other side.

I followed suit, my right shoulder digging into the frame as I pulled out the extendable butt on the SD until the steel rods clicked into position.

I placed the weapon in my right shoulder and swallowed the saliva that had gathered in my open mouth. I could have just let it dribble out, but I didn't want to leave DNA. I adjusted my head so that the cold steel rod holding this side of the butt plate was comfortable against my cheek, and gripped the suppressed barrel with my left hand.

In the torch's gentle glow, I could see that Suzy also had her weapon butt fully extended. Her right hand was locked round the pistol grip, weapon pointing to the floor as she eased the butt into her right shoulder. When I saw that her left hand was back on the door handle, I turned off the Maglite.

There was a burst of laughter out on the street. I pushed down on the safety catch and heard the first click into single-shot. I stepped slowly away from the wall and felt my way forwards until I touched Suzy. I tapped what I guessed was her arm before returning my hand to the barrel.

I heard the handle creak. Butt in the shoulder, both eyes open, sight on, aiming where the door would open, I moved forwards. As the door opened an inch, dull street-lighting penetrated the room through empty extractor fan holes near the high ceiling. I moved left, away from the door frame, both eyes open, and went static. Legs bent, I leant into the weapon, making it a part of me as Suzy moved in and right.

We were both clear of the door now, both inside Jim's kebab shop. Street-light from Pentonville broke through a six-inch gap in the chipboard that covered the tops of MTC's windows. There was a door to our right, half open. Suzy went towards it, moving as quickly as she could without clattering into debris. I followed as she took up position at the hinged side, facing the opening, weapon up, waiting for me to back her.

I was just behind as she took one pace into the next room. I followed, going right, my thumb continuously checking single-shot.

MTC was small, with just an old counter and shelving. Raised voices filtered through from the other side of the chipboard barrier, an argument between a minicab driver and a bunch of clubbers. My eyes followed the voices – a man leaning against 297 was telling the driver he could shove the ride up his arse because twenty-five quid was way too much to get to Herne Hill. The door was bolted, one up, one down.

I turned back towards Jim's, weapon still in the shoulder, picking my way through the shit on the floor. Now that some night vision was kicking in I could make out a sliver of light coming from the bottom of our entry-point doorway into the corridor. A couple of cars passed.

Suzy covered upstairs while I pulled some of the scaffolding pieces from my jeans. As quietly as I could, I wedged three of them firmly between the door and its frame. I didn't want to hang around: I jammed one in about a third of the way up, another a third of the way down. A third went underneath. There was no way this door would be opening in a hurry.

We picked up the bags and moved back into Jim's. Suzy covered her hand with the fleece again to close the door behind us. The room was so dirty and caked with grease I could taste it.

An emergency vehicle drove fast down Pentonville the other side of MTC, its blue light bouncing off the ceiling. I moved to block the door to 297 with the remaining scaffolding joints as Suzy started to get into her NBC kit.

43

I joined Suzy and got the NBC kit on. My SD was never more than arm's length away, lying on its left side, so I could just lean down, grab the pistol grip and flick off the safety catch with my thumb. My eyes never left the closed door into the corridor.

I was soon ready, apart from my respirator. The pistol went into the smock's chest pocket, and I checked the spare SD mags in the map pockets, making sure the rounds were facing down and the concave shapes of the mags were facing backwards. If I had to change mags, all I'd have to do was shove my hand into a pocket, drag out a mag, and the rounds would be facing up and the mag the right way round so it was ready to be placed into the weapon. That was the theory, anyway. In reality, the mags would twist and turn in there, but I liked to feel they were at least in the correct position to start with.

My mind shrank even further as I checked for the last time that the mag was on tight, and that the safety catch moved freely all the way to three-round burst. As Suzy bent to put on her boots, I tested the extended butt to make sure the two rods were still locked. It wobbled a little on its joints, but these things never give you the firm fire position you get with a solid one.

I'd have preferred to be clad from head to toe in Kevlar body armour, but apart from that I was ready. One final check with my thumb that safety was on, and, with my respirator in my left hand, I started moving, picking my feet up carefully as I tried to get used to the big rubber boots again.

A clatter of high heels and laughter passed Jim's kebab as I reached the door. I moved to the right, by the handle, before kneeling down to lay my SD on the floor. I checked the respirator's pressure valve was still tight, pushed my hair back from my forehead and fitted the respirator over my face, making sure I had a nice tight seal and the canister was on firmly.

I took slow, deep breaths to oxygenate myself, inhaling the strong smell of new rubber. Then I stood up. Pistol grip in my right hand, butt in the shoulder, index finger straight along the trigger guard, thumb ready to flick off the safety catch, I checked the SD sight.

Suzy adjusted the butt of her weapon into her shoulder, lodging it in the soft area between the collar-bone and ball-and-socket joint, then flattened herself against the wall on the other side of the doorway. I eased myself forward to get my right ear against the door. I could hear nothing but the sound of vehicles ploughing through puddles in the street. I stood back, adjusting myself into a fire position, legs shoulder-width apart, leaning forward with my left leg bent, hunched over the weapon, making it part of me once more. Suzy reached across and grasped the handle. I nodded, and she eased it down.

The door creaked open a fraction; two inches, then three, then four. I could see nothing but darkness. When the gap was about a foot and a half wide, I moved my left foot very slowly over the threshold, letting the edge of my boot down gently into the corridor. I felt a small chunk of plasterboard press against the rubber, and shifted an inch or two to one side until I found a clear area. I did the same with my right foot, probing for a nice bit of bare concrete. To my right, a sliver of light glinted beneath our entry-point, and just the other side of it two more vehicles splashed through a rain-filled pothole.

Sucking air through the canister, I made my way towards the staircase, five paces to my left. I had both eyes open, weapon at forty-five degrees, pointing up into the darkness.

I reached the bottom of the stairs and peered up into the darkness. My lungs strained to fill themselves with air.

I could hear the faint rustle of Suzy's NBC suit and checked behind me. She was in the doorway, weapon up, covering the darkness above me. She was going to be my one foot on the ground during this tactical bound. While I concentrated on getting up the stairs as quickly and quietly as I could, she'd remain static. When I went firm, she'd come up to me. If there was a drama it would be difficult for her to return fire without hitting me, and the higher I went the more I'd fill her sights. If it went noisy, my plan was to fall flat and slide back down the stairs, letting her take on whatever was up above me.

Time to go for it. I took a slow, deep breath, every muscle in my body tensed to keep the weapon in a really tight firing position.

I moved to the right of the stairway to give Suzy a slightly better arc of fire, and, lifting my right leg, moved it slowly forward, wary of old cans or crisp packets, anything that would make a noise. Once my toe touched the wall, I trod down on the first step, easing my weight on to the ball of my foot. The bare wood creaked louder than the noise of my breathing. I stopped in mid-stride, and listened. Nothing.

I put the rest of my weight on my right foot, repeating the process with the left on the step above, swivelling my body against the wall. My skin prickled with sweat as my eyes scanned upwards, adjusting slowly to the darkness. It looked like there was a landing up there; I couldn't tell whether there was a door as well. I stopped on the fifth step, rolling my eyes, trying to distinguish any shapes or figures in the darkness. It wasn't working: I couldn't see anything yet. We could have done with some NVGs in the ready bags.

I probed further up the steps with my feet, stopping each

time there was a creak, waiting to see if there was any reaction from above me. My face was now soaked: the respirator seal felt as if it was floating over my skin. My muscles were close to cramping as I used all the strength in my legs to move and keep balance, while still keeping eyes and weapon up.

I'd got half-way to the landing, maybe ten or twelve steps up, when I felt my right foot start to wobble and had to lean my shoulder against the wall for support. I sucked in oxygen like a deep-sea diver. The respirator sounded like a waterfall. Sweat trickled down my back; the thighs of my jeans were soaked and tugging against my skin.

The landing had no doors, just plastered walls. There was a different kind of light above me now, probably fighting its way through the first-floor windows from the street. It came from the right, which meant the staircase probably turned back on itself.

I wrestled my way up, still leaning against the wall, focusing completely on the quality of light, trying to detect any shift in its consistency that might indicate movement on the next flight.

A few more steps and I finally made it to the landing. I moved across Suzy's arc of fire, weapon still in my shoulder, and pushed myself back into the far left-hand corner of the stairwell.

I could see six or seven steps from there, leading up towards the light, but I wasn't going to move all the way round and risk showing myself to anyone higher up; I wanted Suzy here to back me. I looked down and saw her dark shape emerging gradually from the shadows. She would have her weapon down now, concentrating instead on keeping as quiet as possible.

I strained my eyes and ears for movement or sound, but all I could hear was the odd creak from below, myself trying to breathe through this fucking respirator, and the sporadic murmur of traffic.

I stayed static, weapon up, feeling the sweat pool at the seal.

I hated this gear, but it always seemed to me a miracle that there was never any condensation on the eyepieces. I opened my mouth and leant forwards to listen again, trying to ignore the stream of saliva that dribbled down my chin.

A couple of minutes later Suzy was two steps away from me, her back against the right-hand wall, SD across her chest. I gave her another minute to sort out her breathing.

She nodded and I moved, my back against the wall, weapon up, edging my way until I was bathed in the soft light coming from above me.

I stayed to the left side of the staircase this time; Suzy kept right as I started to climb, my back drenched and hands soaking inside the rubber gloves. I kept wanting to use them to wipe away the sweat that stung my eyelids.

As my head came level with the first-floor landing, I could see the source of the light – a grime-covered, six-foot-tall window facing on to the street.

Rain pelted against the glass, camouflaging the traffic noise and, I hoped, the sound of our progress. The rooms above Costcutter directly opposite were at the same level, their droopy window nets showing no sign of life.

I was half-way through my next step when I heard a sound, a scraping sound, from above.

I froze, mouth open, holding my breath.

A truck roared past below us.

Had it just been a wooden beam settling down for the night, or a rat? Maybe.

I lowered my foot to get stable, and started to breathe again, swallowing a mouthful of saliva. I stayed static, waiting to hear if it happened again.

Six, maybe seven minutes passed. My muscles were close to cramping. The odd vehicle moved below me and a couple of dossers growled at each other in a doorway. Then the rain got heavier again, and started to pound against the glass.

I looked down at Suzy, still on the first landing, weapon up towards me. It didn't matter if she'd heard it or not. She would know something was wrong because I was static. She'd just react to what I did.

I gave it another thirty seconds, then moved again, weapon up, butt in the shoulder, thumb checking single shot. I kept close to the left-hand wall until I reached the landing and moved into the left-hand corner to keep away from the window. Dull globules of light and shadow streamed across the bare floorboards as the rainwater ran down the glass. Opposite me, past the window and stairs that turned back on themselves once more, there was a closed door. A cheap, light-coloured interior type with a handle to the left.

Suzy began to move up as I dragged some more oxygen through my respirator. She stopped just short of the landing, her back against the right-hand wall as she waited for my cue.

I moved sideways, hugging the wall, weapon up. The light from the window died about a third of the way up the next staircase. I stopped with the window frame against my left shoulder and could see street level as far as the still-closed police station. As a truck rumbled past below, Suzy bent low and moved across my arc to take position by the door. Fuck the window, it just had to be crossed. I joined her, ready to make entry, my thumb checking single shot, my left hand adjusting itself on the barrel, the pad of my trigger finger taking first pressure.

I nodded, and Suzy's hand closed round the handle and gave it a twist. There was the tiniest of squeaks as the door inched open. My eyes saw light, first from the window one side of the ship's bow, then the other. I moved over the threshold, going immediately left, sweeping the room, keeping low, clearing the doorway for Suzy to come through just one pace behind.

Three paces in, I went static, leaning into the weapon. I could see the whole bow of the ship. The floor wasn't subdivided as it had been below; it was just one big open space. There was an old steel desk near the windows, and a couple of upturned plastic chairs. On its side in the middle of the room was a knackered old satellite dish, a solid plastic meshy thing about five feet in diameter. The rest of the place was in similarly shit state. The windows were really getting hammered by the rain here, and it sounded like we were inside a snare drum. The sign for King's Cross station shone at us opaquely from across the street.

I took a couple of deep, noisy breaths and was turning back towards the door when I heard a dull knock above us.

Suzy was rooted to the spot, her head cocked upwards.

I tried not to breathe. Saliva streamed down my chin.

It had come from above us, no doubt about it.

They were up there. The fuckers were up there, directly above us, somewhere on the second floor.

44

I stood rigid, my head still cocked towards the ceiling.

I closed my eyes to concentrate harder, but the noise didn't come again. All I got was the drumming of the rain, and the odd splash of traffic.

Two or three minutes passed. I was sure the sound had come from my right, over towards the Pentonville side of the ceiling.

Still nothing. Finally I headed for Suzy, lifting my feet carefully to avoid making the same mistake as someone upstairs. Squeezing her shoulder, I gestured towards the right side of the ceiling, then shrugged questioningly. She moved her hand more towards the centre, wiggling it to show she wasn't certain.

But wherever it had come from, we both knew it was definitely human.

We were wasting time: there might be locks up there, obstructions to find a way past or early-warning alarms to defeat. No need to tell her that, she was already moving towards the still open door. I just turned round slowly, butt in the shoulder, thumb checking single shot, and followed on.

I veered to the right of the frame and bent down until I could see about half-way up the stairs. I adjusted my cheek on the steel rod of the butt and flicked my eyes across to the sight. The circle and dot were reassuringly in place. As I moved on to the landing and up the left side of the stairs, Suzy came through behind to cover me.

I stopped every few stairs and paused to listen before taking a few more. The light from below was just about good enough to allow me to make out the second-floor landing. This time it extended left and right.

As my head came level with the top step, I dropped my left hand, weapon up towards the ceiling, safety catch back on to avoid an ND [negligent discharge]. What I wanted now was a good firm position from which to look left and right along the landing. It ran about five or six metres in either direction until blocked at each end by a solid fire door with a big aluminium handle. The creasing rubber of my overboots squeaked gently as I lowered myself on to the stairs and beckoned to Suzy. I didn't know what was on the other side of these doors, but I'd already made a pretty good guess, and I wanted her alongside me before we continued.

Soon she was lying beside me on my right, pointing her thumb left to indicate the way she thought we should be going. I motioned agreement and headed left on to the landing, keeping my weapon up. I didn't want it banging into her or, even worse, the metallic clash of two weapons. Suzy took up position behind me, covering the other entrance and the stairs until called for.

The door was fitted flush against the wall, hinged on the left, with a pressure arm, and would open towards us from the right. I moved closer, the SD back in my shoulder, eyes on rapid blink to try to clear them of sweat before I got my head against the door. To avoid banging the wood with my canister, I used my right ear, just below the handle, at the point where it met the frame. For several seconds, it was like listening to a big shell and hearing nothing but the sea; then, somewhere on the other side, I heard a door creak, and footsteps, coming towards me.

I took two swift paces back and hunched over the weapon, eyes straining, no more blinking. What if two came through together? What if there was only one, but covered by someone behind? It all boiled down to the same thing: if anybody came through the door, I had to go for it. No time to check on Suzy: she'd know the score from my reaction and would be backing me.

The footsteps got closer. I took up first pressure.

The footsteps stopped. I took a breath and stared at the door, ready to drop whoever appeared through my head-up display.

Still nothing.

Then, from just the other side of the door, came a familiar sound. The bastard was pissing into a bucket.

It seemed to go on for ever. Sweat flowed down inside my right glove and dripped off my left eyelid, stinging and blurring my vision.

I took another breath and heard a murmur. It didn't come from whoever was having the piss; it came from further back. The stream slowed and, after a few short squirts, finally stopped.

The footsteps retreated. I released first pressure, and returned to my position against the door, safety on, finger along the trigger guard. I heard a cough, then nothing but the sound of the sea once more.

The bucket was good tactics. Even if the water supply hadn't been cut off, they wouldn't have been flushing toilets.

It was time to get in there. I moved backwards away from the door, until I got my head level with Suzy's. She was leaning into her weapon and covering the other way.

I could hear her sucking air through her canister. I held up my middle and index finger, gave her a thumbs-down, pointed at her face, and then the door handle. She turned and moved towards the target door as I got into a fire position, giving my head a quick shake to try to clear the fucking sweat out of my eyes.

Keeping left, Suzy made a final check with me and slowly pulled open the door. The pressure arm creaked, not much, but it sounded to me like a pistol shot.

The moment there was enough room I slipped slowly through into the darkness, hunched down. There were no windows, just solid walls each side of me. My face was soaking wet, my throat parched as I inched forward, eyes wide, trying to breathe slowly to control noise. I heard the gentle click of the fire door closing under Suzy's supervision, then felt something soft and slippery beneath my boot. They'd done more out here than just piss.

There was mumbling ahead of me, voices maybe ten metres away, perhaps further. I froze. I couldn't see anything apart from the soft glow of the SD sight, even though my eyes were starting to adjust. I leant forward to listen for more.

Three or four minutes passed and I began to make out a closed door a few feet away on my left. I edged nearer. What if they weren't together? What if they were split, in different rooms? There was no light coming from the crack beneath the door.

I could hear muffled sounds from further down the corridor: two, maybe three voices talking in low tones. I couldn't make out the language, but what the fuck did that matter? I didn't know if Suzy had heard what I had, but if I went static so would she. Time to get the hoods on.

Pointing the weapon to the ceiling, I rotated slowly, so as not to cut into her arc or bang into anything.

I'd only taken two paces back towards her when Suzy was flooded with light from behind me. As it flared off her eyepieces I dropped to my knees to give her more arc. I was still turning back the way I'd come as the pressure wave of her burst hit the side of my head.

Thud thud thud.

The light came from another doorway, no more than ten paces away to the left. No body on the floor, just a dropped hand-light, and smoke curling into the corridor.

A barrage of screams and shouts erupted inside the room, and Suzy was already ahead of me as we ran towards the light, weapons up. No time to mince about, she went straight in and turned right.

There was a blur of a target: she moved towards it.

I ducked left as she let off another three-round burst.

Big room. Pools of light from the floor. Hazy with cigarette smoke. Lots of shadows. Stuff all over the place. Writing on the walls. Target left – coming from behind a pile of plasterboard, left of another door.

Everything slowed. He was no more than ten metres away. I stopped breathing. My eyes followed him as he ran left to right, not looking about, just hunched up and focused. I followed him, left foot forward, leaning into the weapon, swivelling with him, checking safety was on single shot as I brought the weapon up the last two inches, first pressure already taken as the sight broke into my line of vision and the target hit the screen, but still moving right. I caught him up, watching the circle come from behind his body until it was centre of body mass.

Thud thud.

The double-tap took him down. Real time returned.

Breathing now, I moved towards him, double-tapping again, into his back.

Then I saw what he'd been going for. On the floor, behind a box, were the bottles.

A body hit me from the left, grabbing at my SD. We both went down.

45

His bodyweight smothered me. I kicked out, tried to head-butt him, the SD pinned between us.

Jeaned legs jumped over us – an Indian woman. She grabbed a couple of bottles and ran for the door.

That was the last thing I saw. The mouthpiece of my respirator was wrenched back over my eyes, and my hand torn off the pistol grip. I could smell cigarettes on his breath as he twisted the muzzle towards me.

I bucked and kicked.

The weapon fired. No one was hit. Shit, he had the trigger.

Screams echoed down the corridor.

I felt the barrel of the SD coming round, raking across my chest. My eyes were still covered. I tried to flick the respirator off by rubbing it against whoever was holding me down, as I bucked and kicked to keep the muzzle away from me.

From above came a three-round burst and the weight on top of me squirmed and let out a scream. I pushed and kicked myself away, ripping the respirator off my head. Suzy was standing over him as he crawled towards the bottles, a mush of blood and bone where his right foot used to be.

Suzy got astride him, and gave him another three rounds into the skull. Blood exploded over the lino.

She picked up a bloodstained battery-powered camping lantern from the floor and went back through the escape door to check on the runner. I grabbed my weapon. Fuck the respirator, it was too late now. If there was any of this shit in the air those antibiotics had better get working.

She reappeared carrying two bottles, which she placed carefully alongside the others. 'There's three down and clear.'

Her chest heaved, hungry for air through her canister, as she looked me up and down with the lantern. 'You OK?'

I looked around at the haze of cigarette and cordite smoke. 'Yeah, think so. Fuck that, I thought, you know . . .' I took a second to recover before lifting my boot to show her what had attached itself to the sole, then tapped her canister. 'If we hadn't had these fucking things on, we could just have followed our noses all the way from the kebab shop.'

It wasn't that funny but she started to laugh anyway and we couldn't stop as we inspected the bottles. Blood was pooled around their bases, but all twelve looked intact, their foil seals undisturbed. I felt much more than relieved as I freely breathed in the cordite and tobacco. It made sense that they wouldn't have opened the bottles and risked contaminating themselves until the last minute before they attacked. If the attack was delayed a couple of days, they would be too ill to carry it out. Three large, identical nylon sports bags with shoulder straps were alongside them, and four sets of new clothes and shoes. There were Underground maps and Zone One carnet books sitting on top of all four piles, but only three had cell phones.

I went down on one knee to investigate the bags. Each contained what looked like a fat steel bottle of compressed air, about two feet long. There was also a hard plastic cylinder, maybe two feet by one, connected to a tube that was fed through the fabric and concealed in the mesh pocket where you'd normally put your trainers.

Suzy picked up the bottles one by one and wiped the blood off them with one of the shirts. I picked up an Underground map. I could see at least twelve mainline station signs in Zone One. Four were ringed in pencil, including King's Cross. All were served by Underground lines. I threw it over to Suzy and picked up another; that, too, was marked, this time with stations further to the west including Paddington and Victoria.

About the only thing I'd learnt at school was that the tube's ventilation system worked like a piston: the trains pushed air in front of them as they went. It was why the tunnels were only just big enough, and there was a rush of air every time a train arrived at a platform. If you were in the DW business, there was no better way of spreading the good news.

Suzy let the map fall to the floor and picked up the nearest book of tickets. Three or four had already been used. 'They'd done their recces, then. Bastards.' She went back to cleaning the bottles as I took a look around. In days gone by the room had probably been an office storage area, about fifteen metres square, no windows. NBC boots had left a trail of blood and shit across the lino. Sheets of plasterboard and old grey metal filing cabinets littered the area. Four brand new sleeping-bags had been unrolled in one corner. Rubbish, both old and new, was strewn all over the place.

Empty aerosol cans littered the floor, and the walls were sprayed red with a series of messages in Malay, Arabic and Chinese, punctuated from time to time with vivid red-painted handprints. There was even a Kiblat pointing east.

I looked over at the Chinaman who'd jumped me, now sprawled face down on the floor. The holes in his head weren't leaking any more, but his jet-black hair was matted and glistened in the lantern light. He was no older than thirty, and dressed in jeans, new multicoloured Nikes and a dark blue jumper.

We needed to get going. 'Fuck checking upstairs – they'd have been down here by now. Let's get the bottles and fuck off. Throw me a sleeping-bag, will you?'

She tossed me one from the corner, the sort that could unzip all the way round so it turned into a blanket, and set about pulling the plastic cylinders out of the sports bags. I moved back to the stash of bottles and placed the first carefully in the bottom of the sleeping-bag, gave it a couple of protective turns, then put in the next and gave it two more.

'Everything else will stay here,' I pointed over at the clothes, 'including the cells. If the Yes Man sees them moving without knowing we have them, he'll take action, thinking we've fucked up. Besides, he'll already have every number these phones have called. We're just here for DW.'

Suzy frowned. 'Including King's Lynn, we've got four down, four sets of kit, but only three bags?'

'We'll have a quick look after packing. I want to get out ASAP and get this shit handed over.'

Three bottles later, Suzy took the roll from me and placed it in the first sports bag. It wasn't long before the two others were full. We couldn't find a fourth bag, so headed downstairs. The wind and rain were still going for it, big-time. I could see the Metropolitan Police sign lit up outside the station, through the window on the landing. 'That's all we need.'

We moved swiftly across and started down the stairs. Suzy was still on a high. 'Fuck 'em, we'll just box around it back to the car.'

We slipped back into the kebab shop, ripped off the NBC kit, rolled it up and threw it into the ready bags. The sweat had cooled on the back of my neck by the time I pulled out the jams in 297. We didn't bother unloading the weapons. I could hear Suzy breathing rapidly through her nose, trying to calm herself.

With all the kit stowed and the Browning back in my sweat-soaked jeans, I shouldered my ready bag, and one of the bags of DW, and carried another in my hand.

Suzy still had her rubber gloves on and was using her fleece to wipe the prints off the lock and key. I wasn't going to rush her. Finally she stood up and smiled. 'What's keeping you?

Let's go.' The padlock and key went into her fleece pocket, then she pulled her cuffs over the rubber gloves to disguise them. 'I don't know about you,' she said, 'but I've got an urgent appointment with Mr Nicorette.'

I used the Maglite to locate the steel fixings wedged in the door, pulled them out and threw them into the bag. Then all torchlight was extinguished, ready to exit.

Suzy was behind me with her two bags. While I listened, she leant forward, ready to pull the door back. There was nothing out there but the wind and the rain. I nodded and she opened up. Light poured into the hallway and the first thing I heard was rain bouncing off the pavement.

I waited as the wind attacked my sweat: there was no rush. We wanted to get out quickly, but also do it correctly. I listened for footsteps, heard nothing. I looked out. Two people were hunched under a collapsing umbrella, walking away from us, no one else in sight. That was it, time to go. I stepped out into the rain with two bags over my shoulder, the other in my hand, my eyes fixed on the police station. The wind was cold as it attacked my wet clothes, which were getting even wetter.

I heard the door close behind me and the shaft click back into the hasp. 'All done.' We turned left, away from the station towards King's Cross Bridge and the stern of the ship. Suzy put the key away in her fleece just as sirens started in the distance and two police officers, a man and a woman in bright yellow fluorescent jackets, appeared from round the bend of Gray's Inn Road. Luck was with us: they were on the other side of the road and bent over, protecting themselves from the driving rain. They weren't bothered at the sight of us and our bags, or even Suzy dumping the key down a drain. There were plenty of people like that around here, normally trying to find a doorway to sleep in.

46

We slid the three sports bags carefully into the rear footwells of the Mondeo, then slung our ready bags into the boot.

Even though she was soaked to the skin, her hair plastered against her head, Suzy was still on a high. 'Did you see all that writing and the handprints?'

I nodded. 'Yeah, same as the nine/eleven crew, I reckon – these fuckers wanted the world to know who they are and why they did it.'

Suzy got the key into the ignition. 'It can't have been DW in those spray cans. The girl must have gone back to spray the place up.'

I reached under my seat and retrieved the moan-phone. Suzy's priority was her gum: she got chewing as soon as she'd pulled away from the kerb. Her jaws and the wipers were working overtime.

Rainwater dripped from my hair and nose on to the phone keys as I tapped in the Yes Man's number.

'Yes?'

I wondered if he'd ever thought of putting himself through charm school. 'It's done, we're mobile. Three dead—'

'You have Dark Winter?'

'Yeah, twelve bottles. Three vaporizing kits still in the building, but four sets of tube tickets, and maps targeting mainline stations. It's the tube, it was going to happen tomorrow for sure.'

'Any of the bottles open?'

'No, all still sealed. They've sprayed the place and ID'd themselves with handprints. Same cans as we found in King's Lynn. What about the fourth bag? You reckon we should lift the source? Find out what he knows? There's something wrong there.'

There was a pause. 'There's always something wrong with those people. We have control of Dark Winter – that is all that matters for now. Wait out.' His voice went muffled; he must have put a finger over the mike, but I still heard him. 'We have possible Underground systems, get a message out.' He came back to me loud and clear. 'How far are you from Pimlico?'

We were passing Madame Tussaud's, heading west, the wipers still in a frenzy. 'Maybe fifteen minutes, twenty at the most.'

'Yvette is on her way. I want you to leave everything in the car and give her the keys. You're now weapons free – understand?'

'Yep.'

'Wait out at the flat. I'll be there later.' There was a pause. 'Excellent work, both of you.' The phone went dead before I realized he was talking to me.

Suzy powered down her window and turned up the heater, then wiped condensation off the windscreen as rain hit the side of her face. 'What now?'

'We're weapons free. The Golf Club's taking the car, and we have to wait out at the flat. He'll be arriving later to hand out tea and medals.'

She smiled ruefully. 'We did well, Norfolk boy – we really did.'

I opened the glove compartment and took out a blister pack

279

of antibiotics as her window went back up. 'Here's a thing,' I said. 'He finished off by saying we'd done an excellent job. Either he's had a personality transplant, or he had an audience.'

'He's hardly going to be sitting there on his own.'

'That's not what I'm getting at. There were American and German voices in the background earlier today, and when I told him about the tube maps, he called out to someone close by that it was the Underground systems. Systems, plural. We've only got one here . . .'

She thought for a while, rolling the gum between her front teeth with her tongue. 'I reckon if there are other targets we deserve extra medals and even more tea.'

'You'll definitely be getting permanent cadre now, won't you?'

She didn't reply. With that grin on her face, she didn't need to.

I popped four capsules from the blister pack and passed two across to her. 'Listen, thanks for helping me out back there. I couldn't see a fucking thing.'

'You looked a bag of shit.' She gave me an extra big smile before concentrating once more on the road. 'But don't worry, I won't tell anybody.'

She was silent for a moment. 'I suppose you'll be back to the States soon, seeing Kelly, sorting out stuff?'

'Yeah, and you'll be watering your hanging plants and all that shit in your conservatory and poncing around in your Blue Lagoon, or whatever it's called.'

This time she gave me the sort of expression mothers in supermarkets normally saved for their small children. 'The conservatory's only half built, and it's Blue*water*, dickhead, the shopping centre. If it was the Blue Lagoon, I wouldn't worry about seeing it from the kitchen window.'

We drove into the square.

'Nick?'

'What?'

'What if you're right? What if they are planning attacks in the US? Where does that leave Kelly?'

I nodded as the white Transit came into view, parked and two-up. I'd been asking myself the same question.

Suzy found a space nearly opposite the flat, close enough to see the light on in the front room. She killed the engine and we sat there for a moment, listening to the drumming of the rain. 'Tell you what, Suzy, I'll stay in the car until the Golf Club comes down. We don't want any of this lot getting nicked, do we?'

She pulled out the 9mm from her pancake holster to add to the rest of the ops kit scattered around the car. I shook my head. 'Better hang on to that, just in case there's a drama.' I drew down my own pistol, and stuck it under my thigh. 'Behind us, further down the road, we've got the Transit, two-up. They might be with the Golf Club, but then again they might not. I'll keep an eye on them, just in case.'

She checked safe and reholstered. 'See you in a minute.' She smiled. 'Don't drink the merchandise.'

She headed for the flat, and as she disappeared inside the hallway I checked traser: it was nearly five. I got my own phone out and called Carmen, keeping an eye on the two-up as best I could through the rain-splattered windows.

The phone rang and rang, before BT told me that no one was available to take my call but they could take a message. Shit, she had turned off the phone.

Yvette came out of the front door and down the steps, just her eyes visible through her Gore-Tex storm hood. She was carrying the Packet Echo suitcase.

I cut off the power, shoved the phone in my bumbag, and checked that the keys were still in the ignition. The Browning went back down my jeans as she opened the driver's door, put the case in the back and climbed in. 'Well done, Nick.' Her voice just about made it through the fabric of the face shield. She pulled it down and I saw her tight cheeks crease into a smile.

281

Not sure how to respond, I explained what was in the car and where. She nodded avidly, as if she had more to say and was dying to tell me. 'This has saved so many lives, Nick.' She put her hand out and shook mine sheepishly, as if I was royalty. 'Well done, and thank you.'

I felt a strange pain in the centre of my chest. I wasn't used to this sort of treatment: what I normally got was a bollocking, and an instruction to get back under my rock until next time. 'What now, just wait out?'

'He should be here soon.'

'How many attacks have been planned? This isn't the only one, is it?'

It was worth a shot, but she was too much of an old sweat. Her cheeks creased once more. 'I have to take the vehicle away now, and you have to stay in the flat until he comes.'

She pushed in the clutch and found first gear. As she turned the ignition key, I pulled the stick back into neutral. 'Look, I need to know if there are attacks planned in the States. Kelly's going home to Baltimore this morning. I need to know, should she stay here? Please, she's just fourteen. She's already had more than enough shit in her life.' I suddenly understood how Simon must have felt. I knew begging wouldn't work, but maybe she had children of her own. It was my only chance: the Yes Man wouldn't tell me jack shit.

She lifted her left leg and she released the clutch. 'You put me in a difficult position, Nick.'

I fixed her eyes with mine. 'I'm sorry, she's all I have. I need to know if she should go back tomorrow or if she'd be safer here.' It was pointless saying any more.

She looked out of the windscreen at nothing in particular, and took a couple of uncharacteristically deep breaths. I sat and listened to the engine ticking over for what seemed like for ever. 'Nick, I think it might be better if she stayed in the UK for just a few more days. Thanks to you and Suzy, things should be resolved by then. You'll be staying here for a while anyway. I'll contact you.'

I opened the door as the clutch went back down and she got in gear. 'Thank you.'

She didn't answer, busying herself with the headlight switch as I got out. As I turned to close the door, another set of lights came on. It was the Transit.

'Nick?' I bent down so that I could hear her above the noise of the engine. 'You didn't mention leaving your weapon . . .' I jumped back in and pulled the Browning from my jeans and two spare mags from under the seat. 'It's still loaded and made ready.' I couldn't hold my gratitude. 'Look, I really want to thank—'

She waved it away. 'I just hope Kelly responds well to her therapy.'

I closed the door, and the car pulled away from the kerb. Sundance and Trainers stared straight ahead as they passed in the Transit. They'd have probably preferred to stay and give me a good kicking, but they had a more important job to do – to make sure no one rammed the Golf Club in the back and damaged the bottles. They were probably heading for one of the Firm's secure buildings dotted around the city – or maybe the Battersea heliport, *en route* to Porton Down in Wiltshire, where Simon's mates could play about with the microbes.

Now that we were weapons free, that was it, finished, job done.

47

Hitting the cell once more, I got the answering-service. 'Hello, Carmen, it's Nick. Change of plan – she'll be able to go to Chelsea on Tuesday after all. Don't take her to the airport, she needs to stay here. I'll call later, just don't go to the airport – it's important she stays here. I'll still pay the Mastercard bill.'

If we got the debriefs done sharpish, I could be in Bromley before they left.

I pressed the intercom by the front entrance. 'Hi, honey, I'm home.'

It was only as I began to climb the stairs that I realized how exhausted I was. The only good thing about being soaked in sweat was that it put a layer of grease between me and my rain-soaked clothes. My eyes stung and my hands stank like a rubber factory as I rubbed my face to get a little life back into it. I needed a good dig out and was gagging for a brew.

I knocked on the door and she opened it. 'Nice day at the office, dear? Cup of tea?'

'Good call.'

I followed her into the kitchen. 'There's an attack planned in the States as well. The Golf Club pretty much told me.'

She turned and leant against the cooker. 'Oh, shit.'

'Nothing to the Yes Man, OK? She did it for Kelly.'

She nodded. 'She say anything about Germany?'

'No, but I bet there is one. This is outrageous. They'd have to co-ordinate so there was no early alert.'

We both went quiet. She was probably doing the same as me, thinking about the nightmare of just one attack, let alone three. And, as we'd discovered, it wasn't rocket science. All the ASU needed was DW, some aerosol kit and a few cell phones.

I cut away from thinking about it. Our part was done. George would have another team out on the ground in the States, trying to locate DW before having to go to government. I guessed the Germans would be doing the same. I thought about Josh and his kids, and what I could do for them.

I went to the fridge, pulling out two lots of shit-in-a-tray we'd bought after the first source meet. As I ripped off their cardboard sleeves I thought how strange it was that I couldn't think of anything to say now. Maybe Suzy felt it too: she was certainly concentrating a bit more than necessary on positioning teabags in the mugs.

I stabbed the Cellophane covering with a fork while she fiddled with spoons and milk cartons.

'What's for breakfast?'

'I don't really know.' I inspected it. 'White stuff.' I couldn't be arsed to check the cover. 'Chicken, maybe?'

Her face screwed up in disgust. 'I'll give that a miss, I think.'

Still not looking at me, she busied herself pouring the kettle, then we both just stood there, watching the microwave, waiting for it to go ping. This was getting stupid. 'Things happen like this, you know.' I gently touched her shoulder. 'You're just beginning to get to know someone, then it all stops. That's just how it is.'

She sighed as she squeezed a teabag against the side of the mug. 'Never mind, Nick, we'll always have King's Cross, eh?' She still wouldn't look up.

'I suppose I'd better say it was wonderful working with you, something like that.' It sounded corny, but actually I meant it.

'It was all right, wasn't it?' She took half a step towards me, her eyes still down, seemingly intent on avoiding mine at all costs. I wasn't too sure what she was going to do, but whatever it was, I wanted her to.

She put down the spoon on the worktop and took another step towards me. I didn't know what to do. I didn't want to get it wrong: to open my arms, only for her to walk straight past and check the microwave.

She was just a couple of feet away from me when the door buzzer went. That rueful smile came back as she diverted to the hallway intercom.

'It's me, open up.' The Yes Man obviously hadn't brought his audience.

She hit the buzzer and came back into the kitchen. 'Saved by the bell, eh?' We both laughed, a little too self-consciously.

The microwave pinged as Suzy filled the kettle to get a fresh brew on and I went and opened the front door.

The Yes Man looked as if he'd been doing a bit of overtime. The suit and shirt we had first seen him in were badly creased now, and his tie was loose. I was very pleased to notice a boil developing nicely on the back of his neck.

He took the settee and Suzy put his tea down in front of him, but he didn't thank or acknowledge her in any way, just waited for her to sit in the chair opposite him. 'Right, step by step.'

I shifted in my chair until first light as we went through the whole job, giving Suzy credit for saving my life and for the DW not getting smashed. The Yes Man took it all in, then nodded at her, and for once there was a smile on his face. 'Well done.' She deserved nothing less.

He looked over at me and the smile disappeared. 'You're weapons free, but you will stay here in the flat. You are to stay here until I release you. Got it?'

I nodded. He'd have to get the OK from George before he let me off the hook. 'What about the States? Are they hitting the west coast, or the east?'

I was thinking about Josh and the kids. Maybe I should be DHLing them a shit load of doxycycline.

He pointed at Suzy, totally ignoring me. 'You can go home. No point in keeping you here. Just be on call.'

'Yes, sir.'

He stood up and repeated his congratulations to Suzy, then hesitated. 'In fact, well done, both of you.' I could almost hear his teeth grinding. He picked up his briefcase and made to leave.

'When do you think I'll be able to go, sir?'

'When I'm ready.'

'Can I have a sub then? I am getting paid for this, aren't I?'

'Take it out of your cover documents.' His lip curled. 'It's just cash for you, isn't it?'

'That's right, sir. Just cash.'

The moment the door was closed, her eyes flashed. 'He was trying to say thank you.'

'Not hard enough.'

She stayed where she was for a moment, then hauled herself up. 'Thanks for all that credit stuff. You didn't have to.'

'Yes, I did. You're going to need as much help as you can get, working for that arsewipe full time.'

She walked past me, laying her hand on my shoulder for a second. 'Thanks anyway.'

She turned into the bathroom and a few seconds later the electric shower kicked in. She came out again and headed for the bedroom. I finished the Yes Man's brew, hoping his boils weren't contagious, as I listened to her padding about. I checked traser. It was nearly six thirty. Surely Carmen and the gang would be up by now?

I hit my cell yet again as Suzy came out of the bedroom wrapped in the green towel. 'Kelly?'

I nodded as the BT service came on, and Suzy disappeared into the shower. I told myself there was still plenty of time: they weren't leaving until eleven.

I stretched out in the chair, rubbing my temples. What now?

First thing, go to Bromley, see Kelly, and get my documents and antibiotics. Fuck the Yes Man – and George, for that matter. I'd leave my cell here so he couldn't track me, be back here by the afternoon, and with luck they'd never know I'd left. Did we stop taking the antibiotics now? Nobody had told us. Fuck it, I'd carry on for a bit longer.

I was half dozing in the chair when Suzy reappeared. 'You need a shower, you're minging. Get through?'

'No, I'll go there as soon as I've cleaned up.' I went into the kitchen. The door to her bedroom was still open a little as I dragged the shit-in-a-tray from the microwave and pulled back the film. I fished about in the drawer for a spoon and took a mouthful. 'I was wrong.'

''Bout what?'

'It's fish.'

She was somewhere behind the door, still in dead ground.

'You going straight home, then?'

'I've got a conservatory to build, remember?'

'You sure you can resist one of these?'

She came out, her hair scraped back, dressed in black cargoes and a jumper. 'I'm not eating that crap.'

'No problem, I'll eat it for you.' I put the tray down on the side and reached for the next one. She seemed to have other ideas. I felt her hair, wet against my face, and her breath on my neck. I put my arms round her, but an inch or two away as hers moved tightly round my back. She smelt wonderful, and all I could think about was that I smelt like a wet fart.

I ran my fingertips slowly down between her shoulder-blades. She nuzzled into my neck and I could smell apples again and feel her skin against mine. Then she put both hands on my chest and pushed herself away, blushing with embarrassment. 'Nick, I . . . I'm sorry.'

'Don't be. Beats breakfast, anytime.'

'No, really, I'm sorry – I shouldn't have done that.' She turned and went back to the bedroom.

I picked up the second tray, looked at it and put it down.

When she reappeared a couple of minutes later she was wearing her short black leather jacket and carrying her bag. 'I'm off. Maybe we'll see each other again?'

I nodded. 'Yep, maybe.'

But we both knew we never would.

She held out her hand, and as we shook she pulled me to her once more and her lips brushed my cheek. ' 'Bye.'

I let go of her hand and she left.

48

The traffic crawled through south London. I listened to the same news on LBC's nine o'clock bulletin that I'd watched a couple of times on BBC24 while I cleaned myself up. Most of it was about SARS and Iraq, but the breaking story was that the USA had heightened its terrorist alert state to amber, just one away from closing down the country. It looked like George couldn't risk keeping his operation covert any longer, now he knew the UK ASU had been in their FOB, ready to attack.

There was nothing about Germany. Maybe I'd been wrong about that, or maybe their people had been successful too. If so, I thought fleetingly, Suzy and I might deserve some of the credit. Nobody would ever know, of course: the few who did would be taking that information to their graves, along with a lot more where that had come from. They knew that if they ever decided to open their mouths, people like Sundance and Trainers would be digging that grave for them much earlier than they had expected. That was just the way things were.

There wasn't anything about three bodies being found near King's Cross station either. The clean-up team would have been sent in quick before Zit Girl or her mates broke in for shelter and found more than they'd bargained for. By now all four bodies would have been burned, along with every shred of evidence in that room, and any lumpy bits left over would be floating about in the Thames estuary, waiting to feed the fish.

I'd hired a Vectra from Victoria station using my covert documentation, then maxed out on one of the Yes Man's cards at a nearby cashpoint. What was he going to do? Sack me?

I was feeling surprisingly good on not very much sleep as I reached Bromley high street. I'd shoved my clothes in the washer-dryer at the flat while I'd showered, and even my Caterpillars felt OK.

I didn't know why, but I always felt depressed as I entered the prim and proper road they lived on, with its miles of neat hedges and bungalows with shiny Nissan Micras and six-year-old Jags that got the good news with Turtle wax every Sunday. It was probably the thought of people being retired that did my head in. I'd rather be dead than land up trimming hedges and pruning roses. Or, even more depressing, maybe I'd get to like it.

I turned into the engineered-brick drive and stopped in front of the red garage door that Jimmy had had to repaint recently because the coat underneath hadn't been quite shiny enough for Carmen. I got out and hit the bell push. A nice traditional bing-bong echoed from the hall.

No answer. I tried again, then fished into the shrub pot just to the left of the double-glazed PVC door and pulled out the key. People never learn.

I bing-bonged a few more times as I turned the handle. 'Hello? It's me – anyone home?' I was hit by the smell of polish and plug-in air-fresheners, and a lot of silence.

They couldn't still be in bed, because Jimmy deadlocked the front door every night. Maybe they'd left early: the way Jimmy drove, eleven would have been cutting it a bit fine.

It was shit, but not a big problem. I'd call the American desk at Heathrow and say there was some family drama and Carmen needed to call the house.

I went into the kitchen and was surprised to see the table still laid for breakfast. Carmen put the things out every night before bed, and whisked them away the moment the meal was over – sometimes even before. If the multigrain toast was getting the better of Jimmy's teeth and she was anxious to get on with the Hoovering, that was just tough shit.

I grabbed a handful of Mini Shreddies, Kelly's favourite, and tipped them into my mouth. I could see my two brown Jiffy-bags on top of the fridge-freezer, where all the mail was kept. I picked up the phone and got the dual tone. Why couldn't they just check the thing now and again? It would have made life so much easier.

Chomping away, I dialled 1571 and wedged the receiver between my shoulder and ear. BT told me there were two messages. I grabbed the first envelope, gripped the top of it in my teeth and started to tear it open, showering myself with bits of Shreddies. It felt quite good getting my life back, no matter how fucked up it was, as I listened to myself waffle away to the answering service.

I glanced into the hallway. From this angle I could see that the door into the garage wasn't quite closed. That Jimmy had dared leave a door ajar was strange enough, but I could also see a highly polished section of his Rover still sitting there.

Shit.

The envelope and phone went down slowly on to the kitchen worktop and the last bits of cereal fell from my mouth as I let my jaw drop. Stretching out my hand, I grasped the handle of the cutlery drawer and eased it open. Everything was in its place: potato peeler, bread-knife, forks and spoons. I pulled out two vegetable knives, one for each hand, and moved into the hallway, placing my feet carefully on the Amtico tiles so the Caterpillars didn't squeak.

Throat constricted, I checked the corridor and turned right.

No sign of forced entry anywhere. The only ambient light came from the kitchen and the half-glazed front door.

The door to the living room was only about three paces to

292

my right. The place was empty: everything where it should be, magazines tidied, cushions still puffed up and curtains opened from when she'd gone to bed. All I could hear was the grandfather clock, ticking away in the corner.

I moved back into the hall, closing the garage door and locking it before I headed past the bathroom. There were no signs of morning life in there, no condensation on the mirrors or windows, no smell of soap or deodorant. The shower tray was dry, and so was the bath. Dry towels were folded neatly over the radiator rail.

I came out into the hall again and turned left towards the bedrooms. The next door down on the right was Carmen and Jimmy's bedroom, and the one beyond that was Kelly's. Both were ajar.

I gave the first a gentle push, stepping back out of the way, not wanting to present myself as a target.

The room was in darkness, just a few slivers of light fighting their way past Carmen's immaculately interlined curtains. But I didn't need to see that they were in there: I could smell them.

The metallic tang of blood. The cloying stink of shit.

There was a heavy pounding in my chest.

Oh, shit, no. Not again . . .

I ran down to the next door, my feet unable to cover the six or seven paces as quickly as my head needed them to, wanting to get into her room before the video started up.

Not bothering to check before bursting in, I hit the light switch.

The room was empty.

I checked under the bed, checked the wardrobe. Nothing.

'Fuck, fuck, *fuck!*' I screamed it over and over inside my head as I ran back into Carmen and Jimmy's room. I had to make sure she wasn't there. I switched on the bedside light and pulled back the duvet. They looked like they'd been in a road accident. Jimmy had shit himself, and he and Carmen had both been stabbed and slashed far more times than it must have taken to kill them. Carmen's eyes were still open, dull and

293

glassed over like a fish too long on a slab. She had a curious half-smile, exposing toothless gums, and blood had dried in the deep lines in her face that even Lorraine Kelly hadn't been able to make disappear.

I looked under the bed: just slippers. Maybe she was hiding? I opened the wardrobes, but everything was still perfectly in place, nothing had been touched.

My own voice screamed inside my head. 'Not again . . . this can't be happening to us again.'

Disneyland.

I ran back to the garage, the same terrible feeling clawing at me that I'd had being chased by my stepfather as a kid.

I fumbled with the lock.

'Kelly? Kelly?' I pulled it open. 'Kelly, it's me! It's Nick!'

I let the knives clatter to the concrete floor as I dropped on to my stomach and checked under the car. I even opened the deep-freeze. She wasn't there.

Feeling like a six-year-old lost in a supermarket, I ran back into her bedroom, a sinking feeling in my gut. There was no sign of a struggle. Her duvet was pulled back neatly. The bed-side lamp was upright. Her suitcase and shoulder-bag were packed and by the door. My own black leather bag was stuck in the corner.

I emptied her shoulder-bag on to the floor and her passport fell out with her ticket, some coins, her CD player and an envelope. The only thing missing was the Old Navy T-shirt she always slept in. I looked under the bed again: I didn't know why, I could already see there was nothing and nobody there.

My stomach was jumping all over the place, my throat so dry it ached. I sank on to the carpet, dropping my head into my hands. This had to be connected with the job. Shit, it could even be the Yes Man – maybe I'd asked one question too many last night and Sundance and Trainers had been sent to tidy things up.

I had to shout at myself to cut away. 'Stop! For fuck's sake, stop!' Flapping wasn't going to help me – or her.

I had to secure this place. Nobody must know what had happened here – not yet, anyway.

Did they have milk delivered? I wasn't sure. *Fuck, I should know these things.*

I got up, feeling a little better now I was doing something. I didn't know what, but that didn't matter. I opened the front door. No milk on the doorstep. I went back in and checked the fridge, found a litre plastic bottle from Safeway.

What about post? The top half of the door was frosted glass, so no one was going to see letters stacking up on the carpet, and I knew they didn't have a paper delivered. Jimmy walked to buy one, taking his time, for some peace and quiet.

If not the Yes Man, then who?

Who was I kidding? My head was flooded with names and reasons why.

I stopped, gathered my thoughts. Let's not worry about why, just concentrate on the here and now. First, I'd take her bags and remake the bed, so if this place was discovered at least it was going to be a while before the police worked out who was missing. I didn't want them screaming around trying to do their bit to find an abducted child just yet. It might put her in greater danger.

The smell from Jimmy and Carmen's bedroom was creeping into the corridor as I headed back into Kelly's. Sitting on the light blue carpet, surrounded by flowery wallpaper, I picked up the stuff I'd tipped out of her bag and started to repack it. I opened the passport and was unable to resist looking at her picture. She never allowed me to see it. She was two years younger then, and her blonde hair was a bit longer. I felt myself smile: she'd had a zit on her chin, and had tried to cover it up all morning before I'd finally dragged her kicking and screaming into the photo booth.

I flipped it closed, slipped it into my back pocket and shoved the ticket into the bag, just as a neighbour came out from next door. I could see him clearly through the net curtains, trying to manhandle a black plastic refuse bag down the path. He dumped it into a wheelie-bin, then disappeared back inside.

As I moved the purple envelope out of the way to pick up her purse, I saw it was addressed to me. I sat against the wall and opened it.

Dear Nick,
By the time you read this, I'll be back at Josh's. That's if I remember to put this out with your other letters before I leave!! I'm sorry we argued on Saturday. It's just that I really miss you when you go away.

Remember you asked me what I think, and then your phone went and I didn't get to answer? Well, here's what I think. Here's the deal. When I get back home, I'm really going to get myself together, I'm going to get help, I'm going to go to school, and I'm going to work things out.

My eyes were stinging badly. I must have been more tired than I'd thought.

I know I always go on at you for being at work all the time and now I feel really bad because Josh told me why. I didn't know that you gave him money all the time and that seeing Dr Hughes and the school costs so much. I didn't realize that's the reason you have to work all the time. So that's why I'm going to sort myself out. I figure you won't have to work so hard to pay for me, so therefore I get to see a lot more of you. OK, deal?
See you when you finish work.
Love, Kelly.
PS This letter was the stuff I was doing when you called.

Tears had begun to fall down my cheeks. I panicked. I didn't know exactly what part of this nightmare I was panicking about, but I just couldn't help it. I couldn't control it. The pain in the centre of my chest came back, and a heavy thudding soon joined it as I read the letter over and over again.

I forced myself up, I had to get moving. I wasn't yet sure what, but there were things I had to do.

I folded the letter and put it into my back pocket with her passport and went into the kitchen for my two envelopes. Shoving them down my sweatshirt, I headed back to the bedroom for her kit and mine.

49

Heading north fast, I stopped the Vectra at a public call-box and made a frantic but hopefully calm-sounding call to Hughes's office, bluffing it by asking if Kelly had called to say goodbye. Maybe she'd managed to escape and made her way to the clinic, or even left a message.

They hadn't heard a thing.

I knew the Yes Man's contact number would now be non-existent but tried it anyway. I was right. I thought about calling George, but what good would that do? He would have been part of anything the Yes Man was up to, for sure. I had to get back to where I belonged, the flat, and wait out as I'd been ordered. It wouldn't be long before the Yes Man contacted me and gave me another little job that I couldn't refuse.

I parked in Warwick Square, trying to think of a way to get hold of the Yes Man. I couldn't wait. I needed to know one way or the other. Then it came to me. I'd hit the panic button: that would get the QRF screaming round, with the Yes Man not far behind.

A young couple walked past, Habitat bags overflowing with bamboo plants. I crossed the road, pulled the key from my leather bomber, and was running up the steps when I heard a clipped Asian voice spark up behind me. 'Hello? Hello?'

I turned. Grey had materialized from nowhere, same clothes on, smiling at me as if I was a lost child. 'Do not be alarmed.' He raised his hand. 'Your daughter – go to the coffee shop, go now. Go, go.'

He was almost apologetic, making it sound as if I would be doing him a favour. All I wanted to do was grab his neck and twist it right there to find out more, but that wouldn't help her. 'You talking about Starbucks in Farringdon?'

'Yes, go there now.'

I had to remain calm. 'You know where she is?'

'He will help you, go there now.' With that he turned and walked away.

I ran to the car.

Why would the source know where Kelly was? Why would he even know she existed? Was the source fronting for the Yes Man? But at least something was happening. This is good, I kept trying to persuade myself. *This is good.*

Abandoning the Vectra a block away, I ran to Starbucks, stopped, walked in, got myself a brew, and sat facing the front windows, wanting to be seen.

Ten minutes went by and I needed a piss, but I couldn't leave my seat. I couldn't risk missing him.

I pulled the letter out again and started to read it. That was a mistake. It went back next to her passport, and I concentrated on sipping the brew. Under the table, my heels started to bounce. I couldn't control my legs – it was as if they wanted to be on the move, they wanted to be doing something. I needed him to fucking well turn up, and right now.

Another couple of minutes and Grey walked past, right to left, eyes scanning the inside of the coffee shop.

Two girls, juggling their coffees and cells in one hand and recent purchases in the other, came and sat at the table opposite. Then there he was. He walked past the coffee shop, right to left, and disappeared. I knew he'd seen me, I knew I

299

had to stay where I was. He'd just be confirming with Grey that I hadn't turned up with a big bunch of mates. As if. I didn't have any.

Less than a minute later I heard the door open from the courtyard. I didn't turn round.

A hand fell gently on my left shoulder. 'Hello.'

I turned back and saw Grey now covering the rear of the shop from the courtyard. Where was Navy? Was he with Kelly?

The source continued walking past me to the counter and placed an order. We got eye to eye again as the steam machine hissed into his cup.

My heels continued to bob as I watched him pick up his change, pass the girls sending texts, and come and sit directly opposite me at the small round table. He seemed to take for ever.

I could smell at once he was a smoker.

'What's happening with my—'

He held up a hand and showed me a mouthful of yellowing teeth. 'Your daughter is safe.'

'Why have you—'

'Everything is OK.' He tried a sip of coffee, but it was too hot so he put the cup down.

'What the fuck do you mean, everything is OK? I've just been to the house.'

He nodded slowly. 'Oh, I see.' He looked down at his cup, as if considering another sip, then back at me. 'Have you informed anyone about this?'

My feet stopped jiggling, my heart stopped beating. Even if I had done, I would have lied. 'No, nobody.'

Two teenaged boys arrived and waved to the girls. We waited for them to settle down. I knew I had to stay calm and listen to every word he said. I normally did in these situations, but it wasn't so easy now it was so close to home.

He pushed his cup gently to one side and leaned forward. 'I need to keep her while you do something for me. It is a very simple task. You will go to Berlin, collect five bottles of wine and deliver them to me tomorrow night.'

Aggression wouldn't help her, but a bit of it would help me. 'Why can't one of your fuckers go and get them?'

'Because life is difficult now for dark or slant-eyed men trying to bring duty-free into this country – I'm sure you understand why.'

'How do I know she's OK? How do I know I'll get her back alive?'

'You don't. But what choice do you have? It is a very simple task, and therefore a very simple threat. If you betray me or fail to deliver, you will learn what it's like to see your child killed like an animal.'

He kept his eyes fixed on mine as he pulled a creased white envelope from his pocket. 'Tell them you've been sent from London. They're expecting you.'

He tapped the envelope with his right forefinger. 'Call me once you are back. I have a new number, just for you. Just make sure I have those bottles before two a.m. Tuesday morning.'

'To give you time to prepare the fourth bag before the morning rush-hour?'

'Ah, you understand.'

I took the envelope. 'Berlin been cancelled? Just the US now, unless I give you some help?'

His smile told me I was right. 'My brothers in Berlin are experiencing a problem that means their martyrdom will prove swifter and less glorious than they had planned. They are disappointed, of course, but will experience Paradise all the same. And there are still nearly three million journeys a day taken on your tube system. A target worth the effort. As I'm sure you can appreciate.' His bloodshot eyes narrowed. 'Let me ask you something. How did you find out about King's Cross? Did you meet Yasmeen?'

I said nothing and drank my brew.

He nodded slowly, his lips pursed. He was angry. 'I warned

them I'd be telling you people about the house once they had left.'

'So that you could continue to be best mates with my boss?'

'It was important to sustain my credibility, and keep your eyes away from what was really about to happen.' He sighed. 'Poor Yasmeen. So intelligent, so dedicated, but so unthinking in some areas. I told them to write their messages before leaving, though I do not approve of such gestures myself. Actions speak louder than words, do you not agree?'

I did, and wanted to give him a demonstration this very minute.

He took another sip and smiled. The fucker was actually enjoying this. 'They feel they have to do it, because you people know nothing. The West is all about the here and now, it is all about nine/eleven. Up there, on the walls, Yasmeen and her brothers and sister talk about things that happened in the fifteenth century, but you don't have a clue what they're talking about, do you?'

I looked away. This wasn't getting us anywhere. It certainly wasn't getting me any closer to Kelly.

'We're all on a journey, and I am near the end of mine. We in JI are the architects of a new world. You people are still in the old, lovers of the Jews and the US. You still want to control Asia. The only way to stop you is with *jihad*, the Holy War. And so Bali, and now this.'

'Why are you fucking about? Why didn't you just warn them we were coming to King's Cross? You knew what was going to happen, you gave them up. Why are you playing these fucking games?'

He interlocked his large brown hands and rested his forearms on the table. 'I never play games. I have kept up this pretence for you people because you have threatened my family. I have two sons and I have been made to do things I would never have dreamed of to keep them safe.'

He waited for some kind of acknowledgement, but I didn't have any to spare.

302

'But now that you and your woman have discovered my brothers and sisters before they could carry out their operation, I must do it myself. It wasn't a difficult choice to make. You see, I could have warned them, and of course they would have escaped. But what would have happened then? What action would have been taken? Close the system down, heighten the state of alert? You see, they had to die once you had discovered where they were. I simply took a bag from them before you arrived. They knew nothing then, but now they are in Paradise and understand the reason for their sacrifice. God understands what I have done to carry on the fight, and that my family will be killed by you people.'

His right index finger straightened and pointed at me. His eyes were fixed on mine. His voice had become very calm. 'That is the reason we will win, and you will lose. You are all about now, wanting to live, wanting your child to live above all things, and that is what makes you weak. That is because you have no understanding of what lies beyond this world.'

He was right about life, but wrong about winning.

He got to his feet. 'I will not detain you any longer.'

He turned and departed without another word, leaving me to gaze at his back, and then at the envelope on the table.

I pulled up the flap. It contained a Polaroid head and shoulders of Kelly in her Old Navy T-shirt, hair glued to her face with dried tears. I could only just make out her red and swollen eyes. Her head was resting against a TV showing BBC 24. There were several glass and brass religious ornaments lined up along the top of the cabinet.

The time bar in the corner of the screen said 8:47 and today's date. I'd been watching this programme at exactly the same time her picture was taken. I turned it over. Handwritten in felt pen were his cell number and an address: Apartment 27, 22 Bergmannstrasse.

50

I sat where I was, nursing my coffee as the boys big-timed it and the girls laughed and kidded about. My mind was spinning. How had he known where Kelly was? Grey and Navy must have followed us back to the safe flat, then tracked me, Jimmy and Carmen back to the bungalow.

It was pointless rushing around or going ballistic. The first thing to do in these situations is accept that you're in the shit. Stop, take a deep breath, get yourself into some kind of order, then work out what to do. Flapping wouldn't help me to sort out this nightmare, so it wouldn't help her either. I took a mouthful of brew, deliberately slowing myself down.

Did this still have to be done without any help from the Yes Man, now that it seemed everything was OK in the state of Spookdom? My legs had stopped bobbing about. I had no energy to waste now: my head needed to suck up everything it could get.

Fuck worrying about whether the Yes Man could help. Of course he could, but I wasn't going to ask him and risk a fuck-up as he sacrificed Kelly to get DW and the source.

I needed to stay focused on what to do next, but I couldn't. I looked at the Polaroid again. Not knowing what was happening to her, that was the worst feeling of all. I thought about her being scared, hungry, thirsty, maybe tied up after the picture was taken and dumped somewhere dark and derelict. That strange thudding pain came back in the centre of my chest. As the teenagers discussed where to go clubbing tonight, I stroked her frightened face with the tip of my thumb.

I went to take another gulp of the brew but realized the cup was empty. I put away the picture and pulled over the source's from across the table. I had no option: delivering the bottles was my only chance of making contact with Kelly. The best way to help her was to get myself over there and do what was required of me – then work out what the fuck to do after that.

I put the cup back down on the table. All I knew for sure was that I had an address to go to in Berlin, stuff to pick up, and a cell number to call once I got back. All right, I could do that. I could bring DW into the country. The real problems would arise when I tried to lift Kelly and make sure that shit didn't get chucked about the Underground. If I fucked up, we'd both be dead.

I slumped against the seat, totally shattered. When I got back from Berlin, I'd need someone to back me. I'd be thinking on my feet, and four were better than two. My only hope was Suzy. There was a strong chance she'd refuse, possibly even go straight to the Yes Man. At least that bit was easy. At the first sign of hesitation, she'd be spending some time locked in the boot of the Vectra.

If I found her, that was.

More people came into the café and the steam machine went into overdrive. I felt a little better now there was some sort of plan.

One thing went right for me. The Vectra hadn't been clamped. Sitting behind the wheel, I tried to remember everything she'd said about where she lived, and Bluewater was the obvious start point. I jumped out again and went to a phone box. Directory Enquiries gave me the number, and I was soon talking to Bluewater's information desk.

'I want to do some serious shopping, but I don't know where you are.'

The girl recovered swiftly from her astonishment, and slipped into auto-waffle. 'Well, sir, it's very simple and convenient to travel to and from Bluewater. We are located one mile east of the M25 and one mile west of the A2-M2 interchange. Signposting is clear in all directions.'

'So you're in Kent?'

'Yes, sir. We have a very wide range of shops for your convenience and enjoyment. Parking is—'

Cutting her off in her prime, I got back in the car and headed east towards Docklands and the Dartford crossing, probably driving over the Thames estuary at about the same time that the remains of the ASU would be flowing under it. I checked traser, and it was just after two. What if I didn't find her? It was mental slapping time: 'Just shut the fuck up and get on with it.'

I'd have to fix a cut-off time for the first flight tomorrow morning. After that I'd be on my own.

As the gleaming towers of Canary Wharf went past on my right I stopped at another phone box and called Directory Enquiries again. 'Air Berlin, please.'

A minute later a crisp, fast-speaking female voice fired a barrage of German at me. I cut in. 'What UK airports do you fly to Berlin from, and what's the earliest flight tomorrow and the latest back?'

The German instantly transformed into far better English than I'd ever be able to speak. 'The first flight leaves London Stansted at 0730 and arrives at Berlin Tegel at 1005. The latest return I have is 1905 from Berlin Tegel, arriving at London Stansted at 1940. Would you like to make a reservation?'

'Yes, please. One seat.'

I shoved a hand down my sweatshirt to get out my Nick Stone docs, and my new German girlfriend booked me a flight.

Back on the road, I was soon being directed into the right-hand lane for the M25 and the Queen Elizabeth Bridge. Pretty soon I couldn't move for signs to Bluewater, just as I'd been promised. I just wished there had been one saying, 'Bovis house with half-built conservatory and kitchen window overlooking Bluewater'.

The complex was one big car park, as far as I could tell, radiating out from a huge central mall, surrounded by high ground of sorts. The developers had moved in big-time. This was Commuter Central: if you didn't want to drive to London on the M25 for a day's work, Gravesend station was just a few miles away.

I cruised through Bean, Greenhithe and Swanscombe, scanning passers-by just in case my six numbers all came up and Suzy walked past with a bag of bananas and organic muesli bars.

Every building company on earth was throwing stuff up around here, and for all I knew she might have been using Bovis generically. I drove around a few of the huge estates. Each had a single entrance, which branched into a cul-de-sac with a name like Chancel View or Orchard Way, but without a church or apple tree in sight. Some of the houses were so new that the front lawns were still just piles of rubble.

I spotted two carpet-fitters coming out of a semi and pulled in. 'You know where the Bovis estate is, mate?'

The older of the two lit a cigarette and conferred with a younger lad in an England shirt with his hair pushed forwards in a gelled fringe. It didn't look promising. 'Not sure.' He took a drag. 'All these fucking places look the same to me, know what I mean?'

I waved my thanks and did a three-point turn to get me out of the estate. A service station appeared and I took the chance to fill up with petrol and a meal deal, cheese and pickle sandwich, crisps and a bottle of Coke.

The traffic built up as I made my way back towards Bluewater; hundreds of cars seemed to be streaming out of the car parks. I finally found a space.

The inside of the mall looked and sounded much like any other – piped music and acres of glass, rubber plants and

307

escalators. Getting online was easy: there were BT Internet phones dotted about on each floor. I shoved my 50p into the machine and logged on to Google. The Bovis homes site it took me to was stuffed full of pictures and sales pitch; there were any number of developments in Kent, but none around here. The nearest was on the border with Surrey. I played about, trying to see if someone like the Department of the Environment had a register of construction under way around the county, but came up with nothing.

I picked up a slice of spicy hot pizza and some more Coke, then made my way back to the car. There was nothing I could do at the moment, except try to resist the temptation to get out the Polaroid.

I wiped my greasy hands on my jeans, walked round the car park and drank the Coke, checking out the line of sight of buildings in the distance. It was just after four – leaving me about four more hours of daylight to check out the clusters of buildings in my line of sight, plus all night if I needed it.

I got back into the car and drove. After an hour, all these new builds blurred into one as I cruised area after area of new red semis, with the odd bit of upscale mock-Tudor and yellow-brick executive thrown in, all with nice double garages and BMWs and Freelanders filling the driveways. I landed up in a cul-de-sac with a large turning circle called Warwick Drive. This place was a few years older than the rest; for a start, grass had taken root. Everything looked manicured – I was expecting the Stepford Wives to appear any minute for a spot of synchronized shopping.

I carried on along Warwick. Bluewater was no more than three or four Ks away, across the fields. There was a possible in front of me, down in the turning circle. Mick Davies and Son Conservatories had a Ford Transit flatbed parked outside, and there was a well-worn path across the grass that disappeared down a narrow alleyway between the house and its neighbour.

There was no car in the drive so I parked up and walked round to the back, homing in on a radio knocking out a boy-band tune. The one I guessed was Mick was at the top of a ladder, screwing fixings into the dark-wood frame of a conservatory, and the son was at the bottom, holding it steady. The back garden looked small for the size of the house, and a line of newly planted trees just inside the fenceline wasn't doing a particularly good job yet of blocking out the mall in the distance. The rest of the garden was in shit state: next to a pile of sand there was a concrete mixer with a hosepipe thrown into it leading from a tap on the wall. Water overflowed from the bucket.

Dad upstairs was getting busy with his mastic gun in the gap between the wood frame and the brickwork, so I nodded at the son. I had to speak up over the boy band. 'I live just down the road here – thought I'd come and have a look. I'm thinking about having one myself. Is she in?' I pointed to the house. 'You know, the blonde girl? Short hair?'

I had a peep through the left-hand window, into the dining room. A dark brown table and chairs were stuck in the middle of the room. There was an arch through to the living room.

'Nah, I think she's got brown hair, mate.' He let go of the ladder with his right arm and traced a line just above his shoulders. 'About there.'

'You're right, I'm thinking about next door. It's Suzy who lives here, isn't it?'

To the right of the dining-room window there was a half-glazed door and to the right of that the kitchen, with brown wall units and a chrome mixer tap sticking up above the window-sill.

'Think so.'

'But she's not in?'

'Nah.'

'Do you know when she's back?'

The conservatory footings and six courses of brickwork were already in place, encompassing the back door and kitchen. The frame was nearly up.

He shrugged.

'What about her husband, is he about?'

'Never see anyone, mate.'

'OK, cheers.'

I checked traser as I walked along the narrow gap between the two houses. It was five eighteen, time those boys were packing up. I'd keep on looking for other possibles, but I had a feeling I'd already scored.

As I drove out of the estate my eyes were stinging big-time with tiredness, and my vision was getting blurred. But, fuck it, I could sleep next week. One thing puzzled me: the house had looked too big for just one person, but everything she'd ever said, and done, indicated she lived on her own. There was no one she'd wanted to phone, and she hadn't been worried about anyone or anything. Maybe she'd bought this place as an investment.

But what if she hadn't? What if the reason she had a big house was because she had a husband and kids? With a house full of people, how was I going to stop her if she chose to do a runner to the Yes Man? Fuck it, I'd cross that bridge when I came to it.

I started to check out other possibles. I'd come back here at dark o'clock.

51

Warwick Drive turned out to be my only hope; I couldn't find any other possibles. I went back to the car park at Bluewater and wound the seat back, but couldn't sleep. I just nodded off for the odd five minutes, waking up to every shout, every moving vehicle, every banging tailgate.

When I finally opened my eyes, they were as blurred and watery as ever. My mouth tasted like a dustbin, and the cheese and pickle sandwich had made my teeth feel like they had little fur coats on. At least it was now dark. I checked traser. Shit, I was nearly late.

I went back into the mall and shoved a couple of pound coins into a wall phone. I got a very bright, upbeat 'Hello!' from Josh at the other end.

'It's me.'

The tone soon changed. 'Oh, hi, we're just on our way.'

'Listen, don't bother – change of plan. She's not coming back just yet.'

'You're kidding? I spoke to her only last night and everything was cool. What's wrong? She OK?'

'Course.' I tried to sound as casual as possible. 'She's just going to be here a little longer. I think it'll be better for her.'

Bible college clearly hadn't worked its magic. 'What are you saying? You've changed your mind, or she's changed hers? She's already told me she wants to come back and sort herself out.'

'I know, I know, but she's not going to come back just yet. I'll give you a call later. I've got to go, mate – work, you know what it's like. I just wanted to catch you before you left for the airport.'

'What's going on here, man? You worried about her flying with the alert on? Come on, man, look, the chances are—'

'Sorry, mate, gotta go, gotta go.' I put the phone down and walked away.

I felt such an arsehole. I wanted to tell him to stay at home with the kids, I wanted to tell him he needed to get a truckload of antibiotics, but I couldn't – I couldn't risk a leak. The best chance Josh and the kids had of keeping safe was for me to keep quiet and give George the best possible chance of lifting the ASU. Whoever was out there working for him, they'd better be fucking good.

Back at the car, I got the seat back into its driving position and rolled out of the mall, the only vehicle without shopping bags piled on the back seat.

There was a small parade of shops on the edge of the estate: an off-licence, a Spar 24/7 and a dry cleaner's. I parked and went into the 24/7. An old couple were sitting behind the counter, the woman chewing a KitKat. They both watched me intently while I picked up a pie and a couple of cans of Red Bull.

I left the car where it was and walked the rest of the way, filling my face with cold steak and kidney, or so it said on the packaging, and caffeine, trying to wake up and get myself in gear.

A few people were out walking their dogs, but most were probably bathing their kids: the place had that end-of-weekend feel about it. The street lighting was enough to see by, but not as bright as on the main drag. The developers had probably installed the minimum requirement, which worked in my favour.

The TVs glowed in the the front rooms of row upon row of new brick detacheds and semis. I turned into Warwick Drive. I could see lights on in what I hoped was Suzy's place, up at the top of the turning circle. There was a vehicle shape in the driveway.

I left my second empty Red Bull can on the front wall of one of the mock-Tudors and checked that my cell was off, then ran through the options as I approached the house. What if she had a husband and he was at home? What if she had kids? What if she was alone but her husband came back while I was there? What would I do if she said she was going to tell the Yes Man?

As I got nearer I could see light through the crack in the front-room curtains, to the right of the front door, and from the upstairs landing.

The vehicle turned out to be a muddy Honda 4x4. I headed down the alleyway to the rear of the house, stopping at the brickworks corner to scan the garden. The landing light was strong enough to help me dodge the cement mixer, and the piles of sand and wood that lay beside it. Coldplay were going for it big-time in one of the upstairs rooms next door; Kelly would have approved.

I followed the fence to the new trees at the rear of the garden, keeping low enough to stay in its shadow. I could see Bluewater in the middle distance across the fields, so brightly lit the car parks looked like a UFO landing site. I had a complete view of the rear of the house from there. The curtains were drawn in the living room, but the oak-fitted kitchen was on full display. Between them was the back door, surrounded by a two-foot-high brick wall that formed the base of the conservatory.

I glanced over the fence to make sure the Coldplay fan wasn't hanging out of the window having a sneaky smoke, then set off towards the dining-room window, keeping my distance from the wooden frames and piles of other building shit. I didn't want to leave sign in the sand.

Movement to my right, inside the kitchen; no time to check, just to drop, and crawl into the shadow of the brickwork. Fuck leaving sign now. Face full of grit, I crawled to the corner to see what was moving.

Suzy was filling the kettle. She was wearing a white towelling dressing gown and her hair was slicked back. Her lips weren't moving, and she was giving her full attention to the tap. I would probably have heard if somebody else had been anywhere near. Moments later, she disappeared in the direction of the hallway.

I crawled backwards, keeping on my stomach, then turned and got back on my original course. My bumbag was dragging along the ground, so I stopped to adjust it. Once below the window I sat up, my back against the wall. I shook the sand out of my sweatshirt and tried to ignore the damp and cold that was working its way through the back of my jeans.

I waited for her to return to the kitchen to finish making what I hoped was just the one brew. Coldplay weren't helping much, but I was pretty sure there was no sound from inside her house, no TV, no talk, no music.

A shadow fell across the garden the other side of the back door. I swivelled on to my knees and lifted my head far enough to see through the corner of the window. The dining room was dark, and I could see just a sliver of light falling from the living-room doorway across the hall carpet.

Suzy appeared, mug in hand, then vanished from my field of view. I got down on my hands and knees, crawled to the other side of the window, then bobbed up again. She was lying on the settee, reading a magazine. The mug was next to her on a small coffee-table and a few more magazines were scattered about on the carpet. She was surrounded by smart-looking shopping bags, and a selection of new clothes was draped over an armchair, their tags still dangling.

I stayed in position and checked traser as she turned the pages. It was just after eleven. She must have been as

314

knackered as I was. Why wasn't she going to sleep? Was she waiting for her boyfriend or husband to come home, after all?

I kept watching her, making sure my mouth was far enough away from the glass not to leave any condensation.

Keeping on my hands and knees, I worked my way round the conservatory to the kitchen window. The sink was empty, and there weren't any pictures on the fridge, or happy snaps on the yellow flowery walls.

Some letters were piled further along the worktop. I tilted my head to try to read the writing. I couldn't make out the name, just that it wasn't Mr and Mrs.

I slid back down below the window and rested against the wall. I tucked my legs in, wrapped my arms round them, and lowered my chin on to my knees, checking traser once more as my arse got resoaked. It wasn't even midnight.

The flight was at seven-whatever, so I'd have to be at the airport a couple of hours before. That meant I had to leave here at about three or, even better, half two-ish to build in flat-tyre time. I had just under three hours to grip Suzy and get her to back me – or put her into the boot of my car – before I got myself cleaned up for the flight.

I sat in the wet grass, feeling the sand I hadn't managed to remove from under my sweatshirt scrape against my back, and thought about Kelly. Maybe she was sitting in a corner of a filthy room, with nothing but her Old Navy on, cold, wet and frightened. Was she hungry? Did she have anything to drink? Had she been hurt? Would she know what was happening? There were other questions rushing around in my head too, questions I didn't want to ask.

I felt completely fucking useless. I wanted to get moving, take action, do something positive. I gave myself a good mental slapping. This was the best way to get her back. I needed Suzy to help, and that was why I was here. That was positive action. That was the only action.

I held my breath to see if it would stop the pain in my chest,

315

but it didn't. I filled my lungs instead to calm myself down, but that didn't work either. Why did I always fuck things up?

Time to get on with it. I stood up slowly, making sure I was still in shadow.

Keeping clear of the windows, I went back to the front of the house and suddenly realized she was probably as lonely as I was.

The curtains were still drawn.

As soon as I stepped under the porch the overhead security light flicked on. The door was solid dark wood. I pressed the buzzer, and eventually saw some movement in the hall.

'Who is it?' The voice wasn't scared, just curious.

'It's me – it's Nick.'

'What?'

'Nick. I need . . . I need some help. Open up.'

She turned the locks but left on the security chain and her face appeared in the gap. It was only a few inches wide, but that was enough for me to tell that she wasn't remotely impressed. 'What do you want?'

'Just let me in. It's important. Please?'

The door closed, and the chain rattled before it was opened again. I wiped my sandy boots on the welcome mat and stepped inside. The hallway was light blue and I could immediately smell new paint and carpets. Flowery wallpaper ran the length of the corridor, above a dado rail, punctuated by prints of trees, sky, things like that. It felt like a B&Q showhouse.

There was another door on the left, just short of the staircase, which I guessed led to the garage, as it did in Jimmy and Carmen's. Good: if she didn't want to help me, I could get the car in there and bundle her into the boot without an audience.

'What the fuck are you doing here, Nick?'

I put my hands up in surrender. 'I'm dying for a brew.'

'Fuck that. How did you know where I live?'

'I didn't. The view from the kitchen over to Bluewater? The conservatory? It was all I had to go on.'

She looked down at my clothes.

I shrugged. 'I had to wait and see if you were alone. Look, I need to talk to you about something – but first I need that brew.'

'It better be good.' She turned towards the kitchen. 'Get your boots off.'

I heard the kettle being filled as I obeyed.

My feet stank. I stopped at the door.

Even from behind, her body language was clear. She was probably angrier with herself than with me: she couldn't believe that she'd given herself away. Back in her Det days, a slip like that might have cost someone's life. 'What do you want?'

'Kelly's been lifted . . . by the source.'

She spun to face me, the kettle still in her hand.

I kept my voice low and slow, wanting her to take every word on board. 'I went to see her at her grandparents' this morning. They'd both been stabbed to death. Kelly was missing. No note, nothing.'

We just stood there, Suzy still with the kettle in her hand, as I ran through what had happened next. 'So, it's a simple trade. I go to Berlin and do a pickup, and he gives me Kelly back.'

'Pick up what?' She plugged in the kettle.

'Five wine bottles.'

She turned, a look of horror across her face. 'Oh, fuck – you've got to call the boss.'

'No.' I shook my head.

She turned to the tree of yellow mugs that matched the wallpaper behind her, and for the first time I noticed a wedding ring on her finger. My mind worked quick time.

She knew what I'd seen. 'Relax, I'm on my own here.'

I took a step closer. 'Look, I really need help. I could lie to you and say this is all about keeping control of DW, but it isn't. This is about getting her back, and then trying to control DW. I can't do it on my own. You're the only one I can ask. But whatever you decide, no one must know about this.' I lifted the third finger of my left hand and flexed it in the air. 'No one.'

The kettle stopped boiling and she dropped a teabag into the mug, poured the water, dug out the bag almost immediately and threw it into the sink.

I followed her into the living room with my brew as she hit the main lights. The curtains matched the settee, and the other soft furnishings. It was all a bit too flowery for my liking, and certainly not the sort of thing I'd have expected Suzy to go for.

A selection of family photographs stood on a highly polished sideboard in the dining room. A smiling naval officer took pride of place in two or three of the silver frames. Two boys in muddy rugby kit, more or less the same age as Kelly, grinned out from the others.

She tapped one of the pictures of the uniform. 'That's why I didn't have to call anybody. Geoff's still floating around the Gulf somewhere. These are his sons. They live with their mother in New Zealand.'

Geoff looked much older than her, and was obviously big-time in the Navy. I'd never understood the hierarchy, but there was a lot of gold stuff dripping off his jacket. Her face broke into a smile as she headed for the settee. 'See, I told you, relax. I really am on my own.'

She threw her *Hello!* on to the carpet with the rest of the magazines and sat down, bringing her legs up on to the cushions then covering them with the robe. I stayed standing to protect the furniture. I nodded towards the shopping bags. 'Been to Bluewater?'

'Yeah, I couldn't get to sleep. I was dying to, but what with all the work going on round the back . . .' She adjusted the robe round her thighs again, then looked up sharply. 'So tell me, what's the story on this girl of yours, if she isn't your daughter?'

52

It took me an hour, but I stood there and told her everything. I fumbled my way through that day in Hunting Bear Path and our weeks on the run together afterwards, and how she'd ended up living with Josh and his family in Maryland after her therapy sessions in London.

Suzy seemed to understand. 'She's never fully recovered, then – that's why you came back to see the same doctor, yeah?'

'That's where I disappeared to on Saturday. Seeing your whole family head-jobbed takes some getting over. But she's just like her dad was, a fighter . . .'

I told her how she had managed to fight her way back from being a curled-up bundle of nothing to being able to function outside the clinic where she'd spent the best part of ten months. 'And just when I thought she'd got straightened out, she's developed a habit with painkillers, and she's bulimic, and fuck knows what else.'

'That little performance in St Chad's makes sense now.'

I fished in my pocket and pulled out the Polaroid. 'This was her this morning.'

Suzy kept her eyes fixed on Kelly's face, but they looked slightly glazed, as if she was elsewhere. 'Beautiful . . .' She handed back the picture. 'You're sure about not going to the boss?'

'That job I told you about, the one I did for him a couple of years ago? It was in Panama. He threatened to have Kelly killed if I didn't do it. The two guys in the Transit – they're the ones who'd have done it. If I go to him now, I'll lose what little control I have. He won't give a shit about anything but the DW – fair one, but where would that leave Kelly? The only way I'm going to get her back is by going to Berlin and picking up those bottles.'

'You sure he won't just kill both of you once he's got them?'

I shrugged. What could I say? She was right.

She studied my face. 'You're going to do this regardless, aren't you?'

'Don't have much option, do I? The thing is, will you help me? I don't know how yet – all I know is I'll need backing once I'm in the UK.'

She shifted about a little on the settee, as if looking for something, then smiled to herself. 'Force of habit. I was just about to reach for a fag. It's going to be hard for me, Nick. I'm in a delicate condition.'

'Look, if everything goes well, your permanent cadre won't be jeopardized. I don't think—'

She lifted a hand. 'You know, for a highly trained observer, you can be amazingly stupid sometimes. I said condition, not fucking position. Look, I was smoking in Penang, right, but next time you saw me I'd stopped – me, the girl who could describe to you every cigarette she ever smoked. Then that being-sick thing. Nerves? And did you ever see me taking any doxycycline? Think about it, Nick. Hurry up . . . yes, well done, that's right. Two months. Geoffrey's fond farewell before the Gulf.'

'Why didn't you tell me? How long have you known?'

'None of your business – but I found out after we got back from Penang.'

'The Yes Man know?'

'Definitely not. I'm hoping I get PC before I show, then it's thanks for the promotion, and next day – shock horror, so sorry, I just found out I need some maternity leave.'

'He'll fuck you over, you know.'

She shrugged. 'Geoff's done that already. Anyway, we'll see, won't we?'

I couldn't make out if the Geoff thing was a joke or not. 'What does he think about all this?'

'He doesn't know yet. I'm not too sure whether I'm keeping it.' She looked away and had a moment to herself. 'Our marriage is a bit of a nightmare, to be honest. I thought what I needed was stability. But look at this place, this isn't me – you know what I mean, don't you?' She waved her hand at the flower fest around us. 'I've tried. I always thought I'd want all this, but I'm not made for this shit. You understand, don't you? You're the same.' Her eyes were starting to well up.

I hated situations like this. What was I supposed to do now? I never knew if it was listen, hug, or go and put the kettle on.

'I get the feeling he blames me – you know, if he hadn't met me, he'd still be unhappily married just the once.' She took a deep breath, exhaled noisily, and tears fell down her cheeks. I took one of my own, ready to ask if she wanted a brew, but I was too late. 'Goodness knows why he married me.' She gave me a little grin as the tears fell gently on to her robe. 'Oh, no, hang on, I remember now – I'm such a fantastic fuck.'

She motioned me to sit down and dirty an armchair. 'Fuck it. Never liked the pattern anyway.'

I moved new sweaters and coats off the back and sat down. I'd been nodding ever since her announcement, but I still had no idea where this was leading.

'I was thinking about the abortion when you rang the bell. Shall I tell you where I'd got to?'

I carried on nodding.

'My marriage will not survive, but I still want this child.'

'That changes everything, Suzy. I can't ask you—'

'Why the fuck not? I'm pregnant, not disabled. Anyway, don't worry, I have a secret weapon.'

She was willing me to ask her as she gripped herself and the tears stopped.

'Don't tell me – you're one of the X Men . . .'

She gave me the same sort of look Kelly always did when I said something embarrassing. 'My condition, you dickhead.'

'That's what's worrying me.'

'Not *that* – RUC syndrome. Heard of it, Det boy?'

I hadn't, and now got to shake my head.

'It was first diagnosed in the police over the water. If they survived a bomb attack or a hit, some of them started believing they could survive anything. That's me. I'm invincible.'

'What turned you into superwoman, then?'

'Did you ever hear about the female operator that nearly got lifted in Belfast in the nineties? You remember, August 'ninety-three. You were still in the Regiment then, weren't you?'

I was, and I did remember a few vague details.

'I was working two-up on a serial around the West Belfast estates. Just part of a normal team. I dropped off my partner, Bob, to do a walk-past of the target's flat. I parked up the other side of the estate and waited to pick him up. But we'd been compromised and I ended up trapped in my car by a road-digger. The fucker used the bucket to try to crush it, with me still in it, as a few boyos got together to tear apart whatever was left of me.'

I was going to make a funny, but then saw the look on her face.

'Don't ask me how, but I got out of the car with a broken femur after the bucket had gone down on the car two or three times. I shot the digger driver and one of the players who was trying to batter my head in with an iron bar. Then I held the rest back by grabbing one and jamming my pistol into his gob and just held on until the rest of the team rammed their cars into the crowd to get me out. I was shitting myself. Bob got dragged away and kicked to death in the estate.'

I did remember now: it had been a big deal at the time. She even got decorated for it. 'So you're the famous digger girl, then?'

'Yep, that's me. Big-time hero.'

She sounded a little sardonic, but surviving was something to be proud of, without a doubt. Others in similar situations were now dead, including Bob. The whole Ashford and the MOE school thing made sense now. Her cover had been blown big-time, but the Det would have wanted to keep hold of someone of her calibre.

'Does the Yes Man know you have this head-banging RUC whatever-it's-called?'

'Nope, no one. Just you.' She smiled briefly, checking that the robe still covered her legs. 'You want to know something else no one knows? You want to hear the real story?'

I shifted awkwardly in my chair, thinking that it might be time to go and make a brew.

'It was my fault we got compromised.' Her voice was drained of emotion, her head was down, hair falling forwards and blocking out her face as her hands flattened out the white towelling over her legs. 'I stopped the car for a casual drop-off, but as Bob got out, his jacket must have got tucked in behind his pancake. His Sig and mag carrier were showing. I didn't see it until he was half-way over the road.

'I tapped the horn and he came back, ready to lift off. I said it was OK, don't be stupid, no one's seen it. Fact is, I was more worried about the serial being cancelled and looking a dickhead than being compromised, know what I mean?'

I nodded, but not really meaning it.

'Anyway, he took my word for it, covered up and started again. I went the other side of the estate to pick him up. Next thing I knew that fucking JCB started rearranging the bodywork. So I did my stuff and the green army went into the estate in riot gear and brought out Bob's body an hour or so later.'

Her face was still covered by hair, but I knew she was fighting the tears again. 'Look, you can't blame yourself. He should have checked himself before getting out of the car. It's no one's fault, things fuck up.'

'No, you're wrong. It fucked up because I was more worried about admitting to myself we were compromised. It felt like a failure and I didn't want to accept that.' She sat upright, swinging her feet off the settee. Her eyes were wet, her cheeks red, and she didn't care about the robe now: it fell apart, exposing her legs. 'I couldn't tell anyone – maybe guilt – but I saw Bob, I saw them kicking and punching him to death. We could see each other, he was screaming at me for help. I was out of the car by then but couldn't get to him. I watched them drop a fucking paving slab on his head because of me, but I couldn't do anything about it . . .'

The tears just kept falling, but there was no noise from her now. Maybe she had already made enough over the years.

My heart quickened: I needed to know. 'Do you have dreams about it – you know, like a film in your head?'

She went quite still, not even bothering to wipe away the tears. 'You know, don't you? You have them. I can't stop it sometimes – even watching a TV fight will do it. You understand . . . It's like, I replay it over and over again in my head, and it totally fucks me over. I can't help it.'

Shit. This was more than enough. I stood up, cutting away there and then. 'Want a brew?'

She nodded. 'Yes, you're right. Better shut up now before we become normal and talk about shit – you never know, the floodgates might really burst, and then we'd be totally fucked.'

She followed me into the kitchen and leant against the worktop, wiping her face with a teacloth as she watched me fill the kettle and fumble about for the teabags.

'Ever since then, Nick, I've been the first to jump in. No task too small, Suzy's your girl. No cheap psychology required – I survive even when I fuck up, even when I don't deserve to. That's why I'll go to Berlin with you.'

I found the tea on the worktop behind her and got pouring. 'I just need you when I get back.'

324

'Think about it. It's better for cover and, anyway, you don't know what you're going to find. Apart from that, of course –' she grinned '– you're fucking useless. How many times have I saved that lardy arse of yours?'

I passed her brew over and saw that scary look on her face again. Good, things were back to normal. No more talk of videos and gates bursting open. I was planning on keeping mine well shut. 'So you've got a real syndrome? I just thought you were a fucking fruitcake.'

I got a laugh, but then her eyes narrowed. 'What were you going to do if I'd said no? Kill me?'

'I'd just have lifted you until I got Kelly.'

'Look, I won't lie to you. If I'm on my own and I have to make a choice between Kelly and DW, you know which I'm going to go for, don't you?'

I nodded. 'I've got two important questions.'

'They'd better be.'

I pulled at the neck of my sweatshirt. 'Can I use your shower and washing-machine? I'm covered in sand under here. And can you get on the phone to Air Berlin and book yourself on to my flight?'

53

The seats on the Air Berlin flight were small and cramped, but we were both so exhausted it didn't really matter. Suzy had the window-seat and her head rolled against the side of the aircraft. The gallons of coffee we'd thrown down us all night hadn't been enough to keep us going. It wasn't long into the ninety-minute journey that we were both doing neck-breakers, mouths wide open, saliva dribbling down chins, much like every other early-morning passenger off for a day's business in Berlin, except that they reeked of aftershave and sported suits and pressed shirts.

Suzy had driven us to Stansted in the runabout Geoff used when on leave, a beaten-up old Micra that chugged out of the garage and I replaced with the Vectra. It was better to be disconnected from it as I entered a new phase.

While the suits had been catching up on their beauty sleep, we'd been working out the plan for the pickup. We kicked round and round the possibility of replacing the bottles with others containing inert powder. In theory, it would be no problem to work the switch: we'd both done it enough times with weapons and equipment against other players in the past. But to do the job properly takes time, something we didn't have. Any player worth their salt would have placed tell-tales on the bottles; maybe a small pin-hole in the foil that the replacement wouldn't have, or maybe a taste. Rubbing ginger or a wet boiled sweet around the foil, or the cork before it was resealed, would leave a trace that could be picked up with a wet finger. But even if there were no tell-tales, what if he had the capability to test the contents? Could I afford to take that risk? The source would need to know that he had DW before he'd even think of handing over Kelly – not that I reckoned he planned to – and delivering it intact was the only way I had even the remotest chance of getting to her. Fuck the inert business. Dark Winter had to be delivered.

We had to travel on our own passports because there was no time to do otherwise. Her real name was Susan Gilligan or, at least, that was her maiden name. She'd never got round to changing her passport, even though she'd been married nearly four years now.

My head rolled with another neck-breaker that woke me up as abruptly as if I was having the falling-off-a-building-and-just-about-to-hit-the-ground nightmare. The day's papers had slipped off my lap long ago and got ripped to pieces on the floor as we'd twisted and turned in the confined space to try to get even more uncomfortable. They were full of post-war Baghdad, America's amber alert, which was being blamed on the Iraqi situation, and pictures of Canadians walking about in face masks to avoid contracting SARS. Nothing in the national pages about King's Cross or King's Lynn.

I wiped some saliva from the side of my mouth. The pre-landing announcements started in efficient German, followed by accented but perfect English. The aircraft began to lose height and we tried to find where our seat-belt buckles had hidden themselves.

I copied Suzy as she adjusted her watch to Central European time, then craned my neck to look out of her window. The sky was sunny and cloud free, and I could clearly see the Brandenburg Gate, surrounded by burgeoning high-rises.

The whole of the centre of the city looked like a field ready for harvest, except that the yellow stuff wasn't wheat, it was tower cranes.

'Looks like a nice day for it.' We hadn't talked about the job itself since we entered Stansted, and wouldn't again until we got out of the cab at the other end. We didn't want to be overheard, and talking in whispers attracts too much attention.

Suzy had bought a guidebook at the airport, so we knew Bergmannstrasse was in the old Western part of the city, in an area called Kreuzberg, which I thought I knew from my time as a squaddie in the early eighties. The book said it had a large Turkish population, and Germans went there to escape National Service and become artists, punks or anarchists instead. That sounded about right. I wasn't too sure about having seen any artists, but I'd spent a good few nights in West Berlin getting ripped off by Turkish bar owners and trading punches with German punks.

We landed and everybody stood up and clogged the aisle as soon as the seat-belt sign flickered off. The suits revved up their mobiles to start the day's work. When we eventually disembarked, we were channelled towards two control booths immediately at the top of the ramp. They were manned by German Immigration police in dark-green jackets and washed-out yellow shirts, their spiky hair and stern faces making them look as if they'd be more at home sticking out the top of a tank than checking passports and watching for illegals.

Suzy made sure she had the guidebook in view as the two of us stepped forward. A guy in his late twenties, with a blond crewcut, flushed cheeks and rectangular frameless glasses, took our passports, looked at us, then snapped them shut before passing them back with a nod. We muttered thanks and entered Germany, following signs for taxis. Checkpoint Charlie was just a couple of Ks to the north of Bergmannstrasse, and a major tourist trap. It was as good a destination as any to give to a cabbie, before walking into the target area.

We stepped out into bright sunshine as I took a couple more

antibiotics, not bothering to offer any to Suzy. The temperature was still a little cold as we lined up at the rank with about thirty others, mostly suits with their phones stuck to their ears. White Mercedes cabs filtered forwards to run the fares the dozen or so kilometres into town. We didn't talk: there were still too many spare ears around.

When our turn eventually came, we climbed into a six- or seven-year-old Merc with plastic seats. The driver, an old Turk, didn't need to speak English to understand Suzy's 'Checkpoint Charlie, mate.'

'*Ja, ja* – Checkpoint Charlie, OK.'

We headed out of Tegel, straight into urban sprawl, and soon passed Spandau prison. We arrived at the older part of the city, driving along wide boulevards with cobbled pavements. I stared out at the place the wall had once cut through the heart of Berlin, at Potsdammer Platz. Brand-new buildings were springing up everywhere like crystal puffballs where the wall and its corridor of no man's land, the Death Zone, had once stretched. This had to be the only major city on the planet with so much space for new development at its centre. Billions were being poured into its regeneration, with futuristic buildings, brand-new boulevards and landscaped open spaces everywhere you looked. The last time I'd been here all I'd seen was the wall, rolls of barbed-wire and the bricked-up entrance to the metro. Now Potsdammer station was shiny and new, and speeding passengers all over the city. I wondered if it was on the ASU's list of targets.

There were no glittering puffballs springing up on the other side of the square just yet; there were derelict factories and warehouses instead, fenced off and surrounded by wasteland where other buildings had been demolished, awaiting their turn for an injection of chrome and spangle.

Then, just as quickly, we were driving past Porsche show-rooms and Hugo Boss boutiques, and when we turned the next corner, Checkpoint Charlie was ahead of us. Now preserved as a monument, it looked much the same as I remembered it, only without the wall and its phalanx of armed soldiers. The white guardhouse in the middle of the road was still surrounded by sandbags, and they'd even kept the sign up warning that you were now entering the American sector or, on the flip side, that you were leaving it for East Berlin.

Tourists poured out of a coach and into the museum. As I paid the driver, an old American guy caught my eye, pointing things out to someone I guessed was his son. His uniform, these days, was jeans, a suit jacket and a pair of white tennis shoes, but he clearly still had a full stock of Checkpoint Charlie war stories.

The area on the eastern side was flattened and awaiting redevelopment, and seemed to be lined by Turks and Bosnians with stalls selling Russian fur hats and East German peaked caps and badges. Everything looked suspiciously new and had probably been knocked out last week in the same Chinese factory that supplied Penang with its ethnic masks.

We leant against the wall of a bar facing the museum and guardhouse so Suzy could get the map out. I grinned. 'Two Brit tourists seeing the sights, moaning to each other in crap German accents that they can't get a decent cup of tea – what could be more natural?'

She laughed as I checked traser. It was just after eleven a.m. She pulled her cell from her black leather jacket. 'Better check comms.' I got Geoff's out of the bumbag and powered it up. After a few seconds of roaming, the displays on both said Deutsche Telekom. I tapped in the international code and her number, and her phone rang. We exchanged a few words before closing down.

'Right, let's keep an eye out for a chemist.'

Following the map, we headed south through former East Berlin, the monotonous brick buildings now covered in gig posters, graffiti and 'Stop the War' slogans.

We passed a housing estate of grey, depressing, rectangular chunks of concrete with windows, which they'd tried un-successfully to brighten up with murals of the sun, sand and sea. There was even one with a moth-eaten old Union Jack sticking out among the graffiti.

A Trabant passed us, handpainted in psychedelic colours, with posters in the windows advertising a cyber café.

A section of the wall nearby had been fenced off as some sort of monument.

Two policemen sat in a marked BMW police car alongside a line of shops, one of which had a large red Gothic letter A sticking out from its wall.

'*Apotheke.*'

Suzy was pleased. 'Perfect.'

As we got nearer, I could see that one of the officers had a big walrus moustache and more than his fair share of blubber. He reminded me of someone, and I couldn't help but smile.

Suzy raised an eyebrow. 'What's up with you, Norfolk boy?'

'I was in Berlin for a while as a squaddie. Me and a mate came here for the weekend once on the Hanover troop train. It was our first trip, we didn't know where we were going, what we were doing – just anything to get away from the garrison for a few days. We were bumming around the bars, and got into a fight with the resident battalion. The Turks piled in as well, and the German police came and started making arrests, throwing us into the backs of vans.

'Me and my mate – I can't even remember his name now, Kenny, I think – landed up sitting on the benches facing each other by the rear doors. This big fat copper, just like him over there, came round and slammed them on us, but the lock didn't engage. Kenny and I just looked at each other and, fucking right, madness not to. We pushed open the doors and started running down the road, and all we could hear was this big German trying to waddle after us, waving his truncheon, hollering and shouting for us to stop.

'I turned round and could see him trying his hardest to catch up. No way he was going to – we were young squaddies, he looked like Hermann Goering. I don't know why, but I stopped, turned round again, and started yelling back at him,

331

"Wanker, lardarse!" that sort of stuff. Anyway, he was getting really pissed off. I gave him another couple of paces before I turned round to run, and bang – next thing I knew I was face down on the cobbles and Lardarse was breathing all over me. The bastard had thrown his truncheon and got me smack in the back of the head.'

Suzy shook her head and smiled. 'Comforting to know I'm in such reliable hands.'

We entered the chemist's and didn't exactly have to hunt for masks and gloves. The SARS scare had hit everywhere, and the boy had plenty of choice on display. I picked up a pack of ten green ones, looking a bit like thick J-cloths. I couldn't tell if they were N-whatever number Simon had said. Fuck it, I'd just hope for the best. Right next to them were ten-packs of latex gloves. Not quite the full NBC suit I really wanted, but better than nothing.

Suzy checked out the household section. When we met at the counter she produced two pairs of swimming goggles, and a set of four different-sized stainless-steel knives in case the hand-over didn't go to plan.

Once outside we continued south. 'You said Geoff was married before. What about you?'

'Yeah, while I was in the Navy, just a kid, really.'

We stopped and checked the map together at the end of a housing estate. 'I fucked it right up. Don't even ask. I was eighteen, he was nineteen. There should be a law against it. Two blocks to go.'

We moved off and there was no more chat about failed marriages. Everything went serious now.

Either the buildings on Bergmannstrasse and the surrounding area had survived the Allied bombing, or they'd been perfectly restored in its old style. It looked like we were walking through a movie set for old Berlin.

Bergmannstrasse turned out to be a major thoroughfare. The kerbs on the south side were solid with cars, and the pavements were wide. It was tree-lined all the way down, with a mixture of eighteenth-century-style houses and a few newer apartment blocks. The ground floor of every building seemed to be a shopfront with an awning out, and the pavements were packed.

We stopped on a corner and had a look at the numbers. We seemed to be up in the high hundreds, so twenty-two was going to be somewhere down to our left. We walked on, merging with the crowds of Monday-morning shoppers. It looked like half of Berlin's mothers were out and about, holding back their toddlers with baby reins.

I got the feeling I'd been here before, though it was hard to tell now the area had gone upmarket. It was definitely ex-Bohemia. Every other shop seemed to sell Indian tablecloths and shiny cushions, hemp clothing and candles. Pumpkins were strewn outside organic food shops as a come-on for anyone not already seduced by the New Age music. Boxes of books were laid out on the pavement, alongside bric-à-brac and rails of used clothes. The Turkish influence was obvious, the smell of coffee wafting out of every other shop.

We carried on until we saw numbers forty-eight and forty-six across the road, then stopped under an awning and leant against a wall. Suzy browsed through rails of old leather jackets and jeans while I tried to work out where twenty-two was. When I did, I stared at it in disbelief.

She followed the direction of my gaze. Number twenty-four was a large fruit and veg shop, with trays of produce piled up outside and guys selling from them as if it was a market stall. To the left of it was a plain, off-white apartment block with large square windows set into its façade. There was a central doorway that I assumed led to the apartments, with a shopfront either side. The one to the left was a café called Break-out; the one on the right had an illuminated sign, and you didn't have to know any German to understand what Evangelisch-Freikirchliche meant. Josh would have liked it here.

As we came out from under the awning and moved closer,

Suzy pulled on my jacket sleeve. 'It gets better.' She nodded towards the top of the building, at a neon cross maybe twenty feet high, then got out her gum. 'Say what you like about these arseholes, but they do a nice line in irony.'

'Let's do a walk-past.'

We crossed the road, Suzy's right hand in my left, and her guidebook prominent in the other. We passed the fruit and veg place and looked through the glass front of the church. White stone steps led up to what looked like Hotel Heaven's reception desk. There were quite a few people checking in. The entrance to the apartments was a large glazed door with two glass side panels, and a stainless-steel push-button intercom system. Names appeared in only two of the slots.

Break-out was dark inside, with bare floors and stainless-steel tables, about half filled with coffee drinkers. We meandered on, not knowing where we were going, but it didn't really matter. All we wanted to do was move clear.

We carried on along Bergmannstrasse and turned right as soon as we could to get out of line of sight of the flats. After the rush of the main street this was a bit surreal: we were in a cemetery.

Old grannies placed flowers on graves, while their grandkids played quietly. Paths were dotted with reflection seats, many filled with young couples who seemed to be doing precious little reflection. Suzy and I found one from where we could see the back of the apartment block, and sat down.

54

As the church filled up on the first floor, Suzy's hands worked inside the carrier-bag, pulling away the cardboard and plastic packaging from the knives. I ripped the plastic away from the goggles, masks and the ten-pack of latex gloves, and stuffed half of them into my pockets. The rest were for Suzy.

'This is how I see it. I'll try to leave the front door open in case you need it. I'll collect DW, and meet you back here. If I'm not back in thirty, or you don't get a call, come and get me. If the front door is closed, there might be another way in through the church, or maybe round the back here. You need to check it out.'

She nodded and one of her hands jerked against the side of the bag as a knife suddenly parted company with its wrapping. 'OK, thirty – then I'll come and save your arse, yet again.'

I took off my bumbag and passed it over. I was going in there sterile, apart from the cell. She slipped me two of the shorter vegetable knives and they went into my jacket pocket.

'Thirty, then?' I got up, kissed her cheek, then started walking. I turned left out of the graveyard, back on to the busy main, then left again towards the building. Break-out had got busier and so had the church: people were filing in munching on sandwiches, or fruit fresh from the stall. I stopped by the bank of call buttons for the flats. The organ was thumping out a happy-clappy tune next door as I used a knuckle to press twenty-seven. It took for ever, but at last the speaker crackled. I heard someone coughing, then nothing apart from a burst of static. A truck roared past and I had to put my mouth right up to the intercom. 'I've been sent from London. You're expecting me.'

There was a delay, then the door gave a buzz. Once inside, I used my foot to stop it locking again, and had a look round. There was no CCTV: the only visible security was the intercom and door lock, a Yale-type device that couldn't be overridden. I folded one of the masks over the bolt and pushed the door closed so it wedged in position.

I found myself in a white fake-marble hall that smelt of pine cleaning fluid. According to the signs, twenty-seven would be on the second floor. As I climbed the stairs, listening to a dim murmur from the happy-clappies and the squeak of my Caterpillars on the shiny floor, I started to pull on a pair of gloves.

The steel-and-glass fire door to the second floor opened into a clinically white corridor. There were apartment doors on both sides; I put on the goggles and all four masks as I squeaked down towards number twenty-seven. It was at the end on the left, which meant it faced the main.

Checking my protection one last time, I knocked on the door, making sure my face was directly in front of the spyhole. I was standing there for a good fifteen seconds before I heard the sound of gaffer-tape being stripped away. It opened eventually, just a quarter of the way, and what I saw made me step straight back against the wall on the other side of the corridor. Six foot, my arse: I wanted to be a hundred from this fucker.

The face at the door belonged to a young Turk or Arab, mid-twenties maybe, his hands stained red with paint. That didn't worry me. What did was the state of his face. His eyes were bloodshot and he was soaked with sweat. He panted rather than breathed, and snot poured from his nose. I lifted my hand to stop him coming any further towards me. 'You speak English?'

He nodded, then disappeared behind the door and gave an agonizing cough. Even through the masks, the smell of shit and decay seeping out from the flat was overpowering.

His head reappeared, framed by lank, greasy hair.

'Bring the bottles to the door, OK? You get that?'

He nodded slowly, wiped his nose with his sleeve and shuffled back into the flat, leaving the door ajar. The happy-clappies were still doing their bit for God down below.

I moved left along the opposite wall until I got level with the doorway. The hall was small, square and empty, apart from the vomit covering the carpet and splashed up the walls, and the lengths of gaffer-tape that had probably been sealing the gap between door and frame. I heard more vomit hitting the floor and moved further left. Some of the living area came into view; I could see a big square window, curtained off with cheap material that let in the light. The walls were covered with the same red, spray-painted lettering we'd seen at King's Cross. I moved a little more to the left to try to see more, and wished I hadn't.

A dark-skinned body was sprawled on the carpet. I couldn't tell if it was male or female, because it was in an even worse state than Archibald. On the floor next to it were two shoulder-bags. I didn't need Simon here to tell me what was inside.

I could feel myself starting to gag.

The stomach was so bloated that it had burst through the vomit-covered shirt. All the exposed flesh was covered with saucer-sized scabs, weeping pus that glistened in the light. More vomit clung to the face. I couldn't tell if he or she was still alive; if they were, it wouldn't be for much longer.

I heard the noise of retching from another room, followed by a wet, phlegm-laden cough that sounded like a drain being cleared. My guy was still trying to make it to the door.

The body's head moved, rolling to one side so that its dark eyes looked at me. The mouth smiled, just for a second or so, before it spewed its guts up, probably for the last time. Fuck 'em, they didn't look or sound like martyrs to me.

He made it to the door, carrying a six-bottle wine carton. One of the spaces was empty. Maybe they'd had a breakage. That would certainly have explained why these two were in shit state.

I pointed to the corridor between us. 'Down there.'

He coughed up a gobbet of phlegm the size of a golfball and bent down to do as I'd told him. As he turned back he spat it into the hallway, then moved back inside and coughed up some more. The door closed. Everything went quiet. The happy-clappies were obviously taking a break.

I couldn't see any phlegm, vomit or shit on the bottles or box from where I stood. Not that it mattered: I still had to pick the fucking thing up.

My boots squeaked the three paces. I picked up the wine carrier with my gloved hand and started back down the stairs, my right arm held out so the cardboard didn't touch my clothes. It wouldn't make a blind bit of difference, but somehow it made me feel better.

I got to the front door and placed the box carefully on the floor. I took off my mask and goggles, making sure my gloves didn't touch my face. The door opened with a gentle pull and the mask blocking the bolt fell into the street. I leant down, picked up the box and walked out, breathing deeply to try to rid my nose and lungs of the stench as I headed for the cemetery.

Suzy wasn't anywhere to be seen in the graveyard. Clutching the goggles and masks in my left hand, I pulled off the glove so it enveloped everything, and dumped it in a bin. I found myself a free bench and began to feel a little worried about contamination – well, a lot worried. I knew I'd been reasonably protected, and had kept well away from them, but what about the bottles? What if one was leaking? I told myself there wasn't time to think: there was still too much to do.

I pulled off my right glove, powered up the cell and called Suzy, but just got the messaging service. I cut off and tried again, with the same result. What was going on here?

I tried once more, and this time she answered. I could hear traffic, and the sound of her walking. 'Where are you?'

'On the main.'

'I couldn't get you.'

'Must have been in a dead spot. I've just been having a look round the front.'

'I'm back in the graveyard. I've got 'em. Bring some carrier-bags.'

'I'll be there in a couple.'

As I cut off the power and put away the phone in my bomber, people streamed past the windows on the first floor of the block. It was back-to-work time for the happy-clappies.

I had to assume the bottles were airtight. They wouldn't have wanted the job getting fucked up more than it was already. They wanted the London attack to go ahead. That was why they'd sealed themselves in. They didn't want to raise the alarm.

Suzy came in from the wrought-iron gates as I swallowed another couple of capsules. I gave her a casual-contact wave, and got a happy smile back as she sat down next to me. We greeted each other with a kiss on the cheek, and she put her arm in mine. She handed over two white supermarket carriers, still stuck together at the handles.

'It's in shit state up there.' I described what I'd seen. 'Let's get a cab and fuck off. Who knows? Maybe we can get an earlier flight.'

I started to pack the box into one of the carriers, but Suzy wasn't ready to go just yet. 'What about those two up there? Maybe there's even more. They could decide to—'

'No way are they going to compromise themselves and fuck up London.' I wrapped the second bag around the first. 'Let

339

the fuckers weep themselves to death. Fuck 'em, they're not going anywhere.'

She wasn't having any of it. 'But the rest of the bottle could still be up there. You've seen what that stuff can do. Come on, Nick, we've got to do something.'

I took a deep breath. 'Listen, you get any bright ideas, just tell me. Until then, the best I can do is get this shit back to the UK. Kelly, remember?' I picked up the DW and we walked out towards the main. 'Sorry, but that's how it is.'

We avoided the front of the apartment block, in case any of the ASU were looking out. I didn't want them to see us together – we didn't know if they had contact with the source.

It wasn't long before we were in the back of a cab, heading for the airport.

There was no problem changing to an earlier flight. The last plane out was the busiest, so they were only too happy to have two passengers giving up their seats. We went straight into Departures, where Suzy bought some scent and two huge Toblerone bars, so that we ended up with two Berlin duty-free carrier-bags, one inside the other, for the wine box. It looked completely at home among the sea of red plastic bags that were waiting for our flight.

We took off for Stansted with the DW packed tightly into the luggage lockers, inside our coats. The flight attendant wouldn't let us keep them by our feet. I made a mental note to get to the locker before the suit the other side of me when we landed.

55

We turned our watches back an hour as we headed up the ramp to Immigration, and joined the line of suits and sunburnt holidaymakers making their way through UK passport control.

I clutched the carrier of DW in my left hand. Suzy stood immediately the other side of it to give a bit of protection, and we both had our passports out ready, open on the last page.

I'd cleared my head of any thought of danger. You have to, like an actor getting into character, otherwise it will show. I'd been on a nice day trip to Berlin, and now here I was, going through Immigration with my partner, a few bottles of duty-free in my hand and her with a bellyful of chocolate.

Suzy stood shoulder to shoulder with me for the next few minutes as we shuffled forward. When we were about five or six people away from the desk, I looked up and caught the eye of the woman behind it. She was looking directly at me. She quickly shifted her gaze, but the damage was done. She wouldn't have known what was going on: she would just have been told to make sure we got through without any drama.

I shifted my passport into my left hand, still holding the bag, and pulled out a bottle with my right. Suzy watched me without saying anything. I looked back at the woman as she checked the slowly moving line. When it was nearly our turn, a whole bunch of us got waved through; she didn't look at either of us as we passed the desk.

We carried on walking, joining the others heading for the luggage carousels. 'What's the matter, Nick? What's happening?'

I kept looking around. There had to be a lift team somewhere. 'Fucking bitch! You know very well what's happening.'

'What?'

I moved away from her, gripping the bottle by the neck as if I was about to throw it. She had an expression of complete incredulity on her face as she started looking around the hall, trying to see what I was searching for. 'What's happening, Nick? I need to know, tell me.'

I nodded towards the carousels. I could see them, Sundance and Trainers, still in sweatshirts and jeans, but now under three-quarter-length coats. They also had small shoulder-bags, carried across one shoulder and down the other side so they could run or fight and still hang on to their respirators.

She followed my gaze. 'This isn't me, Nick. Believe.'

I walked straight past the carousels, like most of the suits from our plane who had only briefcases and laptops.

Sundance and Trainers were about thirty metres to my right as I headed for Customs. We had eye to eye: all three of us knew what was going on. They weren't going to risk calling my bluff with all these people around. They'd bide their time: they had no choice.

'There's another two up there.' Suzy's voice came from just behind me.

I picked them out, hovering around the Customs channels, making a meal of putting bags over their shoulders as they kept their eyes constantly on target.

I stopped in my tracks and turned on Suzy. 'I'm getting out of here with all five bottles of this shit. If you, or these boys, try to stop me, I'll throw them. Got that? You'd better go and tell them.'

'I haven't told anyone anything. I don't know how they know.'

Sundance and Trainers shadowed me, and the other two moved out of the way, as I lifted the bottle to reinforce the threat. 'You called it in while I was getting this shit, didn't you?'

She came up level with me. 'No. It was just a dead spot. Why would I call this in?'

I could think of plenty of reasons. The words 'permanent' and 'cadre' topped the list. We joined the stream of trolleys overloaded with suitcases and duty-free bags aiming for the blue EU channel.

'He could have had the tickets flagged up to him or tracked the plastic – who knows?'

We got to the chicane and were caught in the bottleneck. I wanted to push through and run, then just keep running, but I couldn't risk attracting any of the overt security, who probably had no idea this was happening. Running would turn the whole thing into even more of a gang fuck. I just had to act normal, while feeling the pulses in my neck doing their best to burst out of my skin.

I fell in behind a group of four women in their forties, all pushing trolleys. They looked like four mums who'd been away by themselves, all tanned up in shorts and T-shirts, laughing and joking as they clung to the holiday mood, but pissed off that they had to be back in the office tomorrow morning.

I turned round. Suzy was about three paces back, with Sundance and Trainers another twenty behind. I hoped they weren't going to try it here. What could I do? Break a bottle over one of the women's heads? Throw this shit on to the floor? I stayed just a pace or two behind the girls, the bottle slightly raised in one hand and the bag in the other.

The sliding doors parted and we came out into the terminal,

only to be channelled immediately by steel barriers past rows of seats with people bent over laptops or drinking coffee from the nearby Costa franchise. My eyes were drawn to the coffee shop. The other two guys were already waiting this side for me.

I kept close to the four mums as they wandered across the busy glass, steel and concrete concourse, giggling about how lucky their husbands were going to be tonight after two weeks without. 'Of course, that's not two weeks for all of us, though, is it, Kate?' The other two burst out laughing.

Kate didn't like it. 'I don't know what you're talking about, Andreas and I only—' I lost the rest as a family hurried between us, on their way to Departures.

Kate and her friends wove their way through the foot traffic heading for the lifts that would take us down to the car park and railway station directly under the terminal.

My head spun as I worked through the options. I wanted to stay near these four, but if they got out at the car park, the first floor down, I'd have to carry on to the station level and latch on to someone else. No way was I going to get myself isolated in the car park, or get into the Micra and drive. I'd be on my own. They could control me when I got out on the road.

I could see both teams, flanking me about thirty behind. Suzy was still following me, and we had eye to eye.

'I'm staying.' She pointed behind her. 'You're wrong.'

I ignored her. We got to the lifts, and as soon as they could see what I had in mind, Sundance and Trainers took to the stairs, leaving the other two to keep eyes on target.

The large steel doors shuddered apart and the women added to the scrapes on the sides as they wedged in their trolleys. I squeezed in behind them. Kate pressed the button for the station. 'What do you want, love?'

'The same as you.' Her friends had another fit of giggles.

I felt an elbow in my back: Suzy had pushed in just as the doors closed. I kept my hand clenched round the neck of the bottle, making sure she saw it. 'Don't fuck me about.'

344

When the doors opened again the women gave us both a bit of a sideways look. They understood: they'd had plenty of rows of their own. I stepped out and to one side to let them pass, then kept right behind them as they pushed their trolleys into the station cavern. No doubt Suzy was behind me somewhere. I couldn't be arsed to look.

Sundance and Trainers were waiting, gulping in oxygen, as their two mates came down the stairs three at a time. I lifted the bottle and got eye to eye with the shorter one. He made a calming motion with his hands.

By now the girls had got to the touch-screen ticket machines and were buying singles to London. I got out my card and bought one too, then followed them towards the waiting train. The platform was alive with the buzz of Italian and German voices. The tannoy announced the imminent departure of the train for London Liverpool Street in three languages, to the relieved nods of the tourists. Trolleys rumbled, kids shrieked. I watched the four-man lift team staking me, but caught a glimpse of Suzy, ticket in hand.

The women dumped their trolleys and heaved their far-too-big suitcases into the blue interior of the worn-out train. As I followed them, Sundance and Trainers boarded the next carriage. Sure enough, the other two ran past me and got into one further along.

Our carriage was packed with bags, people, and even a rat dog being carried in its own shoulder-bag by a doting Frenchwoman. All the foreigners had their travel guides out, and some were already dozing off. I stood near the public credit-card phone, next to the toilet. Suzy worked her way past some cases and a three-wheeled baby buggy to the opposite side of the train.

There was a tannoy announcement in English that the train was going direct to London, stopping at Tottenham Hale. Translations followed as the buzzer went, the doors closed and we started to move.

Suzy came within a few paces of me.

'Just keep your distance, OK?'

'Nick, I didn't—'

We were plunged into darkness for a second or two before the lights came back on. I couldn't hear the rest of what she said as we went through the tunnel: there was too much noise. I just leant back against the telephone, bottle in hand. I wasn't going to throw it, but I had to look as if I was ready to.

As we came out of the tunnel I heard another estuary voice, male this time. 'Tickets, please.' The guy was working his way towards us on auto-pilot. 'Tickets, please.' I looked down the lines of heads towards the next carriage. Sundance and Trainers had come through the connecting door and were leaning against the luggage racks. I understood the look on their faces only too well. Sundance was talking into his cell. The QRF would be fast-balling from in front of the TV and heading for Liverpool Street.

The train rumbled on, not very fast, shunting us from side to side. Suzy's phone rang as some kids went running past and their father yelled after them in German. She looked surprised. I wasn't.

She put the phone to her ear and listened. 'Hello? Yes, sir. We have it.' There was a pause. 'No, we can't do that, sir. I'm sorry.' Another pause. 'I understand the risks, sir, but there are reasons for this happening and I'm not going to— No, sir, I can't do that. Everything is under control.'

She held up the cell between us and I heard him ranting, 'I want Dark Winter handed over now! Do not disobey me – do not waste your career for this man! What on earth do you think you're doing?'

I managed to get my mouth up against the mike. 'You can have it once I've finished. I'll explain later.'

'Stone, I know what's happening. You were not at the flat this morning, we went looking for you. Where is the source? He's missing – does he have your child? Does he intend to use Dark Winter? I can help you, but I need that agent now.'

346

'Tell the team to withdraw. If they try a lift I'm going to throw one of these bottles. What have I got to lose?'

His voice went steely calm. 'Listen to me. You will not do any such thing. The team will not withdraw, and you will not throw anything, anywhere. I know what is happening; I've opened up the old ops number so we can talk. I can help you. Do you understand me?'

I matched his tone. 'Do *you* understand *me*?'

'Hand the bottles over, Stone. Only then can I help you with this situation. I will get your child back, but I must have control of the bottles.'

'Can't do that. Listen in: there are at least two contaminated bodies in Berlin, and maybe a bottle already opened – smashed, whatever. Flat seven, twenty-two Bergmannstrasse. You got that?'

There was a slight pause. 'Got it. Now, come in and we can help you. I understand the situation with your child, but we can work together and—'

I pulled down the little window next to me and threw the phone out, then dug around in my jacket for Geoff's and got rid of it as well. 'Looks as if I came up with the bright idea instead, didn't I?'

She was happy now as I turned to face Sundance and Trainers. Suzy looked the other way, past the toilet and towards the other two somewhere in the next carriage. 'I thought you'd called from Berlin. I'm sorry.'

She moved closer to me: we must have looked like a boyfriend and girlfriend who'd just had a row and were busy making up. 'What now?'

Sundance was still on his cell, his eyes not leaving mine.

'We can't go to Liverpool Street. You know Tottenham Hale?'
'Nope.'

'Me neither. OK, we'll RV at Smith's in Sloane Square – that's the only location not known to anyone but us, right?'

'Shall we split the bottles?'

Good call. If only one of us made it to the source, we might be able to carry on with the job. I nodded slowly as a woman squeezed past us and opened the toilet door, only to be put off by the smell and turn away. Suzy took off her jacket and knelt by my feet, peeling off the outer duty-free bag and putting two bottles into it. I kept my eyes moving between the two teams. Sundance was redialling, pissed off that he'd lost his signal, and the German kids ran past again as she stood up, the bundle under her arm.

I still had the carrier-bag and two bottles in my left hand, the other on display in the right. 'We'll keep the RV open until eleven thirty tonight. If either of us doesn't make it, the other one's got to get to Fuck-face with their bottles. It's Kelly's only chance.'

She nodded.

'No matter what, don't get the Yes Man involved.' I looked past her to see Sundance on the phone again and Trainers adjusting his bag and just staring at me, really pissed off. 'He won't give a shit about her. Will you promise me that?'

She nodded again and looked back down the carriage. 'I'll do my best, but ultimately DW has to be controlled – you know that, don't you?'

56

Ugly grey tower blocks sprouted from among the greenery as the tannoy announced the joys of Tottenham Hale, just twenty minutes from Oxford Circus via the Victoria line. Tourists could get to many parts of London from here more quickly than by going all the way in to Liverpool Street. I looked out of the window as the train lost speed, trying not to make it obvious what we were about to do.

Soon we were pulling into a mishmash of glass, Perspex, concrete and billboards, surrounded by office blocks and open space. I caught a glimpse of a main road and a large car park, busy with shoppers.

Quite a few people stood up in our carriage and started to make their way to the doors: women in airline uniforms after a shift at a ticketing desk, holidaymakers on their way home. A black woman put her baby into the three-wheeled buggy behind Suzy and busied herself with the straps.

Sundance and Trainers were still at the far end, looking even more pissed off. I couldn't see the other two, but had no doubt they were getting ready to take us from the train.

I checked that the bumbag was zipped up, and that nothing was going to fall out of my pockets. Suzy started doing the same, not trying to hide the fact. 'Fuck 'em, what does it matter?' She was right: they would still proceed as if we were going to do a runner, so waiting until the last minute wouldn't help us any. The train slowed enough for me to read the billboards. The woman negotiated her buggy round the suitcase and rucksack slalom and we fell in behind her. It squeaked to a halt and the automatic doors opened, our last chance to talk to each other. I put my mouth close to her ear. 'Smith's, half eleven.' She nodded, and we followed mother and baby on to the platform. She had that scary look in her eyes again.

The only way out was via a footbridge, enclosed by scratched and graffiti-covered Perspex. Sundance and Trainers tucked in behind us as we mingled with the crowd of people heading in that direction. The other two were in front of us, but staying near the train in case we jumped back on.

Suzy tapped my shoulder. 'Good luck. I'm going for the tube.' As she jogged on up the steps, the other two peeled off and followed her.

I continued behind the mother with the three-wheeler. She had a large bag over her shoulder and was leaning away from it to get a bit of leverage. Through the Perspex, I could see Suzy hurrying across to the other side of the tracks.

I caught up with the buggy at the bottom of the stairs. 'You want a hand with that?' She flashed me a grateful smile. I picked up the front with my right hand, still clutching DW in my left. The baby looked about a year old, totally zoned out, half of his face covered by a blue plastic pacifier.

I glanced over the hood before starting to head up the steps. Sundance and Trainers were on the phone again, about twenty paces away, their bags in front of them now, more or less on their chests. They probably wanted ready access in case I dropped DW by accident as I walked backwards with the buggy.

When we reached the top of the stairs I set the front wheel down and got more grateful thanks from the mother. I smiled, turned to my left, and legged it across the walkway. Through the Perspex I could see my new friend clip Sundance accidentally on the side of the head as she adjusted the bag over her shoulder. He didn't stop long enough to hear her apology. Glancing ahead, I could see the ticket office and the tube-station entrance beyond it. Ticket machines and turnstiles led on to a wide set of escalators that disappeared into the ground. There was no sign of Suzy or the other two.

I went straight through and out into the station approach, past a taxi rank, and ran left, making for the main drag about twenty metres away.

People try subconsciously to get as much distance as they can between themselves and their pursuers, and whether it's in an urban environment or a rural one they think that means going as fast as possible in a straight line. In fact you need to put in as many turns as possible, especially in a built-up area. Every time you hit a four-way junction, it makes the pursuers' job more difficult: they have more options to grapple with, a larger area to cover, and have to split forces. A hare being chased in a field doesn't run in a straight line: it takes a big bound, changes tack, and off it goes again. Just as its pursuers are getting straight-line momentum, they have to change direction too, which means slowing down, re-evaluating. I needed to be that hare.

I emerged on to what turned out to be quite a big junction. To the left was a couple of hundred metres of straight road, bordering a huge retail park, a large open square lined with all the regulars, B&Q, Currys, Burger King. It was heaving with trolley-pushing shoppers, and vans and cars in search of parking. Loads of confusion, loads of movement, loads of cover.

I didn't want to go all the way down to the crossing: that would put me in line of sight with the entrance to the ticket office. Instead I jumped the guard-rail and started to run, dodging traffic. I got half-way across, waited on the hatched lines for a gap, then ran again.

Sundance and Trainers were doing the same thing as I reached the retail park. I kept to the paved area on the left of the open square, moving through the shoppers to the opposite corner by a carpet warehouse.

I checked behind me again. They'd split. Trainers was about forty paces back, moving more slowly now I was static. To his right, moving out into the parking area, Sundance was trying to get up level and parallel to me.

I clutched the DW package in both hands now. No way was I going to drop this shit. I followed the paved area to the right, by the carpet warehouse's glass doors. Sundance was gaining on me, trying to cut me off, so I turned hard left, into B&Q.

I pushed through the turnstile and into a space the size of an aircraft hangar, with aisle upon aisle of paint, drills, workbenches, all sorts, stretching away from me. I was already drenched with sweat, my chest heaving. The two boys were moving purposefully towards the front entrance. I had to put in some angles, had to get that confusion going.

I turned right, trying to get into dead ground, looking up at the signs for a way out. There'd be fire exits, but they'd be alarmed.

I headed for the rear of the store, looking for loading bays, open windows, anything. I realized too late that it seemed to be one big sealed unit, and they'd soon spot that too. One would keep a trigger on the exit point. The other would be coming in to get me.

From a corner of the power-tool section, I watched Sundance come in, also gulping oxygen as he moved past laden trolleys and men in cement-covered overalls.

There was a gardening area through a big hole in the wall to my right. I ducked into a world of fencing and lawnmowers, pre-packed sheds and stacks of paving stone. I felt immediately better being outside: I could kid myself I had a better chance of escape. A forklift truck vanished through a gap about twenty or thirty metres ahead of me. Maybe a storage area – or, better still, a customer pickup point.

I looked behind me again. No sign of Sundance. I joined the trolley pushers heading for where the forklift had disappeared but, shit, it took me nowhere: it was just another cul-de-sac, blocked off this time by lines of rubber plants and small trees. The sprinklers were working overtime here, and the concrete floor was wet.

I turned to go back out again, but Sundance was on to me, his eyes fixed on mine. I moved towards the corner, edging past a small group of shoppers with unsteerable trolleys. Maybe I'd be able to get through the fence. I didn't run: on top of everything else, I didn't want to attract the security guards. I might already be in the shit, but it could only get deeper if the real world got involved.

It wasn't going to happen. I brushed aside a potted palm and hit the fence, but there was no way out. Sundance was closing in.

I turned to face him, holding up the bag. 'I'll throw it.'

'No, you won't, boy.' He opened his jacket to show me a revolver in a hip holster. 'Give me the bottles or I'll drop you here and now.' He took another couple of steps, then stopped as the tannoy announced that assistance was needed in the paint store. I was cornered, my back to the fence. We were no more than three or four paces apart. He held out his hand. 'Gimme.'

Beads of sweat glistened on his scalp before tumbling down his face. I held the bag even higher. He moved his hand slowly to his short and drew down on me. It was suppressed. He kept the weapon low, his eyes never leaving mine. He brought back the hammer with his thumb. 'It's worth the risk . . .'

I couldn't tell if he meant it or not, but the look on his face worried me. He had Suzy's kind of excitement in his eyes. I leant back against the galvanized steel with the DW in my right hand, and slid down to place it on the wet floor. The sprinklers pattered on the duty-free bag and I could feel my jeans getting wet. The forklift speeded past, the other side of the row of palms, beeping its hooter to clear some trolley-pushers out of its path.

What next? I knew he wouldn't want me to move past him

so he could pick up the bag. We'd get too close in the narrow aisle, and he couldn't guarantee we wouldn't land up fighting. He needed to control me while he took control of the bag.

'Open your mouth.'

I would have done the same.

As I let my bottom jaw drop, he took a final step and moved the weapon up from his waist towards my face. My eyes were glued to its muzzle, my brain shrinking by the nanosecond. The sounds around me blurred and receded as it neared my mouth.

I didn't want to take a breath, I didn't want to move my eyes. The hammer was still back, the pad of his first finger on the trigger, the suppressor almost brushing my face.

I shot my hands up to the point where my eyes were fixed, grabbed the barrel, turning it up and to the left.

He swivelled to punch me with his free hand. I didn't have time to dodge the blow. Pain exploded in my temple and my eyes blurred.

The weapon was just inches from my face, pointing into the air. I wedged a little finger in front of the hammer and turned him so his back was against the fence. He pulled the trigger and the hammer slammed into my skin. Locking my bent arms tight, I brought his wrist so close to my face that I could feel the fat barrel alongside it, then I collapsed my full bodyweight on to the ground.

The yell I gave as my knees crashed into the concrete was almost as loud as the one he did as his arm was pulled out of its socket.

He went down like a bag of shit. I clung to the weapon, twisting it out of his hands, sticking my finger in front of the hammer once more to squeeze off the action and keep it at half-cock. He grabbed at DW, saliva flying from his mouth. 'Fuck you, fuck you.'

He knew what was going to happen next, and I wasn't going to disappoint him. I gave one well-aimed kick to his face, and left him writhing on the floor as he tried to protect his right arm and not breathe too hard through a mouthful of broken teeth.

Pushing his short down the front of my jeans, I picked up the duty-free bag, got back into the store proper and headed for the opposite side. I kept my eyes on the exit, waiting for Trainers to appear.

In he came, moving towards the garden section, shoving his cell back into his pocket. Sundance can't have been speaking too clearly, but Trainers had certainly got the message. His eyes scanned every aisle.

I started towards the front of the hangar, not running, trying to remain casual. People behind me were starting to mutter about something going on, and they weren't talking about the offer of the day.

The tannoy sparked up, a young man's slightly strangulated voice asking for the duty first-aider to go to the garden section.

I left the building, passing an Indian security guy in an over-sized shirt collar and a peaked hat balanced on his ears. Thank fuck just one of them had come in after me. If they both had, or if I hadn't been quick enough with Sundance, it might have been a different story.

57

Kelly's eyes stared out at me from the Polaroid as rain pounded the tarmac and drummed on the roofs of the parked cars. It looked like the storm was back, and here to stay for the night. I was sheltering in the doorway of an expensive shoe shop just off Sloane Square, surrounded by scaffolding for the building works next door. A row of skips blocked the kerb, laden with sodden plaster and old, very wet bricks.

Traser told me it was eleven sixteen as I slipped the creased photo back into my bumbag, alongside Sundance's Brazilian Taurus .38 revolver and suppressor. I peered out towards Sloane Square tube station. It was closed. In fact all the tube stations I'd seen on the way here after about eight o'clock had had a couple of bored-looking policemen standing in front of their gated-off entrances. White marker boards told pissed-off travellers that there'd been a power failure affecting the whole system. Something to do with the wrong kind of rain. London Underground was closed until further notice.

I hoped Suzy was around here somewhere, waiting like me, standing off until the RV time. If not, my options in the next fifteen minutes were going to be limited. I'd have to try to use the fact that I didn't have her two bottles to my advantage: I'd tell the source I was only handing over three, that the other two would come when Kelly was released. Not that it would do me any good. That kind of threat only worked in Hollywood. If I was the source, I'd take my chances with the ones I'd got, and drop both of us anyway.

The foot traffic at this time of night was busier than I'd have expected, maybe because of the tube shutdown. At least the taxis were enjoying themselves. There was a never-shrinking line of umbrellas at the rank on the square.

I was dressed in tracksuit bottoms and a Fila nylon jacket to match the Fila baseball cap that was hiding my face from CCTV. The outfit was rounded off with a new pair of trainers, already wet and dirty after my trudge through the City. The DW was next to me in a Nike daysack, nestling inside my rolled-up leather bomber and jeans. I'd got a no-insurance, no-licence minicab about a quarter of a mile away from B&Q. The driver spoke just enough English for me to direct him south as the ancient Rover's clapped-out exhaust rattled below us. He'd dropped me off at Bethnal Green, where I'd gone shopping in the Indian discount clothes shops before hitting the tube at around the time the Yes Man must have decided the situation could no longer be contained in-house. I'd only gone two stops before we were all chucked off at Bank and the station was closed.

My eyes were glued on the bus stop, but none of the people waiting under their shiny wet umbrellas, or sheltering against Smith's windows, looked remotely like her. I checked traser again, and at twenty-six past, head down, daysack over both shoulders in case I had to do a runner, I ventured out into the rain. Two minutes later I had my back pressed against Smith's windows and the daysack between my feet, keeping under the four-inch ledge to help kid myself I was out of the rain. About thirty metres to my right, the other side of the crossing, one male and one female police constable stood outside the closed tube gates, already bored, but probably pleased to be under more cover than I was, and certainly happy about the overtime. The pair of them had a good laugh about something the woman had said. If they'd known what was really happening, there wouldn't have been any jokes.

Two men walked past from right to left, still in their office clothes, carrying briefcases and contorting themselves beneath one small fold-up umbrella. My eyes followed them towards the Kings Road, then switched to a woman coming in the opposite direction. Thank fuck for that. She might have her head down, but it was definitely Suzy.

A guy in his twenties came to share my ledge. He still had his NatWest suit on, collar up, logo on the breast pocket. He lit a cigarette: the smoke drifted the few feet between us and I smelt the alcohol on his breath.

I looked left again. Suzy had pushed her hair up into a ball cap, and her jeans jacket and baggy cream cargoes were soaked. She'd slung a large leather bag across her shoulders.

As she got closer, I lifted my head so she could see me. She was all smiles. 'Hello. How are you?' She gave me a friendly kiss on both cheeks.

'Fine. Enjoying the weather. Just on my way home.'

'I'm parked round the corner. I'll take you.'

It would have been unnatural to go back the way she'd just come, so we carried on towards the tube, taking the junction right that led south towards the river. We followed the bend in the road until we were in dead ground from the police.

About half-way towards the next T-junction, Suzy's head lifted just enough for me to see her lips move under the dripping peak. 'You seen all the closed tubes?'

I nodded. 'Got kicked off one at Bank. Power failure, my arse. It's just like when they're moving nuclear weapons along the motorways. All the junctions get closed off at three in the morning because of some mysterious accident further on, which suddenly clears as soon as the convoy has passed.'

Her lips curled into a wry smile. 'Looks like the boss had to come clean with Number Ten after all. Fair one. I wouldn't take any chances now – would you?' She gave a slightly surreal giggle. 'Bet Tony's flapping big-time. Can you imagine the spin that's going on in there?'

'They'll never keep it buttoned. It's going to be a nightmare this time tomorrow.'

She glanced quickly behind her. 'I spent the first half of the evening in the lobby of a Marble Arch hotel to keep out the way, but I got kicked out. They thought I was a hooker. So I did a quick couple of laps round the shops, got changed and here I am.'

'I almost got caught in the B&Q the other side of the station. Sundance? Fucker drew down on me. Anyway, we're here.'

'What now?'

'I've got to make the call.'

We arrived at the T-junction. Victoria station and Pimlico were signposted left, but we didn't want to go there. I knew a right and a left would take us past Chelsea Barracks and on to the bridge.

There was a lot of activity on the other side of the wrought-iron main gates, behind the Gore-Tex-covered, SA80-carrying MoD police guards. Trucks were lined up on the vast parade square, lights on and engines revving.

Chelsea Bridge came into view, and so did a phone box. We dug around in our pockets and between us came up with about four pounds in change. Squeezing into the box beside her, I got the Polaroid out again to phone the source. Suzy took it from me and studied it.

Three police vans packed with uniforms screamed towards us from the other side of the bridge. It was nearly midnight, maybe time for a change of shift. She handed Kelly back. 'It's going to be a fucking sight slower tomorrow, when everyone gets to know about this shit.'

The Cabinet Office, at number seventy Whitehall, had a suite of rooms for the use of government ministers and officials referred to as COBR, Cabinet Office Briefing Rooms. They were lettered rather than numbered, and emergency meetings tended to convene in room A. They'd be having one right now.

The Chief of Defence Staff, heads of the intelligence and security services, the Met and fire service, every man and his dog, would be sitting round a table in crumpled shirts, working out what the fuck to do about these five bottles of Y. *pestis* on the move around the capital, while at the same time trying to keep everything looking as normal as possible for as long as they could. With Tony presiding, the Yes Man would be trying to explain his way out of the shit. That boil on his neck would be glowing nicely by now. It couldn't have happened to a nicer guy.

I dialled the number, picturing the chaos in the rooms adjoining A: phones ringing, people running around with bits of paper, others instructing the military to stand-to, but not explaining why just yet, others still trying to get the official yes or no on their actions-on for bio attack.

My phone rang three times before the source answered. I didn't give him a chance to speak. 'It's me. I'm back. Where do you want it?'

He was trying to sound calm. I heard him take a breath, and made out the voice of a TV announcer. 'Do you have all five?'

'Yes. Do you still have what I want?'

There was another pause. The News 24 theme tune blared in my ear and the newsreader piled straight into the headlines. Not surprisingly, it was all tube-station closures and power failures. 'Things are extremely tense at the moment, aren't they?'

'They know about you – they know what we're doing.'

'Of course. I wasn't expecting otherwise. Go to the usual coffee shop, and call me as soon as you get there. Someone will come to meet you. Do you understand that?'

'Yeah, I got it.'

The phone went dead.

We got out of the box and into the shelter of a small mews. As we dodged the rain in the overhang of a small garage, I opened my bumbag and pulled out the pistol. 'Here, it's Sundance's.'

She opened the chamber to check it wasn't just full of empty cases.

'OK,' I said, 'I'll go and meet Fuck-face's man, you follow me to wherever. Chances are they're not going to release us till they've dumped all this shit around the place.'

Rain flicked off her cap as she nodded. 'That's if they plan to let you go at all.'

I shrugged. There was nothing I could do about that until it happened. 'Give me an hour wherever I land up. If I'm not out by then, or you hear the shit hit the fan any earlier, you come and get Kelly, DW, me – whatever's left.'

Blue flashing lights passed silently along a nearby street. She put the revolver in her bag. 'Right, we'd better get a vehicle, then, hadn't we? You keep dog.'

MOE girl moved away from me and began to check the cars squeezed into the narrow mews. The older the better, that was what she'd be looking for: easier to break into, easier to wire up. She stopped by a battered V-reg Renault 5, and five minutes later we were driving south across Chelsea Bridge. At the far side we turned left, heading east towards Westminster. After Tower Bridge, we'd cross back to the north of the river, skirt the ring of steel around the City, and head for Starbucks.

58

Smithfield was a hive of activity. Vans and trucks jostled for position alongside the brightly lit market, loading and off-loading everything from small boxes of whatever to halves of cow. Men in white coats, hats and wellies milled about, having a fag and rubbing their hands together to stave off the cold.

The clapped-out Renault came to a halt, and so did the wind-screen wipers. They hadn't been much help anyway. I jumped into the public phone-box we'd stopped beside, fishing in my pocket for change. I got the Polaroid out of my bumbag again, thumbed a coin into the slot and dialled. It rang several times before he answered.

'Hello?' He sounded as calm as though he was contemplating a walk in the park.

'I'm nearly there.'

'Good. A white van will meet you.'

'I'll be in the alley next to it.'

'Make sure you're facing the road. He'll be there soon.' The phone went dead.

Rain cascaded down the windscreen as I got back into the car. I gave Suzy the pickup point. She listened with a sad smile on her face, then leant closer and kissed me very gently on the cheek. 'This really might be the last time.'

There wasn't a lot I could say back. I returned her smile, then checked my documents and bumbag and climbed out. My wet tracksuit bottoms clung to my thighs as I adjusted the daysack on my back. 'Hope not.' I gave a little wave.

'Me too. Maybe out of work . . . you know, I come and see you, you come and see me, that sort of thing.' She revved the engine.

'That'd be good. I'd like that.'

She finally found first and drove off to get a trigger on Starbucks, while I set off on foot.

There was hardly anyone around as I walked towards the coffee shop and turned into the alleyway. The whole area was shut down for the night; everything was dark apart from the street-lights that shone weakly through the downpour.

A car splashed past, and a couple of people under umbrellas hurried towards Farringdon station. I didn't know why: you could see it was closed. I didn't see uniforms, but they'd be under shelter somewhere.

A white Transit, as knackered as the Renault, came slowly downhill and stopped opposite me. I squinted through the rain to try to identify the driver. As he lowered his window, I stepped out of the shadows. It was Grey, still on his own, still looking benign, the ultimate smiling assassin. 'Give me the bag, please, and get into the back.'

That wasn't going to happen. If I controlled DW I had a better chance of seeing Kelly. 'No way. It stays with me.'

He smiled as if he was my host for the evening, and pointed to the side door handle.

After two attempts I eventually got the thing open, and the interior light flickered on. I climbed in. The van was the same inside as out, the steel floor rusty, dented and scraped. It smelt like a spice counter. He pulled the door shut, and I got down on my knees in the darkness to keep DW stable. I leant the side of my head against the cab bulkhead and listened to him climb back in. Almost as soon as we started rolling he was gobbing off in Indian or whatever, probably telling the source that everything was all right, he'd got me.

What now? Was I going to get dropped? I'd convinced myself they wouldn't risk it, just in case I'd switched the bottles. Surely they'd want to keep me alive until they knew what they had. I fucking hoped so, but what choice did I have? I just hoped Suzy was out there following.

Less than a minute later the van stopped. The cab door opened, and after a couple of goes so did the side door. The light came on. He'd pulled up alongside a builder's skip, in front of a red-brick wall and boarded-up windows.

I had to get in quick. 'Whatever you've got planned, mate, think about it. What if this stuff isn't real, what if I've swapped—'

Grey's smile told me he didn't give a fuck. I could talk all I liked: it was all the same to him. He threw me a roll of black bin-liners and stepped in next to me, a Sainsbury's cardboard wine carrier in his hand. 'Undress. Please, undress.'

He hit the light switch so it stayed on when he'd closed the side door. I hadn't noticed before how deep-set his eyes were. 'Have you the picture of your child, please?'

It was obvious from his tone that we weren't going anywhere until I complied. I took off the daysack and placed it on the floor, then gave him the Polaroid from the bumbag. I started to get undressed. This was a good thing. He wasn't taking any chances that I might have some kind of surveillance device on me – and now, whatever happened to my kit, the picture and number wouldn't be among it. It meant that only my clothes were heading for the skip – for now, anyway.

He opened the daysack while I got my kit off, and the bottles clinked as he unrolled them gently from my old clothes. He lifted each one up to the light and examined it carefully, then peeled back the corner of the label with a thumbnail, and checked again. If there'd been tell-tales, maybe a scratch on the glass, he would have found them.

I was down to my boxers and socks. It was a cold enough night, and being wet didn't help. He waved at my shivering body. 'Everything, please. Undress.'

I did as I was told and threw them into a bin-liner, along with my bumbag, documents and traser.

'Move back, please.' He motioned for me to get further inside the van, and delved into his pocket. Out came a pair of surgical gloves and a tube of KY jelly. I knew exactly what was coming. I'd had it done to me enough times. Devices have to be small to stay up there, but even so, they can have a few hours' battery life.

Without needing to be told, I bent over and touched my toes. The rubber glove snapped on behind me, then came the KY. The inspection only took a couple of seconds. When he'd finished, he slid the door open, picked up the bin-liner and threw it into the skip. The gloves followed.

That was it: I was completely naked, no kit, just five bottles of DW sitting in a box on the floor with labels hanging off them.

The door slid closed again, but at least the light stayed on. Then off we went, Grey gobbing off on the cell, even laughing from time to time. I didn't know what he found the funniest: the KY-jelly trick, or me flapping about getting dropped.

We stopped at lights, slowed at junctions, turned right and left. Pedestrians splashed past in the rain. Sometimes I could hear car radios, or vehicles ticking over next to us. I tried to ignore the cold and my plucked-chicken skin, and just kept a tight grip on DW. I had no idea how far we'd gone – for all I knew he could have been circling two blocks continuously, trying to disorientate me.

We came to a standstill again, but this time the cab door opened and I heard a chain rattling, and the creak of gates. The van rolled forward, then the engine died and all I could hear was the endless drumming of the rain. Wherever we'd been going, I got the feeling we'd arrived.

The side door opened. We were in a yard. Two steps in front

of me was a wall of brown, wet, grimy bricks. Set into it was an open door that led into a very small, grungy hallway. There was another door a few steps inside, and some stairs to the left of it.

'Come, come!' Grey ushered me in as if I'd just arrived for a dinner party. I stepped out on to the cold wet tarmac. DW was in my right hand. I couldn't see anything but high brick walls and the shiny slate roofs of neighbouring houses. We couldn't have been driving for more than half an hour, so we must still have been in London. I didn't have a clue where, though. I just hoped Suzy did.

59

A couple of paces got me into the hallway. I could smell mildew and spicy cooking. The staircase was steep, narrow, and covered with greasy carpet that led up into the darkness. Grey stood behind me and pushed open the interior door. We were in a derelict restaurant kitchen. There was no direct light, just whatever sneaked through the square of glass in each of the two swing doors the far side of the room. It was strange that it still smelt: nobody could have cooked here for years.

He curled his finger in front of my face and whispered, 'Come, come.' We moved past a series of old pots and pans and all sorts of other kitchen stuff that still sat on the oven and worktops. The floor tiles were freezing under my bare feet.

He stopped just short of the doors and turned to face me. I could just about see his eyes in the quarter-light, and the finger that went up to his lips. 'Look.' He pointed at the window. 'Look.'

I put my nose against the glass, still keeping a firm grip on the bottles. Most of the furniture in the old restaurant was stacked against the walls, but Kelly was sitting on a chair in the middle of the room. She had her back to me, facing the street.

Navy stood over her. One of the unstacked tables had a little lamp on it, illuminating his face and the knife in his hand. I wondered if it was the same blade that had dealt with Carmen and Jimmy.

Even if she'd been facing the other way Kelly wouldn't have seen me. She was blindfolded, her hands and feet tied, still wearing her Old Navy T-shirt, her hair a knotted mess.

I took a deep breath. I wanted to call out to let her know I was there and she was safe. But I knew I had to stay calm. She was alive, and we were in the same place. That would have to do for now.

Grey started pulling on my shoulder. 'Come, come.' He was sounding even more excited. Maybe he wasn't taking me to dinner after all; maybe we were going to a fucking funfair.

I followed him back to the bottom of the stairs. This time, light was coming from the landing above. The outside door was still open, letting in the rain. He invited me up the narrow steps. 'This way, this way, please.'

When I was about half-way up, the source appeared on the landing. Without acknowledging me, he switched off the light, then went back into a long, narrow lounge. I paused in the doorway. The red velour curtains were closed, but there was no mistaking the TV, which still had BBC News 24 on mute, and the line of ornaments. I'd had a picture of them in my bumbag for the last couple of days. The rest of the room was new to me. A green three-piece was arranged around the TV, and his raincoat hung over the back of the nearest armchair. Against the wall, to the right, was a small dark-wood table with two chairs.

The fireplace was decorated with grey 1930s tiles, and an equally ancient gas fire was fitted in the grate. It wasn't on. Arranged along the mantelpiece were more ornaments like the ones on the TV, chunky brass or glass replicas of mosques. Hanging above them was a picture of Mecca during the Haj, along with family photos: a silver-haired couple and a marriage in traditional dress. Two other doors leading from the room were closed.

'Come in. Your child is OK, yes?' The source was on the settee, watching the silent TV. A cell phone rested next to him on the arm. He still wore his suit jacket, but he'd taken off his tie and left the top shirt button done up. The fourth sports bag was lying at his feet.

Ken Livingstone was live, his hair soaked, dozens of mikes shoved in his face. The caption told us: 'Mayor has no information of attack, all efforts directed at restoring power to tube'.

The next caption was a news update. Unnamed Foreign Office official informs BBC of imminent biological attack on tube system. Government withholding information about public safety. Government spokesman says report unfounded, calls for public to stay calm.

The Yes Man must have let Simon out on Sunday, thinking the job was done. Maybe Simon had too, until he heard about the tube closures.

It wouldn't be long before Sundance and Trainers found him. Sundance would have his arm in a sling, but that wouldn't hold him back. He'd nearly kicked me to death two years ago; Simon wouldn't last long. Sad, but I did warn him.

I waited in the doorway, using the opportunity to check below me. The white-painted door from the kitchen was just opening. Shadows fell on the bottom of the stairs. 'Please . . . please let me go.'

They were carrying her out to the van.

Fuck 'em, I might never see her again.

'Kelly!'

The box went down on the carpet and I jumped down the stairs.

'Nick! Nick!'

I virtually fell into them in the hallway. My hands grabbed at her blindfold as she thrashed about, her hands and legs still tied. 'It's OK, I'm here. Everything's OK.'

Her blindfold came down as a pair of massive hands closed round my neck, forcing me to my knees. I glimpsed her

369

petrified face as she was picked up again by Grey and Navy. Tears streamed down her cheeks. 'Sorry, Nick, I'm sorry . . . no Disneyland . . .'

I couldn't answer. I couldn't even breathe.

Navy's hand went over her mouth, and all I could see was her eyes, jumping about with fear. A second or two later, she was gone. The door closed and the hands released me. I lay on the floor, fighting for air.

The source stood over me as I recovered.

I looked up. 'Why can't she stay with me here?'

'She's not going far. Why are you so stupid? You need to stay calm, for her sake. I have stopped them killing her. Those are their orders. If you wanted to talk to your child, you should have just asked. Come, come with me.'

I followed him upstairs, coughing up stuff and trying to breathe. I had to keep calm. He was right. Sparking up wasn't going to help her.

He picked up the bottles and went into the lounge but I stalled in the doorway again, listening for the van.

Shit, how long before Suzy gets here?

He waved a hand at the family shots above the fireplace. 'She is going to the son's house, the son of our hosts here. I just wanted you to see her, to let you know she is still worth saving. Your actions have proved I was right to keep you two apart. It should ensure there is no more irrational behaviour while we wait.'

His voice was still calm, very much in command, as he headed back to the settee, his eyes glancing at the TV pictures of bored and bedraggled police officers outside Earl's Court tube. 'As you can see, things are not as straightforward as I would have hoped.'

The van started, ready to take her away.

I walked into the room. 'You going to light that fire? It's freezing.'

'But of course.' He knelt and clicked the ignition button as he turned on the gas. 'I'm going to explain why you still need to

370

know she is alive.' He was talking to the fire. 'You see, I have no technical way of checking that you have in fact brought the *Y. pestis*. The bottles, they are genuine – but their contents? That will take a little while to ascertain, but it is not a problem. Your mayor says the underground system might be closed for a day or two. So –' he got up, waving both hands in the air, then settled back into the settee and let them drop on to his thighs '– so, we have to play a waiting game. I know you are a sensible man. That moment of stupidity –' he gestured towards the stairs '– that was just weakness. I know you won't do anything like that again, because if you did, they would simply kill her. So we just wait.'

The source lit himself a cigarette and I heard footsteps on the stairs behind me. Grey came in, and I could hear the van. He walked past me as if I wasn't there.

The source got up and opened the nearest of the closed doors. I saw a 1960s-style gas cooker standing next to a stainless-steel sink and draining-board. Lying on the brown carpet tiles at its base were the silver-haired Indian couple from the fireplace photographs. He wore a grey cardigan over a white shirt, buttoned to the collar, and his lined face and silver moustache gave him a quiet dignity. She looked pathetic in comparison. Dressed in a green sari, she also wore a cardigan, and her husband's socks to keep out the cold. They looked a devoted couple, and probably had been right up to the moment they were killed. There was no blood. They hadn't been cut up like Carmen and Jimmy. They had probably been strangled or suffocated to keep the noise down.

The source studied my face as I took in the dead couple. 'Do not feel sorry for them. They are in Paradise. They are happy now they understand the reason for this family sacrifice.'

Grey stopped at the door and took the bottles. The source held his face in his hands, smoke from his cigarette curling up into his hair. They stared into each other's eyes for a few seconds as the source mumbled something, then Grey headed

371

for the fridge. He placed the bottles on the carpet, then bent down to empty it. The source closed the door on him and sat down again, drawing on the last of his cigarette.

'This son you're talking about, where she's going – he's dead as well?'

'Yes, he, too, has that honour. And perhaps he has you to thank. We needed two houses for this new, unexpected phase of the operation.' Smoke leaked from his mouth as he waved me towards one of the chairs. 'Sit. We're going to be here for quite some time.'

I could hear the clink of bottles. I picked up the dry raincoat and put it on, then went and sat in the armchair closest to the fire.

The source was still in explanation mode. 'You see, the only way we can check that you have delivered the *Y. pestis* is for someone to consume it. So, if you've exchanged the bottles, please tell me now. Your child doesn't have to die just because you are lying to us. I'll give you the opportunity to go and get what I want.' He paused. 'Well, are the contents of the bottles genuine?'

I nodded.

'We will soon see.' He looked at the closed door as if he could see through it. I heard a cork pop, followed by some hard, aggressive coughing. Grey must have taken a very hard and dutiful snort.

The source looked at me and smiled. 'That is the sort of commitment to God that will make us victorious. We will all go to Paradise.'

The door opened and Grey appeared with a mask on. The fridge was closed, no bottles to be seen. Just a pack of butter, a carton of milk and some Tupperware containers lying beside the old couple. They nodded at each other once more as he closed the kitchen door and headed downstairs.

That was it, then. We were going to wait until Grey showed signs of contamination. Only then would the source prepare the kit and get out there. Maybe the other two would join him for a while, chugging their lungs up on the tube during rush-hour.

What about Kelly?

She'll get contaminated by him.

Shit, shit – cut away from that. Think only about what you're going to do now, this minute, to stop it happening.

'You're going to get caught, you know. They're out there looking for us. Just let her go. I promise you, they're the real bottles. You know I wouldn't fuck about with her life. Why let her get contaminated? Let her go – she doesn't know where we are. Drop her off at a library or something. Keep me – she's just a kid, for fuck's sake.'

The outside door slammed and the Transit's engine revved. The source leant towards me, smoke escaping from his nose and his mouth. 'You people didn't think so much about my children. Both of them are about the same age as yours.' His expression hardened. 'Maybe they do not matter as much as white people. It's me who's fighting the *jihad*, not my children – but they will pay the price because of you. So why is your child so much more important than mine?'

'She isn't. But she's mine.'

'You are exactly right, and you still have the opportunity to keep her alive. If the bottles really do contain *Y. pestis*, your child will most likely be contaminated. But you have the power to keep her alive by waiting patiently until I carry out my duty. Then you will be able to collect her and give her medication.'

He picked up the cell and dialled. 'And you are helping us because all those thousands of people you don't know mean nothing to you – only your child means something. Maybe she will live, maybe not, but you will stay here. That is because, unlike me, you are simply weak and want to save your child.'

He finally stubbed out the dog end that had remained stuck between his fingers, and spoke rapidly into the phone. I didn't have a clue what he was saying, or even what language he was saying it in, but the phrase 'National Guard' was easy enough to pick up – and the reason he'd said it. His eyes were glued to the News 24 coverage of events in the US. He seemed to be reacting absolutely calmly to the caption that state amber still held. The National Guard were filmed patrolling bridges and other key locations, and it appeared all police and fire-service leave had been cancelled. They threw in some shots of Americans panic-buying even more frenziedly now that the BBC's reports of the possible London attack had hit the US networks. Hundreds of people were lined up at checkouts with trolleys laden down with bottled water, canned food, plastic sheeting and duct tape.

The Yes Man had been wrong about there being panic on the streets if the attack was successful. It was here already.

He put the phone back on the arm of the settee but his eyes didn't leave the TV.

'Was that the American team?'

He didn't look at me. 'As you can see, they may be delayed. But God is with us.'

The cell rang as the picture switched to lines of UK buyers in a twenty-four-hour Tesco, doing exactly the same as the Americans after seeing the late-night news.

He wasn't fazed: he just checked the number, pressed the connect button, and started to talk again. The conversation went on for several seconds. The TV showed the talking head of a politician, probably appealing for calm.

The phone went down. I needed to know who he'd been talking to. 'Is she at the son's house now? Is she OK?'

He nodded. 'Of course. We are not animals.'

60

What the fuck was I going to do now? What about Suzy? Had she kept up with the Transit on the way here? Was she still outside, or was she following it again?

She'd have stayed put. Even if she'd seen Kelly being bundled into the van she'd have let her go. Fair one, I couldn't blame her for that: she hadn't seen me, or, more importantly for her, DW.

How long had I been here? Thirty minutes, maybe forty, I didn't know. She could be about to burst in at any moment, fucking up whatever was going to happen.

What *was* going to happen?

I had to do something, and I had to do it very soon. What if Grey and Navy were checking in with the source every half-hour – even every quarter? What would happen to Kelly if a report time went unanswered? I knew the answer, and it was one I couldn't cut away from. They'd kill her.

Our eyes were fixed on the TV, a metre or so to my left, as panic, conjecture and downright lies unfolded silently on both sides of the Atlantic.

The source was a couple of metres to my right. He slipped

his cell into his pocket as he tapped out another cigarette from the pack.

I looked back at the TV, measuring the distance between me and the brass mosque on top. It was about the size of an SLR camera.

I breathed in slowly, deeply, psyching myself up. I had only one chance.

I counted, one . . . two . . . three . . .

I sprang forwards, eyes fixed on the shiny metal lump.

There was a muffled shout behind me.

In grabbing it, I tipped over the TV, and sent the rest of the ornaments flying across the floor.

I swung my head round to fix on target. My body followed, the fistful of metal raised like a hammer.

His face didn't register surprise or fear, just anger, as he cleared himself off the settee. 'You idiot! Your child!'

I brought the mosque down hard on his head, bending my knees for more power.

It didn't connect. Starbursts filled my eyes and I went down, tumbling over the settee. Fuck, that hurt.

I had to keep moving.

I forced my eyes open, tightened my hold on the weapon. One side of my face burned with pain and I tasted blood. I felt teeth where they shouldn't be. All I could see were his feet, bouncing up and down on the carpet like a kick boxer's, waiting for me to get up.

Blood trickling from empty tooth sockets, I pulled myself up on my knees using the back of the settee. I forced snot from my nose so I could breathe. My jaw was almost too painful to move.

He was still bouncing. 'You want more games? Or just to sit – it's up to you.'

'OK, OK. I'll sit.'

I dropped the mosque over the side of the settee and it landed quietly on the carpet in front of the fireplace. I limped towards the chair. The TV news rolled on, Dubya

376

and Tony Blair mouthing hollow promises to the ceiling.

'Idiot. Next time I will really hurt you. Now sit.' Standing over by the curtains, the source wasn't even out of breath. The only reason he hadn't killed me was because he didn't know if he yet had genuine DW. Thank fuck for that.

The mosque was lying on its side, out of his line of sight. I moved round to the front of the settee – then rushed for it again.

There was a blur of movement to my right as I tried to get upright. I was too slow: I had to get in close to him before he could do any more jap slapping.

He buried his head in my stomach and pushed me towards the fireplace. We stumbled over the TV and my back jarred against the tiles, knocking the wind out of my lungs. Blood spluttered from my damaged mouth.

I kept an arm round him. If he managed to detach himself and got to use his hands, I'd be fucked.

I brought down the mosque as hard as I could. I didn't care where it hit him, just so long as it did. There was a loud groan and I held on to him tight, keeping him close.

I wanted to target his head, but it was too far into my stomach. I lifted the mosque again and punched it down between his shoulder-blades.

I could smell burning, then I felt heat. My hair was singeing against the fire-guard.

I jerked away from the wall and we rolled. I bucked my way on top, pulling my arm clear so that I could smash the base of the mosque down on his head.

I missed, but I got his neck.

Down again, got his face.

Down again. There was a dull crunch of bones. Blood. A muffled moan.

He was only semi-conscious now, his blood soaking into the carpet. I kept astride him. 'WHERE IS MY CHILD? WHERE IS THE HOUSE?'

He turned his head and tried to smile, but he couldn't

377

get the muscles to work. 'Soon, in hell.'

I twisted the metal ornament in my hand so that the crescent moon on the tip of the muezzin tower was pointed towards him, and hammered it into his blood-soaked face, again and again.

The heavy brass crunched against his head twice more, my arm juddering as I made contact, then his skull caved in.

The little bubbles of blood stopped coming out of his nose. His eyes had a vacant stare, pupils fully dilated. A pool of darker blood thickened on the carpet, which couldn't absorb the amount leaking out of him. I left the tower embedded in his temple.

Swallowing more blood as I fought for oxygen, I plunged my hand into his pocket, feeling for his cell. There wasn't time to fuck about looking for the son's address. I wouldn't know it even if I saw it.

The phone was smeared with his blood but still powered up. I couldn't call the Yes Man from here – I didn't want him to know where the bottles were. Not yet.

I swallowed a tooth, nearly choking as it tore its way down my throat. I got to my feet and ripped back the curtains, trying to control my breathing.

Rain rattled against the windows. There was a main drag outside but no road signs. Directly opposite was a Victorian corner pub converted into a mosque.

Where the fuck was Suzy?

I lunged down the stairs, and out into the rain.

The gates were corrugated: I undid the bolt, but they wouldn't open. They'd been secured by the padlocked chain.

I put the cell into a coat pocket and started a frenzied climb. Adrenaline sorted out the pain in my face as I slipped and slid on the angle-iron frame.

I managed to wedge my right foot on the crosspiece, but as I pushed down on my heel to propel myself upwards, the skin split and I felt metal grate against bone.

I threw myself over and collapsed on the pavement the other

378

side, my whole body in pain. Curled up on the ground, trying to recover, I pulled out the cell to make sure it hadn't got damaged in the fall. The power was still on, everything was OK.

To my left, fifteen metres away, was the main, and on the other side of it the mosque. I hobbled towards it and saw a sign. I was at the junction of Northdown and Caledonian.

Shit, I was just the other side of King's Cross, the way Grey and Navy had gone when we followed them.

Come on, Suzy, come on!

I started dragging myself up Caledonian, the main, past the disused Indian. I had to get some distance between me and DW.

Rain poured into my mouth as I gasped for air. Mud and grit worked their way inside my injured heel with every step.

I dialled the Yes Man. He was on the line before I heard it ring.

I jumped into the doorway of a Bangladeshi community centre at almost the same moment as Suzy drew up alongside in the Renault.

'It's me. Dark Winter – one of the bottles has been opened, but I've got them all contained.'

'Slow down – say again?'

I dashed across the pavement and into the car, slamming the door behind me.

'Where's D—?'

I held up my hand to silence her, then plugged my free ear with a wet finger to cut out the roar of the heater and the drumbeat of the rain.

I took a deep breath and held it a second. 'I say again, I've got all Dark Winter contained.'

'Where are you?'

'Get a fix on this phone. I'll keep it open.'

'Is it with you?'

'No. Shut up and listen. The ASU have split. They're bound to have check-in times on this cell. One of the team is

379

contaminated. I need to get there now – if they report in and there's no answer . . .'

'Report to who? What has happened?'

'Doesn't matter. Look, if they call in and don't get an answer, fuck knows what they'll do. I repeat, one of them is contaminated. This is the source's cell. I'll give you his numbers. You tell me where they are, and I can get there now, before they report in. You've got to get your finger out – I don't know the check-in time. You understand?'

Suzy revved the engine and dropped the clutch. 'Let's find that van.'

I went through the menu to 'calls made' as the Renault screamed down the road. Suzy attacked the condensation on the windscreen as the wipers thrashed ineffectually on the other side of the glass. 'Fucking car!'

We passed a warren of roads through a housing estate.

Three numbers came up. I knew the Yes Man would be on to it now he had this one, and would be checking its history, but it would take them a couple of minutes. This was quicker.

Shit: 001212.

The American call.

I got back to him. 'I've got a Manhattan number. He spoke to them less than thirty ago.' I recited it, then reeled off the other two UK numbers.

'Got it. Wait out.' He cut off.

Suzy slowed as we passed a service road for a run of shops, and wound down her window. I did the same, my eyes shooting all over the place, trying to ignore the pain in my foot.

'I was just coming in to get you, then I saw you pile over the gate.' She was virtually shouting at me, her head stuck out of the window so she could see ahead. The windscreen was thick with condensation. 'I had to stay with DW. You know that, don't you?'

'Kelly is with them, they took her in the van.'

'Tell the boss, he needs to know.'

380

'Why? This is the only way I might get to her. He won't give a shit about her. I just can't take any chances.'

We sped towards the junction, having cleared the service road. 'I saw them – they went this way for sure. Fuck, fuck!' She hit the brakes as the headlights caught a set of bollards blocking off a rat-run through the estate.

We both turned and squinted through the rain-covered rear window as she reversed. 'They can't be more than five minutes away. They called in to the source when they got there. We've got to find them before their check-in time, or that's it. Come on, throw this fucking thing round.'

As we turned at another junction, my hands were on the dashboard, rocking backwards and forwards, willing the car to go faster.

We saw plenty of vans, but none of them was the battered Transit. 'Why hasn't he called yet? It shouldn't take this long to locate these fuckers. Faster, Suzy, for fuck's sake.'

'Shut it. He'll call, don't worry. But we need to check these roads. Keep looking, we'll find them, we'll find them.'

I kept checking the cell's signal. What was taking the Yes Man so long?

We came to another junction. Rain flew in through the windows. 'Down there. Look, go left, left.'

She turned, driving hard towards two white vans parked further up the road. 'Got it!' she yelled. 'Look right – the carport 'bout five houses up.'

She threw the Renault sideways and it bumped up on to the pavement. I fell out of the passenger door and used the parked vans as cover. The house was end-of-terrace, with a corrugated plastic lean-to down its side.

The cell rang.

I checked the number before hitting the green button and the Yes Man was immediately talking at me.

'Listen in. Do not go into the house, you understand me? Both of you stay outside. Contain the area. A team is on its way. I repeat, stay outside.'

How the fuck did he know where we were?

I spun round, looked up and found it. A CCTV camera at the end of the road, less than fifty away. The arsehole had located the numbers within a minute of me giving them to him and had just fucked us off and taken over.

Suzy kept eyes on target from behind the van as I bent down to protect the phone from the rain.

'You bastard! Kelly's in there!'

'Where is Dark Winter?'

'Go fuck yourself. Find it yourself.'

'Do not go in, Stone. *Do not go in.*'

I brought the phone down, but she grabbed my hand before I could jab the red button. 'Tell him where it is. Tell him. You can't take any chances, remember?'

Shit. I brought the cell back up to my ear. 'It's above the disused Indian on Caledonian Road, opposite the mosque. Have you got that – opposite the mosque?'

I could hear plenty of commotion going on behind him, even above the lashing of the rain.

I cut the call, and immediately got another series of short sharp bleeps.

61

The number displayed was one of the two UK numbers.

'They're checking in! They're checking in!'

She broke into a run, heading straight for the house. I hobbled after her, the cut in my heel widening until I felt tarmac on bone.

I was only metres behind her as she squeezed into the gap between the van and the side door. I went straight for the front, barging into it with my shoulder. Three times I tried to ram it in, but just bounced off. I checked the windows. No good – double-glazed.

Suzy was breaking glass. Slipping and sliding on the muddy grass I limped as fast as I could round the side to her. She had an arm through the smashed pane. Her wrist jolted upwards as she fired a round, the report drowned by the suppressor and the rain.

She pulled her weapon away, screaming, 'I've missed! He's gone left, left, left!'

I pushed her out of the way.

My raincoat sleeve rode up my arm and jagged shards of glass cut into my skin as I fumbled for the lock and Suzy jostled for position, weapon up, shouting in my ear, 'Come on! *Come on!*'

My fingers closed over a Yale. I turned it and half fell inside, my arm still in the frame as Suzy barged past, weapon up, running through the inner door.

Almost immediately she was screaming. 'Fucking hell! Fuck!'

I followed her into the hallway, my mouth still filling with blood. Street-light shone through the panels either side of the front door.

Two young dark-skinned bodies lay on the floor. Suzy must have fallen over them and was now scrabbling to get up the stairs. Her feet thumped on to the landing as a frantic shriek echoed somewhere above me.

'KELLY! KELLY! I'M COMING!'

I jumped over the bodies and took the stairs two at a time. My legs couldn't go fast enough.

A door was open ahead of me.

The bathroom.

Empty.

Suzy was standing a few paces further down, weapon up, hammer back. It was gloomy, only the street-light filtering up from the hallway, but I could make out three or four further doors, a couple each side of the corridor. Suzy was trying to work out which one she was behind.

I grabbed the handle of the first left and she went for the right.

It was dark in there, but I saw movement. I dived towards it, crashing into furniture on the way. As we fell between two beds, sharpness penetrated my right thigh.

'Suzy! Suzy!'

The muscle seized up immediately, in spasm round the blade.

We tumbled on to the floor and his hand was wrenched away, leaving it embedded. He got on top of me, his head rammed into my neck, biting, trying to get flesh.

I smelt cologne, cigarettes, coffee, as his teeth sank into my neck.

I bucked and kicked as I tried to reach the knife in my leg. Blood ran down the side of my neck.

Another scream from next door. *Good, she's still breathing.*

I added a yell of my own as his head jerked away from me, taking a mouthful of my flesh with it.

For a moment all I could hear was his grunting and growling, then Suzy's voice. 'Get away! Move away from her! Now!'

Kelly's screams took over as bodies thumped against the connecting wall.

My fingers reached his eyes. I wanted to gouge my way through to his brain.

He flicked his head and tried to bite my hand. I grabbed a fistful of his slippery hair, yanking it back, trying to keep his teeth away.

The room filled with next door's screams. I shut it out of my mind, concentrating on the knife.

I head-butted him, and his teeth cut into my face.

I did him again – 'BASTARD!' – anything to distract him as my hand stretched down again for the knife.

Suzy was still trying to get control. 'Let her go! Let her go!'

My fingers closed round the hilt and I pulled.

I screamed at him again as I pulled the blade free, then rammed it into him as hard as I could. I didn't know where I'd hit, but he stiffened, his muscles tensing to fight the pain.

I pulled it out and thrust it down again and again, into his back, into his arse, anywhere I could reach.

His screams reached a crescendo as he jammed his head down on my face and tried to bite my cheek, never giving up.

Another high-pitched scream next door.

'KELLY, I'M COMING! KELLY!'

He was leaking over me – our blood was burning into my eyes.

I dug the knife into his back, keeping it there, jerking it forward, backwards, left, right. His breathing was getting laboured, but he still hung on.

I churned my hand up and down and round in circles, any way I could. My head was over his left shoulder and I was breathing through clenched teeth as he screamed just inches from the side of my face. He tried to bite me again, then hollered into my face like an animal.

But his bucking and writhing were less violent, his cries softer.

Kelly's screams bounced off the walls again, then just stopped.

I felt as if I was drunk. I was aware of what was happening, but it was taking too long for the message to reach my brain. All I could see were bubbles of red light in front of my eyes, and starbursts of white.

I have to get to her . . .

Our faces were just millimetres apart when his grip loosened completely and his movements weakened to no more than a spasmodic twitching.

My software started to kick in as I tried to focus and get up, but the raincoat was tucked underneath him. I pulled as best I could until his body slumped to one side.

The back of my neck felt as if it could no longer hold on to my head. The starbursts and bubbles returned. I scrambled over the single bed and fell out into the darkness of the landing.

I'm losing too much blood, I'm going down . . .

No other noise from anywhere, just the rain on the windows.

I stumbled to the door and reached for the handle, but I just couldn't make my trembling hand take hold.

I turned for the stairs, wanting to get away, but my feet just froze.

Falling to my knees, my head against the door, I could only sob weakly as I smelt the metallic tang of blood.

Feelings of nausea and helplessness crashed over me. 'Kelly . . . Kelly? Suzy? Please talk to me – please. *Please.*'

Why didn't I get here quicker? I could have stopped this fucking nightmare . . .

I didn't want to go in. I just wanted to crawl away, pretend this wasn't happening. But I had to.

I started banging at the door, screaming at it, begging for an answer. 'Suzy open the door, please. Kelly, Kelly . . .'

I slid to the floor, collapsing in a heap.

But I needed to see, I needed to be sure.

I had to go in.

I can't run this time . . .

A sliver of light came from under the door. I tugged at the handle, and tried to push my way in. It wouldn't budge.

I pushed again, harder, and it did shift this time, but no more than a few inches. I knew why, and felt the tears roll down my face.

My hands shook and I lost control of my breathing.

My sight was fading. Blood dripped from my neck and leg as I pulled myself to my feet. I pushed the door again, and the dead weight behind it gave way some more.

It was Suzy who was blocking the door. A knife had been stuck into her neck; the tip of it was just visible the other side. Her eyes were closed, but on what I could see of her face through her blood-soaked hair, she seemed to have a little private smile.

I sank back to my knees, my vision blurred, and crawled through the gap.

The other two lay on the double bed. Navy was slumped face down across her, the back of his white shirt red with blood from the site of the exit wound.

'Kelly, I'm here now . . . Everything's fine, I told you I was coming . . .'

I crawled over and knelt at the edge of the bed. Tears, snot and saliva splashed off my face as I hauled at his arm with my last reserves of strength.

Sirens were approaching. Tyres screeched to a halt outside.

He fell to the side, half on top of me. Whimpering to myself, I kicked him off, then climbed on to the bed.

Orders were being shouted. The front door was getting rammed.

She lay perfectly still, as I'd seen her lie so many times when she was asleep – stretched out on her back, arms and legs out like a starfish. Except that this time there was no sucking of her bottom lip, no flickering of her eyes under their lids as she dreamed. Her head was twisted to the right, at far too unnatural an angle.

I could hear the rear-entry team in the house now as blue lights bounced against the windows and the front door finally gave in.

As I leaned over her, my tears fell on to her hair-covered face. I knew it was futile, but checked for a pulse anyway.

She was dead.

I dragged her to the edge of the bed and gathered her in my arms, trying to hold her as best I could as I stumbled back towards the doorway.

I placed Kelly gently beside Suzy, as the rooms below were cleared. They would be coming up the stairs soon, NBC kit and respirators on, weapons up.

I pulled the knife out of Suzy's neck and threw it at the wall, then lay down between them, gathering their ragdoll heads in my arms and pulling them on to my chest.

With their foreheads touching, I buried my face in their hair.

62

Hunting Bear Path
Thursday 17 July, 11:12 hrs

A plume of black smoke belched from the JCB's exhaust as it lined itself up on the corner of the house, churning the recently cut lawn beneath its giant wheels. Sunlight glinted on its steel bucket as the arm rose to first-floor level, then began to extend.

I folded Kelly's well-creased letter into the photo page of her passport, and took another look at her face. Fuck knows how many times I'd done that since collecting the Vectra before Geoff could get back from the Gulf and find the wrong car in his garage.

Josh's expression was unreadable behind his mirrored shades. He turned to the woman the other side of him and muttered, 'Looks like a scorpion's tail.' Mrs Billman said something back, but I didn't catch it above the digger's roar. We were the only three this close to the house. The other neighbours were clustered on the road, too respectful to come further up the drive.

The bucket seemed to hesitate a second or two, then jerked forward. Mrs Billman raised her camera as steel crashed against weatherboarding. She'd asked if we minded her taking a photo or two, and how could we say no? It was a big occasion for the community. It wasn't every day they got to buy a house for peanuts and then demolish it. The landscapers would be coming in soon to replace it with a fun park, complete with rubber floor and drinking fountain.

The whole house seemed to shudder, then Kev and Marsha's bedroom wall surrendered to the sound of splintering wood and breaking glass. It had taken a while for me to decide to come and see this, but I'd known I had to. I needed to see this fucking nightmare through to the end.

I had brought Kelly back to the US the day her grandparents were cremated in Bromley, following the tragic gas leak at their bungalow. I didn't know if Carmen's sister had managed to make it over from Australia.

Josh had buried Kelly alongside the rest of her family. It was his first official engagement. There was standing room only in the church. I didn't know whether she'd have been proud or embarrassed.

I recognized the principal's secretary and her maths teacher, and I met her friend Vronnie afterwards. She'd looked strangely serene: I assumed she was fucked out of her head on Vicodin.

The funeral itself didn't matter that much to me. I'd said my goodbyes as we lay there on the bedroom floor. In time I'd probably get a few words added to the stone, but I didn't really know what yet.

The undertakers had managed to make her look so peaceful: her hands were folded across her chest, and it was hard to believe she wasn't just sleeping. As I sat beside her coffin and read out her letter, I'd half expected her to open her eyes, grab it out of my hands and say, 'Hey, chill. Just kidding.'

The bucket scooped out a big chunk of roof and dumped it to one side, then the arm extended again and began gnawing away at a wall. Mrs Billman started to cry, and I looked down and kicked a stone to the edge of the drive.

The tube was running again, and London was back to normal, whatever normal was, these days. The Manhattan number had led George straight to the US ASU. They were lifted with twelve intact bottles, and were probably floating down the Hudson within hours.

My injuries were going to take a while to heal, but at least I was alive. I supposed that was a good thing.

There were more splintering noises and I looked up at what was left of the house. The whole roof and upstairs section had been flattened, and the bucket was at work on the ground floor. They'd said it would only take an hour or two to demolish; the carting away would take the time. They didn't know the half of it.

Josh had played the game and not asked how any of them had really died. He knew better than to ask. I'd given him all the proceeds of the house sale, and told him it was a down payment on my place in heaven.

The mess I'd left behind in the UK had been cleaned up by the Yes Man and Yvette with their usual efficiency. Suzy was cremated in Kent, after a fatal crash on the M20. No other vehicles were involved. Apparently a steel bar went straight through her neck, killing her instantly. It was a well-attended affair and I lost myself easily enough at the back of the chapel. I saw the Golf Club doing the same, and we had a few words. She told me they'd known she was pregnant, but had been waiting for her to tell them, just in case she chose to abort. Either way, she would still have got permanent cadre.

Geoff was flown back from the Gulf. He'd have known the accident was nonsense, but also that there wasn't a fucking thing he could do about it. He, too, knew it was always better not to ask questions. I left the service as he stood up to say a few words about his wife and unborn daughter. It looked as though the Golf Club had had enough as well, because we stepped out on to the pavement together.

Sundance and Trainers seemed to have kept themselves busy since that last night in London. Simon had been carjacked and killed in Namibia as he drove from the airport to meet his family. All the thieves took was his camera. According to some papers, an unnamed doctor had come forward and announced that he'd been treating him for some months, for depression. I felt sorry for his kids, but you can't fuck about with information like that. It wasn't as if we hadn't warned him.

The de-luxe colonial was fast becoming a pile of debris. I turned to Josh and saw a tear roll down from under his sunglasses. I checked traser; it was nearly eleven fifty. 'I've had enough, mate. Fancy going?'

We said our goodbyes to Mrs Billman and started down the drive. She said she'd contact us with details of the opening ceremony for the park, and we nodded, but I knew neither of us would be going.

Josh was aching to talk. 'Hey, listen, man, why don't you stay for the night – maybe a little longer, long as you want? You don't look too good. You could sleep in her room . . .'

'It's OK,' I said. 'I'm fine. I'd rather just go back to the apartment. I'm only just recovering from six years of *Pocahontas* – I don't want a headful of Eminem for the next six . . .'

The community might be getting a swing park but they wouldn't be using Kelly's as one of them. We got to the Dodge and checked that the dismantled lumps of wood, the chains and the tyre were lashed tight on the back.

'What you going to do with it, man?'

'Don't know yet, just keep it in your garage, I suppose, until I think of something. I just wanted to keep it, that's all.'

'No problem, man. I hear you.'

We climbed into the gas-guzzler, and as it roared into life I took my last look. I was never coming back. I'd done everything I needed, these past few months – apart from sorting myself out, of course.

Josh hit the main and headed home to Laurel. 'So, what you going to do in that apartment of yours? Just bang your head against the wall? C'mon, why not stay, just for the night?'

'I'm thinking about going away for a few months. Don't know why. I just want to pack, get a few things organized . . .'

He gave that all-knowing nod. He knew very well why I was going, and where.

The digger might have knocked the house down, but it couldn't erase the video. And now I had a couple of new sequences to add to the collection. A good few more cold and sweaty nights lay ahead if I didn't get my life of shit together. I'd thought a lot about going back to Dr Hughes. The zoo gates had really burst open this time, and the animals were going wild. Maybe she could help me.

The dash clock said 11:58 as I got out my cell and checked the signal.

Josh was impressed. 'You getting the hang of those things at last?'

'Just expecting a call, that's all.'

Dead on midday, my cell rang. When George gave a time, he carved it in stone. 'That house business go OK, son?'

'Yeah, left a few minutes ago.'

'Good. I can't let you go to England. Strange things can happen in therapy. The security risk is too great.'

My body slumped. Even admitting you needed help was a fight.

'But here's the deal, son. There's someone I know here. He's a good man and understands work situations like ours. Hey, he's even helped me in the past. And you'll be getting the benefit of that pension fund earlier than you thought. The guy's exorbitant.'

'Thanks, George.'

'No need, son. The fact is, I still haven't found anyone better. And you aren't quite dead yet.'